7/14/14

POCO
BUENO

To David Kelley,

Mr. Kelley,
Hope you enjoy
the story.

—

POCO BUENO

CHRIS PARKS

STORYARTSMEDIA

Published by Story Arts Media
PO Box 1230, Boulder, CO 80306
www.storyartsmedia.com

ISBN: 978-0-9889754-0-8 (paperback)
Library of Congress Control Number: 2013932374

Cover and Interior Design: Joseph Daniel, www.storyartsmedia.com

First Edition
Printed in the United States

THE INVITATION

Every spring since 1970, an odd ritual has taken place in Houston. On a specific date, which shall remain unstated and held in confidence, the invitations to The Port O'Connor Offshore Invitational Fishing Tournament are mailed out. Professional assistants and secretaries who work for some of the city's wealthiest and most powerful men have the event marked on their calendars. Their assignment on this day is one of the most important things they will do all year—*people have been fired for screwing this up*. Each must obtain an advance copy of the invitation, complete its entry form, and deliver it to the office from whence it came, with the entry fee, before 5:00 p.m. The successful completion of this task secures a prime dock space for the boss's sport-fishing yacht, and one of only ninety spots in the tournament. This is the invite to the Poco Bueno.

CHAPTER ONE

S tokes rested a silver razor on the marble counter and turned on the hot water in the sink. Squinting at himself in the brightly-lit mirror and noting the dark half-circles beneath his eyes, he waited for the water to flow warm.

His temples pounded. His lips narrowed. The water ran.

On the counter sat the pewter frame his mom had recently sent him for his birthday. The photo inside had been taken by his brother and published in *Fly* magazine. It showed a determined, thirteen-year-old Stokes standing in the middle of a mountain stream, casting a fly. Clothes hung on his skeletal limbs: long-sleeved shirt, straight-legged jeans. The boy behind the glass–all elbows and teeth–stared out at himself from the picture.

Stokes cupped his hands and raised a portion of hot water to his face, then spread shaving gel over his day-old beard. He rinsed the razor and looked toward the glass. Moving slowly from the bottom of his throat toward the line of his jaw, he made his first stroke. He ignored his deltoid rolling across the apex of his right shoulder, paying no attention to his bicep flexing, or his tricep extending and then contracting. Even if he had been watching, the movement of his muscles would have made no impression upon him. The physical obsessions of youth had long since been replaced by the mental strains of adulthood. Besides, he was focusing on his razor–just the right amount of pressure–he did not want to cut himself. Three strokes, side by side. Rinse.

He stood straight. A swimmer's body stood, unnoticed, in the mirror. He raised the blade to the left side of his foam-covered neck.

When Stokes was that kid in the picture, there was an old Coliseum behind the YMCA in his neighborhood. He rode his bike past both buildings from kindergarten through fifth grade, when he decided he wanted to learn to box: not a surprising goal for a kid who stood five feet tall but tipped the scales at only sixty pounds. He stopped at the Coliseum, watched the boxers train twice, then asked the coach if he could join the team.

He joined the boxing team. There were no try-outs.

They trained three days a week for an hour. He learned how to throw a punch, how to conserve energy, how to deliver a direct blow and step into it. But he had no power. He gained two pounds. He grew an inch. He lost a pound.

He got hit in the head, a lot.

So he learned how to move. He thought of a chicken yanking its head back and forth.

I must have looked like a chicken–rail thin, head bobbing.

His head moves got quicker and his coach complimented him once, "Nice head work." Stokes remembered the words still. The coach forgot he said it a half-hour later.

Stokes thought he had a knack for ducking punches and for boxing, but he didn't win many rounds.

Never expected to win–just wanted to box.

He pursed his upper lip and shaved beneath his nose.

He was eleven years old when his coach finally told him he had a lot of heart, but was a hopeless boxer. The term "hopeless" was never used, but that is what Stokes heard. The coach told him to put on some weight and come back. Stokes rode home on his bike, sobbing. That night he perched on the side of the tub in his white brief underwear–with the bathroom door locked and the water running–examining his body in the mirror above the sinks. The toes of his bare, size-twelve feet clung tight to the porcelain, gripping the edge like a tree frog, while tears welled in his eyes and rolled down his gaunt cheeks. Water flowed noisily from the faucet, drowning out his wheezy gasps–or so he hoped. He looked hard at his bird legs, his matchstick arms, his big ears and his buck teeth, wondering why he couldn't look like other kids. Then he cried himself to sleep.

A few days later, he joined the swim team at the Y. His friend William was on the team and they were always looking for members.

The team practiced six days a week. Seventy-two lengths of the pool made a mile, and they swam one to warm-up, every day, flipping and turning every lap. It was no race. His face hurt where the goggles circled his eyes. No matter what design of goggles he used, the bridge of his nose hurt. The lens fogged over and he couldn't see. The very definition of monotonous. Stokes added numbers in his head as he swam; he had forgotten about that. It occupied his mind: *Two plus two equals four; four plus four equals eight; eight plus eight equals sixteen; sixteen plus sixteen equals thirty-two . . . sixty-four plus sixty-four equals one twenty-eight . . .* Monotonous.

Stokes played football in the fall; split end, but he could not catch. He started swimming again after football stopped.

Rubbing the tips of three fingers along his neck, he felt some stubble and eased the razor across his throat. *Better.* He rinsed the razor and looked again at the picture. Eleven-year-old Stokes kept hiding in the bathroom with the door locked and the water running, thinking he would never gain weight. But instead of just feeling sorry for himself, he turned his back to the mirror and started doing calf raises on the side of the tub, saying aloud: "Down, even, up, one. Down, even, up, two . . .". He did that for years. A decent swimmer, not a star. He earned a few medals, but never went to state. His calf muscles grew–a little; his thigh muscles grew–a lot.

A year after being dismissed from boxing, he found himself in the gym at the Y, trying to shoot baskets. Two eighth-graders loitering in the weight room targeted Stokes and William and a couple of smaller boys. They ordered them inside; a command performance. Everyone knew they were going to get teased. There was nothing they could do.

"We're going to teach you munchkins how to lift weights," one said.

"You have to start with this," added the other, pointing at a forty-five pound bar with two plates on the ends. The eighth graders had been struggling with it.

"Who's first?"

Stokes stepped forward to take the brunt of their taunts and save the others. William was little and fat, the rest were even smaller. Stokes was a string bean, but at least he stood eye level with the two older boys. Expecting nothing but humiliation, he lay on his back on the bench press. The eighth-graders monitored the sides of the bar. Stokes pushed the bar up off the rack, moved it toward his waist, then lowered it. When the bar touched his chest he pushed up. Amazingly, lifting it was easier than he expected.

As he finished raising the bar, one of the bullies said, "Do eight."

Stokes pushed out five reps in quick succession.

The eighth-graders were stunned. Not nearly as stunned as Stokes.

The swim team kids screamed, "Come on Stokes, two more, two more."

He dropped the bar to his chest, then pushed furiously. His right hand went up, then contorting his body, he lifted his left.

"Come on Stokes!"

He finished seven. It felt as if the bar might crush him when he dropped it again.

"Come on Stokes, come on!"

Pushing with all his might, his right hand went up, his left barely moved. The bar was winning. His right hand came back down.

One of the eighth-graders now stood at the head of the bench, spotting him. "Suck in the deepest breath you can," he commanded.

Stokes did it. The little kids got quiet.

"Come on Stokes," William said in a small, determined voice.

"Now let it out and push hard when you do," the spotter said.

Stokes exhaled. The bar went up. His right arm extended and locked, his left stopped halfway and shook.

"Push it, push it! Finish this!" the spotter yelled.

"I can't," Stokes said.

"You got it! Push!"

Stokes sucked in another deep breath, focusing his eyes and his efforts on his skinny left arm–his bony shoulder, his straining bicep, his nascent tricep–all of it. He blew out slowly, *willing* his left arm upward until it locked.

Cheers erupted from the munchkins.

One of the eighth-graders slapped the side of his head. "Good job," he said as he and his buddy headed for the door. Stokes's gang congratulated him.

He changed a great deal that day, and that year. That, he remembered.

Stokes splashed hot water on his clean-shaven face, then pressed the tips of his fingers firmly against his closed eyes and held still. After a moment, he pushed his fingers across his eyebrows, stretching his eyes open. His fingertips came to rest on his pounding temples. He looked again at the eager, ambitious, hopeful kid in the picture frame, then back at the captive, worried soul he had become. He leaned in, eye-to-eye with his image, and asked: "What the hell happened to you?"

CHAPTER TWO

I hate this fucking elevator.

The car slowed and the bell emitted an anemic ting. The chamber seemed to exhaust itself with a final lurch. The door sighed open. Stokes stepped into the dim foyer, traversed the shadows beneath the vaulted panel ceiling, and dragged himself toward the entranceway. His temples throbbed.

When he pushed open a walnut door marked "O'Donnell Oil," the seven a.m. sunlight assaulted his eyes. He made his way to his office, dropped into his chair and sat motionless, breathing in and out slowly through his nose, feeling the pain and listening, with each incoming breath, to a muffled click in his head. He visualized the spot: an inch behind the eyes, about a thumb's distance inside the temples. With a few fingers he quietly drew a folder across his desk, picked it up, considered it, and tossed it back.

How long will this take?

He glanced around the room and shook his head, first at the thought of the work before him, then at the confinement of the walls surrounding him–walls that declared his dreams had vanished, his ambition replaced by *this job* and *this life* and *this fucking office*.

He slipped a key into his center desk drawer, removed a plastic sheath of sinus pills and broke two squares free.

In the kitchen, he filled a shiny blue O'Donnell Oil mug with water, popped the little orange pills into his mouth, and drained the cup.

That's a start.

"Good morning, Sunshine." Linda, John O'Donnell's leggy secretary, breezed in and snatched a mug from the shelf above the sink. "How are you this morning?"

"Wonderful," Stokes answered in a strong voice.

He poured a cup of fresh-made coffee and took a solid belt. His shoulders convulsed as he turned his back on Linda, nearly dropping the cup of scalding coffee on the counter. He sucked a breath across his front teeth. "Is he in?"

"Oh, yes . . .".

Stokes forced himself down the hall, past the busts and urns and oils and the vacant secretarial carrels that would fill up punctually at eight. *Time to move. Get to work. Talk to John. Close this deal. Park your ass back in that chair. . . then get the hell out of here.*

The faint tinkling of metal on ceramic briefly broke the silence. He looked to his right while passing Danny's open office door, glancing out at the shimmering mirrored windows of a building across Fannin.

You've got to help yourself. No one can do it for you. You can't feel sorry for yourself.

He stopped for a moment, then walked on.

What the hell am I worried about? I'm set; mission accomplished.

The distant ring of the spoon started up again but was drowned out by a booming voice. He stepped into his father-in-law's half-acre suite just as Big John told someone to call him back.

"Morning."

"You coming tonight?" John asked without looking up.

"Of course. This is a big anniversary for you two. Mimi and I will be at the house around five and we'll follow you over. Listen John, I need to talk to you about the Emmit deal. There was—"

"Do you have all the signed votes?"

Stokes stiffened, then quickly decided to ignore the interruption and instead focused on John's huge hands flipping through the pages of a magazine. "Not yet, but I'll have them by noon. I need . . .".

Stokes froze.

John had turned the magazine sideways.

Linda swooped into the office, weaved around Stokes and set John's carefully prepared coffee on his desk, atop a brown leather coaster branded with an oil derrick and the words "O'Donnell Oil." She then spun and made a beeline for the door while Big John lifted the magazine off the desk to get a better view of an eighteen-year-old in a perfectly airbrushed centerfold photograph. Linda had acted as if he were reading *The Wall Street Journal*. John seemed heedless. Of course, he knew looking at pictures of fully nude women in front of other people in an office was not quite a social norm. But John really liked looking at naked women, and John didn't give a rat's ass what other people thought.

"We need every member's signature before we close," John barked, holding the magazine at arm's length to better focus his seventy-year-old eyes above his glasses.

No shit.

Stokes already had thirty-two of the thirty-six signed votes on his desk. He had spoken to the other four signatories, and they had all promised to send in their ballots this morning. But there was a slight possibility something could go wrong.

"And we close by noon." John shut the magazine and tossed it onto the middle of his desk. A gorgeous, double-take blonde gazed out from the glossy cover.

"I know John, I've got it handled, but we need to talk about the bucket structure of this deal. I want to ask you . . .".

The phone behind John's desk rang. Not the office phone sitting on the corner of his desk with twenty buttons that lit up every day like so many Christmas lights–the riot that phone produced never disturbed the hush of this realm. Instead, the old-fashioned brown phone, in the little brown box on his credenza, was ringing. Big John spun in his chair, tie flying, jacket straining, as if letting it sound one more time would cause it to burst. He slapped his tie straight and raised the receiver.

"Yeah." The back of his collar bounced above his chair. "Yes . . . which one?"

A light began blinking on John's office phone. A few seconds later another light blinked on the phone's panel. The lights glowed red. Linda walked in, clipped noises emanating from her high heels striking the hardwood floor. Stokes turned to look at her legs.

"Mr. O, I have your wife on line one and Mr. Kaplan is calling on line two."

John spun again in his wing-backed chair. "I'll talk to Kaplan. Tell Lovey I'll call her back."

Spin.

"Just tell Jose to weed the beds and get the pool guy there today before people start showing up. You can take the Mercedes in Monday."

Stokes clenched his teeth, kettle-drums boomed in his temples. He turned to leave, then closed his eyes and relaxed both fists.

"I'm sorry son, I have to talk to Kaplan."

Stokes thought of saying, *Maybe so, but you took a call from your fucking errand boy while I'm trying to discuss business and you would rather discuss the weeds in your fucking yard than an important fucking sentence in a contract that could result in a huge fucking lawsuit down the line for this fucking company,* but, instead, he just said, "Are you going to be here later?"

"Sure." John picked up the handset.

In the hallway, Stokes met up with Dennis, the pilot. Dennis used hearing aids in both ears, the result of a previous life on aircraft carriers. He also wore lenses so thick and convex his eyes appeared comically large.

How can he pass a flight exam?

"You coming with us?" Dennis asked.

"Where's that?" Stokes avoided the bulge of Dennis's eyes and glanced at the raised scar on his right earlobe.

"We're flying to Corpus to check out a ranch."

"When?"

"Now. We're late."

"I don't think so."

Again, with the drums.

The fucker just said he would be here. He doesn't have the patience to even talk about the details of this deal and we're going to close by noon. Of course, John did not say *he* would be here for the closing. He just said he would be here *later*. That was the thing about John. He never actually lied, he just never told you any details unless you asked specifically or you absolutely needed to know. So while Stokes stayed here slugging it out, getting the signatures, baby-sitting the lawyers, tying up every possible loose end and landing the deal, John, once again, would fly off to play. Both temples thumped. He entered the men's room.

CHAPTER THREE

Stokes walked up to a urinal and his cell phone rang inside the chest pocket of his jacket. He did not have to look at the phone to know who it was. He looked anyway. *Jean Paul.* He let the call go to voicemail and proceeded with what he had come in for. He closed his eyes, tilted his head up and felt the cool air from the ceiling vent washing over his forehead. It eased the pain in his temples, at least momentarily.

When he pulled the door open to leave, the phone went off again. Again, he knew who it was. After last night, Jean Paul was calling to gloat.

Stokes flipped open the phone and held it to his ear. "Yes?"

"Bueno, señor. Como esta dude?"

"Bueno is not a greeting, *dude.* Bueno means 'good.'"

"What's your problem man? I thought you'd be happy with your new *girl-friend.*" J.P. sang "girl" and "friend" like a child taunting a playmate.

"Shut the fuck up, J.P. She's not my girlfriend."

"Calm down dude, I'd kill if she were my *girl-friend.*"

"You're a dick. And my head is killing me. Let's change the subject. How was your evening?"

"Dude, how fine were those two? We went to three bars after the banquet and each time we walked in a door, guys just stared. I was in heaven."

"They were just as advertised. Those two probably doubled the take for the club." Stokes lowered his voice, stepped into his office and closed the door, "And that little blonde has the best tits I've ever seen in my life."

"You have no idea partner."

"You didn't?" Stokes said, only slightly surprised.

"No, but I will. Suzanna has them brainwashed with her rules."

"What rules? The banquet was over."

"Doesn't matter. According to Suzanna, if anyone screws a guest at an event, they're fired. If they even talk about doing it, they're fired. She's all uptight about her reputation. She's afraid of being accused of running a string of hookers rather than a stable of goddesses."

"Well, she's got the goddess angle down cold. Seriously, those girls beat any group I've ever seen at any fundraiser, bar, party, strip club– anything. They were fucking beautiful."

"Tell me about it. Angie, the blonde, worked in New York for three years as an aerobics instructor then got the world's greatest boob job and started doing covers for fitness magazines. The other one was a Dallas cheerleader for three years after Suzanna."

"So what're they paid to work a deal like ours?"

"Two grand for four hours, plus tips."

"Jesus . . . . For that kind of cash, I'd avoid fucking the pigeons too."

"Sí, señor, and Angie made over two grand in tips."

"No shit?"

"No shit, Cisco. But I have some bad news. You're going to be mad."

"What?"

"I think your truck is dead."

"What's wrong with my truck?"

"The transmission crapped out. I could get it to move, but only in reverse. We backed up for six blocks down Bellemeade, then backed onto Westheimer and left the truck at Chuy's. It was hilarious. I'm just glad I didn't get stopped by the cops."

"You thought I'd be pissed? Hell, I'm happy. Let's get a new truck. I'm sick of the maintenance on that thing."

"I'll buy this one from you," J.P. said. "How much do you want?"

"I tell you what. You take it to Jay--"

"You're getting another Suburban?"

"Yep, I already picked it out."

"Wait for the new models. They'll be out this fall."

Stokes stood before his window, surveying the hazy, humid, morning skyline of downtown Houston. "No, I don't care about the year. This one's fine. White, camel leather, four-wheel drive, awesome sound system; loaded. It's on Jay's lot. Don't tell him you're buying mine, but see what he'll do on a trade. I'll sell it to you for whatever he offers."

"Deal. I'll do it today because, señor, we have Poco Bueno next week."

"Sí," Stokes said. A smile leaked from the corners of his mouth. For a split second he forgot about his headache. Just the words "Poco Bueno" caused a grin to puddle on his face. Then he remembered the anniversary party tonight and the closing today. The puddle evaporated.

"J.P., I need to get some work done, but if you go by Jay's, call me."

"Dude, I'm pulling into Jay's right now. I'll call you, but you just sold your truck to me. Don't forget."

"I won't. Are you in reverse?"

"No, I'm in my truck. I'll call you back."

The line went dead.

Stokes closed the cell phone, set it on his desk, spun it with two fingers, then took a seat. The silhouette of his secretary, Molly, had walked by the frosted glass panel of his office door a couple of times since he closed it. She now knocked lightly.

"Come in."

"Good morning, Mr. Summers. I have a scanned copy of every signature. I thought you'd like to know."

"How'd you do that?" Stokes looked at the clock: 7:35.

"Well, Dr. Howe sent an e-mail with an attached signature page just a few minutes ago and we already had the others. I made calls and got two of them last night after you left. I picked up the Miller Trust signature on my way home. By the way, how was the fundraiser?"

"Great. I avoided buying anything except a tag stick, which I actually needed. Listen, Molly, I really appreciate your effort. You just saved several hours. I'll call Pat and see if we can move the closing up so I can get out of here. My head's about to explode."

"Oh, I'm sorry."

Stokes heard the genuine sympathy in her voice. He felt guilty.

"Is the pollen affecting your sinuses again?"

"I'd like to blame something in the air, but it probably has more to do with smoking three good cigars and several really shitty cigars. That, and the scotch, bourbon, beer and red wine sort of kick started it. Oh, and I had two or three margaritas. Anyway, I have to be charming tonight for the shindig so I'm going to go hide if Pat can do the closing. You can leave too if you like."

"Thanks, but I have to leave at noon anyway for a doctor's appointment. I already filled out a request."

"We won't tell bookkeeping. You worked hard on this. I appreciate it. Go enjoy yourself. If Pat can do this earlier, we're both going to get out of here."

"Pat can't do anything earlier–unless you pay him double."

Patrick Shofner of Vincent & Gump walked into Stokes's office, dropped into an armchair and propped a pair of black crocodile boots on the glass of the desk. Then he repeated what he had told Stokes twice that week–once they had the signatures in hand, they could close. Stokes had sent him an edited copy of the agreement with a revision clarifying part of the future distribution of profits on the "bucket" feature they had dreamed up many deals ago. All the buckets depended on future revenue, drilling and production benchmarks, and this was the edit Stokes had tried to discuss with Big John. Pat had the fax in his hand, which he waved at Stokes.

"Glad you caught that," he said. "You should've been a lawyer."

Stokes, whose law degree slept in the bottom of the drawer next to his left knee, chuckled at the backhanded compliment.

"Will Centek bitch about the change?"

"I don't see how they can. It follows the general intent of the parties. But if they do, I'll call you. By the way, you're making your family a fortune."

"This is chump change to Big John."

"Bullshit." Pat removed his boots from the company desk, straightened up in his chair and swept a hand over the spot where his heels had just rested. "There's more than four million in this deal for the O'Donnells, and my bet is it yields at least ten million over time. The last three partnerships you created have netted more than ten million already."

"Yeah, and ten million might cover the down payment on John's next Gulfstream."

"Don't kid yourself." Pat stood and scanned Stokes's bookshelf while he talked. "Big John has always been lucky and he's always had money. He may know how to hold on to it, but you, my man, are making new scratch here. Even if John can't appreciate it, your partners sure as hell do. And I, your smallest partner, sure appreciate it. If you have any doubts, don't." He picked up a clear glass plaque etched with the words "U.S. Long Cast Championship" and held it to the light.

"Thanks, Pat. I tell you what. You let me win at golf and I'll consider us even."

"Fuck you." Pat laughed and replaced the trophy.

Stokes laughed as well.

Pat was merciless on a golf course. He had played at the University of Texas and could have gone pro but, like Stokes, he wanted to make money. Practicing law was a sure thing, whereas a career spent competing on the links was full of risk.

Stokes stood, eyes heavy. "Listen, if it's okay with you, I'm going to disappear for a while today. My head is killing me and I have to be at John and Lovey's house early tonight before the party."

"No problem. I'll call you if Centek bitches about your changes. Either way, I'll call you when the deal is done. See you tonight."

"See you tonight. Thanks."

Pat exited and Stokes looked at his phone. He needed to make two phone calls before his escape. He dreaded the first. He sank, along with his mood, into the tufts of his chair.

His temples began pounding again. The pain was tucked somewhere in the back of his mind while he talked to Pat, but now, calling home to talk with Mimi, the throbbing intensified. He looked down at his red silk tie, studying its interlocking stirrup pattern while listening to the droning ring signals in the earpiece of his office phone. *How can anyone spend so much damn money on a tie?* He heard his sinuses click deep inside his head.

In college he drank more than his share. He had smoked cigars, mostly cheap ones, since he was fifteen–usually while hunting and fishing. Yet, his sinus problems had started only recently. Now, instead of drinking and smoking and dealing with a normal hangover, he had these killer sinus headaches that sometimes lasted all day. This one hit around three in the morning and woke him up. He had lain in bed with the pain banging in his right temple for the rest of the night. By the time he rose and showered, both temples were thumping and the pain had grown worse.

He picked a piece of lint off the gray, chalk-striped crotch of his suit and thought of something else: getting up twice last night to pee. *I'm falling apart, getting old-man problems.* He intended to age gracefully and not bitch, just as his dad had done, but he had not anticipated going to seed at thirty-one. All this went through his mind in seven or eight rings. A maid answered.

"Summers residence."

"Hello, this is Mr. Summers. Is my wife up?"

"No sir," the Hispanic voice answered in careful, measured English. "Should I wake her?"

"No, just tell her I called."

"Yes, sir, Mr. Summers."

He hung up, picked up his cell phone, hit "send," saw Jean Paul's name, smiled, and hit "send" again.

"Bueno," Jean Paul answered.

Stokes knew he had started something. J.P. would use "bueno" for a greeting until something else replaced it.

"I'm thinking about your *girl-friend.*"

"If you liked her so much, why didn't you sit with her?"

"Dude, she's out of my league. Besides, it was your table. I just invited her to sit down because she was obviously alone. Anyway, Angie started coming on to me after I spoke to Suzanna."

"Angie was coming on to everybody but only to empty their wallets, and it sounds like she did a really, really good job."

"Yeah, dude, but I think Suzanna is fine. I'd like to see her in the same outfit her girls were wearing. I swear, I would have never guessed a man's fishing shirt tied at the bottom could make a girl's tits look so good."

"Speaking of," Stokes said, "how much did you spend last night?"

"I have no idea. I had four hundred cash when we got to the Country Club and I have zero now. I also used my credit card at the bars, but it was worth it."

"What was the brunette's name?"

"I don't remember. I was working on Angie. Anyway, your *girlfriend* is fine."

Stokes looked at his open office door. "J.P., please shut the fuck up. I'm married. The last thing I need is to be accused of having a girlfriend."

"Your marriage ended a long time ago dude. If it were me, I would have told the bitch to haul ass four years ago but, no, you have to be the gentleman all the time."

"Thanks man, you're a real help." Stokes adjusted his tie.

"Seriously, why the fuck are you still married? She drinks all day, she doesn't ever want to do anything, and your mother-in-law is a bitch from hell."

"How do you really feel? Go ahead, dude. Don't hold back."

"I'm serious. You're a great guy. You have a charmed life. But, you need to get back in the ring. You fucked up marrying Princess. Why don't you just admit it and move on with your life?"

"I'm going down to the boat," Stokes said. "Where are you?"

"I'm at Jay's, waiting on him to get back from the used car lot. But I'm meeting Angie for lunch."

"Good. I'm in the manager's Volvo. Please don't come to the boat, I'm going to take a nap."

"Bueno. You take a nap old man, I'm going to do Angie."

"Ten-four," Stokes said, admiring J.P.'s enthusiasm.

Stokes stood and walked into the hall. Molly sat at her desk, typing.

"Leave. Go home," he begged as he passed her carrel. "Pat's secretary can type any changes."

"I'm going after I finish this."

"Good. I'm gone. Have a great weekend," he yelled.

Stokes looked around. It was just after 8 a.m., yet the whole floor bristled with activity. At every carrel, secretaries and bookkeepers talked on phones, made notes and typed on computer keyboards, drafting the letters and spreadsheets and distribution reports they would send to their investors and to the multiple state and federal agencies that watched over the oil and gas business.

Stokes pulled open the door he had come in an hour earlier and stepped into the elevator lobby, wondering how he would ever leave here for good. His index finger trembled as he pushed the button with the down arrow on it, something he had done thousands of times in the last six years. He had come here at night, on weekends, and on holidays, working for weeks without stopping, to make his deals succeed. He knew all the cleaning people by their first names. He even knew the weekend time sequence of the air-conditioner. Many nights he had left completely crestfallen, with some huge obstacle threatening to end months of work and planning, yet he was proud he consistently found a way to salvage every looming tragedy.

But this shit is killing me. No, no . . . think positive.

He forced the more pleasant episodes of his past struggles at O'Donnell Oil into his mind by starting at the beginning:

The first project he worked on, less than a month after taking the Bar, was a lease scheduled to expire. There were no drilling rigs available and John hoped Stokes could figure a slick legal maneuver to extend their deadline. Instead of pursuing a legal angle, Stokes forfeited some of his own interest, used it to persuade a competitor to loan them a rig, and spudded the well in time to preserve the lease.

That made him think of last year, when he hired a Mexican labor crew to build a board road in Nueces County, but they drug up and went home for Christmas. To finish the road, Stokes recruited J.P.

and a group of high-school kids. They worked through the holiday weekend, at the last minute, in the rain, and forty miles from the nearest town, but they did it, allowing drillers to reach the location and break ground before the term ended. The O'Donnell's were now making money off that well. Stokes had sold his interest at a deep discount to pay off loans.

He also thought about his big gamble: his wager in western Colorado that had gained him the only public recognition he'd received while at O'Donnell Oil. It was the one time in the last six years that he'd felt he had accomplished something on his own, and it could have easily ended in disaster. But, as it worked out, it made him rich, and the O'Donnells richer.

As the company man, Stokes had been on location for over a month. They'd broken a pipe string, had to fish it out of the hole, and were way over budget. The geologist declared they'd missed their sand, but Stokes disagreed. He and the mudlogger thought they were still above it. Stokes also thought the geologist was relying too much on the seismic. When they called Big John to settle their argument, he ordered them to stop drilling. John told Stokes, "If you can't take a dry hole, you shouldn't be in the oil business." The triumphant geologist caught his flight home.

But Stokes had other ideas. *If you don't have the nerve to follow through on a bet,* he thought, *you shouldn't be in the oil business.* So he called Mimi and told her he was going fly fishing. Then he made his play, the riskiest decision of his young life: he kept drilling. The day rate on the well totaled $125,000 and he figured he could borrow enough to cover four days, max. It took two days to make the next three hundred feet. Six days after the geologist flew home, in the middle of a March snowstorm, and with everyone, including Stokes, thinking they had a dry hole, they hit their sand–full of gas and fifty feet thick. That well ushered in a sixty-well field that was still being developed. The O'Donnells, Stokes and their partners had been receiving fat checks ever since.

Every early wildcatter in the oil business could relate to betting it all, but few modern oil men had ever done anything close. Hence, the story spread from the card table in the grill of the Petroleum Club to the local cocktail circuit, and Stokes enjoyed celebrity status for a month or two.

Pat was right. Stokes had found a way, repeatedly, to make money for their partners and, most of all, for the O'Donnells. He had earned his keep.

The elevator door opened and Stokes stepped inside. *But I'm not in charge–and never will be. I'll always be the son-in-law down the hall, at least until Danny takes over.* He thought of Danny and his oily black hair, his milk-white face, his dark suits with the ever-present dusting of dandruff on his shoulders.

Stokes shook himself. Instead of worrying about the future, he decided to think about the present and figure out how to change things. But as the elevator door closed, the vise of his worries closed in on him as well. Money. His debts were making it impossible to change anything. He had to work here. He had to make more. That much was certain.

He zoned out for a minute, thinking of his marriage, his life, and all he owed. Mimi's question from yesterday still stung: How could you spend three million dollars on a four-hundred-thousand-dollar toy? He glanced at the ceiling. *For that matter, how can I spend my life like this?*

The elevator stopped and the door opened; his head throbbed. He made his way through the crowded main lobby, thinking he would never be able to salvage his marriage to Mimi. He adjusted his tie, then heard his own voice say: *Because she is a fat, pasty, lazy bitch, just like her mother.* The words had a disconcerting effect on him and were echoing in his aching head while he stepped inside the garage elevator. He had never allowed himself to agree with J.P., yet he just said that silently. And what *he* said was worse than any of the things J.P. had ever said. Then again, J.P.'s talking about Mimi's faults never bothered him to the extent he thought it should. He pushed the button and looked at his tired eyes in the mirrored gold metal of the elevator.

Mimi has become her mother. His phone rang.

"Hello."

"Stokes?"

"Hey Pat."

"The deal is signed. No problems."

Smile.

"Thanks." He snapped the phone shut.

I am now square with the O'Donnell family.

CHAPTER FOUR

Stokes exited the Robicheaux Bank building's dark, underground parking garage in downtown Houston at 8:15 a.m. By nine, he entered the sanctuary of the Lakewood Yacht Club where *Princess* sat at her berth. Stepping out of Mimi's Volvo, beneath the live oaks of the parking area, he gazed at the flowing lines of his sleek, freshly-waxed boat sitting in the shade of her covered stall. His headache barely lingered and the pressure had left his temples. He attributed at least part of the cure to the relief he now felt. He had finally paid a huge debt.

Stokes began dating Mimi while he attended law school and she was an undergrad. Her parents lived in the affluent River Oaks subdivision of Houston. A month after they met, he went home with her for a weekend. They arrived late on a Friday night, and the next morning, Stokes woke to a quiet house. He stepped out the front door, intending to take a walk around the neighborhood to see how rich people lived. The ancient gardener, Jose, was trimming the hedges. Stokes introduced himself, then commenced picking up branches and bagging them. Jose despised rich gringo brats, but his joints ached and he silently welcomed the help.

An hour later, Big John O'Donnell drove into his driveway and walked into the main kitchen where Mimi and her mother were having coffee by the fireplace. Big John hugged his daughter, then asked his wife when Jose had gotten so busy he had to hire help. Neither Mimi, nor her mother, knew what he was talking about. The three of them trekked down the central hall and looked out the front door. There, on the steps, sat Jose and Stokes, sweating from their efforts in the heat and humidity, and sharing water from an old plastic milk jug. Both clambered to their feet when the O'Donnells opened the door.

Mimi was embarrassed, but she bravely proffered an introduction: "Mom, Dad, this is my boyfriend, Stokes Summers."

Lovey held her nose a little higher and crossed her arms.

Stokes stepped forward and firmly shook Mr. O'Donnell's hand.

"I love your house Mr. O'Donnell. Your yard, the azaleas, these huge old magnolias, the cobblestone driveway, everything is really just awesome."

Big John O'Donnell sized up Stokes, who wore a tattered, gray, Jesuit High School football jersey with the sleeves cut off. Mimi's younger brother Danny came down the stairs and lurked in the hall behind them, like an apparition.

"This one's a good worker," Jose said cheerfully. "*And* he got an arm the size of my leg." He laughed, patted Stokes on the shoulder, then shuffled off to his rusted pickup truck.

"What's going on?" Danny asked, still skulking inside the dark vestibule.

"Something …. Something I have never seen in twenty-two years of you kids living here." Big John turned and swatted Danny across his pale head. "Someone just did some work," he said as he lumbered into the house.

That sealed it.

John was impressed with Stokes, and Mimi had always wanted Daddy's approval.

Four months later, they were engaged; fourteen months after the engagement, they married.

For a solid year before the event, they went to parties thrown by the O'Donnell's friends, business partners and sycophants. Stokes's mother hosted one of the smaller gatherings, but she actually paid for it with her own money and cooked all the hors d'oeuvres herself. Most of the other catered affairs were expensed on business accounts, or paid for by corporations, or law firms, or somehow financed with other people's money.

By the time the wedding rolled around, both Stokes and Mimi wondered just how compatible they were. In Austin, Mimi stood out as the vivacious girl in a crowd of regulars; but here in Houston, she filled the mold of Lovey O'Donnell's daughter: mean to the help, condescending to anyone who didn't belong to the same country club caste, and–thanks to her mother's generous pouring–a sloppy drunk. After months of parties, hundreds of lavish gifts, and a slew of comments like, "Oh, we just know you two are going to make it," Stokes and Mimi felt they had an obligation to try and "make it."

On the other hand, his engagement had an added benefit Stokes had not anticipated: He hunted and traveled with Big John as much as he dated Mimi. On one of their first trips, opening weekend of deer season in south Texas, John sent a company jet to Austin to pick up Stokes on a Friday morning. It was to be Stokes's first deer hunt, but at the last minute, he called John.

"I'm sorry Mr. O'Donnell, but I just can't go. I really want to, but Mimi and I had a fight earlier this week and I haven't spoken to her since. I don't think I can go hunting with you if I'm about to break up with Mimi."

He still remembered John's reply: "God-damn it son, I invited you to go hunting, not my daughter. I hope you two stay together, but even if you don't, I like having you around. Now get on that fucking airplane because I have a proposition I want to discuss with you this weekend."

That is how his business relationship with John O'Donnell began. Stokes was aspiring to land a job as an associate at a top Houston firm. But John offered him a job paying more than any law firm, plus a percentage bonus, and he was specific about one thing: the position was separate and apart from whether Stokes ever became his son-in-law.

"This isn't family," John said, "it's business."

So now John, the boss, had been paid in full. John the father-in-law was another matter.

CHAPTER FIVE

His cell phone rang. Stokes went rigid and felt a dull ache in his right temple. Was the pain coming back? Maybe it was just the phone ringing that set him off again. Or maybe the thought of talking to Mimi triggered it. He knew that was it. He wished he had already turned it off. He flipped the phone open, then remembered that with this new phone, all he had to do was look at the window on the front to see who was calling. *Too late.* He pushed the green button to answer and held it to his head. The phone stayed silent.

"Hello?"

Nothing.

Off to his left, a sea gull cried out above the dock.

He held the phone away from his ear and studied it. The little screen seemed perfectly content. The bars in the top corner indicated he had a strong signal. Next to those bars, mysterious hieroglyphs told somebody something, but Stokes had no earthly idea what they stood for. In the other corner of the screen, an icon showed the battery as fully charged. The date and time were displayed at the bottom, but there was no indication of Mimi's calling him. He felt the sun burning the side of his face while the phone rang again in his hand. Momentarily baffled, he looked at the screen. It showed Mimi calling from her cell. He tentatively pushed the green button and held it to his ear.

"Hello?"

"Hey, you called?"

"Oh, hey . . . Yeah, I called earlier. I took your car this morning. I let J.P. use mine last night after the Safari Club dinner."

"Why do you insist on hanging out with your employee?"

"Don't start."

"Seriously, the guy's an embarrassment, living in that filthy little trailer in Dickinson–"

"Not everyone is lucky enough to have their parents pay for everything, Mimi."

"Oh . . . so you have a problem with my family's money now?"

"I was thinking of *my* family. My mom and dad paid for my college and part of law school. J.P.'s dad beat the shit out of him and he left home at the age of fourteen. Just because he doesn't live in River Oaks, doesn't mean he's not a good person."

"He's an embarrassment Stokes. You have lots of friends who are doctors and lawyers and successful businessmen. Why can't you just hang around with them?"

"Listen to yourself. What does someone's wealth or family status have to do with who they are? How the fuck did you become such a snob?"

"Stokes!"

Stokes could not remember ever cussing at his wife.

"Sorry. Listen, my head is killing me." (He lied. He actually felt much better and the pangs in his temples had dissipated, especially with that last comment.) "I finished the closing on the Emmit deal early so I took off. I'm at the boat. I barely slept last night. I'm going to take a nap. I'll see you at the house around four."

Lovey's voice harped in the background. Immediately Stokes pictured them in Lovey's chauffeured Town Car, sitting together in the back seat. Mimi seemed to be listening to her mother and not him.

"Where are you?"

"I'm with Mom. She just picked me up in the Town Car. We're going to get our hair done and do some shopping after lunch."

That meant they would split a bottle of wine over lunch at Tony's and the tab would exceed the chauffeur's weekly salary. At this moment, Lovey would be in a panic, fearing the maitre d' might not give her a table worthy of her social status. They would head to Saks or Neimans or one of their ten or twelve favorite stores to shop–out of boredom or fun or whatever–and be fawned over by hopeful sales clerks on commission. Stokes decided he really did not care and would just leave it alone.

"Okay," he said. "Have fun. I'll see you at the house."

He pushed the red button and held it down. The phone made its dying tones and the screen de-animated to black. A covert smile revealed itself. *No one can call and I am free to sleep.*

Stokes crossed the wooden dock and hopped onto the back deck of *Princess*. He walked up the stairs, put his key in the sliding glass door and opened it. The shade covered the opening and he moved it just enough to step around, then slid the door closed. The air-conditioner fan made a steady hum.

He threw his keys on the bar, slipped two fingers between his tie and collar and rocked the knot forward. The half-windsor gave way and he felt the previously unnoticed pressure release, prompting him to yank the fine silk from the fold of the starched cloth. He unfastened his top button and ambled down the steps, stopping at the thermostat to decrease the setting to sixty-five. Then he strode past four separate doors to the master cabin at the end of the hall. Once inside, he pulled firmly on the handle until the bolt caught.

Here, in the master, it was dark. The shades were down and all the lights were off. Stokes fell onto the imported white cotton of the eiderdown comforter that topped the king-sized bed. This was his favorite spot in the universe: his own bed, in his own room, in the private, placid, sublime world he had built—one that floated. Stretching high above his head, he clasped a down pillow in his arms, locked his right hand to his left arm and applied pressure, squeezing the pillow tight against his head with his biceps. Without looking, he kicked off one black-laced wingtip, and then the other, letting them drop. The Italian leather made a soft thud on the carpet. He wiggled his liberated toes inside his black socks, then closed his eyes. His breathing slowed. Within minutes, he fell asleep.

CHAPTER SIX

I t was a good dream: The sun burned hot. Two boys played on a beach and birds flew above. One boy brought seashells to the other. The second boy sat on the hard-packed wet sand near the sea, placing the shells in a row, diligently scrutinizing each in relation to the other like a waiter checking the place settings of his tables before opening. The little boy had to have the shells just so. Then a wave hit the beach and water reached the shells, jostling them around. Some washed away. The boy calmly began his work all over.

Move, thought Stokes. *Don't just sit there; you know another wave is coming.*

The boy painstakingly lined up the shells once more. Another wave. Shells everywhere. Maddening.

Move.

He resumed the line again.

Stokes stopped watching the two boys and looked at his dad. They were sitting in sumptuous leather wing-backed chairs, having a drink at a big, mahogany bar under a palm tree on the beach. A golden-yellow drink, full of ice and topped with a lemon wedge, sat on a coaster on the polished bar. The crystal glass had a deep-cut diamond pattern. Tiny beads of condensation raced diagonally and at random intervals, dripping onto the coaster, mesmerizing Stokes while he tried to ask his dad a question. Before he could speak, a commotion interrupted. A bar fight broke out behind him.

Stokes turned and opened his eyes. The dream . . . was a dream.

Someone or something was in the cockpit of the boat. Stokes rose quickly. Some S.O.B. was about to pay for waking him from a rare dream about his father. He yanked open the cabin door, rushed down the hall, up the steps and across the salon. He pushed the switch to raise the shade. By the time it was halfway up, he saw the cause of the racket and his anger fled. Jean Paul was on the dock and Angie stood in the cockpit next to four large, cardboard boxes. In her tight, white shorts, clingy blue tee-shirt and white deck shoes, she looked even better than the night before. Stokes momentarily lusted over her athletic legs as he slid open the door and stepped outside. She turned and gave him an all-American cheerleader smile.

Stokes was instantly intimidated. *No wonder this girl made the cover.*

"Bueno amigo," Jean Paul said.

Stokes looked at J.P., opened his mouth to reply, then stopped himself and glanced toward Angie while walking across the upper mezzanine deck.

"Hi Stokes," she said.

His brain told him to answer, but his tongue was stuck.

"Sorry to make so much noise," J.P. said, "but I think you're late for your date with the manager."

"Shit," Stokes said, looking at J.P. again as he descended the stairs.

He swiveled. "Hi Angie. I'm a little slow this afternoon." He met her eye, then quickly shifted his attention to the boxes, which he as-

sumed contained their new ice chests and whatever else J.P. had ordered for Poco Bueno.

"What time is it?" he asked J.P.

"Almost seven."

"Oh, Christ. I'm really late." Stokes hopped over the transom and
onto the dock.

"Take your new truck," J.P. said, handing him the keys to the white
Suburban parked next to Mimi's Volvo. "It's more fun to drive than
that Swedish meatball and the phone gets a good signal. I programmed
it. If you want to call Mimi, just hit the button and say 'Manager' real
loud and clear and it'll dial her cell."

"Cute. She'll love that," Stokes said, loping off in his socks toward
the truck.

When he was out of earshot, Angie turned to J.P. "You're going to
get him in so much trouble."

J.P. curled his upper lip. "I hate the bitch."

Stokes cranked the Suburban. A riff from the Rolling Stones roared
out of the ten speakers mounted throughout the truck, blasting into
his ears. He immediately turned down the volume and shot a long,
distant look toward J.P., then shook his head and pushed the buttons
to close the windows and the sunroof.

J.P. looked back at him from the cockpit and held up his arms. He
pointed at his own ears and screamed, "Live a little dude, listen to the
fucking Stones."

Stokes's only reply was to wave briefly while the tinted driver's window ascended and fully filled the recently vacant window frame.

J.P. put his hands to his hips and stared after the truck. "Dude
needs to get a life."

Stokes gunned it out of the parking lot. At the marina entrance, he
drummed his fingers on the wheel while the guard opened the gate.
He felt genuinely surprised at himself. He never overslept. Recently,

sleep meant tossing and turning and waking every hour or so–even on a good night. But he had slept soundly, really soundly, for ten hours. That seemed impossible.

He looked at the dash clock and studied the radio and the layout of his new truck. Then he realized his old Suburban had been parked on the other side of the Volvo. *J.P. must have driven one to the marina, with Angie driving the other.*

But, how did he get the old one working?

He thought of Angie, although he was not sure why. Then he realized his driver's seat was too far forward.

Maybe Angie drove this one.

Stokes pushed the button to move the seat back, but it was blocked. He repositioned the rearview mirror with his right hand. The back seat was folded down and the third seat removed. Slide marks criss-crossed the new carpet. *J.P. picked up the boxes somewhere and brought them to the boat.* Stokes looked back at the dash and entered onto I-45. *Seven-fifteen.* And, he felt great. He adjusted himself in his seat by rocking his butt and his shoulders sideways, squeezing the thick, new leather steering wheel in the grip of his left hand. It felt half again as thick as the old one. *I like this truck.*

Then Stokes remembered his dream. He actually had a chance to talk to his dad. *How cool was that?* He could not remember ever dreaming and being almost able to speak to his father. *And the rest of the dream; little kids on the beach. What was that about? But who cares?* He thought of the other things in the dream: simple things which hit him on a visceral level. *Leather.* He squeezed the steering wheel again and thought of the leather coaster on the bar in his dream, or was that on John's desk this morning? *Scotch.* His dad drank scotch and soda on special occasions, and that included whenever he had a chance to sit and talk with his youngest son, Stokes. *Clear, crystal highball glasses. The sea. Boats.* Stokes's mind had wandered off the dream a bit. He tried to stay in the train of thought but soon concluded he had lost it. *Shame.* It had been a nice few hours.

Stokes drove at seventy-five, along with the rest of the traffic flowing toward Houston. He looped around downtown and exited Allen Parkway, heading for his house. He knew Mimi would have called a dozen times by now, never leaving a message. He congratulated himself for having left his cell turned off. Then he patted his pockets.

"Shit."

He'd left the phone on his bedside table on *Princess.*

He glanced at the dash and the controls above the windshield. One of these was the Suburban's phone, but he was not sure which. It had to be the button with the phone icon. Surely it could not be that hard to use. But he did not want to talk to Mimi now. He would just get there as soon as he could.

Stokes pulled into his driveway, ran into the house and changed into his silk tux. In the bathroom he fiddled with a blue lapis and gold cuff link and said to himself, *Move, move, move,* but the cuff's four layers of highly-starched cotton blocked the link pin from swiveling.

The house phone rang. Stokes ignored it. After seven rings, it stopped.

What's wrong with me? Mimi will be convinced I'm dead in a wreck somewhere, and I'm happy. Damn happy.

The house phone rang again. He reached for the second cuff link and stopped to stare at the pewter frame sitting on the counter. There he stood, balanced in that stream and facing the camera, intent on conducting sixty feet of line, leader and tippet with a five-weight fly rod. According to the caption, it took only a thousandth of a second for the Nikon shutter to capture that image. It had taken Stokes over a year to master that cast.

Move.

The Ritz was only five minutes away. He would explain things in person when he arrived.

But I really should hurry. Move.

Stokes looked at the frame: the boy behind the glass was much taller, older and skinnier than the kids in the dream–and he had never visited the ocean.

The phone stopped ringing. His fingers froze.

Move.

That's what that dream was about.

"That wasn't a beach dream. That was a life dream …. That little fucker on the beach wouldn't move …. I'm trying to line up shells in the surf."

He looked at the mirror. "You need to move. You need to help yourself."

He looked back at the determined eyes of that skinny kid, a kid who had never excelled at anything until he became obsessed with learning how to cast a fly. "You did it before . . . fuck, do it again."

CHAPTER SEVEN

The party did not go well.

By the time Stokes walked into the cavernous ballroom at the Ritz, Mimi held a martini glass containing two forsaken olives, a toothpick and no more martini. He correctly assumed it had not been her first. Of course, it did not help matters that after the valet had taken his keys, Stokes had gone into the Oak Bar, admiring the woodwork and the old English paintings of race horses and sailing ships. He ordered a double scotch and soda with a twist, then strolled into the grand ballroom flashing a smile and a perpetual oilfield tan. His late arrival supplied ample fuel, but his relaxed demeanor served as the flint Mimi wanted for a fire.

She sparked it with "Where have you been?" It ended four hours later with Mimi crying off her mascara and Stokes holding her to his chest while they waited for the valet to bring the truck around.

Mimi saw the new Suburban and pushed away.

"You . . . " she inhaled, "got a new car–an–an–you . . .," she inhaled again, "didn't even," inhale, "tell me–ha–bout it." She burst into tears.

Stokes suddenly regretted having only three drinks the whole evening. Luckily, he had managed to bum two spectacular Cubans from Dr. S. (Samuil Svlatoslavov, M.D.; most of Houston called him "Dr. S.") He continued to enjoy one while Mimi whined about the new truck. He opened the passenger door, which sparkled under the Ritz's portico lights. *Nice paint.* Then he patiently helped Mimi load her silk-taffeta dress and, he noted, her broadening backside into the truck.

Stokes walked around the back of the Suburban thinking he still found Mimi amusing; in fact, he still *liked* her, despite her sloth, her dependence on her mother, and her worsening drinking problems. He felt sorry for her now in her babbling, drunken, pity party. But he could not honestly say he loved her anymore. *Regardless, this is pretty funny.* He smirked, considering how Mimi and her father both hated cigar smoke. He stomped out the lovely, unfinished cigar on the ungrateful pavement, tipped the valet, climbed into the driver's seat, and closed the door.

"Youuuu," Mimi charged.

Stokes pulled out of the drive. "What?"

"Youuuu …."

After a long, hanging breath, she added, "Have a girlfriend."

Stokes stopped laughing. "I do not have a girlfriend, Mimi." He turned left onto San Felipe.

"I can smell perfume in this truck Stokes Marshall Summers, don't lie to me."

"Mimi, I promise you I do not have a girlfriend." Stokes thought he detected a hint of perfume but was not sure. He slowed the truck and eased across the railroad tracks.

Mimi was crying again, but this time in a higher octave. She seemed to have sobered up.

"Look, Princess, I'll call J.P." Stokes fiddled with the controls above the windshield. "I won't even tell him what we've talked about, but I'll get him on the speaker and let him tell you how the perfume smell got in here."

Stokes could smell the perfume clearly now. He recognized it as Angie's and wondered why he had not noticed it earlier. He thought of Angie, then Suzanna, then the task at hand. "I promise Mimi, J.P. had this girl with him and they brought this new truck to me at the boat."

A dial tone sounded over the stereo system. Stokes searched the dash, trying to figure out how to dial J.P.'s number. He couldn't find a key pad.

"You do too have a girlfriend. You don't," (inhale),

"love me anymore and, youuuu . . ." (inhale),

"just think I'm fat and," (inhale),

"Please say number or name," said an automated voice over the speaker system. Stokes turned left into their neighborhood.

Mimi sniveled. "You don't even pre–tend," (inhale),

"to be nice to my muh–huh–huh–huh–ther." Her sobs unleashed another massive stream of black mascara tears. "And I know you have a girlfriend. I see the way women always look at you!"

Stokes braked harder than necessary at a stop sign less than a block from their house. He turned to his braying spouse. "Mimi, I promise, I do not . . . and I have NEVER . . . had a *GIRL FRIEND!*"

Mimi sealed her lips, restraining a tiny hiccup in her thick throat. She sniffed back her tears, looking at Stokes.

An automated voice came over the speaker system: "Dialing Girl-friend."

Stokes gripped the fat, leather steering wheel hard with both hands. His heart leapt. A ring tone sounded; he frantically looked up at the phone button to see how to turn it off.

A refined female voice filled the air in stereo: "Hello, this is Su-zanna."

Stokes stared at the phone buttons above the windshield, mouth agape. He gathered himself, then turned to face his wife.

"Princess, I swear this is all a mistake."

Mimi's jaw hung, locked in a silent scream. Until that moment, she had only been bluffing on the girlfriend thing, trying to gain an edge.

"Stokes," Suzanna cooed, "is that you?"

Stokes blinked at Mimi. She swung quickly.

He could have blocked her hand or moved his head. He had ducked plenty of direct punches–this was just a roundhouse. He let it come.

Mimi slapped his jaw squarely with a solid *whack*. She spun toward the door, her dress rustling and flapping furiously around her, like a flock of silk pigeons taking flight inside the cab. She managed to push through the squab of fabric, yank the handle and shove open the door. Five yards of saffron and a pair of very expensive, tight shoes hit the street.

The truck door slammed.

"*Fuck. You!*" she screamed at the black tinted glass of the closed door.

Stokes stared out the passenger window and watched his life changing. He hit the red button above the windshield, terminating the call, then slowly followed in the truck while Mimi limped the remaining half-block to their house.

CHAPTER EIGHT

Stokes did not bother trying to explain anything to Mimi that night. Once home, she headed straight to the bar. He changed into his jeans and his scuffed cowboy boots. Then he threw some things into a gym bag, including the pewter-framed picture, and walked to the kitchen where Mimi sat, hissing on the phone to her mother. She was slurring her hisses.

"I'm going to the boat."

Mimi glowered at him–phone stuck to her ear.

Stokes wavered, momentarily considering a peace offering. He felt guilty about upsetting her, but the situation would be easy to explain. She turned her back to him.

Never mind. I'll wait till you're sober. Besides, I'm not sure I care what you think.

Back in the truck and headed south, Stokes considered how he and Mimi had lived their lives farther and farther apart for the last few years. The O'Donnell women were social fixtures in Houston, and like most fixtures, they were not easily moved. Mimi belonged to a bevy of clubs and organizations, and every year, she chaired this or that ball.

Lovey served on a committee or two of everything Mimi chaired. In addition, Lovey was firmly ensconced as one of the Grand Dames of the Houston Opera. They attended every ball and fundraiser of consequence, and they "lunched" several times a week with their fellow dilettantes. The only thing about their social lives that aggravated them both was how seldom Lovey's picture appeared in the society pages of the *Houston Chronicle*. Of course, publishing a picture of a woman who looks like the mama pig in the illustrated children's story of The *Three Little Pigs* does not sell many newspapers, but the social editor could not really tell that to Mrs. O'Donnell. Instead, the exquisitely coiffed society women who made the pictures that sold the papers were the ones Houston saw on the front page of section B. Lovey continued to wonder why.

Getting their pictures in the paper, wondering where they would be seated at Tony's for lunch, and thinking about what tent-sized dress Lovey would buy for the next dinner or ball or benefit, those were the pressing issues Mimi and her mother spent their hours upon. Stokes was sick of it.

At first, it had been enjoyable. The engagement parties and their wedding had been Stokes's introduction to Houston society. After that, he secretly relished all the black tie affairs. He felt at ease chatting with the rich and famous. He liked meeting Elton John and the various royalty and glitterati who swept through Houston to attend the parties, mostly to prove their local host was someone special. He especially enjoyed jetting to New York or Washington or L.A. with the O'Donnell air force for an occasional ball or political fundraiser. Depending on who and how many, the O'Donnells would take the G-V or the Lear or King Air or, before they sold it last year, the Cessna long wing. Sometimes they took several planes. It was all genuinely fun–for a while.

Then John's stories began to repeat themselves and Stokes found himself knowing the punch line of every one of John's jokes. As Stokes dug deeper and deeper into the oil business, he found less and less time to make these social trips.

Being in the rough and tumble end of big oil and having a society family and a society wife had numerous advantages, and Stokes exploited them all. He still attended a few of the local parties because they were somewhat useful and bearable. And, he looked for geological prospects that were within a day's drive of Houston. That way, he could spit tobacco into a waxed paper cup all day; drive home, shower, change, and be drinking Piper Heidsieck out of leaded crystal by midnight. Being on location let him keep a firm grip on day-to-day operations, while these parties gave him a chance to give firsthand reports to his partners, promote his deals, and meet and talk with other oil company executives.

But it had grown old, mostly because of Mimi and Lovey. John knew it. Stokes knew it. Even Mimi and Lovey knew it. No one talked about it. Instead, John always managed to be at one of his ranches, Stokes's schedule always placed him on a well location, and Mimi and Lovey soldiered on, escorting each other or dragging one of their "safe" male friends with them as their escort to the next party.

Stokes looked inside the open gym bag askew on the passenger floor. The picture his mom had sent him sat atop his clothes. Inside the frame, the grinning ambition of many years past looked out at him from under the thick, disheveled bangs of a thirteen-year-old boy. Then it clicked. The drive that gangly kid possessed still lived inside him—he just had to channel it: *I'm going to get a divorce.*

CHAPTER NINE

"About fucking time." That was Jean Paul's reaction when Stokes told him about the divorce.

"You used to be a whole lot of fun, but the only time I see the old Stokes anymore is after a few drinks at a fishing tournament."

"That's a problem," Stokes said. He pulled the pewter frame out of his leather gym bag and stood it up on the bar. "I might not have a job to pay for fishing tournaments anymore."

Jean Paul rose from the couch in the salon of *Princess* to get another beer. "You're not going to sell the boat, are you?"

"No way. I'm just not sure how to support our habits. We dropped fifty thousand at the Sailfish Championship in Key West last April, and that was just one tournament. We fished six more."

Jean Paul smashed a lime wedge into an icy Coronita bottle and handed it to Stokes; then did the same to another near-frozen, seven-ounce bottle. He looked at the pewter frame.

"This you?"

"Yep."

"Skinny little fuck."

He sat back down on the couch, looked at Stokes and shook his head. "You pocketed ten thousand from the Calcutta at Key West. You're not counting *that*. Then again, we burned thousands of gallons of diesel getting there and back and you paid a crew for two weeks while we pre-fished the tournament. You put them up in nice hotels, you paid a forty-three hundred dollar entry fee, and you paid that old Cuban dude to teach us the subtle art of kite fishing, *for a week*, at *twice* what you should have paid him. I know you're counting all *that*.

"But, you're not counting the fact that besides you and me, we had Judge Kenzie, your oil partner Myers and those two Centek dudes on our boat as registered anglers. Those goofy bastards cost us a higher money place in the tournament screwing with dolphin all day when we should have been fighting sails. And you let them do it. No captain would let them do that."

"I'm no captain."

"We could have won the tournament Stokes."

"That wasn't the point J.P. I wanted those two to have fun."

"That's *my* point. You said that trip sealed the deal with Centek. So how, in God's name, do you figure you lost money fishing that tournament?"

"My point is that when Mimi and I get divorced, O'Donnell Oil and I get divorced."

"Maybe."

Jean Paul drained the beer he just opened. He set the empty bottle on the surfboard table and let out a deep, purposeful belch.

"But maybe not. John loves you. You're his golden boy. He just won't ever let you know that to your face."

"That doesn't mean Mimi and Lovey won't see to it that I'm out of the company."

"Guess again," J.P. said, heading to the refrigerator for another beer.

Stokes took a long draw on his half-finished bottle to catch up.

"John needs talent to keep that big office open and you, my man, have more talent in your little finger than anyone in that family. Plus, John hates the pig woman as much as you do; he's just dug in so deep he can't escape. I'm sure that big bastard tunes Lovey out the minute her lips start moving." Jean Paul handed Stokes a Samuel Adams.

"I can't drink this."

"Sure you can. We're out of Corona."

Stokes emptied his Corona and looked at the label of the Sam Adams, then took a sip.

"Anyway," J.P. said, "don't you have a share or royalty or something?"

"This is pretty good," Stokes said. "I do. I have, or had, a thirty-second share of all the deals I've done. That's why I've been doing so many of them. But I sold all the overrides to pay for refurbishing the boat. All except this last one and the Colorado play, but that will run out quick."

"So why not open your own shop?"

"Because, up to now, I've had the O'Donnell's name and connections. I work for the fucking O'Donnells J.P.–everyone in Texas knows that name. I've got a salary and all the benefits: the planes, secretaries, insurance, office–shit, you name it. There's a ton of overhead I don't have to deal with. Plus, the deals were given to me. It's not like I had to go find them. Not to mention the capital. It takes a million just to drill a well nowadays, another million to set pipe, and more if you have trouble. I can't just open my own oil company tomorrow."

"Why not?"

Stokes tried to talk and J.P. cut him off.

"Seriously, you know the business. You can use your contacts and go to work on your own Monday morning."

"Cash. You need a moving van full of hundred-dollar bills to be on your own in the oil business. The O'Donnells keep a fifty percent interest in the wells they drill. The reason they get to see so many deals is that everyone knows they can develop anything. They have an ocean of cash. All I have is debt." Stokes shifted in his seat uncomfortably.

A series of twenty or thirty firecrackers exploded outside. J.P. jumped up to look out the window. With his back to Stokes, he took a sip of his fresh Corona.

"Needs lime," he said, turning toward the counter where a small pile of cut-up lime sat in a puddle of juice on the granite.

"I thought you said we were out of Corona."

"We are. This is the last one." J.P. stuck his grinning face close to Stokes's as he walked by his seat. "You didn't think I'd waste our last good beer on you, did you? By the way, did you buy some fireworks before the Fourth?"

"Yes. A shit load."

Stokes rose and slid open the first door of the stacked sliding glass doors. Lights were on throughout the marina, but the parking lot stood empty. He stayed inside and shut the door, but continued to look out.

"I'm so tired of working there." Stokes shook his head and noticed the movement of his reflection in the dimly lit glass. "If I could just get out of debt, I'd go lay on a beach."

"Wrong. You're not the beach bum type."

Stokes caught J.P.'s eye in the glass. "Oh no, I'm a bum alright."

"No you're not. You're a fighter. Deep down, you know the best part of it all is the fight."

"The best part *of what* is the fight?"

"Of anything. Like a ball game. When you're in it, before you know how it will end, that's the best part. Of course, you don't think that; you're just trying to win. But when you look back at all the work and struggle you went through–"

"The work doesn't mean shit, unless you win."

"The struggle's when we grow," J.P. said.

Stokes walked to the bar and picked up the pewter frame. He sipped his beer and studied the boy in the photograph.

"Spare me the philosophical bullshit."

He set the picture down on the bar and returned to his position in front of the doors.

"What do you see there in the glass?" J.P. said.

Stokes spun and faced J.P. "What the fuck are you talking about?"

"People look at you and see a rich, successful, educated guy. Is that what you see?"

"I'm not in the mood for this."

"Do you really think you'd be happy if you dropped out and sat on a beach?"

"I know I would."

"Wrong amigo. That's my whole point. You don't know yourself. We don't fish Stokes, we *tournament fish*. Why do you suppose that is?

"Soon as you rested up on that beach, you'd want to do something. Build something, break something, hunt something. What makes you happy isn't sitting on a beach or in a finished yacht. It's the unfinished yacht you dig. It's not just landing the fish, it's the fight, the anticipation."

"No offense J.P., but I hear this kind of mystic shit all the time. If I could ditch all this and sit on a beach, I'd damn sure do it."

"So why can't you sit in a room all day and do nothing?"

"That's not the same thing."

"Bullshit. Same thing. Sit and stare at something. If you'd try it, you'd realize I'm right and it's not mystic bullshit."

"So what?"

"So deal with it. Life's a game and you're gonna have to fight if you're in it. The only question is: Where're you gonna direct your efforts? The boat's finished. So's your marriage. You're bored. You have nothin' to focus on but work. You like the recognition for doing a good job, but the problem is, John ain't pattin' your head and saying 'good boy.'"

"Fuck you! That's not true."

"Yeah it is. You know it is. And, bumming on a beach isn't the answer, because that's *not* what you like."

"I'm so glad I have you around to tell me what I like." Stokes turned and looked out the glass door again.

"You think you're the first guy to wrestle with an angel?"

"What the–"

"Look it up." J.P. swigged his beer.

"You're gonna die Stokes." J.P.'s voice suddenly sounded flat. "And when you do, you're gonna score your life by your experiences, and most of that experience will be struggles. It'll be like looking back on a ball game and reminiscing about how hard you worked to win it."

Stokes swallowed and summoned his most caustic tone. "Careful, you might lose me here."

"The struggle is where ninety percent of life is spent. Learn to enjoy it."

Stokes stood at the glass for a long moment, finished his beer, then focused again on his reflection, trying to think of a pithy response.

"J.P., I'm going to bed."

Through the door of the head he heard J.P. yell a muffled, "Night, night."

Stokes went to his room, but rather than lie on his bed, he sat at his desk. He switched on the brass wall lamp, swung it out over the antique mahogany writing desk and opened a drawer. He removed a black leather binder that contained a stash of papers: sheets from yellow pads mostly, some typing paper, a few printed reports from his broker. He sensed a tingle near his upper molars and felt the saliva his body instinctively sent to his mouth. His heart beat faster as he set the binder in front of the computer screen and contemplated the contents. The top paper, torn from a yellow pad, featured a hand-drawn, blue ink line dividing the page into two vertical columns. On the top left of the page, in bold script, was the word "Assets," on the right, "Liabilities." There was a date at the top as well: June 14, 2001, last month. He had written this right after the family meeting with the O'Donnells.

I'm getting a divorce. No more safety net. I'm on my own without the backup of Mimi's money.

That thought hit hard. He had grown dependent on the security Mimi's money provided. He had not worried about their long-term future much; there was nothing to worry about. He had only worried about the short-term. But now, on his own, he damn sure had to worry about both.

Stokes concentrated again on the papers. He swallowed and thumbed through them. The last page was the oldest; it showed thirty-five thousand in student loans under "Liabilities." Under "Assets," he had written the word "Stuff" in parentheses and then listed: "Truck, Clothes, Guns, Rods, Furniture," and placed what now seemed like an inflated value next to each. He wrote it six years ago, when he began working for the O'Donnells. He hadn't initiated the real borrowing then, but he was about to. *Big time.* In fact, once he'd grown accustomed to being a member of the O'Donnell family, he'd given no more thought to filling out a loan document than most people gave to calculating the tip on a bar tab.

He turned back to the first page, the most recent. One million, six-hundred thousand in debts. *And I've paid that down from where it was.*

He had made personal balance sheets like this since college, saving every one since moving to Houston. It seemed as if he sat and thought about money on a Sunday almost every month. He stopped and counted the pages. Eleven. *Eleven in six years is not too obsessive.*

Stokes looked at the front sheet from June again. Next to the entry "Cash/Savings" he had written the figure: $340,000. *Everyone thinks I'm rich . . . but I'm deeper in debt than I was when I came here. Deeper*

than I ever imagined I could be. My job, my house, my savings, and Princess are my only real assets. The clothes, guns, rods and furniture all meant so much to me, but they're just garage sale junk to anyone else.

Another wave of anxiety gripped him. *I can't afford to get divorced. I'll go broke.* His right hand shook, accompanied by palpitations in his chest. He swallowed again, tasting fear in the metallic tartness of his saliva.

But I'm gonna die miserable, and soon, if I don't make a radical change right fucking now.

He decided to do the math on two million–that exercise used to comfort him. If he had two million, what income would that generate? He pulled the calculator out of his drawer and punched in the numbers: 2,000,000. He paused, feeling tipsy and trying to think of what to do next. *This is stupid.* He turned off the calculator and put it back in the drawer.

In school he thought two million would be enough to live on forever. He believed if he ever had two million cash, he would retire: live on a beach, exercise, eat right, love life, and let his biggest daily dilemma be whether to refrigerate the Baileys.

He thumbed back through the sheets, looking at the dates and the cash entries. There it was–the total on the left column under "Cash" was two million dollars. That had been the high water mark for him. July, three years ago. He actually *had* two million. He had auctioned all of his overrides beginning the previous July and concluding that spring and summer. They were working on the boat. The Colorado field had just come on line. Back then, he had done the math–correctly–and realized he could not live forever on two million dollars, not if he spent three-quarters of a million a year. His conclusion at that time: I either need to spend a lot less, make a lot more, or die in two years, five months and sixteen days.

He thumbed forward. The cash stayed at 2 mill, then 1.4, then 820, now 340. It had all gone into the boat and his lifestyle. He had tried to spend less, but cutting back meant not keeping up. So he had decided to hell with it. More would come in. He could work. Focusing on work beat being at the house with Mimi. He put more money in the boat. More still. He would do it right. The boat may be a twenty-by-seventy space, but it filled a void. Every inch was going to be fucking perfect.

He tried to focus on the present. *Think positive. I'm young. I can work–if I have a job. The boat has value.* He removed a cigar from the heavy crystal ashtray and held it in his mouth. He considered lighting it, but decided it would rev him up. He needed to sleep.

J.P. is right. I need enough to go on my own.

CHAPTER TEN

Stokes woke to the smell of bacon frying. He pulled on his jeans and walked out of his bedroom, down the short hallway of *Princess* and up the stairs, expecting to see J.P. Instead, as he turned left and rounded the corner to the galley, his vision fixed on the smooth, granite-firm curve of a woman's bare ass. He was instantly awake, fully alert and a tad embarrassed. His gaze locked on the flawless nude bottom for a beat or two, then slowly followed the contour of her hips and the gentle sway of her lower back. Angie turned around–a spatula in one hand and a pepper shaker in the other–placing her large breasts in the center of Stokes's narrowed field of vision. He raised his eyebrows and took a deep breath.

"Hey baby," she purred, standing on her tip-toes, expecting a kiss.

Stokes held still, unable to exhale. Her breasts pressed against his bare chest. When her face was only inches from his, with her lips drawn together in a small, sensual "o," she opened her eyes, unpuckered and blinked–but she did not move.

"Oh, hi Stokes! I didn't know you were here," she said. Then she backed up two steps.

The extra space didn't help.

Stokes stood paralyzed. He did not expect a comfortable, even happy, response from a totally nude woman who, only seconds before, thought herself alone with her new lover. He stared down at the perfect breasts that had just massaged his chest.

He didn't say anything. He couldn't. He heard the bacon frying on the gas stove. He smelled the biscuits in the oven. The warm light made him aware the sun was up behind the blinds, and he heard Sinatra's "Summer Wind" playing on the stereo. Still, he could not, stop, staring.

Angie remained there, fully exposed, smiling up at him. After a moment, he forced himself to stop looking at her tight, shapely legs and her ample breasts, which would have been at home in any of the centerfolds of John's magazines. He looked her in the eye. She shrugged her shoulders and turned to the stove. Stokes heard *"tap, tap, tap,"* when she pressed the piezo switch, igniting a burner. She leaned over the counter, standing on her toes again, arching her back and reaching across the stove. His cheeks flushed as he watched her finely-chiseled rear end. She set the spatula on a stainless spoon holder behind the stove, then picked up her glasses and slid them on. On anyone else, the thick, black, rectangular spectacles would have been hideously ugly, but over azure blue eyes, framed by her striking face and luxuriant blond hair, the eyeglasses only magnified her beauty.

"I can't really see very well without these," she said.

Angie turned and saw Stokes's gaze directed at her breasts. He quickly looked up. She saw his blush and smiled.

"Hold on," she said, calmly brushing past him, bare skin on bare skin, a velvet cloth dragging across a canvas tarp.

Stokes watched her, enthralled, while she tip-toed down the hall steps and disappeared into one of the guest rooms. He shook his head from side to side in disbelief. This woman presented the most perfect specimen of a nude, human female he had ever, *ever*, had the absolute pleasure of looking upon. *She could have modeled for Vargas.*

He took a brilliant blue bottle from the mirrored bar behind the stove, put a scoop of ice into a whiskey tumbler, poured a shot and a half of vodka into the glass, and watched the clear, square ice cubes melt and shift. Then he opened a fresh bottle of Bloody Mary mix and filled the glass.

Angie returned wearing one of J.P.'s long-sleeved blue work shirts, the front and tail of which hung to her knees. Her firm thighs flashed when she bounded up the steps. She curiously eyed Stokes's drink.

"Mind if I have one?"

Stokes held out his drink. "Just made this one."

"Oh no, you go ahead. I can make it."

"No. On *Princess,* one of the rules is everyone takes care of the cook and the captain. You keep cooking, I'll make the drinks."

"Deal," she said. "I cut up some celery last night."

Stokes opened the door of the ice maker.

Angie knelt to open the under-counter refrigerator, then reached inside, grabbing a plate. In the process, her shirt fell open. Seeing movement out of the corner of his eye, Stokes looked away from his newly iced glass and into her open shirt. There, he fixed his gaze on the full profile of her exposed left breast. He also saw the shirt had ridden up on her hip. She wore nothing underneath. He froze, again. She stood up and handed the plate to Stokes.

"Got to have celery with Bloody Marys," she said, waking him from his trance.

"And Tony's," he said, recovering.

He grabbed a spice can off the counter and shook it over both drinks, then plopped a stick in her glass. She stirred her drink with the celery then chomped it. Turning back to the stove, she raised the steel mesh screen above the pan of frying bacon. She leaned over on her tip-toes, arching her back again and reaching high over the burners to pluck the spatula from its holder. Stokes watched the blue tail of J.P.'s shirt drift away from the back of her pretty thighs, and realized what she was doing before was trying to avoid getting burned, not seductively posing for him. He walked around to the other side of the bar and took a seat, to enjoy a new vantage point.

"I love your boat, Stokes."

"Thanks. She's a lot of fun."

"I'm sorry you caught me in here like this. I didn't mean to be rude walking around naked."

Stokes swallowed hard. "Oh, don't apologize," he said, then choked. Coughing lightly and not knowing what to say, he added, "It's not"–he coughed–"a problem." He felt like an idiot.

"I just like being naked sometimes," she said.

Stokes detected a Southern accent in her voice when she drawled, "nay-kid."

"Where are you from Angie?" he asked, moving to safer ground.

"Charleston. And, Virginia and North Carolina, but mostly we lived in Charleston when I was little. I'm gonna wake Jean Paul. The bacon's ready."

Angie turned briskly, skipped down the hall, and disappeared into the guest room again. Stokes heard the rhythmic noise of fabric and mattress crunching together.

"Waa–hoo. Get up lazy bones!"

Whack.

Thud.

Thump.

"Ouch!"

In short order, J.P. stumbled out of the room, wearing only boxers. His straight, sandy-blond hair stuck out from his head in odd directions.

Angie trailed him, growling, "That huuurt!" as she planted a girly fist in the middle of his broad back. Her expression fell to a pout.

"Shouldn't wake people up by jumping on the bed. Don't you know about the monkey song? *Three little monkeys jumping on the bed . . .,*" J.P. chanted. His long frame topped the stairs.

Stokes picked up the stereo remote from the black granite bar, held it toward J.P. and punched the volume four times. Francis crooned about the very good year in one hundred fifteen decibels, drowning out J.P.'s horrible singing voice while J.P. screamed, "*. . . one fell off and busted his head!*"

After breakfast, J.P. and Stokes stood in the cockpit of *Princess,* watching Angie drive off in J.P.'s new Suburban, which was now Stokes's old Suburban. A rare summer cold front, or rather "cool" front, was pushing through Houston, and the humidity level today felt bearable. Although the temperature had already reached ninety, the humidity remained less than fifty percent.

"Mind if I ask you some questions?" Jean Paul sat on the gunnel.

"Shoot."

"Whose name is the boat in?"

"Mine."

"Does Mimi's family or company or trust or whatever still have any interest in her? You still use her for company business."

"We set up the entertainment stuff as simple reimbursement. Pat's firm had originally suggested I not buy the boat from O'Donnell Oil but, instead, let the business keep it to take advantage of some tax pro-visions."

"I remember all that. What I'm asking is, since you're married to Mimi, doesn't she own half the boat?"

"No; at least I don't think so. I decided to buy her before we tied the knot. Plus, Mimi couldn't give a shit. John was the only one who ever used the boat. I was the one who wanted to buy her and Mimi has only been on board twice. She always refers to it as 'your' boat."

"And you don't think that's going to be a problem?"

"Let's hope not," Stokes said.

"So, what's the plan?"

"I'm going to talk to Mimi today. After she's woken up, taken her pills and downed some food to dry her up, I'm going to explain what happened. Then I'm going to nicely tell her the truth: We have no business staying married and we should get a divorce. After that--"

"After that, we change the name of this boat."

"Amen partner. And after that, I don't have a clue."

CHAPTER ELEVEN

Stokes spent well over an hour talking with Mimi. When he broached the subject of divorce, she stayed surprisingly calm and composed, and they had a long, frank discussion. Afterward, they hugged when he left their home with a full suitcase. He kept telling himself Mimi had problems. Most of those problems, he reasoned, were related to Lovey.

Being with Mimi had once been fun. She was cute, she could tell a joke better than most, and she was always up for some mischief. They first met at a house party where they both had dates but ended up talking to each other all night. Stokes had gone to high school with several O'Donnells who lived in Shreveport and he asked Mimi if she was related to them. They were, she said; in fact, they were first cousins.

Stokes then fascinated Mimi with a story about her grandfather Dutch. It was folklore in Shreveport, the story of how Dutch O'Donnell got his start, but Lovey had never allowed John to tell it. It revealed the nouveau nature of the O'Donnell family fortune, hardly appropriate for children of the Robicheaux empressarios who'd lorded over a cattle empire for generations.

In the forties just after the war, Dutch O'Donnell was an aspiring engineer hoping to make it rich in the oil business. Unfortunately for Dutch, he didn't have any money. But he did have the moxie to join a poker group with Walter Gossett, a good-natured Shreveport oil man who was exceedingly rich. Walt was a Louisiana sheik. He owned a collection of hotels and controlling interest in oil and gas fields all over Louisiana and Texas. He loved to gamble and held a weekly poker game at his suite in the ornate La Maison.

Dutch had a hot prospect on a wildcat and he just knew it would make a well. He did not want to take on investment partners, but no bank would loan him the money. One night Dutch banged on the door of Walt's suite. Walt—who was bald, mustached and built like Buddha—appeared wearing only a towel around his huge girth. He wielded a straight razor and shaving cream covered his face.

"What the hell do you want Dutch?"

"Walt I need to talk to you and it's urgent."

Walt let him in.

While Walt shaved, Dutch explained the prospect. He wanted to borrow the money from Walt's bank, The Pioneer Bank of Shreveport, but the loan officer had turned him down. Dutch wanted to know if Walt would co-sign a loan.

This bold request appeared to aggravate Walt. He grabbed a piece of hotel stationery off a desk and, without saying anything, and without even wiping the remaining shaving cream off his fat cheeks, he scribbled out a note and handed it to Dutch.

"Now get the hell out of here Dutch. I've got a piece of ass lined up."

He ushered out young Dutch and slammed the door. In the gilded hallway, Dutch read the note:

Give Dutch O'Donnell any amount of money he wants.
                                                    W.T.G.

That nine-word note launched one of the largest family fortunes in Louisiana history.

Dutch O'Donnell once recounted to Stokes's mother how he broke into the oil business. He teared up while he carefully removed a yellowed, creased leaf of La Maison stationery from his wallet, the worn ink barely visible below the fleur-de-lis on the rag paper.

Mimi had never heard that story, but a day later, she called her father and confirmed it; word for word.

Despite their shared Shreveport roots, the Summers and O'Donnell families had little in common. The Summers' family's idea of wealth consisted of enough money to eventually have their three-bedroom, brick house paid for and to educate their four boys. The second and third generation of the O'Donnells lived in a world where money was "managed" rather than made. The O'Donnells had split into several family sections, all of which were still very wealthy. The wealthiest, by far, was Big John's clan in Houston. Lovey Robicheaux's family owned banks and vast stretches of land all over Texas, having arrived over a decade before Santa Anna's bugles called the Degüello at the Alamo. Robicheaux banks were notorious for pressuring ranch owners to take out excessive mortgages, upon which the bank later foreclosed, adding to their holdings. When Big John and Lovey married, the amalgam of her land and his oil forged a nearly impenetrable ring of wealth which protected them and their two children–and anyone lucky enough to marry into the family.

Contrast that with Stokes, who lived in a rented house with a group of hard-charging buddies. Mimi, having grown up swathed in designer clothes and courted at debutante balls, found Stokes's world refreshing. Stokes's roommate, Kelly, was a master chef of the backyard barbecue. He'd dig small holes in the yard, fill them with charcoal, then take the racks out of the oven to make a pit. Mimi loved the lack of pretense. In Stokes's social circle, no one really cared who she was or how much money she was worth. If they did, they at least had the good graces not to show it. Mimi's childhood friends, with whom she had attended private schools and summer camps, were driven toward preserving their positions and living off their parents' money. But Stokes and his crowd were all striving to improve themselves; they were intelligent, independent, and driven to excel. Most of his law student friends ranked near the top of their class and worked summer jobs with the biggest Texas law firms. Even as interns, they pulled down eye-popping salaries. Mimi was drawn to their energy and enthusiasm, and she saw Stokes as the most promising of them all.

Stokes moved to Houston, passed the Bar, and, to his eternal frustration, Mimi reverted back to debutante mode. While Stokes went to work in the family oil business, Mimi went to Mom's. Lovey was an alcoholic in denial and she recruited her daughter into the fold. Stokes hated her for that. She had been so miserable a person, and so lonely, that she brought her daughter down with her. Whether she did so consciously Stokes was never sure, but it was a pathetic situation nonetheless. His once vibrant and fun-loving wife was stolen from him by her calculating, attention-starved mother.

Stokes drove out of River Oaks, down Kirby Drive. He needed to talk to someone, but talking to J.P. about Mimi never ended well. He decided to call Pat.

"Pat man. Where are you?"

"Let's see. It's Saturday. The weather is beautiful. I'm in town. Where the fuck do you think I am?"

"How're you swinging the sticks?"

"Not bad. I took Sanders for forty dollars and I wasn't playing that well. Holman is buying the next round of drinks so I'm happy."

"You at the club?"

"No. We played at Ravenwood, but come on over. We're watching Tiger on the tube and we're going over to Holman's later to cook some steaks. You and Mimi are welcome to join us."

"Well, if you don't mind, I think we'll have to pass on dinner, but I would like to chat with you in person for a minute."

"Come on. We're in the bar next to the pro shop. I'll buy you a beer."

Stokes hung up and accelerated through a yellow light, mulling over his feelings again while he drove. He felt a sense of relief that he'd finally confronted Mimi, but he also saw the big, black cloud of insecurity building on the horizon—and he was barreling straight for it. In the last six years, bonds had been carefully woven, and he could clearly hear the fabric of those bonds tearing. Mimi, John, his business relationships, even Lovey, had been his life. Could he really go on from here? And if so, where would this lead? But maybe this could work out. He relaxed his grip on the steering wheel and let out a breath. Then he thought about the money, and his fingers locked around the leather like talons. *No. Please no, not now. I need a fucking drink.* He swallowed, trying to settle his heaving chest.

He swept the cab with his eyes, foraging for something to calm him, something to chase the butterflies out of his stomach. His glance came to rest on the console and he pursed his lips, remembering the present from Dr. S stashed inside. What he really craved was tobacco, but not the chewing kind. He wanted a nicotine buzz combined with the distraction of a tactile, primal ritual that included the crude pleasures of sharp objects and fire.

Watching the road, he blindly felt around in the console box and withdrew a neatly wrapped cigar, a box of matches and a pocket knife. The heavy scent of Connecticut Shade wrapper filled the cab as he held the cigar close, drinking in its aroma. Just the smell of the pungent, aged tobacco soothed his nerves. After merging into the congested traffic of highway 59, Stokes steered with his knee, removed the red and gold band, unwrapped the thin, yellowed tissue, and squeezed the barrel of the cigar, feeling it flex. The claro leaf remained moist and full of its analgesic oils. He opened the knife and effortlessly made a deep slit in the tip of the cigar, marveling at the fine razor edge of the blade.

Caught up in the act, he allowed the truck to drift. A horn blared and a semi roared past, forcing him to yank the wheel as the trailer's draft rocked the Suburban from side to side. He ignored the near-death encounter with the single-minded obsession known only to an addict intent on a fix. He merged right to take the loop, then turned off the air-conditioner and struck a Ritz match: a thick chunk of wood with a solid glob of bright blue sulphur on the tip, carefully chosen by the image-conscious consultants who managed the world-wide reputation of the hotel.

"Now that is a damn solid match," he muttered, the cigar clenched in his teeth.

Drawing on the cigar, he watched the flame suck inward. He released the draw and the flame reset itself, burning high and bright and yellow, without a flicker. Cigar smoke swirled in a great looping cloud that hung in the air, and the woody, rich smell mixed with the odors of brand-new leather seats, untouched carpet, and a hint of acrid sulphur. Deep in the recesses of his brain, endorphins escaped and danced through his veins. He drew on the cigar repeatedly, grinning like a true pyro while watching the flame draw in and then resume its strong burn over and over. Then he felt the strong, solid, hot, *damn hot,* flame singe his forefinger.

"Shit."

He shook the match, dropped it in the opened ashtray, then swerved right, cut across the graveled median, nearly took out a safety barrel and exited onto Westheimer.

"What a dumb shit."

He glanced at the whitened end of his scorched finger. With the air-conditioner back on, he opened the sunroof and turned up the stereo. He rested the tip of his finger in the cold stream blowing from the vent, and drove on to Ravenwood smoking a fabulous cigar.

"Hey Pat," Stokes shouted out his open roof as he pulled alongside Pat's BMW. Pat was sitting in the front seat with his door open, changing his shoes. Stokes parked, climbed out, and walked around to Pat's door.

"Does every vehicle you buy have a cigar vent?" Pat nodded toward the Suburban's open sunroof.

"I'm glad I caught you out here."

"Oh don't worry, they'll let you smoke on the patio of the bar."

Stokes smiled and scrutinized the cigar in his hand. "No, it's not that. I just had a long talk with Mimi. We're getting divorced."

"Oh . . . I'm sorry Stokes."

"Yeah, well, some things don't work out the way we plan. I have some questions and I need some advice."

"I don't think I--"

"I'm not asking you. There's an obvious conflict with you and the O'Donnell family. I don't want to burden you with any information, but I'm just wondering, do you think I should hire a lawyer?"

"You know, Stokes, for a really smart guy sometimes you ask some really stupid questions."

"Seriously. That's why I'm asking you. You know all the details. Mimi and I have a pre-nup and a post-nup. Your firm drafted it all. I don't think there's going to be any argument about who gets what. I'm licensed. I don't want to pay another firm three hundred fifty dollars an hour to make one court appearance and do ten hours of office work. And I'm perfectly capable of reading an agreement and signing it."

Pat stared at Stokes with a serious, contemplative look on his face.

"Get a lawyer."

"I–"

"We never had this conversation. I never told you this. Get a lawyer. Now let's go in and get a beer."

"Pat . . . I think I want to go drive around."

"Do that. The guy who drafted your pre-nup was a goofball. We fired him two years ago."

Stokes looked at him, considering what that meant. "Thanks," he said, turning to leave.

"By the way, you look happier right now than I've seen you look in years—like a weight's been lifted off your shoulders."

"Yeah, people kept telling me that last night at the party. Hell, you told me that last night at the party."

"I did? Must have been wasted, I don't remember . . . . You shouldn't listen to me when I'm drinking."

They both laughed.

Stokes drove out of the parking lot and down the short drive. He did not like Pat's answer. For one, he did not want anyone else knowing his business. Second, he knew he needed a lawyer without having to ask. Truth was, he just wanted someone to talk to. *So why didn't I talk to him?* He took another long draw on his cigar. *Maybe if I had a few drinks I could talk about this, but not now.*

Part of him felt great. Another part felt like a failure. Stokes's parents were married for almost fifty years before his dad died. Big John and Lovey just celebrated forty. In his dad's family there were seven brothers and two sisters and, of the boys, five of them had married in their twenties and were still married now in their seventies and eighties. But there was no possible way he was staying married to Mimi any longer.

He blew a mouthful of Cuban smoke at the road ahead. *Failure or not, I'm going to change some things. I'm going to rescue what's left of that little kid; at least I'm going to try. I'll be god-damned if I'm going to sleepwalk through the rest of my life.*

CHAPTER TWELVE

Stokes found himself on I-45, southbound again, headed for the boat. His stomach rumbled, so he took the NASA Road 1 exit. Frenchie's would be open. On his way down east NASA Road, he passed a one-story, brick and glass building with a sign out front that read: "Morgan & Witt, Attorneys at Law." He knew all the major law firms in town, but he'd never heard of Morgan & Witt. *That might be a good thing.* A car sat in the parking lot and lights were on inside the building.

Stokes drove the ten blocks to Frenchie's and pulled in. Then he placed his nearly-finished cigar back in his mouth, gripped the steering wheel and made a hand over hand u-turn out of the lot. When he pulled into Morgan & Witt's drive, a woman who looked to be around fifty was unlocking her car. A large stack of papers sat on the roof of her sedan.

"Excuse me," he said through the open window of his truck. "I hate to bother you like this, but are you Mrs. Morgan?"

She smiled. "No, it's Mr. Morgan, but I'm Mrs. Witt."

"I'm Stokes Summers. Do you handle divorces?"

"Mostly. That's why I'm here today." She chuckled lightly.

Stokes liked her. She seemed sharp, cheerful, and she worked on Saturdays. "Well, I'm getting divorced and I might want to hire you."

Melinda Witt plopped her papers on the front seat and closed the passenger door. "Well, I just happen to be in the market for more business Mr. Summers. Why don't we go inside and talk?"

Mrs. Witt wasted no time. She explained up front that she charged one hundred and fifty dollars an hour and wanted a retainer of one thousand dollars. Stokes had that much cash in his wallet. Poco was next week. He wrote her a check.

For the next two hours, Stokes talked; Melinda took notes. He laid out the marital assets: their home, artwork, furniture, a few cars, his truck, and he explained the situation with the *Princess*. He also told her about his pre and post-nuptial agreements, and the complicating factor of his powerful in-laws and their equally powerful lawyers at Vincent & Gump. Melinda asked for the name of the O'Donnell's accounting firm, which Stokes provided. He knew she needed a clear picture of the finances if she was to protect him in the divorce. He also asked her to call Molly if she had any questions regarding his compensation package. He outlined the O'Donnell Oil businesses, their many family trusts and the broad network of other businesses owned both by the family members and their trusts.

It impressed Stokes that Melinda listened passively and seemed unaffected by the large amounts of money involved. His position was simple. His employment contract with O'Donnell Oil was straightforward and entered into before the marriage. It specified Stokes was entitled to a salary and a percentage of profits on deals he originated or handled himself. The nuptial agreements ratified the employment contract and categorized all employment income as Stokes's separate property. Stokes had asked for this since Mimi's side of the agreement listed many millions in assets and trusts set up by the

Robicheaux family and by Dutch O'Donnell, and later John and Lovey O'Donnell, for Mimi's benefit. Obviously Mimi would be well provided for, even in advance of the staggering inheritance she would split one day with her brother.

Stokes did not remember much family law from school, but he thought there might be a case on whether the contract could validly classify proceeds from the wells as separate property since he obtained his interest during the marriage. He told Melinda that as far as he was concerned, Mimi could have the house and everything in it, but he wanted the boat. He also assured her this would be the easiest divorce she had ever handled.

"I hear that a lot," she replied with more than a touch of cynicism. "You know, of course, there's no such thing as a legal separation under Texas law. It takes at least sixty-one days to get a divorce, even if both sides are in agreement. So you're still married until the court says otherwise."

Stokes slumped in his chair. Prior to this, he had not allowed himself to seriously consider a divorce, even though he had been unhappy for much of the last six years. But he was determined to pull the trigger and wanted out as quickly as possible. He slid to the edge of his seat and picked up his checkbook off the desk.

"I want to start the proceedings immediately."

"I'll call Vincent & Gump first thing Monday morning."

For a brief moment he appeared to puzzle over her words, then he laid his checkbook down again.

"Better yet, you get me out within seventy days, I'll triple your rate and throw in a bonus."

"I'd love to take your money, but unless I take a judge hostage, I'm not sure I can make that happen. Still, I'll give it my best shot."

With that, Stokes said good night and Melinda locked herself in.

Outside, a northwest breeze swept leaves across the parking lot.

The sun was down, but the clear July sky still held a soft radiance. *This might be a step off the end of a plank, but it's a step.*

He decided to take *Princess* out in the lake and anchor for the night. He stopped at Frenchie's and ordered two spaghetti dinners, but when he reached the boat he was disappointed to find J.P. was not there. He turned on the television, sat on the couch, ate dinner and fell asleep. Around midnight, he woke up and went to bed.

CHAPTER THIRTEEN

Before daybreak Sunday morning, Stokes heard J.P. say, "Get up fuckhead." Without opening his eyes, he grumbled: "Why?"

"We're going to church."

"What?"

"St. Paul's has an early mass. Don't you want to hear the good news?"

J.P. cackled and smacked on the plastic tip of a small cigar.

Stokes smiled, opened his eyes and swung his arm, whipping a pillow in J.P.'s direction.

J.P. stepped out of the path of the airborne assault-pillow; its wind made the cigar's end glow red momentarily.

"Seriously," J.P. said. "We have a busy day. We've got Poco Bueno this week. I need to leave today to get to Rockport. It may take a day to get everything done there, and then I'll go to Port O'Connor. You can come down and meet me early Tuesday to pre-fish for a day. I can't get Pete down here to service the gen-sets because he went on vacation without telling me. So we're going to change the oil and filters. Then we're going to change the impellers on the engines and the generators, change every fuel filter and clean every water strainer on the boat. We're going to do all that by noon. Then we're going to run to Smith Point for a shake-down cruise and I'm going to leave by 3:30."

"Let's don't and say we did." Stokes threw the comforter to the side of the bed. "Anyway, don't you have that little baby doll Angie to play with today?"

"I just left her apartment. By the way, we took the Volvo to your house last night. Angie's going to ride to Rockport with me and then fly out of Corpus. She has a photo shoot on Tuesday for a nutrition bar that wanna-be health nuts are buying by the truck load. The bars weigh eighty grams and thirty grams of that is sugar. Go figure."

"Not everyone has the nutritional scruples that we do J.P."

Stokes rolled out of bed. J.P. puffed on his cheap cigar and handed Stokes a Bloody Mary.

"Want a Swisher?"

"Not yet."

They chinked their glasses together. "To divorce," J.P. said.

"And good nutrition," Stokes said.

CHAPTER FOURTEEN

*P*rincess – the boat, not the wife.

Because of her lines, her paint job and the ridiculously expensive stainless steel trim highlighting her every curve, she captivated everyone who saw her. She was truly a graceful yacht – but this was *after* she met Stokes and J.P.

During his engagement to Mimi, Stokes heard John tell stories about his boat. He assumed she had fallen to ruins from the way Big John described her and he repeatedly suggested to Mimi that they at least go look at *Princess*, but she could not have cared less and he eventually quit asking. For the first busy six months he worked for O'Donnell Oil, all Stokes knew about her was John owned a big sportfisher he never used. Stokes bided his time, hoping for an invite to go fishing. Then, in January, five months before the wedding, John mentioned at lunch he was about to sign a contract to sell *Princess*.

"How about selling her to me instead?" Stokes asked, forgetting for the moment that he was already in debt up to his eyeballs. He had always had an adolescent obsession for boats, and four hundred thousand for a seventy-foot Hatteras had to be a steal, even if she was eighteen years old.

John jokingly consented to sell *Princess* to Stokes, thinking his future son-in-law wasn't serious. But after lunch, Stokes drove to Kemah with the keys. Far from the wrecked hulk John described in his cocktail stories, *Princess* looked more like a dirty orphan in need of a loving parent. She showed more as a yacht than a fishing boat and he went from room to room, exploring. The steering wheel in the enclosed flybridge refused to move, and he had to put his full weight on it before it would budge. Once loosened, hydraulic fluid leaked out below the dash. None of the toilets had water in them, and none of the faucets worked, but Stokes remained undeterred. The electronics functioned and he had fun just flipping switches and finding out what they did.

Smitten, he left the marina and went straight to the bank to set up a loan.

Then he talked with Mimi.

True to form, Mimi could not understand why Stokes would want to buy an old boat, especially her family's old boat. All Stokes had to do was ask John not to sell her. But Stokes did not want to fix up a boat someone else owned, even family. He convinced Mimi *Princess* was worth the investment and she decided his childish fascination with the boat was cute, so she consented.

John offered to give *Princess* to Stokes as a wedding present, but he insisted on buying her. Big John did persuade him to sign a note, payable "on demand," which–to John–meant Stokes only had to pay back the loan when–and if–he could afford it.

So John sold *Princess* to his new son-in-law, and felt fortunate when he stopped paying dock fees and insurance on a boat he never used. He felt doubly glad Stokes bought her and he looked forward to fishing again, maybe once per season, on a big, long, stable boat someone else owned.

In October of that year, returning from his eighth or ninth trip, Stokes maneuvered *Princess* past the jetties of Seabrook harbor. When he turned, the tide and wind sucked her sideways. He threw both engines into reverse, but this swung her long bow and she hit the rocks, sending a sickening shudder through the boat and everyone aboard. Once docked, Stokes inspected her, and as far as he could tell, the rocks had not pierced the hull.

That night he placed three extra pumps in the bilges and the next day he called a local shipyard to arrange the haul out of *Princess*.

That is when he met Jean Paul.

The shipyard manager recommended Jean Paul Gilpin to do fiberglass work. But when Stokes called him, Jean Paul immediately said, "No thanks, I'd rather step on nails and eat glass than screw with fiberglass again."

"I'll pay for your time if you'll just come by and give me an estimate of what needs to be done and tell me who can do it."

No response.

"She's a seventy-foot Hatt and I keep a supply of cold beer and cigars on board."

"I'll try and swing by later."

That evening, Stokes concluded the chances of this Gilpin guy ever showing up were slim to none. He put on a mask and snorkel and went swimming, expecting to find a gouge in the green, hair-like slime covering her hull. He found only a shallow scratch. While he climbed a ladder onto the dock, a truck pulled into the parking lot. A tall, broad-shouldered fellow stepped out, staring at *Princess*.

"You Stokes?" he asked as he walked toward the boat, still staring and clearly enamored with her. Without waiting for an answer, he added, "I should take a beer and a cigar from you right now, shoot you and leave. Anybody that puts a hole in a boat like this deserves to die."

"I'd agree with you, but I've just spent the last hour rubbing her belly and I can't find anything more than a few scratches. So don't shoot."

Jean Paul removed his sunglasses and gazed at the white hull.

"She's a wide bitch. How long's she been under this cover?" he asked, glancing up at the shed.

"Years. I really don't know how long."

"Sitting covered like this, her glass should be in good shape above the water. Below would depend on the quality of the original work and her last bottom job. Let's have a look."

Stokes held out the mask but Jean Paul did not take it.

"I meant from the inside."

For the next five hours, they walked, climbed and crawled over every accessible inch of *Princess*. Stokes explained he'd had difficulty backing her in a cross wind. Jean Paul was not surprised.

"You need a thruster to control that swinging bow. This is a boat worth preserving." J.P. crouched next to the transom and pointed with the clear neck of his bottle. "These numbers show she was the initial hull in her series. After fairing, she was probably used as a template.

"This number," he indicated the last two numbers in the series, "tells you her birth year. Back in '78, Hatteras had been building fiberglass boats for eighteen years, and they knew how to impart strength to their materials. Their best trade secret was hand-laying the thinnest fiber possible, soaking it completely in resin, and then squeezing out all the excess before the glass hardened. All the manufacturers know that now, but back then, no other company had the expertise, or the crew, for such a labor-intensive job. If there was ever a firm foundation on a boat, this is it. She needs to be fixed up right."

Jean Paul was an expert, or so he sounded, and he commented on everything. They discussed electrolysis and the destructive power of saltwater on props and exposed metal parts. He rattled off information on anodes in encyclopedic fashion. They talked about floor paint, engine room paint, bottom paint and wall paint until Stokes grew so tired of trying to understand which two-phase acrylic or epoxy paint Jean Paul recommended for which job that he quit trying to listen. Jean

Paul also insisted Stokes haul her out immediately, explaining that a "bottom job" on a fiberglass boat is a vital part of regular maintenance.

After only a few hours, Stokes offered Jean Paul a job restoring *Princess*, thinking it would take less than two months to pull her out, do the work, and put her back in the water. Jean Paul figured it would take at least three, maybe as long as four. After considering it for a day, he accepted.

Then they decided to fix a few more things.

An entire fishing season came and went. Every time they ordered something, they realized they needed something else. Every time they pulled out a wall or stripped a wire, they had to replace it. Every project created a project. They ended up gutting the hull, and Stokes turned into his own worst enemy, visualizing the luxury interior he wanted and stubbornly setting his mind toward making it happen. But the more he worked with Jean Paul, the more frustrated he became. Despite little formal education, Jean Paul had a quirky, savant-like ability to process numbers, charts and graphs. In addition to reading every issue of every yachting, boating and fishing magazine, Jean Paul would read the label, the engineering statistics, the warnings, the ingredients, the performance charts and package inserts of everything they bought. And he understood them. Stokes did not. Every day it seemed Jean Paul spoke on the phone with a manufacturer of glue or paint or wire or sonar, asking technical questions that only their most senior product representatives or engineers could answer. At least once a week, he would relate that something on a performance graph was wrong or something about a radar or radio could be modified to work easier with something else. The months drew out.

Stokes never intended to completely refurbish *Princess* and neither did Jean Paul. Two years later, they were ready to kill each other.

CHAPTER FIFTEEN

"So what's it going to be?" J.P. asked.

"What are you talking about?" Stokes said.

"The name dude. What are you going to name her? Whatever it is, I want to change our registration at the tournament. You said you're definitely getting a divorce so you ought to take the next step. Dropping the name 'Princess' off this boat would be a really good start."

"I already told you the new name J.P."

"Stokes, my boy, you don't have the huevos to call her that."

"You're wrong, amigo. It may say 'Princess' on her stern right now but we just changed the oil and filters on the 'Break Wind.'"

"Now you're talking. I have a present for you."

J.P. washed his hands in the cockpit sink, went to the back door, kicked off his flip-flops, then disappeared inside. A few seconds later, he returned holding a cardboard cylinder about four inches in diameter and three feet long.

"What is it?" Stokes asked.

"You've gotta clean your hands."

Stokes walked over to the sink.

"Is that a flag?"

"Nope."

Stokes reached for the cylinder.

J.P. yanked it away.

"Dry 'em."

Stokes rocked his head and dried his hands on a white embroidered towel hanging from a metal clip in front of the sink.

"Okay?" Stokes held up his hands for inspection like a television doctor prepping for surgery. "They're clean. What's in the tube?"

J.P. pulled a metal stopper out of one end and reached inside. He spun his hand to tighten the roll, then slowly removed a white paper pipe.

"Hold both corners," J.P. said, "and don't let go. This is important."

"Yes sir."

J.P. and Stokes stepped apart, unfurling the roll of paper. Stokes chuckled as the letters "D," "N," and "I" appeared.

"You dog," Stokes said.

"I picked it up yesterday at the sign shop. It's the same size, style and font of the lettering we used the first time."

"Let's look."

They raised the full length of waxy paper over the fighting chair and positioned it on the transom.

"Whatever you do, don't let it touch the water," J.P. said.

"No problem. We need to put this on right now."

For the next hour, J.P. and Stokes peeled and razored the letters P R I N C E S S off the back of the vessel and then taped the white paper to the stern. They slowly burnished the blue vinyl letters B R E A K W I N D from the paper to the boat. Stokes completed the last of the letters while Jean Paul took a call from Angie.

"Stokes, Angie has three gorgeous friends who want to take a boat ride today. Okay with you if I ask them to ride to Corpus with Angie and I?"

"That's totally up to you, but . . . ," Stokes paused and checked to see if the "E" had adhered clean without any bubbles, "how are you going to survive, just you and four girls?"

"Actually, you should go with us. It would do you good to make the run. Life is short dude. We could have a *really* good time."

"No. The attorney told me I'm married until the divorce is final and that will be at least two months. If I ran to Corpus with you, Angie and three of her friends, Mimi would shoot me. Let me correct that. She would have me shot."

"Fuck her. In fact, let's invite our tournament crew to leave early and make a week of it."

"No," Stokes insisted.

"Answer a question for me. Since the day we met on this boat, what have we always wanted to do? What have we always talked about doing?"

Stokes knew immediately what J.P. was getting at and he recited their mutual dream in a monotone voice, sounding as tired and bored as possible: "Get some strippers, take the boat out for a week, and have a wild, naked, drunken fuck-fest."

"Exactly. And you are *never* going to do it. So let's do the next best thing. Let's go with these girls, today, right now, and have a party."

Stokes looked up at J.P. and then went back to burnishing the "R." He rubbed the wax paper with a rubber spatula and peeled back the paper again to inspect his work.

"What time is it?"

"Nine," J.P. said.

CHAPTER SIXTEEN

By 10:30 they had a crew.

Stokes first called Pat, who could not make the trip and had to unexpectedly cancel for the tournament because of his work schedule. Next, he phoned Wayne Stearman. Wayne and his brother Blaine were fourth generation Texans and "to the manor born," just like the O'Donnell children. They had inherited most of their assets, including a large family fortune and a strong passion for the outdoors. Wayne was the eldest by a year. They were partners on three of the oil and gas deals Stokes had structured for the O'Donnells and they held interest in the Emmit deal Stokes had just closed.

The Stearmans had purchased controlling interest in "Spider Arms" several years before and had recently taken the company private. Running it was not terribly taxing since Spider had run itself for one hundred and forty years. They did quite well selling shotguns, rifles and ammunition to sportsmen all over the world.

Wayne was his usual, exuberant self and eager to call his brother. He rang Stokes back in less than a minute to confirm they could both make the trip since they had planned to be out of their offices

Tuesday through Friday. For them, leaving today simply meant missing one additional day of work. Wayne also asked if he could bring
someone along.

Stokes then called Dr. S, who was on the fishing crew for the tournament. Dr. S was in a pissy mood.

"I have to cancel. My wife just informed me she booked our plane
tickets to Europe for Saturday instead of Monday."

Stokes begged him to come with them now for a few days. Dr. S
gave him an unequivocal "no," explaining there was no possible way he
could be out for the beginning of the week.

"I have to work a full schedule Monday and Tuesday. I'll drive
down to Port O'Connor for the dinner Wednesday night and then return to Houston. Sorry buddy, but that's *all* I can do."

An hour later, Dr. S was speeding toward the marina in his Mase-
rati when he called Stokes back.

"I thought about it, called my nurse, told her to clear my schedule
and packed my bag. I'll see you in a few minutes."

That made five or six, excluding the girls. Stokes had not told any
of the men about the women since they had not absolutely confirmed
they were coming. That also gave the married guys cover. If they
were unaware these women would be on the boat, how could they be
blamed? Anyway, of all the crew, only Wayne Stearman would be worried. Dr. S kept a girlfriend on the side most of the time and Blaine was
single. No one would advertise that women went on the boat trip, but
Stokes had learned that word always seemed to leak out.

J.P. held his right shoulder to his right ear, squeezing his cell phone
to the side of his head. He handed Stokes a margarita glass full of orange juice and vodka garnished with a mint leaf. Actually it was more
of a *wad* of mint leaf. J.P. had smashed the pitiful plant between his
forefinger and thumb and rolled it until it gave up its oil. It looked like
a remnant of cooked spinach.

"We're switching to Screwdrivers cuz we're out of Bloody Mary mix and I don't want to pull out the blender," J.P. said.

Stokes held his cell away from his ear and pointed to the green lump floating on the icy orange surface.

"Nice touch."

By one-thirty that afternoon, engines were running, wet exhaust pipes were bubbling and Stokes was primed. Angie had arrived with two other goddesses and Suzanna. Jean Paul hadn't bothered to tell Stokes that Suzanna was one of the three friends.

Stokes fidgeted in his chair. Divorce or no divorce, if word of these girls on the *Princess . . . Break Wind . . .* reached Mimi, she would throw a gasket.

Dr. S was ecstatic. "Don't sweat it Stokesie," he said, reading Stokes's mind and body language while the girls piled out of their car with their bags. "Just roll with it."

Stokes finished a fresh drink in the time it took the girls to walk from their car to the boat, about fifty steps. All that remained in his glass were a few light-orange ice cubes and three wads of tattered mint.

Angie introduced the new girls. First came Sophia, a smoldering Italian beauty who had the dark, olive complexion of her Mediterranean ancestors. Despite a voluptuous body and sexy, curvy lips, her most arresting assets were her eyes: large, dark-brown irises set in clear, white orbs with an electrifying twinkle. The sort of woman who turned sophisticated men into tongue-tied fools.

Elsa, the fourth goddess, stood tall, with a mane of blond hair and Germanic features. She looked as though she had just jetted here from Chamonix. Stokes imagined her, with her statuesque bearing, modeling in a fur bikini in one of those ice-bound vodka ads. He felt confident the ad he visualized could sell millions of gallons.

After introductions, the crowd went inside. Stokes stayed out, his mind working overtime.

Four women and five men on a boat that sleeps five or six guys comfortably is going to be a rowdy crowd. On the other hand, we have plenty of sleeping pads and bed rolls. We've spent more than one night with nine people on board. Wayne said he might bring another guy; if so, that'll be ten. We could stop and get hotel rooms.

Stokes looked at his empty drink, tipped his glass, gleaned a taste of what remained, then lowered his hand.

Wayne could get in serious trouble with his wife.

No one is going to tell anyone.

These things get out.

Wayne can decide for himself whether to ride down. The girls are Jean Paul's friends. Out of my control.

Angie ran outside, bent over, picked up her purse and ran back inside. The booze, and the views, were winning Stokes over. He walked over to the stereo control panel and cranked up the volume. A guitar riff wailed.

Roll with it.

Wayne called to ask if he should get some ice on the way.

"We have three ice makers on board and a freezer full," Stokes replied.

"Should I get some water?"

"You can, but we have two hundred gallons of drinking water in the tanks and a watermaker."

They compromised on extra Bloody Mary mix. Before he hung up, Stokes explained about the girls.

Unfazed, Wayne responded: "My wife doesn't have anything to worry about, and my brother is going to love it. I'll be there in ten. Blaine is right behind me with the other fellow I told you about, Jordan Ansel. He's our marketing director at Spider."

Stokes hung up and sprawled in the fighting chair; a custom rod fitted with a gold Penn International eighty-wide rested in the holder.

He felt no pain as he patted the reel. "This is going to be the trip of my dreams," he said to the shiny, polished cylinder.

Dr. S exited the salon with a bottle of beer in one hand and a cigar in the other. He wore a white linen polo shirt and a thick, gold necklace. Combined with his dark skin and his swept-back, shiny silver hair, he looked like a Hollywood actor.

"Where are the others?" Stokes asked.

"Getting the grand tour. The girls all love the door handles and your steam bath."

"Naturally," Stokes said, trying to be brave.

Two Escalades pulled in to the closest open parking spaces in the lot. Wayne and Blaine climbed out wearing pressed jeans, white button-down shirts and white Stetson cowboy hats. Wayne's guest, Jordan, was a bald, burly, barrel-chested man who moved with the grace of an athlete.

"The arms dealers have arrived," Stokes said.

Dr. S put down his beer and went to help with the luggage. Stokes stayed seated, content to bask in the moment. Within a few minutes, the four men were on the dock at the stern of the boat with arms full of bags and booze.

"I've been hearing about this boat for months now; let me take a picture." Jordan raised a professional digital camera with a wide lens.

"This is priceless," Wayne said.

Stokes lifted his glass to the camera and Jordan took the picture. Then the salon door opened. Angie, Sophia and Elsa tumbled out and saw the camera. They laughed and yelled that they wanted to be in the picture. All were wearing string bikinis, holding unlit cigars, and giggling like children. Boobs bounced, nipples made their presence known through thin fabric, and bare feet pattered across the white-checkered fiberglass deck. Angie came around one side of the fine mahogany fighting chair, Sophia and Elsa circled the other. Jordan snapped a string of six shots while the girls struck poses.

Jordan lowered the camera slowly. The look on his face resembled a stunned spectator at a magic show who had just seen a tiger disappear before his eyes. He stared at his camera, wondering if he had really captured the images he had seen in his viewfinder. Then he looked at his bosses beside him, their eyes bugging under the brims of their Stetsons. Dr. S put his arms around the shoulders of Wayne and Blaine and calmly announced, "*That,* gentlemen, is what every man's dreams are made of: beautiful women, fast boats, a cold cocktail and a whole lot of money. I hope you got the name of the boat in the picture Jordan."

CHAPTER SEVENTEEN

After leaving Lakewood Yacht Club, the only stop the *Break Wind* had to make was to buy fuel from Charlie's. Stokes purchased his diesel there whenever possible because it was an easy in-and-out for a seventy-foot yacht and convenient to their home dock.

Charlie, like most retailers in the area, bought fuel wholesale from O'Donnell Fuel Supply, a small, unprofitable part of O'Donnell Oil, of which Danny was now president. Several vendors had found new suppliers since Danny took over–and he had plenty of excuses for the shrinking business–but Lovey and Big John were oblivious to the fact that the reason for OFS's losses was the complete neglect of its president. Regardless, it was an easy gig and it took no intelligence: perfect for young Danny.

Stokes never paid for fuel at Charlie's, he just signed the tickets. When OFS invoiced for deliveries, Charlie would note the amount Stokes purchased. The fuel Stokes "bought" was noted by O'Donnell bookkeeping and then "off booked" to another invoice. This resulted in Stokes buying wholesale directly from O'Donnell Oil. There was also another bonus to Stokes: the charges were held until the end of the year. Since he paid his bill at the same time O'Donnell Oil paid year-end bonuses, he obtained an interest-free loan on wholesale fuel.

While they filled their tanks, Stokes showed everyone where to stow their gear and gave each a job. Angie, Sophia and Elsa were to spray the dust off the windshields and the foredeck, and hoist the flags. Dr. S and Suzanna took charge of the blender and made margaritas. The Stearmans prepared plates of hors d'oeuvres. Stokes put on some new music. Jean Paul stood at the helm on the flybridge and slowly drove away from the fuel dock, hopelessly distracted by the bikini-clad trio before him on the bow. He zigged and zagged all over the channel.

They motored under the bridge that connects the town of Seabrook with the adjacent township of Kemah and approached the mouth of Clear Lake harbor. J.P. eased along at low speed, without creating a wake, with their flags raised and tunes blasting from their speakers. J.P., Stokes and Dr. S lounged on the flybridge, smoking torpedo-shaped maduros. Angie, Elsa and Sophia finished a quick clean-up of the front deck while enjoying the hot sun and the cool spray of the wash-down hose. The Stearmans, Jordan and Suzanna observed their progress from the cockpit. While they passed the outside patios of the restaurants and bars lining the Kemah boardwalk, heads turned and men hollered at the girls on the front of the boat. All three waved and jumped, loving the attention. Jean Paul blasted the horn repeatedly. Then, as soon as the stern was visible, people sitting at the outside tables pointed at the boat. This reaction continued in wave-like fashion down the quarter-mile boardwalk.

A laughing voice broke over the radio, "*Break Wind, Break Wind,* is that you Stokes?"

"Ten-four. This is Stokes on the *Break Wind*. Who am I talking to?"

"This is Peter at Landry's. We just watched you pass. I wanted you to know that I have a bar full and the only thing that received more attention than the phenomenal babes on the front of your boat was her new name. I love it. Everyone here was most impressed."

"Ten-four Peter. Thanks for the feedback. We'll stop in for a drink on our victorious return from Poco Bueno." Stokes hung up the microphone and looked at J.P.

"I think we started something here." J.P. pressed the throttle forward, leaving the "no wake" zone of the harbor behind.

Once they made the ship channel and turned south, J.P. asked Stokes to take the wheel so he could check the generators and engines. He grabbed a hand-held radio and hit the stairs.

Stokes watched the GPS screen, which displayed both knots and miles per hour. He tapped his palm on the top of the synchronized throttle, slowly increasing their speed. The deep roar of the new twin engines sounded like the jets of a small private plane, their pitch rising progressively as the screen read twenty-one, then twenty-five, then twenty-eight miles per hour.

"You there?" J.P. asked over the radio.

"Roger," Stokes replied.

"What's our speed?"

"Twenty-four knots."

"RPM's?"

"Almost sixteen hundred," Stokes said.

"Okay, hold her there. Nothing's leaking. I want to check some levels."

"What's he doing?" Dr. S asked Stokes. "I thought you spent all morning jacking with the engines."

"We did. And we checked all the levels and looked for leaks too, but that's why I love J.P. He always checks the engines and all the seacocks and even the toilet paper in the heads before a big trip. Hell, before any trip."

"Okay," J.P. called over the radio. "Let her run. I want it full throttle to check our RPM's with these props so I can compare it when we switch in Rockport."

"Ten-four."

Stokes turned to Dr. S. "I guess *that's* what he's doing."

Stokes keyed the mike again: "We have a mile or more clear ahead in the channel but there's a tug pushing some barges after that. I can open her up for a bit."

"Do it."

Stokes switched the mike to the public-address system, then adjusted the volume on the speaker. The three girls were still on the front deck, tanning, on their stomachs with the backs of their bikini tops untied.

"Hold on ladies," Stokes said. "I need to run at full throttle for a minute. Wave if you heard that."

All three held up a hand and waved without looking up.

Dr. S whacked Stokes on the arm with the back tips of his fingers.

"God-damn it. We could've had a free show if you wouldn't have tipped them off. Twenty-to-one said at least one of them would've sat up topless when you nailed it."

"Sorry Doc." Stokes spun around and yelled down at the cockpit, "Hold on," then he slowly pushed the throttle.

"I still can't believe how quiet this boat is," Dr. S said.

"It does make it nice," Stokes said, pushing the last inch of the throttle ahead.

The engines settled into a consonant roar.

At the higher speed Stokes adjusted the trim. The sound of water splashing the hull subsided as all seventy feet of the *Break Wind* lifted another inch out of the bay. The GPS screen read forty-five miles per hour. The girls on the front fastened their tops and sat up for the ride, facing forward and enjoying the headwind. The boat flags popped so sharply it seemed they could spontaneously shred at any moment.

"What's your speed?" J.P. asked over the radio.

"Forty knots."

"What's your RPM?"

"Twenty-one ninety, maybe twenty-two."

"We're only at twenty-two hundred? Cool!" J.P. yelled.

"You picked an appropriate name," Dr. S shouted over the din of the wind and water being assaulted by the big yacht racing south along the Galveston Ship Channel toward the Gulf.

"You're the first to get it," Stokes said.

"We're good down here," J.P. said.

Stokes quickly eased back on the throttle. The girls shot him a disappointed look, and Angie made a thumbs up motion several times. Stokes switched back to the P.A.

"We need to slow down for traffic. You guys can relax and sunbathe. With this north wind, we're going to have a flat sea all the way to Corpus so we should have plenty of opportunities to go fast later. Next time I speed up though, I'm not going to tell you. Dr. S here was disappointed he didn't see some skin earlier."

Angie looked up at Stokes and Dr. S on the flybridge, then grabbed her shoulder straps with her thumbs and peeled her bikini top down to her waist. She held her top there, exposing her breasts, and briefly shimmied side to side, smiling playfully. Then she lay down on her washboard stomach. Sophia pushed at her shoulder to chastise her.

Dr. S grabbed the microphone from Stokes.

"Darlin', you just made my year."

Angie waved again without looking up.

"Slut," Sophia said with a laugh.

"Lay-off."

"You'll show those puppies to anyone Angie."

"Well, they cost enough." Angie raised her head off her towel, rested her chin on the back of her clasped hands and wiggled her feet in the air behind her. "Look at him."

Two lovely faces swivel up toward the flybridge.

"Which one?"

"Stokesie. He saw me naked yesterday morning and he actually blushed."

"He's married Angie, and I thought you had the hots for J.P."

"Oh, I do." Angie waved her feet side to side. "I just can't believe a guy that's in his thirties could blush. He was sooo cute. And J.P. says he won't be married much longer."

"Really?" Elsa said, speaking up for the first time. "He's getting divorced?"

"Yes *really* . . . . But forget it Elsa. Suzanna saw him first and J.P. swears he would never cheat on his wife, even if he is getting divorced."

"Really?" Elsa repeated.

Behind the thick frames of her glasses, Angie's eyes narrowed and her pupils constricted as she turned to Elsa.

"Don't Elsa. I mean it."

Elsa shrugged and laid her head back on her towel. She arched her brow and nuzzled into the plush terrycloth, prompting Sophia to speak up.

"Leave him alone Elsa."

"Oh please pooh-kee. You both act like I'm some sort of pre-dah-tor."

Meanwhile, J.P. climbed the stairs to the flybridge.

"J.P., you're the luckiest man on the planet," Dr. S said, staring down at Angie.

"Nawh, that title belongs to Stokes. But I'm probably the happiest guy on the planet."

"I don't know," Stokes said. "I may have been miserable for a long time but fellas, I have to tell you, right now – I'm pretty fucking happy."

CHAPTER EIGHTEEN

On what turned out to be an extremely busy Sunday on the water, they cruised toward the Galveston jetties, slowing down often to avoid throwing their cresting wake at smaller boats. As Stokes expected, the north wind had slicked off the Gulf and it sparkled blue all the way to the beach in places. After two hours on the bow, Angie and Elsa retreated inside, leaving Sophia to tan alone. Behind the reflective lenses of his sunglasses, Stokes studied their bodies thoroughly while the girls walked the foredeck and disappeared behind the wall of the salon below.

"Perfect. Fucking perfect," J.P. said.

Stokes sat beside him, mirroring his thoughts, but saying nothing. Instead, he looked ahead to Sophia's bronze body, then past her hips, her thighs, and her toes; out onto the smooth ocean with the setting sun glaring in his eyes.

They had a clear path ahead in the calm waters along the Texas coast. The display on the flat screen read: "29 m.p.h." Stokes pushed forward on the throttle. The RPM's steadily climbed to twenty-one hundred, the miles per hour went to forty-two. He pressed the trim button, watching the display. The miles per hour climbed to forty-three, then forty-four and held. Sophia did not seem to mind the increased speed. Her only response was to wiggle her dark toes.

J.P. stood up.

"You want anything?"

"No," Stokes said. "I'm good."

J.P. went below. Stokes sat alone at the helm, enjoying the solitude. The *Break Wind* had ten people aboard but since the boat was broken up into multiple areas, it was possible to have some down time even with a crowd. The wind blew through his hair. He could feel the occasional slight change in the air temperature as the boat raced west, a result of the small thermoclines in the water they were crossing over. The Matagorda water tower was barely visible on the horizon.

They were making good time.

Stokes eased the throttles back to their previous position. He heard the salon door open, footsteps on the stairs, Angie's voice and Elsa's. Wayne spoke to someone from inside. Stokes was startled when J.P. answered from the steps. The salon door closed and Stokes glanced toward the stairs. J.P. was the first up, and he approached the bridge followed by Angie, Elsa, and then Blaine.

"I'm going below," Stokes said as he stood.

"Ten-four," J.P. said, plopping onto the bench.

Stokes turned and found himself face-to-face with Elsa. She stood her ground, blocking his exit. She gave him an up-and-down glance while she peeled off her shirt, revealing her long, taut body. With her arms outstretched, she dangled her shirt in her right hand. "Are you leaving us pooh-kee?" she asked, dropping the shirt on the dash with a flick of her wrist. She grabbed Stokes firmly by the hips, squared her body to his, and eased around the console to claim a spot in the sun.

Stokes took a moment to recover from the unexpected body contact and Elsa's sexy come-on. He had never before been called "pooh-kee" in such an overtly sexual tone, or any tone at all for that matter. The word had oozed from her lips, like syrup from a pile of pancakes.

When Elsa stepped away, but before Stokes recovered, Blaine approached from the stairs. He put his hand on Stokes's neck and leaned close.

"Bless you man," he whispered. "This is better than a titty bar."

Stokes laughed. Blaine grabbed Stokes's face, held his cheeks firmly with two broad hands and jokingly tried to plant a big kiss on his mouth. Stokes swung at Blaine's arms and they wrestled for a moment. Then, freeing himself from Blaine's grasp, Stokes jumped toward the stairs and hurried down. When his head was level with the flybridge floor he yelled, "Have fun." The stereo kicked on and a soulful piano solo filled the air. True to form, J.P. turned the volume up to the eardrum-piercing range.

Stokes went down into the salon to find out what everyone wanted to do about dinner. Inside, Wayne chatted happily with Suzanna in the kitchen, where he was mixing a large salad. Dr. S stopped pulling steaks out of an ice chest in order to silence his phone, and Suzanna poured wine. She handed Stokes a glass when he entered the salon.

"Try this," she said, raising one eyebrow.

"What is it?"

"Latour," Wayne said. "Most expensive shit I could find in my cellar."

"What's the occasion?"

Angie came running into the salon from upstairs.

"Life," Wayne slurred, a cigar in his mouth. "Life its own self." He glanced at Angie's bottom as she stepped by him. "This is wonderful Stokesie; glad you called."

Angie reached the galley and hastily scooped ice into foam cups with the name "Princess" printed on them. Dr. S pecked at his phone. He looked up excitedly. "There's a big smoker tomorrow night at the Petroleum Club in Corpus. We should go."

"What's a smoker?" Angie asked. She dropped a scoop of ice into a cup.

"A cigar party," Dr. S replied. "We have one once a year for the mission. The Corpus guys from our hospital network invite me to theirs all the time but I've never been. But this one tomorrow should be good, Peter Salizar is going to be there."

Stokes pulled several black marker pens from a drawer and placed them on the bar near Angie. "Try to get everyone to mark their cups. It's easier to keep up with them that way."

Angie poured a generous measure of Jack Daniels into each of the iced cups. "Who's Peter Salizar?"

Stokes looked at Dr. S. "Forgive her, she's new."

"Peter Salizar," Dr. S crowed as he stood, flourishing his right arm in a dramatic sweeping gesture while keeping his left hand on his chest, "is only the coolest guy in the history of the world. He killed his wife."

"He divorced his wife," Stokes said.

Angie opened two 7-Up cans and began topping off the drinks in front of her.

"Okay, he dumped the bitch," Dr. S said. "He was working as a dentist in Cleveland, Ohio, and he moved to the Dominican Republic, bought a huge plantation, and opened his own cigar factory."

"He inherited a fortune, including the tobacco plantation. He didn't have to buy shit," Stokes said.

Dr. S continued, "He now makes the best fucking cigar in the universe."

"Can't." Angie shrugged, then glanced down and absent-mindedly adjusted her boobs that were generously spilling out of her tight bikini top. "I gotta go to a shoot."

Stokes met Wayne's eye. They were the only two who had seen Angie re-set her breasts. Angie then picked up four drinks, squeezing them together between her hands and her boobs, and headed back outside. Stokes looked at her well-endowed chest, and then again at

Wayne. Dr. S ran to the door to open it for Angie. As he did so, Stokes and Wayne clinked two fine, crystal wine glasses together in a silent toast to Angie's chest.

They made their salute just as Jordan came up the hall stairs holding a stainless barbecue pit with two blunt pegs sticking out at odd angles from its base.

"Do you know where that goes?" Stokes asked Jordan.

"I'll figure it out."

Stokes turned around and led him out the door. They set the pegs in two rod holders mounted side by side in the gunnel. When the pit locked in place, Jordan shook it lightly. It sat level and rock solid. Stokes took the black hose from the back of the pit, pulled on a coupling and pressed it into a brass receptacle, where it made a "whoosh," audible over the wind and the rush of the hull cutting the water.

Stokes yelled to Jordan over the noise, "The propane line comes up inside this stanchion and through the pipe."

Jordan slapped his thigh. "Now that is slick as owl shit."

"You want to light that?" J.P. yelled from the flybridge. "If so, I'll slow down."

"Yeah," Stokes said. "Do that."

J.P. eased back on the throttle and Stokes and Jordan grabbed the transom to brace themselves. The *Break Wind* came off plane and settled into a fifteen-knot pace.

"I have a small pit, same brand as this, permanently mounted to the rail of my little sailboat. Compared to this rig, it's a piece of junk," Jordan said.

"Yet another Jean Paul innovation," Stokes said, his voice loud and his head swiveled toward the flybridge so J.P. would hear. "The guy knows how to rig a boat."

J.P. turned and shot them an appreciative smile.

* * * * *

Two hours later they were anchored miles east of Cedar Bayou and the Port A jetties. The sun had set. The north wind kept the mosquitos away and the sea flat. J.P. could have easily docked at a marina in Port Aransas, Corpus or Rockport, but he wanted to anchor and double-check all their systems before they went offshore for the tournament. The crew lingered around the dining table. Well into their sixth bottle of wine, they were having a good time getting to know each other. No one wanted to risk changing the mood by clearing the table. They had just finished viewing the photos Jordan had taken earlier of Stokes in the fighting chair, surrounded by the girls. Stokes sat quietly, thinking.

Dr. S stood up, grasping a broad-bladed steak knife. He flipped it over in the air, grabbed it by its wooden handle and tapped his fine, thin wine glass sharply with the thick backside of the blade.

Ting, ting, ting, ting.

"May I have your attention."

Everyone stopped talking and looked at Dr. S.

"Most of you know me, some of you don't, but I hope to get to know you all better very soon." He looked steadily at Elsa and Sophia and smiled.

Sophia giggled, her bright, Latin eyes focused on Dr. S. "Dream on sweetheart," she said, evoking laughter from everyone.

Dr. S ignored it. "I want to propose a toast; not to our host, or this lovely vessel, or to any of you; but to this day. It started out simple enough but the last eight hours have been an absolute blast. I don't know what it is, but every time I'm on this boat with you Stokes, I thoroughly enjoy myself. I want to sincerely thank you for calling me this morning . . . at the last minute."

This prompted more laughter all around.

Suzanna clapped and everyone joined in. When the ovation stopped, Jordan spoke up.

"You know guys, I'm in marketing and every day, all day, I'm trying to determine what people like and why. Today I've determined that this," he waved his left arm expansively to indicate the whole boat, "this is what *I* like."

Again, everyone laughed and there were a few "amens" and "hear-hears."

Blaine spoke up. "I'm with you Jordan. To me, this is paradise. I only wish I could make a living sitting here rather than sitting in a damn office."

"There isn't a man alive who wouldn't have enjoyed our trip today," Wayne said. "Our dad used to always say: 'Give people what they need and you'll make a living . . .'" Blaine joined his brother and their two voices chanted: "give them what they want and you'll make a fortune."

"What business was your daddy in?" Angie asked.

"He sold caskets!" Blaine howled. That broke up everyone at the table. As the chuckles died down, Blaine fanned the flames: "But he sold a shit load of caskets!"

Another outburst of laughter filled the air.

"Well boys," Suzanna said, "I shook it in Dallas for five years on the sidelines and I was in the office for two more selling fantasies to men in the form of pretty girls in cowgirl suits. I'm basically still in that business and I spend my days like Jordan, distilling what my customers like. I can tell you, if you could package today, men would buy it and then thank you for selling it to them."

Everyone nodded and agreed, then Stokes stood up, letting his chair screech on its steel coasters across the cherry floor.

"You can," he said.

Everyone looked at him.

"You absolutely can. Wayne, Blaine, Jordan, I have a great idea. How much do you guys spend on advertising at Spider every year?"

Wayne lifted his hands off the table. "Oh shit, I don't know."

"We spent just over six million last year, counting all platforms,"

Jordan said. "That includes domestic and foreign print, mostly South American in the foreign, plus the web, television, sponsorships and freebies. We're on target to spend about the same this year."

"Well, why not produce a show and direct it at your target market and let that be the bulk of your advertising?"

"We've thought about television a lot," Blaine said.

Wayne nodded.

"But there's not that much money in the budget," Blaine continued. "We can't run ads during football and baseball games in a cost effective manner. Our print ads in hunting magazines are the most effective things we do."

"I said produce a show," Stokes said. "Produce the whole thing, with Spider as the sponsor."

"What do you have in mind?" J.P. asked.

"I have in mind permanent employment for you and me, and a spot for most of the people at this table doing what they love, or, what was it your daddy said Wayne? Giving people what they want and making a fortune?"

"Okay," Wayne said, touching the tips of his fingers together, forming a steeple with his hands. "I'll bite. What's your concept?"

Stokes walked over to the television and pushed a button. The computer shut down. Stokes sighed.

J.P. walked over to help. "Do you want this on?"

"Please," Stokes said.

J.P. pushed the power button, then grabbed the remote. "TV?"

"No, the slide show Jordan just had on."

J.P. hit "monitor" on the remote then went to the laptop on the nav station dash and tapped the touchpad.

"That one," Stokes said. "Hold that please."

The big screen displayed a picture of Stokes, with Angie in her one-ounce bikini on one side, and Sophia and Elsa in their barely-present bikinis on the other.

"What do you see here?" Stokes asked the group. "What jumps out at you?"

Dr. S held his wine glass level with his eyes and said: "Three sets of the most bodacious tatas with headlights on that I've ever seen in my life. Pardon me, ladies, but I am just honestly answering the man's question. But how do I get to be involved with this venture, whatever the fuck it is?" He drank the glass dry.

"I'll answer your question in a minute Doc. But you started on the right track, albeit a little crudely. Come on everyone, what do you see?"

"Beautiful girls and a hot guy," Elsa said.

"A sweet, hot guy," Sophia said.

Stokes wanted to respond to the compliments but Wayne spoke up.

"Three babes and the luckiest man in the world."

"Three babes, a custom rod, and an International reel," said J.P.

"Sex on deck," Blaine said.

"Every man's fantasy," Suzanna said.

"Exactly!" Stokes said, pointing at Suzanna. "That's the concept, Wayne."

"Explain," Wayne said. He laced his fingers together and leaned forward in his seat, returning to the role of level-headed businessman.

"I'm the host," Stokes said, pointing at the screen. "These are my 'assistants.' Or, maybe my 'nieces.' We begin every show the same way from the back of the *Break Wind.* 'Hi, I'm Stokes Summers. I'm your host today for another version of the *Spider Arms Sportsman.*'"

He paused and briefly touched the lids of his eyes. "We have to work on the title. Anyway, we do something like a cross between the opening of *Tool Time* and the old *American Sportsman* with Curt Gowdy. We travel all over the world to hunt and fish with celebrities, and the girls are there as a teaser at the start of the show to attract the guys."

"I'm not watching unless there's a chance to see more pussy later. Again ladies, pardon the French," Dr. S slurred as he poured more wine.

Stokes fell silent and looked at Wayne and Blaine. Neither offered any comment.

"The niece deal was a joke," Stokes said. "Sarcasm."

Wayne appeared to be contemplating the idea while he stared at the screen.

Stokes thought he was being presumptuous, telling his friends how to run their business, and perhaps the bikini concept seemed a little too on-the-nose. But he'd already said it so he pressed on.

"I know it's sexist, but that's your market guys."

Wayne stared at the picture for a moment longer, wrung his hands together, then turned toward Stokes.

"I'm not doubting you there, I'm just picturing all three girls wearing different bikinis in every opening."

Again there was more laughter. Most of the people around the table assumed Stokes was just rambling, but Stokes was thinking he had just discovered a new way to make a living–while playing. It was a job in which he would be his own boss, and one that took advantage of his two biggest post-divorce assets: his boat, and his willingness to work.

CHAPTER NINETEEN

Thirty minutes later, after a group effort to clear and clean the dishes, Jean Paul approached Stokes near the bar. "You are *way* off track here," he whispered.

"Maybe."

"How are you going to produce a TV show?"

"The same way we rebuilt this boat," Stokes said. "One board at a time."

For the next four hours, Stokes wanted to talk about ideas for a show. Everyone else stayed interested for an hour but their attention faded as the margaritas, wine, after-dinner port, and coffee with Bailey's worked their spells. J.P. lowered the dining table into the floor and rearranged the seats. He dropped the surfboard table's ironing-board style legs, slid the table under the couch, then put *The Graduate* on the big screen. Bodies lounged on couches, pads and sleeping bags.

Stokes, Suzanna and Wayne stepped outside to smoke and continue the conversation. They sat on folding chairs in the cockpit under the stars. The bow anchor kept the stern out of the wind.

"Do you seriously want to take on a project like this?" Wayne asked.

"I do. To be honest Wayne, I've always wanted to do something on radio or television. Everybody has some secret dream. Mine has been to do something creative. The reason I went to U.T. was their communications program. I was a film major, but before I graduated, my dad offered to help pay for law school, so I did that. Dad died before I finished my first semester and . . . well, anyway . . . it's six years since I earned my law degree and here I am chasing oil for my in-laws. But, yeah, to answer your question, I'd like to do something like this. If we do it right, we could entertain a whole lot of people and have a helluva good time. I don't want to sound cocky but I think I'd be good at it."

Wayne took a long draw on his cigar and slowly nodded. "If anyone can do it, you can. You're photogenic. You could appeal to a wide audience, but you have no background and no experience with anything in the entertainment field."

"True. When I started with the O'Donnells, the only thing I knew about the oil business was my father was in it. When we rebuilt this boat I had a vision, but no earthly idea how to do anything it required. You know Wayne there are people in this world who are paid piles of money to be boat designers. It's a highly creative process. J.P. engineered the mechanics, but I drew up the interior of this boat, by hand, on paper, down to the quarter inch. And I loved every last minute of it. Hell, rebuilding this boat is the only creative thing I've done in the last ten years. I had a naval architect and two engineers tell me they'd rarely seen a vessel interior with a better layout. They also told me I should license the door handles and patent the floor magnet system that holds the dining chairs. I'm not too worried about making a television show. I've watched plenty of them and I know what I like.

"Besides, there are thousands, hundreds of thousands, of guys like us out there who aren't nearly as fortunate as we are. Most men would kill to live just one day like we did today. And those guys buy your guns. Everyone dreams of quitting the rat race, leaving their job, disappearing with their dream girl, and just . . . you know . . . extending that feeling forever. But no one ever does. How great would it be to let a hundred thousand guys share today with us, even if it's vicariously? And if we put it on film, they can do it again and again. Just like the quirky, romantic experience they're all getting inside right now by watching *The Graduate*. If we get the show exactly right, with great scripts, believable plots, plenty of skin, and we catch a big fish now and then, we'll be making money on reruns for a long, long time."

"I get the feeling you've thought about this quite a bit," Suzanna said.

"I have. Not in these terms, but in general. The escape dream is universal. Plus, with my divorce, I'm about to be out of a job."

"Don't bet on that," Wayne said.

"There was something we studied when I was in high school that I think about all the time," Stokes said. "Freud said we're happiest and saddest when we either succeed or fail in influencing other people."

He took a long drink from a bottle of water. "I know that sounds a little strange but that was the gist of what he said. I always dreamed if I could write a song or a poem that people liked—something that gave others pleasure or an escape, even for just a few minutes—that would be pretty cool. To me, affecting as many people as possible, in a positive way, would have to be my ultimate goal in life. That and making a ton of money." Stokes laughed.

"So you want to influence people, lots of people, by being the host of a hunting and fishing show?" Wayne asked.

"And give up your job or, at least, your profession?" Suzanna said.

"Well, yeah . . . maybe . . . .. And I'm not giving up my job. I just can't see how I won't be fired soon. Plus, the more I talk about it, the more I like this idea. Think about it. We all remember the television shows we grew up with, especially the good ones. The media has a big influence on us. If we produce a positive show about what we love–fishing, hunting, the outdoors–we could help shape the current sportsmen out there and the next generation. We could celebrate the positive aspects: the peace people gain from being outdoors, the camaraderie, the fun of it all. I would personally love to watch a well-produced show on hunting and fishing, but there aren't many that are well produced."

"Because it would cost a fortune to produce just one," Suzanna said.

"Everything costs money, and doing anything right costs twice as much as just doing it pretty good," Stokes said. "I'm willing to put my money on doing it right, but I don't want to waste it on anything less."

"Well," Wayne said, "I'm interested, but I'm not sure how we start."

"Let's start this way. If Spider will sign on to sponsor the show, I'll split the up-front cost of a couple pilots with you. We'll hire a film crew and start writing scripts. If we sell the show to a network or manage to get it on television ourselves and sell advertising, we'll split the profits. The only catch is I want full creative control. I warn you, I'm going to do things right. We're going to get celebrities on the show to keep it interesting, we're going to shoot in exotic locations around the world, and we're going to use high-quality people and equipment to film it, not tape it. That'll give it a softer, more theatrical look."

Wayne was writing something on the smooth backside of the golf towel that had been hanging next to the cockpit sink. The towel had "Princess" embroidered on it in big, blue letters. "Here," he handed Stokes the towel which read: *50/50 cost split between Spider and Summers and 50/50 profit. Summers has creative control. We do it all first class. s/Wayne Stearman.*

"All right partner, you have a deal," Stokes said. He signed the towel with the Sharpie Wayne handed him. "You keep up with our contract."

"So, again, I have the same question," Wayne said, folding the rectangle of cloth. "What's our first step?"

"There are a couple of people who can help us get started. For one, an ESPN crew will be at Poco Bueno. They're doing a one-time special on big-game fishing tournaments and the invite mentioned they would be there. I can also call my friend Cutt Adelman in San Antone. He produces a fitness show and has done TV stuff for years. I helped him with some of his ad contracts and we talk all the time."

"Or, you could ask me," Suzanna said.

"Okay," Stokes said. "What should we do?"

"Call Out Field Media in Albany, New York. They produce TV field sports for the Outdoor Network. Schedule a film crew for whenever you want to start shooting. Then write a script or two as fast as you can and sign up every sponsor you can find."

"I take it you've done this before," Stokes said.

"Sort of. I helped write a show about becoming a cheerleader that aired in Dallas. One of the directors of our show is a close friend of mine and now works for Out Field. They send crews all over the world. They hire freelance videographers and editors all the time and they also have a huge crew of their own. You're going to need an outfit like that. If you film outside the U.S., you have to have a full-time staff just to get the visas and permits you need and to deal with all the foreign embassies and corrupt governments. They also have a full production house. When you call, you might not want to mention your feeling about how poorly most sporting shows are produced."

"If they're that good, I'm sure they'll agree their competition can be awful," said Wayne. "I mean, most of those shows look like Billy Bob took his video camera to the lake after guzzling a couple of six-packs."

"That's true; and my friend Sandra will agree with you on that point."

"Sandra?" Stokes asked.

"Yes, Sandra. She's the director. Why?" Suzanna stared at Stokes.

"Nothing. But I would've guessed a director of a hunting show would be a man."

"Really?" Suzanna folded her arms across her chest. "Well, you would've guessed wrong."

"I'm thinking I may have gotten a lot of things wrong about you

Suzanna. Are you upset with me or something I said? You haven't said much to me today."

Wayne stood, holding his square of terry cloth. "You two work this out, whatever it is. I'm going to the men's room. Can I get you anything?"

"No thanks," Stokes and Suzanna said in unison.

With Wayne's departure, Suzanna let loose: "For starters, where do you get off calling me at one in the morning and then hanging up on me?"

"Oh shit. I meant to explain that to you. J.P. programmed my phone and put you on it as my girlfriend."

Suzanna gripped the arms of her chair and leaned forward, opening her eyes wider. "Excuse me?"

"No, wait, it was a joke. J.P. was teasing me about talking with you all night at the Safari Club banquet. So he programmed the voice commands on my new truck to dial you if I said the word girlfriend. It was a joke, but it backfired, royally."

Suzanna raised her left eyebrow.

"Look, J.P. loves to kid around, it was nothing more than that. Unfortunately, when I called I was having an argument with my wife and I couldn't explain things very well to either of you. I should've called you back. I'm really sorry."

The wind blew a strand of hair across Suzanna's face and she pulled it away, smoothly tucking it behind her ear.

"You look like a hurt puppy," she said, just before she broke up laughing. "I'm the one who's sorry. J.P. and Angie told me all about it yesterday. I promised I would make you sweat a little before we told you I knew."

Stokes stared at Suzanna with his head cocked to one side.

"Oh, don't look so astonished honey," she said, patting him on the knee. "Wayne was in on it too."

Wayne came back outside, followed by Blaine, Jean Paul and Angie.

"So, are we really going to *try* this?" Blaine asked.

"No," Stokes said. "We're really going to *do* this."

Suzanna shot a wry look at J.P., Angie and Wayne.

"What?" Blaine asked. "Did I miss something?"

"I told him," Suzanna said.

"Oh," Angie said, "why so quick? You should have made him squirm." She stood behind Stokes and ran her hand through his thick, wavy, brown hair, purposefully messing it up and making his bangs hang over his eyes.

"I think I've squirmed enough over your little prank." Stokes rearranged his hair with his hands.

"Will someone let me know what's going on?" Blaine asked.

Angie happily explained to Blaine the details of the joke. They all kept talking for another hour before turning in.

That night, aboard the *Break Wind*, Stokes hardly slept. Ideas for the Spider Arms program kept running through his head. He rose from the cushion he had been lying on, sat at the bar and began writing ideas on a yellow notepad. Just before dawn, Suzanna came out of the master bedroom, where she had slept with Sophia and Elsa.

"Morning," Suzanna said. "You have the first episode written yet?"

"No," Stokes whispered, "but I have four or five in my head."

She smiled. Stokes stopped writing and watched her for a moment.

"Where do you keep the coffee?"

Stokes pointed at the refrigerator. "There's some already ground in the fridge."

Suzanna opened the door and knelt down to look inside. She removed a Ziplock bag, put a filter in the coffee maker and poured the ground beans into the filter.

Stokes watched her thin, delicate hands. Her nails were polished and fastidiously maintained. She was not wearing any makeup that Stokes could see. He also noticed there was not a single wrinkle in the polo shirt, or the shorts, she was wearing. Her posture made her even more attractive. *When she knelt just then, her back was straight. Standing in the kitchen, sitting at the table last night, seated outside on the back deck, she's very proper and polished. Polished. Not showy but . . . polished.*

"Did you iron your shirt?" Stokes whispered.

Suzanna bit at her lower lip, placed her manicured hands on the bar and leaned over to Stokes. "Yes, don't tease me. I can't help it. I can't stand to wear wrinkled clothes."

"No, you look great. I just . . . I don't think I've ever seen anyone on this boat wearing an ironed shirt--certainly not at 5 a.m."

"Well, this is my first time on your boat. I'll be back."

She turned and walked down the hall steps, then into the master bathroom. In another corner of the salon, Wayne rolled over on his sleeping mat and opened his eyes.

"Stokesie, what time is it?"

"'Bout five-twenty. How'd you sleep?"

"Really well," Wayne whispered. "These mats are great. I'm gonna buy a couple. It's like you're on a mattress."

"Well, get a little more sleep. We're going to pull anchor early."

Stokes poured a cup of coffee then walked to the sliding door. He lifted a corner of the shade that was holding back the growing light of dawn, and stepped outside.

It was a fine morning. The wind had quit, the humidity was still low and light was showing on the eastern horizon. Stokes went up the narrow, curved staircase to the flybridge. He sat on the couch just as Suzanna came up the stairs with a cup of coffee in her hands.

"This is the only yacht I've ever been on," she said, taking a seat across from him.

"Really? You look like you were born for this."

"Why thank you." She tilted her head to the side, letting her hair fall from her shoulders, exposing her smooth neck. "Actually I was born in Marion, Kansas, a long way from the ocean. My parents thought I was born to be a veterinarian. They were most unhappy when I dropped out of SMU after one year to be a cheerleader."

"Did you want to be a vet?"

Suzanna leaned forward, hugging her coffee with one hand and slapping at the air with the other. "Oh gosh yes. I still do. But when I was nineteen, I wanted to be a cheerleader more. I did go back to college for another two semesters, but night school and my work schedule were too much. So I decided to stay with the team. I can always go back to school. Thing is, I'm not the same person I was at nineteen. I don't want to go to school for six or seven years right now. Right now, I like what I'm doing."

"Which is?"

"Convention models is what we're called." She tossed her hair. "But it's more than that. I'm showing young girls how to maximize their earning potential while they're still young and don't have to work at looking good. I wish someone could have shown me."

"How do you do that?"

"Well, Mr. Summers, let's put it this way. The courses I took in animal psychology were extremely valuable."

"Meaning what? All men are animals?"

"Close." Suzanna laughed lightly. "All men are dogs. Nice dogs, most of them, but they're all dogs."

"So what do you show the girls who work for you?"

"How to make money from the dogs without being bitten." She sipped from her coffee, holding the cup close to her with both hands. "When I first became a cheerleader, I was almost working for free. The league featured pictures of us in their promotions, the networks put us in all their ads, we were on television during the games every week. We were part of a multi-million dollar sports machine and we were paid peanuts. When I moved into the office, I realized how important we were to the image of the team. Men love to look at beautiful women, obviously. The trick is men will watch *for* the women. Even if they only get a two-second glimpse every twenty minutes. It's Pavlovian. You ring a bell and the dog starts to salivate, thinking he will be fed. Same is true with cheerleading or modeling. You show a man a pretty girl in a swimsuit and he starts to salivate. You stop right there. Once you have his attention, you can sell him anything. If you show him too much, the mystery disappears, along with the tension. The timing is critical. If you'd ever worn a bikini, you'd know what I mean."

"I can't say I've ever worn a bikini but I get your drift. It must be fun to have that kind of impact on men."

"It can be fun, but like anything else, you can take it for granted. I guess it's like being rich or healthy. After a while, you forget how lucky you are. I liked being on television. That way, even if men were leering at you, you couldn't see them. But that was years ago . . .". She traced the rim of her cup with her forefinger. "Now it's my turn. Judging by the picture in your bathroom, I'm guessing you're from the mountains."

"So you recognized the kid in the picture frame?"

"I did."

"Well, you're right about the kid, but not about the mountains. I'm a Louisiana boy. That was a camping trip." Stokes paused and tucked his chin toward his chest. "I used to hate that picture."

"Why? It was in a magazine; that must have been exciting for you."

"I guess because I pitied myself." His chin rose. "You know how kids are at that age, you cry over a haircut."

"Been there."

Stokes lifted his face higher still. "I spent years with that rod before my brother snapped that shot. It's a great cast. Everything's in balance. There's constant contact with the line, it's got that beautiful candy-cane shape, it's tight all the way to the fly. And, the depth of field in the photograph is fantastic." He eyed Suzanna and shook his head. "But all my friends saw was how skinny I was."

"Oh, that's just what they *said*." Suzanna tapped his forearm with her fingertips. "They *saw* the rest. All that determination is in your eyes. It comes right off the page."

"Maybe, but I still hated it. The only one who raved about that cast was my dad." Stokes wrinkled his nose and then smiled pleasantly at her. "I've never told anyone about that before. I don't know why I thought of it."

"It's a sweet picture."

"Yeah. My dad was real proud of it. He had that frame on his desk till the day he died."

The blower motors switched on.

"Jean Paul is up." Stokes cocked his head to listen for a moment, then the big twin diesels roared menacingly, their wet exhaust spitting and gurgling behind the boat. The anchor winch motor, or windlass, engaged and the anchor chain clanked and banged against the bow roller, the chain stop, and the cogs of the gypsy.

"So, how can I get in touch with your friend in Albany?"

"I have her e-mail and cell number. I'll find it for you," Suzanna said.

"Great. I'm going to get to work on this today."

"You aren't wasting any time. But . . . aren't you . . . putting the prop in front of the bow, or something like that?"

"No. I want to do this. I need to do this. And, I'm positive it will work. For the first time in years, I'm excited about a job. The only thing I need is some money, some hard work, a vision, and a boat; and I have all that. The next step is to make it all profitable, and I have a bunch of ideas on how to make that happen. Plus," Stokes rose, held out his arms and spun around slowly, looking at the expanse of the boat and ocean, "I'm in my new office."

"Nice office."

CHAPTER TWENTY

An hour and a half later, the *Break Wind* slipped between the walls of the Port Aransas jetties. Unfortunately, half the coastal barge fleet was already there. Traffic was terrible. Having a boat that could run almost fifty miles per hour, even in white-capped seas, had spoiled J.P. and Stokes. Thousands of barges and tugs crawl the Intracoastal Waterway between four and eight knots. Had the *Break Wind* made this trip in the Intracoastal, it would have taken a full day for them to pass all the barges, negotiate the locks and swing bridges, and generally deal with the congestion of the "ditch," as the captains call the ICW. Even this slight interruption in their otherwise fast-paced trip had J.P. anxious. He sat on the flybridge, rapping his hands on his knees, tapping his feet on the deck, fiddling with the VHF radios, playing with the gain on the radar, switching radio stations–doing anything he could to entertain himself while they chugged along in the Port Aransas channel. Everyone else was showering, rolling up sleeping bags and starting their day.

Stokes sat down at the salon navigation station and typed in various searches on the computer. While the yacht motored onward, he read about the Out Field Production Group. Afterward, he called his law school roommate, Kelly, who had recently become an in-house counsel for an ABC affiliate in New York. He figured Kelly could help.

"Little early, isn't it Stokes?"

"I don't have much time. My doctor told me I have less than a hundred years to live."

Kelly chuckled. "I bet he's right. What are you up to?"

Stokes laid out his idea for the show, then asked if Kelly could put him in contact with a producer who would know whether Out Field was a suitable company or if there was another group more appropriate for the job. Kelly gave him some names and numbers. Monday morning turned out to be a good time to be calling. In two calls, thanks to Kelly's introduction, Stokes was talking to an executive producer of ABC Sports. It helped that the producer loved to fish. Stokes again explained his concept and that he already had a sponsor. The producer was impressed: Spider was the second-largest gun manufacturer in the U.S.

Stokes asked about Out Field and several other shops mentioned in the articles he had searched. The producer suggested Stokes try Out Field, but told him they did field sports mostly and he doubted they could handle fishing. Stokes was discovering that television production companies were more specialized than he had imagined. The producer also told him that two of the outfits Stokes mentioned were unreliable, another was recently bankrupt and a fourth was excellent.

When he asked who was airing the show, Stokes told him "no one yet." Stokes was shocked when he expressed interest and asked to see a pilot. Stokes promised to call him back when he reached that stage.

He hung up and turned around in the nav station's chair just as Angie walked into the salon. "Angie, what's that war whoop you use?"

"You mean *waa-hoo*?"

"That's it." Stokes grabbed the radio's interior microphone, switched it to the P.A., turned up the volume, keyed the mike and held it to his mouth.

"*Waa–hoo,*" he screamed.

The crowd in the salon turned to look. Stokes had his back to them. "We just got a bite from ABC–on my first phone call!"

He released the mike transmit button and waited to hear from J.P. at the helm. Instead, he, and the rest of the salon's occupants, all those on the flybridge, and everyone on channel thirteen, heard: "Waa-hoo, this is the *Carol Ann,* westbound with four barges. Everyone on this channel can hear without you yelling. Unless you're navigating the Intracoastal with ABC, I suggest you use another channel."

Stokes closed his eyes for a moment and keyed his mike again. "Sorry Cap, I didn't know I was transmitting."

"No problem," the voice from the *Carol Ann* said. "Have a safe one."

Stokes set the mike down, humbled. J.P. walked up behind him and patted him on the shoulder.

"Technology just kicks your ass doesn't it?" he said in a fatherly tone.

"Aye-aye partner. Repeatedly and often."

"What were you trying to tell me?"

"I was trying to tell everyone but the moment passed. Who's driving?"

"Elsa. Prettiest captain you ever saw. I gotta piss."

J.P. dropped down the hallway stairs.

Stokes decided to call the office and speak to Molly. She had just arrived at her desk. He explained the weekend's events concerning Mimi, then cautioned her to be ready for anything, including his being fired by O'Donnell Oil. He assured her things would work out and asked if she wanted to keep working with him, already knowing the answer would be "yes." Instead, he received a "hell yes" from a woman who had said less than a dozen curse words in her life. Stokes then explained he planned to ignore business calls for a few days, and suggested she call in sick as well.

He hung up and turned around. The Stearman boys were discussing breakfast, everyone was dressed, and drinks were already being poured. Stokes felt too excited to do anything but work on his new project. He headed to the master suite to work at his desk since the rest of the boat was getting busy.

His door stood open. Three girls had slept in the room and it looked as if a burglar had ransacked the place. Clothes were thrown over every piece of furniture; three suitcases were opened on the bed. His blue towels with the white letters "S.O.S." embroidered on them were all over the floor. He stepped inside and met Suzanna coming out of the bathroom with an armful of brushes and sprays.

"Nope," she said, grasping him on the shoulder and turning him around. "You stay out another ten minutes and we'll give you your room back." She pushed him out into the threshold and Sophia slid past him into the hall.

"Hey Stokes," Sophia said. "I love your shower and your bedroom. Thanks for letting us sleep in there." She kissed his cheek with curvy lips that felt like velvet.

Those pouty, sexy, curvy lips. A wave of excitement silenced his brain.

"You're such a gentleman."

The door slammed behind him before he could say a word. Standing at the end of the hallway, he felt his cheek where Sophia had kissed him and watched her tan legs run up the stairs.

"These girls are perpetual flirts," he said to J.P., who was exiting the guest bath. "I can't believe I'm happy they destroyed my room."

J.P. slapped him on the back.

"Dude, these four sweethearts could wreck the boat and you'd still love them. Speaking of wrecking the boat, I'm gonna go check on Elsa." J.P. hurried out of the hallway and up the stairs, with Stokes close behind.

"What can we do?" Blaine asked when Stokes walked into the salon. Wayne, Blaine and Dr. S were sitting at the dining table. Jordan was in the galley.

Stokes thought a moment, went to the kitchen and pulled on a pink Mirror-lure drawer handle, then removed a notepad out of the top drawer.

"Here," he said, tossing the pad to Blaine. It landed with a *whap* and hissed as it slid across the table toward Dr. S, who raised two fingers and trapped it. "Make a list of everyone, at every company you can think of, that we might be able to con into advertising on a show that does not exist yet. As soon as I figure out what it might cost, we'll structure a deal."

Stokes looked at the three of them. They stared back.

"You meant to get ready for the tournament, didn't you?" Stokes asked.

"*Duh,*" Dr. S said. "But I like your enthusiasm Stokesie. Glad to have happy Stokes back. Mopey Stokes sucked. Tell you what. We'll work on this while we spool reels."

Dr. S stood up. "Boys," he said, heading down the stairs, "let's go into the storeroom and pull out our weapons, the new spool and the big, white bucket."

Stokes poured a glass of orange juice and headed upstairs to the flybridge. They were now several miles out of Port Aransas and there was no traffic. J.P. reclined with his shirt off. Elsa—wearing yet another designer bikini from her seemingly endless collection—sat behind the wheel. Sophia observed Stokes's approach with a languid expression as she sat curled up on the u-shaped couch in front of the driving console. She appeared to be wearing nothing but a couple of strings, but Stokes assumed there was a bikini in there somewhere. He walked behind the helm and the driver's bench, taking a strategic position between J.P. and Elsa.

"We good up here?"

"Finer than split silk, bro. Captain Elsa loves to drive."

"I'll drive any time pooh-kee. This is fah-bu-lous."

Just the sound of her deep, steamy voice aroused Stokes. Not to mention the beguiling form of Elsa's body. As Stokes stood over and behind her, he studied her breasts, then refocused.

"Good," he said, patting J.P. on the shoulder, "because until J.P. agrees to use the deluxe autopilot, which he just insisted we had to have, we need lots of good captains."

J.P. shook his head. "This is a good chance to train some new crew members Stokes. There's too much traffic and we can use the autopilot anytime."

Stokes looked ahead. The channel was clear. He looked astern at a solitary pushboat heading for Port A. Then he looked back at Elsa's breasts and glanced again at Sophia's curled-up form; she held her tan, bare legs tight to her chest, her head resting on her knees.

"Ten-four," Stokes said. "I'm going to make some more calls; you mind J.P.?"

"Hell no. I may have to stay up here with girls in swimsuits while you do paperwork, but I'll get us to Rockport. Do what you have to do."

Stokes retreated downstairs toward the master suite. Angie and Suzanna were just exiting.

"It's all yours," Suzanna said.

Stokes stepped inside. The space looked immaculate.

"My God Suzanna, did you iron the room?"

Suzanna raised her right leg behind her and hit Stokes in the butt with a swift side kick. "You promised not to tease me about being a neat freak."

"I never did such a thing. You asked, but I never would promise to pass up an opportunity like this. You even put a flower vase on my desk," he said, glancing at his writing desk.

"It's just a few sprigs of mint in a sherry glass, but look how she arranged it," Angie said, running to the desk and grabbing the glass.

"Again, that has never happened on this boat before. Thank you Suzanna."

Stokes sat down at his desk as Suzanna pulled the door closed. He lifted the thin-walled snifter to put it on the floor, but changed his mind and positioned it to the side, behind his computer screen. Then he slid the thick crystal ashtray closer to him from the back edge of the desk and opened a drawer. Three Havanas nestled together in the small, cedar box atop the log book. He removed one, placed it in his mouth and thought for a moment; the same thoughts he had been thinking for forty-eight hours—when he allowed himself to think them: *I am in serious trouble. I owe sixteen hundred grand. My main income is my company paycheck. I just told Mimi I want a divorce. Ergo–I just told Lovey. Lovey is going to boot me out of the company inside of a week. I have two months, maybe three, before I have to start selling things, and there is really only one thing to sell.*

Stokes turned and looked around his luxurious cabin. *Fuck.*

Fear again. Lots of it. It came over him like a veil. Like a flood. He floundered in a pool of fear, drowning in the deep end.

No. God-damn it. I'm not going to take counsel from my fears. I'm going to do something about this. I'm going to do this something. Focus. Focus, Stokes, focus.

He turned on the computer. It took a while to calm down and concentrate, but he did so. He browsed the internet and made a few phone calls. He was deep in thought when the door to the suite opened and Suzanna told him breakfast was served.

CHAPTER TWENTY-ONE

"So how is the analysis going Sigmund?" Wayne asked while Stokes ascended the hallway stairs.

Everyone sat at the table except J.P., who was piloting upstairs. Stokes looked outside and recognized the white-sand coastline. Key Allegro lay several miles off the starboard bow. He could not see forward, but he knew the Rockport water tower was ahead and slightly port. They were doing less than five knots now. Of course, there was no rush; they had almost reached their destination.

Angie was busy preparing a tray for J.P. From the hall entrance to the salon, Stokes watched the boat's wide wake as they motored toward Cove Harbor in the ICW Alternate route. A cluster of stout rods stood propped against the couch. An eighteen-hundred-yard spool of heavy, blue-green monofilament line floated in a quarter-full bucket of water just outside the storm-glass doors.

"I just rented a van in Rockport," Stokes said.

"For what?" Wayne asked.

"For some dude named Mishka and his entourage. They're going to set up and film us at Poco Bueno."

"Stokes, don't you think we should have a script before we put on a play?" Wayne said.

"Got that too. At least I have the format, and you guys are about to help me tweak the first few shows."

"Sorry Stokesie," Dr. S said, "we alweady tapped our wittle bwains, making a list of possible sponsors. We commenced drinking Bloodys and we were going to clean and spool a few reels next. So you see Stokesie, we's too dwunk to tink."

"All the better." Stokes picked up a pitcher of Bloody Marys and topped off Dr. S's glass, then dropped five yellow pads on the table. "I need you all well-oiled. I want ideas for a show you would actually watch."

"Back up," Suzanna said. "You have a film crew meeting us in Corpus? Today?"

"Not exactly a crew. That Out Field group is the best there is. Unfortunately, your friend Sandra is in some god-forsaken country in Africa and won't be back for a week. Out Field was appalled that I called today since they usually schedule their crews months or years in advance. And the receptionist made a point of telling me she usually deals with directors and not producers."

Stokes picked up the nav station microphone and studied the radio's screen, concentrating intently on the letters I N T R clearly on display. He keyed the mike.

"J.P., I have everyone assembled down here to fill them in on my progress. By the way, I'm a producer now."

"Big fucking deal. I'm a captain," J.P. said. "Put yourself on speaker so I can listen in on this pow-wow."

Angie set her loaded tray on the nav station ottoman and turned to the radio. She pushed a button, flicked a dial, and lifted a black toggle switch next to the radio. Stokes had never used that particular toggle switch. The radio screen now read "Intr/Speaker." Stokes saw it, looked at Angie as she was leaving, had a passing thought, forgot what it was, and then turned back to the table.

Angie opened the back door and hollered, "I'm coming up."

"Bueno." J.P.'s voice blared over the salon speakers.

"Anyway," Stokes said, "Mishka was the only cameraman they could recommend. One of the partners at Out Field had a run-in with him last week and fired him so they figured he was still available and, lo and behold, I woke him up in Fort Lauderdale and he agreed to get on a plane."

"So," Suzanna hesitated, "you hired a reject cameraman and that's what you consider doing this . . . this . . . 'Spider Arms Fishermen' show first class?"

"Oh, they said this guy Mishka is a first-class camera operator, he's just a little hard to get along with. But, I think that's because he's difficult to understand. He's Russian or Chechen or something."

"Russian or Chechen is not the same thing Stokes," Dr. S said. "Chechens sort of hate Russians. We recently fucked up their territory a tad."

Stokes nodded. "I just want the guy to film fish fighting. From what I learned talking to Out Field, it will take a hundred hours of filming to get ten minutes of useable film. So I figured we better start."

"Have you lost your mind, dude?" J.P. had expressed what everyone was thinking, his voice thundering in surround-sound over the stereo speakers. "Twelve hours ago you were up to your ass in the oil business and now you're a television producer?" The word "producer" boomed so intensely the speakers distorted.

Stokes reached over and turned the volume down on the radio.

"Don't worry guys," Stokes said, directing his gaze at Wayne and Blaine. "This works. The first call I made, and I mean the very first call this morning, was to an executive producer at ABC Sports and he was already interested in seeing a pilot. It's doable. I also talked to my buddy Cutt in San Antone briefly. He produced his first ten shows in a borrowed studio that he financed with credit card debt. Of course, knowing Cutt, they were someone else's credit cards, but that's another story."

"Well," Suzanna said, "let's eat and then we can brainstorm. It sounds like things are already in motion."

By the time they finished breakfast, the boat had traveled much closer to Rockport. They would soon angle into the open bay, turn out of the Alternate channel and then into the Intracoastal. Stokes figured he had ten minutes before they reached the harbor. J.P. and Angie were still on the flybridge, communicating with the group by intercom.

"Okay, guys," Stokes said to the assembly. "We open every show the same way; just like the picture Jordan took. I say something obvious like: 'Hello. I'm your host, Stokes Summers, and welcome to another edition of Spider Sportsman.' Again, we need a good name. Then we have some theme music with an overlay of pictures from our adventures. Lots of action shots–only some of the still shots are black and white. We show short film clips in quick succession of fishing, hunting, a flash of skin, a cocktail and a cigar on a table and people talking, more fishing action, a thick crystal ashtray, a heavy, worn leather bag, a Lear jet on a runway, a helicopter, and more skin, and then, when that stops, we begin each show from the back of the boat. We're mixing modern with nostalgic in the opening. Then I'll sit in the fighting chair and give an outline of the show while the girls walk into the frame with a prop or visual as I mention each segment.

"Now I've been thinking about ideas for the content. I have plenty but I want to know yours first. Most of mine are on this notepad." Stokes held up a pad. "But I want to put yours down in writing and then we'll see what we have."

"I thought you already had the concept–fishing and hunting with celebrities," Wayne said.

"I've thought it out. If that's *all* we do, we'll end up with the same thing over and over. Plus, each star will want to be paid and our cost will go up. We should do *some* celebrities, but we can't do *just* that. Look at this magazine." Stokes tossed a *Sports Afield* magazine to Wayne. "The advertising is mostly by companies we know but the ads are all for products hyped as new or improved."

"Right. You have to generate excitement," Jordan said. "Every year we're looking for the next gadget or new model that will sell the same basic rifle we've made for a hundred years."

"Bingo," Stokes said. "So why not cut to the chase? We can make advertising part of the content. The girls, the boat, the celebrities and the location are the vehicle for us to deliver five minutes of incorporated advertising with two or three segments per show. For instance, we'll compare all the hand-held, battery-powered, waterproof flashlights on the market, but rather than doing some boring scientific test, we'll do something fun like," Stokes sat up and lowered his voice, "'This week we're going to test six of the waterproof flashlights on the market,' then Angie walks into the scene in a bikini with a tray of flashlights."

"Not unless she's well paid," Suzanna said.

"And scantly clad," Dr. S said.

Stokes smiled. "I turn to Angie and the flashlights and say--"

"On Angie, they're called headlights," Dr. S said.

"I heard that," Angie said faintly over the speaker.

Stokes laughed. "Shut the fuck up Doc."

Dr. S laughed and held up his hands in mock surrender, then lowered them to his chest and made a groping motion with both hands.

Sophia wagged a finger at him. "You need professional help."

Blaine's cell phone rang. He hopped up and answered it as he disappeared down the stairs.

"Anyway, I say, 'We've set up a real world test. We're going to let Angie try and find the cell phone I dropped in twenty feet of water, at night, using these lights.'"

"Wait," Suzanna said. "Having the girls start the show is a great idea. But using them in the show is different. You can use them to sell swimsuits or to do something feminine or sexy, but when you try and use them as mechanics, or skin divers or near-naked fishermen, they're really just sex objects. You're going to lose your whole audience."

"Why?" Dr. S asked. "I'd watch Angie change a tire and enjoy it."

"Thanks Doc," Angie said again over the speaker, her voice barely audible.

"It's simple, and it's the same mistake most men's shows make over and over. I told you this already Stokes. You can sell a sexy product, like condoms or lingerie, using sex. But if you try and sell motor oil or wrenches or ammunition using sex, then you have nothing but a pin-up calendar that can only be looked at on a wall in the back of a gas station. If you overdo it, you'll have a hard time making a good show."

"I get your point Suzanna, but I need to keep the girls involved," Stokes said.

"No question," Jordan said. "The girls help sell it."

"They're cute," Suzanna said, "and shapely. Just leave most of their clothes on."

"Let's keep going," Stokes said. "This is good. I need to hash this out. But Suzanna you're right, the girls are a condiment, the adventure segments and the product segments should be the meal."

"I never thought of any of my staff as ketchup but we can debate that later."

"You know what I mean." Stokes looked out the window at a group of wade fishermen on the left. *Five more minutes till we dock.*

"Anyway," he said, "my major point is we have different segments. We do a travel segment where we jet off somewhere cool to hunt or fish with a famous person: flyfishing for marlin in Cabo San Lucas, grouse hunting in Canada, red stag hunting in France; you know the drill.

Then we try something new on the market–some new technology like the latest GPS. Then we do a mechanic section, or maybe a nostalgia segment where we pick some type of gear used by old timers or some sort of ancient technique and put it to the test to see how it stacks up against modern gear or techniques."

"It's familiar. The scripts are obvious. What differentiates this show from any other?" Jordan asked.

"The quality of the content for one. We put some story in the program. And some in-depth technical reporting. We write it out and develop the characters. We build sort of a community–like the Cheers bar, only the regulars are our boat and her crew. That way, we're not just doing shoot-from-the-hip, strung-together videos," said Stokes. "Plus, we test products and actually give an honest opinion on which is best."

"That testing will last less than one season," Jordan said. "If I'm the marketing director for Joe's Guns and you slam my rifles or rank them less than number one, I'll never advertise with you again. So if you test eight guns and belittle seven, you're left with one advertiser."

"But that's the problem with most of the magazine comparisons. You read an article's title that says we're going to review this year's new duck guns and the article just lists the features but never gives an opinion."

"That's because they want the ad dollars from all the guns they review."

Blaine came up the stairs, closing his cell phone while Stokes spoke.

"I want to do it differently. Let's call junk 'junk.' We'll endorse what works and slam what doesn't. If we're fair and honest and say what we believe, we'll earn credibility with the audience and allegiance from the people who make the good stuff."

"That will certainly make you different," Jordan said. "You might go broke though."

"I seriously doubt that. An honest comparison that lets a viewer know what you looked for and gives an opinion, a real opinion, will work. Think of a restaurant. I can't stand it when I ask a waiter what's the best dish they serve and I get the response that it's all good. Have a fucking opinion."

"You certainly seem to have one." J.P.'s voice was still in stereo, but it was barely above a whisper.

"I guess I'm getting worked up. What do you think Wayne? Blaine? You're helping to pay the freight. How does this sound?"

"I like everything I've heard so far Stokes," Wayne said.

The boat turned left around a buoy marked '49' and entered the Intracoastal.

"You have conviction and I like the way you deliver the lines. I like what Suzanna said about not overexposing the girls."

"Guys," Blaine said, "this all sounds great to me. I don't know what else to say except, Stokes, I think I have another sponsor."

"Who?"

"Premium beer."

"Come on. How?"

"Bill Busch the fifth was in my dorm at Vanderbilt and we were fraternity brothers. He said they've been looking for a high-quality outdoor show for a while. He's coming to Port O'Connor to talk to us. I invited him to the Captain's Dinner Wednesday night. Can you get another ticket?"

"Wow." Stokes shook his head and then inched himself up a little straighter. "Yeah, I think we can find another ticket."

"I think I signed on with the right crew," Suzanna said.

"I agree," Wayne said. "Suzanna, are you on board to work with us?"

Stokes turned to her. "Please tell me you want to do this."

"Absolutely, but this is your idea. I'm just making suggestions like everyone else."

"Actually, I was hoping you'd participate. Your input could class up the show and keep us from peddling soft porn."

"Fuck that," Dr. S said. "The porn industry does very well, and for good reason."

"You're right Doc, but I don't want to sell porn. I want to produce something that leaves a good impression."

"Hear-hear," Wayne said, raising a glass. "What do we call the show?"

"Let's talk about the look and feel of the show, maybe the name will come to us," Stokes said. "I want to put some romance in the show."

Stokes held a saltwater fishing magazine opened to a black and white photo with a huge marlin in the foreground.

"When Dutch O'Donnell moved to Houston in the late fifties, he lived for big-game fishing." Stokes tapped the page while Wayne and Blaine stood to look over the photo. "And not just for the fish. Look at the caption. This is from 1962. You've got a young movie star, with the obligatory dark glasses, in the fighting chair, and next to him a starlet's cleavage in her 'daring' swimsuit."

Wayne chuckled. The young woman in the photo wore a typical, early-sixties style suit, hardly a match for the string bikinis displayed on the *Break Wind*.

"And this." Stokes tapped the page twice. "A fast-action photograph showing water droplets suspended in the air and a tan, bare-chested mate grabbing the leader of a spent marlin. This was originally published in Movie Magazine. That's what we need to recapture. This is a sexy sport, or it can be. Fast boats. Bare skin. Big money. Sportfishing used to be glamorous. Let's make it that way again. Hell, in the sixties, all the successful oil men in Houston owned a Hatteras or Bertram. Those were the 'it' boats. And they were status symbols at the Petroleum Club. The competition was all about who could have the fastest boat, the best captain and the most tournament wins."

"And Dutch usually led in all categories," Dr. S said.

"Oh yeah," Blaine said. "I've heard the story from John many times about how his daddy loaded up his sons and flew to the Hatteras yard on his eighty-sixth birthday. Ordered the biggest convertible Hatteras could produce, and two days later he died of a massive heart attack."

"I get it," J.P. said over the intercom. "Glamour, romance, nostalgia. But, we need a hook."

"I know," Stokes said softly as he thumbed through the magazine. "You're exactly right J.P. That's what's bugging me."

"I can't hear Stokes. Turn it up," J.P. said.

Stokes stood up, held the magazine at his side with a finger between the pages, then adjusted the volume on the radio.

"I think it's great," Wayne said.

The rest of the crew agreed except Stokes. "No Wayne, it's just the same old thing. We can put it in a nice package but we need something to tie it together. We need to follow the money."

"Meaning what exactly?"

"We need to stress what all print ads stress. Something new or improved, some new feature or design is how you sell cars and boats and laundry detergent. We need to build a show around *that* using everything we are talking about."

Stokes thumbed backward through the magazine, then stopped for a moment, reading. "Look at this. How many articles in this magazine do you think are telling stories and how many are giving you tips? Guess."

"I'd guess there are one or two articles that tell you how to do something and one or two that are just good fiction," Wayne said.

"That would've been my guess, but the answer is zero fiction. The patina of this entire publication is 'stories of the outdoors,' but everything in here is 'how to' or 'where to' or 'what to use.' No fiction, no short stories. Nada. Less than half of the pages are articles, the rest is advertising"

Stokes kept flipping pages. "*Technical*," he said, jumping from his seat. "We use a retro look, but we emphasize the newest, most technical products and show people how to use them. They're *in* the story. Hell, they *are* the story. And it will *contrast* with the nostalgic stuff. It's all technical and gadgets–all new. That's it! That's the hook!"

"Technical what?" J.P.'s voice blared from the flybridge in full stereo–only louder than before. "I missed that."

Stokes picked up the mike and keyed it.

"The Technical Sportsman!"

The deafening squeal of the speaker feedback caused everyone to grab their ears. The salon was silent for a few moments but every occupant around the big, mahogany table heard a fading ringing sound while their accosted eardrums slowly recovered.

"Oh, that's exciting," J.P. said.

The crew in the salon opened their jaws wide to clear their ears as the boat slowed to an idle. J.P. made a right turn into Cove Harbor. Elsa stood up and calmly took the microphone away from Stokes. She hung it on its holder and reset the volume level on the radio. Stokes paid no attention to her.

"Let's call it a working title," he said, rubbing his ear. "But we could use that as an angle in every segment. Hell, look at any magazine: every ad is about the latest and greatest technical advancement."

"You have something there Stokes," Jordan said.

"But," J.P. said at a more natural volume level, "you doing a show on technical stuff is . . ., well, you can't even set a watch."

"I just don't like wearing a watch. But that's what made Tim the tool man funny on *Tool Time.*"

"We don't want to try and produce a comedy show, do we?" Wayne asked.

"No, we don't," Stokes replied, "but a little humor mixed with information, good stories, atmosphere and great action would be something I'd watch, plus Doctor S will watch it for the women."

"All that other stuff is good too," Dr. S said.

The meeting broke up as they approached Cove Harbor. J.P. pulled the boat up to a wooden pier where two mechanics who worked for the Gatewood shop waited. Next to them, a Great Blue heron walked, unconcerned, on long, stilt legs. A smattering of gulls hovered and made laughing calls in the strong wind above the dock.

As they pulled aside, the heron lifted his slender body off the planks and flew away. The mechanics helped tie up lines. A white van pulled into the parking lot above them, next to a low mott of windswept oaks. A teenager sat in the driver's seat.

Sophia and Elsa wanted to stay and tan. They had originally planned to go back to Houston, but the guys were begging them to stay around for the week, or at least until the Captain's Dinner Wednesday night. Suzanna told them they could if they arranged for other girls to cover their appointments.

Angie was headed to Phoenix for her shoot. Suzanna was torn between business, pleasure, and a building case of jealousy over leaving the men with the double threat of Sophia and Elsa. But business concerns won out and she decided to go along with Angie. The nutrition bar people would be at the shoot and Suzanna figured some politicking would be in order. She and Angie made preparations to load their bags into the van.

Stokes and Wayne would ride in the van as well. Jordan, Blaine and Dr. S would stay with the boat, or more to the point, with the girls. They arranged for a cab into town, where they would have a look around and then hit the Key Allegro bar to wait for J.P. to finish with the boat.

CHAPTER TWENTY-TWO

"Tell me again why we came to Rockport?" Stokes asked J.P. while they stood on the dock. "You just put these props on. They're under warranty, so why didn't we just have the guy come to Kemah?"

"Because we have to match the props to the boat and it's easier to do it here. Right now, we're maxing out at twenty-two hundred."

"Why would that matter?"

"Don't you remember when we commissioned the new motors? Pete wouldn't certify the engines for the warranty until we could turn enough RPM's. The first set of props we put on was the stipulated pitch for this hull, but we didn't turn over twenty-one. We went down more in pitch and that still didn't get it. So we had to order another set. Each change meant we had to lift her out. I don't want to pay for prop tuning, or three sets of props at once, or order a new set and have to send it back and wait for another. I sure as hell don't want to pay for three separate lifts. These blades are a new design, and I don't want to waste three weeks screwing with them. There's an open lift in Rockport and we can do all this here in one day."

"I don't remember any of this. When did we pull the boat out and put three sets of props on her? And, why can't we just run at twenty-two hundred with the props we have? That would still be plenty fast." *And, how much is this going to cost?*

"You were somewhere. It was right after we put her back in the water. But I'm telling you, we need to get the RPM's right. These engines were designed to run harder than twenty-two. They need to be pushed. The hole shot, our top end, the cavitation we're getting on our turns, the range on the throttles, the load on the engines–everything depends on the props and their pitch."

Stokes leaned away from J.P., turned his shoulders and scratched his head.

"Put it this way: do you want her to have the best props–bar none?" J.P. said.

Stokes instantly quit scratching and faced J.P. again.

"Absolutely."

"Then we need to get the fucking props right and I think these are the best available."

"Well, since you put it that way, I'm glad we're in Rockport today."

Stokes returned to his cabin and grabbed his wallet, his notepads, and a brown, expandable folder. In the van on the way to the rental car lot, he pulled out the stack of notepads in order to explain more of his ideas to Wayne and Suzanna. Suzanna took one look at the folder and rolled her eyes back like a second-grader with too much homework. Stokes began to speak, but Suzanna held her palm in front of his mouth to stop him.

"One question."

Stokes shut his mouth slowly and dropped his shoulders. The van stopped at an intersection. Wayne and Angie turned in their seats. Even the young driver turned to hear what this question would be.

"Did you sleep last night?"

Before Stokes could answer, Suzanna gently put her forefinger to his lips.

"Tell me the honest truth."

Stokes broke into a smile. "Not much."

"Okay," Suzanna said. "Continue."

Stokes took a breath. "We do a mechanic section, discussing bottom jobs on boats and . . ."

Suzanna turned to Angie, tilted her head toward Stokes with a sidelong glance, then slow-whistled, "Whew."

Stokes did not notice. He just rattled on until their vehicle pulled into the rent-a-car lot, which also doubled as a used car lot and U-Haul franchise.

As they unloaded the van, Stokes considered his schedule: *I have to pick up this fella Mishka and his equipment in Corpus at five. Suzanna and Angie's flight is at four something. If I get them there an hour before, that's three. The Corpus airport is about an hour away . . .*

★ ★ ★ ★ ★

It turned out to be a long day.

Angie and Suzanna caught an earlier flight. Stokes and Wayne drove all day with phones stuck to their ears. They had a few hours wait between dropping off the girls and picking up the camera crew, so they drove to the waterfront in Corpus and had lunch. Stokes stopped by the docks and was glad he did, because the harbor master intended to put them in a slip a good distance from the road. He paid extra for one that backed up to the street.

J.P. had an easier time. The mechanics sized the new props correctly on the first try. J.P. was excited because once they were able to turn their full range of RPM's, they picked up more speed and eliminated their cavitation problem.

J.P. had almost made it to Corpus by the time Stokes left the downtown marina for the airport. Wayne decided just to wait for the boat.

Stokes talked with J.P. on his cell while he drove back toward the airport. As they spoke, another call came through Stokes's phone; the ring tone kept beeping while he was trying to communicate with a man driving an open boat at fifty-two miles per hour.

He hung up with J.P. and studied the cell's screen. Two missed calls. He pushed a button and noted the calls had come from a number he did not recognize in the 713 area code. The phone's time read 4:20 p.m. The calls came in at 4:15 and 4:19 p.m. *Odd.* He pushed the green button and held the phone to his ear.

"Mr. Summers?"

"Molly?" *Must be her cell.*

"Mr. Summers, something's going on here you need to know about."

"What?"

"Well, just before lunch, three lawyers from Vincent & Gump came over here to meet with Mr. O'Donnell. They were in his office behind closed doors all afternoon. I wasn't spying but it was the talk of the office. I assumed it was just business but when I was leaving for lunch, Mrs. O'Donnell, Lovey that is, and Mimi were getting off the elevator. They went down the east hall. Neither saw me but I'm pretty sure they were going to meet with Mr. O'Donnell and the lawyers. Anyway, I thought tomorrow I would just call in sick like you said but I would have to come up here to get my paycheck. I talked to Marty in accounting and she said I could pick up my check early, so I went down there right before three.

"Anyway, I was getting back to my desk and Mr. O'Donnell came up. He was by himself and asked if he could have a minute of my time. I was sort of shocked, you know. I mean, I've never had Mr. O'Donnell ask me to sit down and talk. So we go in your office and he closes the door and we sit down. He was real nice and soft spoken. But I'm worried."

"What did he say?"

"Well, it was weird. I expected him to fire me but he didn't say anything about that. He asked if I'd heard from you. I told him you called and he asked if you sounded okay. I said you sounded fine but you told me that you and Mimi were getting a divorce. As soon as I said it, I couldn't believe I had said that. I'm so sorry, Mr. Summers."

"No problem, Molly. It's not a secret. I'm sure John already knew. Is that it?"

"No, no. I just was worried I shouldn't have volunteered I talked to you or that you mentioned the divorce. What worried me was he asked about *you* a couple of times. Were you okay? Were you upset? Had you been unhappy with him or the company lately? It was really odd, like he was worried you might hurt yourself or something. I kept telling him you were fine but it got me thinking. You are okay, right?"

"Molly, I'm fine, I promise."

"Well, it was obvious something was going on and I got the feeling he wasn't just worried about your health, but I can't imagine what it is. I mean, I think he's genuinely worried about you, but I also think there's something else."

Stokes paused, thinking. "Was that it?"

"No. After that he asked me if I had a key to your office. I said 'yes' and I was going to give it to him, but he asked me to keep it. Then I did something else stupid and, again, as soon as I said it I thought: Am I a mental case or what? But it turned out okay. I told him, I said, 'Mr. O'Donnell, do you realize this lock is not coded like the rest and only Mr. Summers and I have a key?' But he said, and this is a quote: 'I know and that is why I want you to keep it for now.' He said, 'Do yourself a favor and make yourself scarce.'"

"John said that?"

"Yes," Molly said. "Make yourself scarce. So we walk into the hallway and Dennis is waiting. Mr. O'Donnell walked away with him as I pulled your door shut to lock it and as I do, here comes Lovey, storm-

ing down the carpet like a linebacker! She's followed by Mimi and a
drove of gray suits. I tried to duck into my carrel and disappear but as
they walked by, I caught a look at Mimi's face and her eyes were swollen and bloodshot. She didn't even see me.

"Mr. Summers, I've never seen her look worse. Anyway, Mimi and
Lovey went into the Sligo conference room as Big John; I mean, Mr. O'
Donnell; sorry; as he was leaving with Dennis. I guess Mr. O'Donnell's
office wasn't big enough. So anyway, I heard Mr. O'Donnell talking to
Dennis about being late and needing to get to the airport. Then all the
lawyers and Danny file into the Sligo room and there are more people,
mostly paralegals, joining them now and–this is another odd part–
Shawn Coleman, your accountant, just called and asked me what floor
the Sligo room was on."

"Coleman's coming there?"

"That's what I assume."

"But John said make yourself scarce." Stokes paused. "Molly, listen
to me. Leave now. Take the stairs down a couple of floors and leave.
And I mean right now. Don't answer your phone if anyone calls. John
wants you gone for a reason and I think I get it, but go and don't talk
to a soul."

"You got it."

Stokes hung up. He thought of calling Pat but he didn't want to
involve him. He opened his wallet, thinking of Melinda Witt. Her card
rested on top.

"Good afternoon, Morgan & Witt," the receptionist said.

That impressed Stokes. She had a small office, but at least a human
answered the phone.

"Melinda Witt please."

"I'm sorry, she's in court. Can I take a message?"

"Yes, could you tell her Stokes Summers called and ask her to call
me at--"

"I have your numbers Mr. Summers. Can she reach you on your cell?"

"Yes," Stokes said, stalling.

How efficient is this gal?

"Yeah, ask her to call my cell. What's your name?"

"Gail."

"Gail. Thanks Gail, just tell her I called."

"I will Mr. Summers. I don't expect her back until tomorrow morning but I'll be sure she calls you."

CHAPTER TWENTY-THREE

When he met Mishka at the airport, Stokes contemplated renting a second van. He knew they would need a lot of camera gear, but Mishka had mountains of boxes, some four and five feet long. They removed the van's third seat and left it at the airport location of the rental company. After a half-hour of careful loading, they still had to squeeze in all the luggage.

"Why so much gear?" Stokes asked Mishka while they exited the airport parking lot.

"Four cameras, computers, booms, film stock, audio recorders, balance systems. Takes a lot." Mishka grinned. "Tell me again. You never film before?"

"No. Never." Stokes looked at Mishka and his assistant. He had expected an entourage. He received two scruffy looking guys instead. To top it off, the assistant was Mishka's cousin.

"Why you film now? Why not video?" Mishka asked, grinning again. Apparently he found something enjoyable.

"I'm producing a TV show. And, film is better, right?"

"It depend. I still like film. But one hundred time more expensive.

But I like look. I like tradition. Tell me of show."

"It's a fishing and outdoors show. We want to film a tournament this week."

"Yes, we talk before," Mishka said. "Pitch me show."

"What?"

"Pitch. Like baseball. You pitch me show like you want me to pay for whole show. Pitch."

"Oh. You want me to describe the whole concept."

"Yes. Pitch is common term in Hollywood. You never hear?"

"No," Stokes said, "never hear . . . I have never heard the term for a show but I've certainly pitched lots of deals."

"Good. Pitch me deal. I want to know for filming."

Stokes explained his concepts to Mishka, including everything he had discussed with Wayne and Suzanna and the others; his motivation, his ideas, everything. When he finished, he looked at Mishka, who was staring out the window. Stokes then glanced in the rearview mirror at Mishka's cousin. He was softly snoring in the back seat, wedged between a tall stack of black plastic boxes and the door.

Stokes waited for a reply.

"Not fishing show," Mishka said. Stokes wanted to ask him what he meant but Mishka continued. "Life show. This your life, your dream life. You sharing life with audience."

"Exactly."

"I film this. Not just film fish. Film you, film boat, film your life."

"That's it," Stokes said.

"We not friends."

"What?"

"We business men. Not friends. Okay? You let me film all time, okay? Thirty-five, sixteen; you buy stock, I film. I film at meal, at dock, at airport, at driving. We video too. All time, okay? You and I not talk while film. Only talk about film. Not friends, okay?"

Stokes was unaccustomed to Mishka's fractured English. It took a second for the words to sink in.

"Okay. Okay, we'll see if that works out Mishka."

"Will work. Will make good show. You look like rich Texan. In my country, would like show about rich Texan fishing." Mishka looked satisfied.

When they arrived at the dock, the *Break Wind* was settled in her stall. No one was on deck except Dr. S, who was enjoying a smoke in the fighting chair. Stokes, Mishka and his sleepy cousin boarded the boat.

Dr. S struggled to his feet, faced Mishka and held out his hand. "How the hell are ya?"

Stokes could see Dr. S was bombed.

"Mishka Dravost, this is Dr. Samuil Svlatoslavov."

Mishka puffed his chest, stood close and shook Dr. S's hand. Dr. S's eyelids fluttered and he swayed back and forth on his heels and toes.

"You Russian?" Mishka asked in a gruff voice.

"Pretty damn," Dr. S roared.

"Chechen," Mishka boasted.

"Chechen is Russian brother."

Dr. S kept shaking Mishka's hand and put his other hand on Mishka's shoulder.

"Russia shit on Chechnya. Shame on 'em. Shame on my Mother Russia for doing that to poor Chechnia."

"We good," Mishka said to Stokes. He broke free of Dr. S's grip, turned, climbed off the boat, and walked across the sidewalk to the van. His cousin joined him in unloading their gear and luggage.

"What was that?" Stokes asked Dr. S.

Dr. S winked at Stokes and drunkenly bellowed, "Had to meet a comrade!"

Mishka turned, looked at them, and smiled tightly.

Dr. S leaned forward, hugged Stokes and whispered in his ear, "Fucking bunch of terrorists in Chechnia and they hate it when you say *Mother Russia.*"

CHAPTER TWENTY-FOUR

An hour later all the cameras were stored on the boat. Unfortunately, they were now completely out of room.

"Even a seventy-foot yacht can get crowded if you load her with enough crap," Dr. S said.

The men had congregated in the salon and Mishka sat at the bar, intent on assembling a hand-held digital camera. His cousin's snores emanated from a guest cabin. A second digital camera rested on the granite in front of Mishka.

Sophia emerged from the hallway.

Mishka spun around to introduce himself, but instead blurted, "Oh, Got."

Stokes wondered if Mishka realized he had said this out loud. Everyone else clearly heard it. But none of the men could cast blame.

Sophia had tanned to a shade of dark, roasted cinnamon that advanced her from mortal beauty to Roman goddess. She wore a simple, white tunic dress that showed all the curves of her figure and accented her dark tan. Her hair was up, and thick mascara highlighted her already arresting eyes.

Mishka had turned into a pillar of salt; he held a battery aloft in one hand and half a camera in the other.

Elsa followed in a blue business suit. If Sophia resembled a Roman goddess, Elsa favored an ice princess. The indigo suit made her blonder, and the frost of white gloss on her lips, colder.

Wayne, Blaine, Jordan, J.P. and Dr. S stood when the girls entered the salon. Stokes noticed they both had tried to dress conservatively for the smoker. The result was disruptive. Stokes watched the men fawn over them. He decided nothing complimented the looks of these women better than plain clothes. It emphasized their gorgeous, friendly faces. *Of course, the neckline of Sophia's dress is good too.*

"We ready men?" Stokes asked the assembled crew.

No one paid any attention to him.

It took another ten minutes, but Stokes succeeded in waking Cousin, prodding Mishka into finishing the assembly of his camera and herding the entire crew off the boat, down the street, and across Shoreline Boulevard into downtown Corpus. They walked a few blocks to a sixteen-story building.

From the main lobby, their group took two elevators to the top floor and the "Corpus Christi Medical Association's Thirteenth Annual Cigar Evening." At least, that was the title on the sign mounted on the easel in the lobby of the Petroleum Club.

Stokes's elevator arrived at the club first. His group waited for the others while he wandered into the main dining room and spoke to a bubbly, heavy-set woman seated behind a reception desk.

"Hi. I'm Stokes Summers. I called today and bought two tables."

"You did. Thanks for your wonderful donation. A couple members of your party arrived a few minutes ago."

Stokes looked around. There were thirty or more tables arranged in the big room. A podium highlighted the far side, facing him, and it was framed by several long tables packed with auction items. People were standing in clusters throughout the room. Dr. S walked up with the rest of the group.

"Your tables are at the front Mr. Summers. You're a Platinum Sponsor."

Stokes turned back to the happy receptionist and smiled.

"Of course. Thank you so much."

He grinned, knowing Dr. S had set him up. Earlier that afternoon, Dr. S told Stokes over the phone that he would buy the tickets, but Stokes wanted to pay for the tables because he had invited more guests. Dr. S then called, reserved two tables, and called Stokes back. He gave Stokes the number and told him to call and give the receptionist his credit card number.

Stokes never asked how much the tables cost, but he thought it strange that Dr. S had not gone ahead and bought the tables. The money meant nothing to Dr. S, but the subtle joke of making Stokes spend two thousand a table to be a Platinum Sponsor at an event that meant nothing to him–that, to Dr. S, would be funny. Stokes decided to deny him the satisfaction of acknowledging the prank.

"Platinum? Way to go Stokesie!" Dr. S said, lisping the "t" and spitting.

Stokes wiped at the front of his shirt.

"Nothing but the best for us," Dr. S said.

Stokes held his hand to the side, searching his chest for spittle. *He made it through that last part without incident.*

Dr. S threw an arm over Stokes's shoulder and they walked toward their tables. Dennis sat alone at a large, round table next to the podium. Stokes scanned the room, looking for Big John. John O'Donnell's rolling laugh was easily distinguishable; Stokes heard him before he saw him.

"Doc," Stokes said, "I need to talk with John."

"Big John," slurred Dr. S. "Is that him? I thought that was him. I'd know that laugh anywhere. Course that's him. Let's go see him."

"No, no. I need to talk to John alone Doc. You go to the table."

Dr. S looked at Stokes with his eyes half closed. It seemed he was losing his ability to comprehend.

"Look Doc." Stokes pointed at their two tables. "There's Dennis. You know Dennis, John's pilot."

"Oh yeah. Big John's pilot is named Dennis. 'Member that time you caught him in the ear with that back cast?"

"How could I forget Doc? And that," Stokes pointed at Dennis and held his extended right arm in front of Dr. S's face, "*that* is Dennis."

Dr. S looked down Stokes's arm and rocked on his heels. "Lookee there Stokesie. Speak of the pilot and up he pops. There's Dennis the pilot." Dr. S. turned to face Stokes with a sad expression. "That was kinda gross what that pink Mirror-lure did to his ol' ear, but it gave you an idea and we got some nice door handles out of it, huh?"

"Right Doc. Everyone loves the door handles. Why don't you go see Dennis? He's at our table."

"Okay. I wonder what he's doing at our table?" Dr. S said, pitching forward.

Stokes grabbed J.P.'s arm. "J.P., watch Doc, he's seriously fucked up."

"Yep," J.P. replied.

Stokes looked hard at J.P. His eyes were bloodshot.

"Are you drunk too?"

"Bullet-proof!"

J.P. swayed sideways and Stokes caught him by the shoulders.

"S found a bottle of Anjeo in his doc'er bag and we did shots. And brother, it was smooooth."

"Stay sober and watch Doc, okay?"

J.P. kept his lips together and smiled. "Too late on the sober part."

Wayne came up beside Stokes.

"I'll keep an eye on them."

Stokes thanked Wayne and made his way across the room to a small crowd where Big John held forth.

CHAPTER TWENTY-FIVE

S tokes and John left the room together. John was calm and controlled, just as Stokes expected. John handled all problems in the
same manner, whether they were private or public, business or personal. He wanted to hear all sides of an issue before he made a decision
or let himself react emotionally.

Stokes had realized after breakfast that he made a big mistake in
not talking to John about the divorce earlier. John had never screwed
Stokes around. He might not have told Stokes everything he was doing,
he was often a pain in the ass, he had a huge ego, he was blind when
it came to his kids, and he could be extremely self-centered, but John
was loyal and he had always been honest with Stokes. Stokes felt he
should never have put John in the position he had been in for the last
couple of days. Dealing with lawyers was something Stokes dreaded,
despite being one himself. He knew John had been forced to listen to
an eager pack of expensive, pin-striped suits dissecting his family's finances and hyping the issues to justify their fees. And the attorneys in
the domestic section of Vincent & Gump were pricks; especially if they
were discussing something they knew more about than their client. On

top of that, John's little girl was upset and his wife was in protection mode. Stokes had never seen a sow defend her young, but from watching Lovey over the years, he assumed a mama pig could be a vicious bitch if you threatened her babies.

Stokes asked a waiter if there was a private room where he and John could talk. Stokes had some explaining to do. He knew John would have heard about the divorce Saturday evening and he may have been awake to hear about the spat Friday night. Stokes also knew Lovey and Mimi had huddled on the phone into the wee hours Friday and then slept off their hangovers. When he talked to Mimi Saturday afternoon, she had just showered. Lovey had probably kept the same schedule, but not John. Regardless, the first call Mimi made after Stokes talked to her Saturday would have been to Lovey. Then Mimi probably spent all Sunday at her parents' house. Stokes did not know where John had been for the weekend. He should have asked Dennis. John usually escaped to one of his ranches, but since the party was Friday night, he may have hung around Houston. Even if he was away, John would have wanted to console Mimi, so he surely talked to her a number of times since Friday.

But John had told Molly to make herself scarce. He was protecting Stokes. Stokes had figured that out easily enough. If Molly was at the office, the lawyers and accountants would have wanted to snoop through his files and begin preparing arguments against him. John was playing for time and withholding judgment because he wanted to hear Stokes's side. That is why Stokes phoned Dennis this afternoon, why he bought the tables, and why he invited John down here.

Stokes did not give a damn about attending another fundraiser, but this worked out well. John could escape Lovey for the evening, Dr. S and the crew could enjoy the party, and Stokes could talk to John—which he should have done Saturday, or at least Sunday. That had been his plan, until he let J.P. convince him to come out and play. *J.P. and a bunch of beautiful women.* When Stokes closed the door of the little conference room the waiter had ushered them into, he visualized Angie's wide, round breasts and the way they sat high on her chest as she stood nude in the kitchen. The memory surged through his mind while the door made an audible *click*.

"Damn son," John said as Stokes turned around. "Why, the, hell, did you not talk to me first?"

Stokes could see the pain in John's face. John was not angry, but he was obviously hurt.

"I meant to John. I did. But after I talked to Mimi and stumbled across this lawyer in Clear Lake--"

"No, son. I mean *first*, before you talked to Mimi. First. Why the hell didn't you talk to me first? This is a screwed up deal now."

"John, I didn't plan this. It started with Mimi thinking I had a girlfriend after the party Friday and–"

"The hell it did. Mimi's been getting more like her mama every day for the last five years. This started years ago and we both know it. Fuck, how do you think I deal with it? I've been living with her mother for a century! I could've told you anything you needed to know. You just don't say shit except 'yes baby' and you get some nice little darling by the hour or by the day when you're in Vegas. It solves a whole lot of bull-shit, son. Now you've screwed yourself. And do you realize you've made me listen to those fucking snakes from Bubba Gump all day? And her mother! My God, you'd think the end of the fucking world was coming listening to Lovey whine about this shit."

John's face was red, his big Irish nose was splotched redder, and the skin on the side of his neck looked like he had a heat rash. He ran his right hand through his thinning, rust-brown hair.

"Stokes, I love you like a son, but this thing is already way out of hand."

Stokes realized John was talking about patching things up; about him and Mimi getting back together. Stokes had been relieved and happy for two days, almost three, since deciding he wanted out. Now, even the *thought* of staying with Mimi made his stomach twist.

"John, I can't do that. I can't compartmentalize things like that. I just can't cheat on Mimi."

At the word "cheat" John jerked his head up, looking offended and startled. "That's pure horse shit."

"Bopping some whore in Vegas isn't going to make my life with Mimi any better."

John leaned forward, waving his hand. "Wait one minute son. I've dealt with this for years. And it works my way, believe me. There ain't another way to do it. Not with Lovey, anyway," he chuckled.

"John, how many times did you screw around on Lovey before you had Mimi and Danny?"

"Plenty!"

Stokes had seen too many pictures and heard too many stories of John and Lovey when they were first married.

"There's a picture in your office of you and Lovey and the horses in Yellowstone–were you married then?"

"Sure, that was our honeymoon."

"And your family's camp in the Adirondacks, when you guys spent the summers up there, did you have kids?"

"No. You know we didn't have Mimi or Danny for years. Plus, we didn't get married till late."

"Exactly. The two of you used to spend every day of the summer together. You weren't out fucking around on her then. You and Lovey have been together forty years. You can't tell me your marriage had already fallen apart before you had kids."

John sat in a hump, looking at his hands. Stokes could read his body language as clear as any verbal answer John could give. John's head hung, bowed between his big shoulders. He took his hands off the table and folded them over his big gut.

"Son, that is exactly what happened," John said, without looking up.

Stokes let that sink in. It took a while to register. "Why on earth did you have kids?" Stokes asked.

"Because, Lovey wanted 'em. She thought it would keep us together. Hell, I wanted kids. Always did. And it did help keep us together, son. We've been together forty years."

John stopped talking. He was an intelligent man. Stokes knew that John knew he was making a ridiculous argument.

"Don't get divorced son. I want you to stick around. I want you and Mimi to work things out. I want you in my family."

That got to Stokes.

"John, you've treated me better than any man ever has, other than my dad. I should've talked to you. I owe you that and I apologize, but let me tell you what happened."

Stokes briefly recounted the events of the weekend as they concerned him and Mimi. He knew John was not interested in the chronology but Stokes felt compelled to tell it all. Stokes continued up until what he learned today talking with his secretary.

John knew Stokes was explaining what was happening and *why* he was getting divorced–not arguing *whether* he was getting divorced.

"Well, let me fill you in on what's happened at the O'Donnell household," John said defensively. "First, if you ain't fuckin' someone on the side already you're missing a golden opportunity 'cause Lord knows Mimi and Lovey and half the cunts in Houston think you are."

"How's that?"

"Well, you have a boat that looks like a Manhattan apartment. If that's not a stabbin-cabin I don't know what is. Next, you showed up late Friday night and got a call from your girlfriend after the party."

"That's not what happened."

"Doesn't matter! That's what the coconut telegraph has reported to all the Junior Leaguers in the 19 zip code. Anyway, let me finish. You suddenly announce to Mimi you're getting a divorce on Saturday, and by Monday you have a stack of legal documents four inches thick delivered to the Bubba Gump law firm. There ain't no way this was not planned in advance. You show me a lawyer who can produce that much annoying paper on a weekend and I'll show you my next attorney."

John obviously was no longer reporting what Mimi thought or what Lovey thought, but what *he* thought.

"John, I swear I never spoke to that lawyer before Saturday. This was not pre-meditated. I told the gal I'd give her a bonus if she could make this divorce happen quickly."

John grasped at his bulldog jowls with his huge right palm then squeezed his thumb and forefinger across his chin. "I believe that son, but there's a whole lot more."

"What else could there be?" Stokes asked.

"Boy, you are naive if you don't think your wife and her mother haven't dreamt up every possible scenario. And you damn sure helped them."

Stokes took a breath, but stifled his urge to defend himself.

"So Sunday afternoon I came back early from El Toro Borracho and I wanted to finish watching the golf tournament but no, I walked into a god-damned buzz saw at the house. Patsi Mills had a birthday party or some such shit on Sunday. There must have been a zillion of your mother-in-law's friends at that party and they were talking about only one thing."

"Tell me this party was not in Kemah."

"You bet your ass it was in Kemah! And all I heard about was how scandalous it was for a grown man to have a bunch of bimbos on his boat that were young enough to be his daughters and looked like they belonged on the cover of the swimsuit issue."

"I'm only thirty-one John."

"That's not the god-damn point!" John screamed. "These women live for this type of shit and you handed them a plate of it. Mimi is so fucking embarrassed and worked up she's cried her face to twice its size." He paused and lowered his voice. "My poor baby. I swear she looks like her mama now."

Stokes winced at the thought and then hoped John did not see it.

"And Lovey is just reveling in all this and poisoning Mimi at even the mention of your name. They want your blood son. Not just your boat, not just the money, but blood. If Lovey had her way the fucking Princess would've been seized by the sheriff at the first port you landed in today. And I don't even want to tell Dr. S, but his wife was at the fucking birthday party. She says he waved at her on the boardwalk."

"Oh shit," Stokes said quietly.

"Oh shit is right. So, you're telling me you're too noble to cheat out of town, but you're okay with making a spectacle of yourself in your own back yard? And – this is as rich as six feet up a bull's ass – you changed the name of my boat to Break My Wind. What the fuck is that Stokes? Have you gone completely fucking crazy?"

John stopped. He was huffing like a dog, looking at Stokes.

Stokes didn't know what to say.

John broke into a smile, then a laugh, then a hard, deep belly laugh.

"Breaking My Wind! You really changed the name of my old boat to Breaking My Wind? Have you," he slapped his knee, "have you lost," he slapped the table, laughing hysterically, "have you lost your ever-lovin' mind?"

John's laugh was infectious. Stokes began to chuckle.

"The name is Break Wind John."

Stokes broke up laughing as he finished his sentence. They both sat there laughing for a while.

"Oh son. You've fucked this up royally and you haven't even gotten any pussy in the process, have you?"

John burst out laughing again. Stokes laughed with him.

⌣⁄

"John, I don't want to drag this divorce out. And I guarantee you Mimi knows in her heart I have never cheated on her. Not even now."

"Don't be so sure. But I'll talk to her and you need to call her too. Tomorrow. We need to get everyone calmed down and deal with this in a civil fashion. And I don't want my checkbook waved around in court Stokes. Let's keep the money shit private."

"I will call." Stokes watched John and was mindful not to nod his head in any direction.

"So, your mind's made up?"

"No." Stokes lied. He could not bring himself to hurt John. It was a small lie to give his father-in-law some hope that things would return to normal. "No, John, it's not made up. But, I've felt like I was just drifting along for the last couple years and now I have some direction. Part of that has to do with this decision. But, no, my mind is not made up."

"Good." John stood. "Then maybe we can figure out something."

Stokes recognized John left that vague for a reason. *Of course, we can figure out something.* But John was not trying to commit him to anything.

Stokes smiled. "Sure we can."

"Come on," John said, heading to the door. "I'll buy you a drink."

Stokes sat still while John opened the door. He needed to talk with John about the details of the divorce, about his job at O'Donnell Oil, about the deals he was working on, and about how they should handle the divorce lawyers. But John's attention had shifted. John smiled, reading Stokes as well as Stokes had read him.

"We can figure it all out after some whiskey," John said.

CHAPTER TWENTY-SIX

W hen Stokes and John returned to the dining room, it was packed. At each table, eight or more men sat talking and jeering and leaning and gesturing, cigar smoke rising above them all. Only a few women were present. A platoon of white-coated waiters wove through the back of the room, removing plates from serving carts. And a veritable hive of activity surrounded the front tables Stokes had purchased. Peter Salizar, the guest of honor for this evening's affair, sat at one, sporting his signature white linen suit and Panama hat. Among a sea of men wearing dark sport coats and silk ties, he stood out like a caricature of an expatriate American on an exotic, tropical island: a very happy caricature. He was flanked by two local caricatures–a pair of white Stetsons. Salizar laughed it up with Stokes's crew. In addition to Wayne and Blaine, Jordan, J.P., Elsa and Sophia were all at the table with Salizar. Next to them, two bottles of champagne wallowed in the ice of free-standing chillers. Mishka stood nearby, recording with one of the smaller cameras he had been playing with earlier.

John turned to Stokes. "I don't like the idea of anyone filming this."

"Relax. He's working for us and we own the tape. No one's

going to see anything unless we want them to see it."

"All the same, I don't like it."

Stokes and John greeted Salizar while the food was being served. They settled in at the second table, along with Mishka, his cousin, and Dennis. The extra chairs from their table were shuttled back and forth as Wayne Stearman and Dr. S took turns bending Big John's ear. But John was not talkative, he was hungry. He stabbed at a huge slab of prime rib, cut a slice and stuffed it into his mouth. While he chewed, he spread a heavy pat of butter on a roll and then grabbed another roll. He looked at Stokes as he buttered the second roll. He pocketed a bit of the remaining prime rib in his cheek, patted his prodigious gut, and with a hearty laugh said, "Got to keep my weight up."

The doctor who had organized the dinner addressed the crowd from the podium. He thanked everyone for coming and supporting their cause. Then he introduced Salizar, who had just arrived in the States from his plantation in the Dominican Republic. Salizar quickly captured everyone's attention with stories about his life in the tropics. He was selling cigars, but Stokes soon realized his lifestyle and his stories were what people were buying. Holding a Salizar cigar brought to mind the romance of the Carribean and the warm sunshine of a tropical beach.

Salizar gave the audience a virtual tour of his homeland, the island of Hispaniola, located in the Archipelago of the Antilles less than eighty kilometers east of Cuba. With vibrant detail, he walked his audience through the tobacco fields, the drying barns, and the main or "big" house of his plantation, explaining each step in the tobacco growing process while vivid color photos flashed on a large screen. Afterward, the host doctor returned to the podium.

"Thank you for that wonderful presentation Mr. Salizar," the host said. "We're going to take a break now so everyone can finish eating and bidding on the silent auction items displayed on the tables in the back of the room. Now remember, there is a sheet of paper next to each item and if you want to make a bid, you'll need to write your name below the last bid and fill in how much more you are willing to pay than the person before you. We'll start the live auction in about fifteen minutes."

Stokes left to check out the auction items. When he stood, Peter Salizar laughed boisterously at the other table and Stokes looked over. Several people had pulled their chairs to Salizar's table and others waited in short lines just to meet him. He now sat between Elsa and Sophia, and all the men who came up to him checked out the girls as much as they talked to Salizar. If they took a picture, they made sure the girls were in it too.

Stokes made a loop around the perimeter of the room, surveying the auction items. Dr. S had bid on nearly everything: a sterling silver pen set, five hundred dollars; a set of Salizar's stone coasters, two hundred dollars; an ostrich-quill leather briefcase humidor, twelve hundred dollars. All had "*Dr. Samuil Svlatoslavov*" written in his flashy paraph next to the bids. In some cases, rather than just raising the previous bid by twenty or thirty dollars, Dr. S had doubled it.

When Stokes finished looking at the silent auction items, the overhead lights dimmed and spotlights came on. They were starting the main event–the live auction. Three local television crews had come in and set up cameras. Salizar went to the podium again to join the host doctor, only this time, Sophia and Elsa joined him. He introduced the girls to uproarious applause and whistles from the crowd.

A cameraman gently pushed Stokes out of the way while recording a shot of his reporter. Stokes walked behind the camera and studied the view, then looked into the camera's monitor. It captured Salizar in his hat and linen, flanked by Sophia's white tunic, dark hair and dark tan, and Elsa's dark suit and white blouse. *This guy has a good eye for a background shot.*

Rather than cut in front of the lens on the way to his table, Stokes took advantage of this break in the night's action and headed for the men's room. There was a long line. But he had been to this club before and knew its layout, so he headed downstairs to the men's grill. When he reached the bottom of the sweeping, half-spiral staircase, he turned left down the hall. This floor was quiet.

Stokes stepped into the bathroom as another man left. A small partition separated the urinal and the sink. He stepped up to the urinal and heard the door open behind him. A large ox in a blue blazer walked up to the sink. Stokes turned to look but the man paid no attention. The ox man turned on the faucet, cupped his hands under the flowing water, then splashed water on his face.

"You and your friends think you're pretty cute." He huffed.

Stokes heard him clearly.

"Excuse me?"

The ox stood up straight and flexed his shoulders back.

"No, I don't think I will," he said, taking a white, starched cloth napkin from a stack next to the sink. "I don't think I want to excuse you or your fucking friends you piece of shit."

Ox threw the towel in a wicker basket.

He's either joking, loaded or crazy.

Stokes turned his head and watched as the ox man moved behind him at the urinal, ready to face off and fight. Stokes calculated the guy's clothes almost unconsciously: his blazer was not off the rack.

The stitching could be Armani.

He wore a bright purple tie with a yellow design on it that Stokes recognized.

Smartly tied. Probably just drunk.

"You come in here to our benefit, hog our guest and drink our booze, and you weren't even fucking invited you prick."

Stokes eyed him. He wore a large A&M University ring on his left hand and he glared at Stokes, waiting for a reply. Stokes kept peeing, continued to look over his shoulder, grinned broadly and said, "Fuck off," dismissively to the well-dressed Aggie doctor.

A right hand came flying at the side of Stokes's exposed left jaw. Stokes jerked his head reflexively and heard four quick cracks in rapid succession next to his right ear.

The beefy bastard had swung his enormous right hoof, but Stokes had ducked the punch. Stokes never stopped peeing. He was in a fight. *Stay calm. This is how it always happens. One second you think a guy is kidding around and the next second you're in a fight.*

Then Stokes realized he was still peeing and was impressed with himself. *That's pretty fucking calm.*

The ox man had connected his punch, but not with his target. Stokes looked at the wall a few inches from his face while he zipped up. Bright red blood was splotched across the burnt-red and tan tile, and one of the bigger tiles was cracked. *Nice punch.*

The ox cradled his hand and groaned when Stokes turned to face him. He was enormously broad, but he was probably an inch or two shorter than Stokes with a corresponding reach. *He sure as hell moved quick.* Convinced the attack had ended, Stokes made for the door.

"Better have that hand checked Doc. And you ought to be more hospitable to guests next time–you piece of shit."

Ox did not look at Stokes; he just kept looking at his hand and groaning.

Stokes walked out of the men's room, stepped past two young men in suits, and headed back upstairs, thinking this might be a good time to leave. When he entered the dining room, Kaplan was sitting next to Big John. Kaplan's two bodyguards lurked nearby.

Kaplan was one of John's best friends. Unlike John, Kaplan grew up in a two-room shack with a dirt floor, but he made up for it. Kaplan was a street tough, a notorious brawler, a fearless businessman and one of Corpus Christi's biggest celebrities. He was best known for his fried chicken franchises, but Stokes knew he made his *real* money buying and selling insurance companies and loaning money to small island countries with bad credit. The bodyguards were a recent addition–added after the president of some rat-hole republic tried to get out of his debts by offing Kaplan.

The crowd grew more animated. Peter Salizar wandered among the front tables with his microphone. Sophia and Elsa held a three-foot by five-foot picture of the plantation house surrounded by palm trees.

Salizar provoked the crowd: "Come on now. This is for you and seven friends. Four days, three nights lodging as my guest any time you want to come between now and January."

"Thirty-five thousand," someone shouted from a table near Salizar.

Salizar turned and looked at Dr. S.

"Thirty-six," Dr. S said.

"Thirty-six says my friend. Do I hear thirty-seven?" Salizar said.

"Thirty-seven," someone yelled.

"Thirty-seven once," Salizar said.

Stokes settled in next to John and said "hi" to Kaplan, who grumbled "hello." Kaplan made it a point to ignore underlings, and in John's presence, Kaplan considered Stokes an underling. Stokes paid no attention to Kaplan's boorish demeanor but turned back toward John.

"You need to get him out of here before he buys this building." John nodded toward Dr. S. "He's already bought everything in it."

Two sets of camera lights came on behind their table. The auction was the highlight of the evening and the trip to Salizar's plantation was the highlight of the auction. The news crews sensed this would be the best shot of the night.

Dr. S stood up. "Fifty thousand."

Salizar turned to him from across the room. "Did you say fifty?"

"I did. It's for a good cause," Dr. S said as he sat back down.

Polite applause broke out through the dining room. Salizar walked quickly back to the podium where the host doctor joined him.

"Okay. We have fifty thousand from my good friend, Doctor . . . Doctor Slots-vots-ko-vas-las," Salizar said.

The host snatched the mike. "Going once, twice, three times. Sold. Thank you Doctor! Folks that is a new record for us. In thirteen years we've never had a night like this."

The crowd applauded. Dr. S waved to the host, turned to J.P. and leaned in to him.

"What's the cause anyway?" he asked over the clapping.

"I have no fucking idea," J.P. said.

"Come on up here Doctor. We need some pictures," Salizar said as the lights came back up.

People spoke loudly and began to stand all around the room.

"Stick around everyone," the host doctor said to the crowd. "We're going to take a break, then we'll announce the winners of the silent auction."

Dr. S stood and grabbed Big John by the arm. "Take a picture with me Johnny."

"You go ahead," John said.

"John, John, John. Turn around." Dr. S put his face close to John's and rolled his eyes toward the podium. They both turned. Sophia was bending over to set the poster down, revealing her deep, darkly-tanned cleavage and the majority of the surface area of her boobs. John looked back at Dr. S.

"Okay. Come on," John said to Stokes and Kaplan.

Stokes started to beg off but he too had been watching the girls and decided perhaps he should humor John. Kaplan stayed seated. A large crowd thronged the podium while the cameraman positioned everyone for a shot. Stokes was stuffed in the middle with one arm behind John and the other behind Sophia. At that moment, the big ox from the bathroom charged through the mob and, with a booming right hand, blind-sided Stokes, knocking him sideways into Sophia. Ox lost his balance and fell forward, sending the three of them tumbling to the floor. The ox struggled to his feet. Kaplan sprang from the table, rushed him from behind, and seized ox's collar, pulling him away from Stokes. He drew back for a punch as his bodyguards rushed in.

Flash bulbs went off, the crowd closed in and four men grabbed ox. The bodyguards tried to apprehend the photographer whose camera had just flashed, but he slipped through the pack and disappeared. Rather than go after him, they put their backs to their boss, expecting more trouble, but nothing else happened. The TV camera crews had captured the whole incident.

Sitting on the floor beside Sophia, Stokes put his hand to his eye socket and felt it swelling. He looked at Kaplan, who was surrounded by his two thugs.

The guy doesn't even acknowledge I exist yet he jumped to my defense and he is, what did John tell me? Four years older than John, so he is seventy-four.

Kaplan was snorting like a hooking bull. Stokes heard him tell one of his bodyguards to "find that son of a bitch with the camera," then he turned and spoke calmly with the TV crew while he pulled out a roll of hundreds held together by a rubber band. Stokes thought of the Chechens. He looked around, but saw no sign of Mishka or his cousin. Then he looked at Sophia. Her white cotton dress had bright red blood smeared across the front. Elsa was holding her hands.

J.P. knelt down and pulled Stokes's hand away from his eyes. "Oh, dude, you're going to have a shiner from hell."

"Thanks J.P. You always know just what to say."

CHAPTER TWENTY-SEVEN

After the fight, the party broke up quickly. The ox had been ushered away by several men who seemed to know him well and were not at all shocked by his behavior. According to some locals, he was a heart surgeon. Stokes could not stop thinking about him. *A surgeon treats his hands like a fine musical instrument, drunk or sober. He had to be high on drugs to deliver a second punch with that hand.*

Around one in the morning, they made it back to the boat. Wayne and Blaine mixed drinks the minute they reached the galley. Everyone else found a place to sleep.

"Guys, it's Tuesday morning. What do you say we go fishing?" Stokes asked.

"Now?" Blaine asked.

"Yeah, now."

Wayne and Blaine looked at each other.

"I was going to have a nightcap and go to bed," Blaine said.

"Ditto," Wayne said.

"How 'bout helping me with the hookups and lines so we can leave?"

Wayne shrugged. "Why not Stokesie."

Two white felt Stetsons dropped onto the black granite bar and the three men headed outside.

Leaving Corpus before two in the morning was not a random idea. In July, the Gulf winds are usually calmest in the pre-dawn hours, and Stokes and J.P. always embarked on their fishing trips before sunup. The two goals of their trip had been to fix their props and pre-fish the tournament. Now that the props were done, it was time to fish.

Traveling at night from Corpus would be a challenge since spoil islands lurked just off the main channel, but Stokes would move cautiously. He figured they could be in Port Aransas in less than two hours, even moving at a crawl. Although he had not slept much the night before, he did not feel tired. Sharp spasms from his eye had launched a diversionary attack on his consciousness, his bruised ego demanded his attention, and driving the boat would give him time to think. *How could someone get so upset over nothing?*

The night air felt cool and unusually dry; the wind was negligible. The moon waned, a quarter full, but bright. Stokes noted the way the sliced moon's light bounced off the water at the ten o'clock position before him. He drove east-northeast, the *Break Wind* stealing through Corpus Christi Bay, with the lights of Port Aransas reflecting on the mercury surface ahead. Stokes was enjoying the constant, whispering purl of the water when a metallic clunk made him pivot toward the stairs. Through his monocular view–his left eye now completely swollen shut–he saw Mishka, holding a camera.

"I don't want a fucking documentary on my black eye Mishka. Turn that shit off, will you?"

"Nyet. You drive. Forget me. This is good."

Stokes looked ahead in silence. He felt too tired to argue. His head hurt, his eye throbbed, and the salt or pollen or wind–he did not know which–made his battered eye water and sting. Mishka stood behind him, filming.

"How much of the fundraiser did you film?"

"All."

"And why do you think that will have anything to do with a sports-man show?"

"You the sportsman. Show about you. Trust Mishka."

"Why should I trust Mishka?"

"Mishka has camera. You have to trust," he said.

"I think I understand, and that's my point Mishka. Why should I let you film everything? You could edit this and make me look like a fool."

"Yes. Or like big Texas hero. Hero will sell better."

Mishka sat down next to Stokes and turned the camera off. He cradled it like an infant in his arms and rode silently for a minute. "I need this very much. I work eight years in business. No breaks. I slop cameras, edit film, do all. I get zip. Just more job. I under-stand concept of show. I think more understand than you. You give me time, okay?"

Stokes turned to the guy beside him: black, curly, unruly hair; dark, oily skin; a terrible, pock-marked complexion and a thick broom of a mustache. Set inside that frame two keen, brown eyes twinkled at Stokes. Mishka's lips broke up at their corners into a broad smile; his white, even teeth cut a stark contrast across his dark, pitted face, all shadowed by kinky black hair. Even in the dim light Stokes thought he recognized something in Mishka's eyes. Stokes had seen it before. He had it, and he just realized Mishka had it. Stokes was a waiter in high school and college. Most of the waiters he worked with had the same look, the same twinkle. Stokes considered himself a hustler. He would do what it took, whatever that was, to get things done. All the good waiters he ever worked with were hustlers. Mishka was a hustler. Stokes thought Mishka would do whatever it took. At least, he sure hoped so.

"Okay. I will trust Mishka. But let's be clear. When we start editing, it's you and me doing the edits, not just you. Capiche?"

"Capiche comrade."

"I think I was wrong about heading offshore in the middle of the night. What do you say we drop anchor Mishka. I'm too tired to drive."

"I say good idea. Everyone else asleep now."

Stokes increased the light on the GPS. The glow from the brightened color screen hurt his eye, which had adapted to the dark night sky. After his exposed pupil adjusted to the backlight, he pushed the "Chart" button, then "Menu," and zoomed out to the two-mile range. He had a choice. He could pull into the harbor at Port Aransas and tie up, but that would be dangerous alone and Mishka had never crewed for him. Or, he could drop anchor in the Lydia Ann Channel, directly across from the harbor. Any passing boats would throw wakes in the channel but Stokes did not intend to sleep for long. He would have to anchor cautiously since the boat needed six feet of draft. But the channel had a firm sand bottom and he could rely on a clean set.

He anchored.

Ten minutes later he made J.P. move over, then dropped onto the guest room bed next to him. Stokes didn't know who was sleeping where, nor did he care.

Not long after Stokes went down, J.P. got up. Stokes was barely conscious.

"Anybody staying ashore?" J.P. asked.

"Nyet," Stokes said.

"What?"

"No. Or not that I know of; hell, I didn't ask."

"Fuck 'em. We came to fish and fish weees gwanna doo. You cool with that?"

"Uh-huh," Stokes mumbled.

J.P. walked out of the pitch-black guest cabin and closed the door.

CHAPTER TWENTY-EIGHT

Another breathtaking day.

The sun was newly risen. Not a single cloud traced the light blue sky. The air was crisp. Ninety nautical miles from the Port Aransas jetties, the water radiated a deep cobalt blue. The surface was unusually smooth. Off to the east, the blue seawater mixed with the silver-white reflection of the sun to form a pattern of shimmering, horizontal splotches. The sea was placid, but alive. Small waves rolled beneath the sheen. Each tiny undulation momentarily darkened the surface of the water in shadow and then, as the crest of the wave passed, the surface lightened again and the sun flashed. An endless progression of these waves moved methodically in whatever direction each was headed, until one mixed with another and moved in a new direction, repeating the infinite process. To the north, a floating, semi-submersible drilling rig industrialized the onshore horizon of the Mexican Gulf. The *Break Wind* drifted, and inside, J.P. tied a leader to a loop of heavy monofilament line.

"What're you thinking we'll catch?" Wayne asked J.P.

Wayne reclined on the couch where he had slept. A Tom & Jerry cartoon played on the television screen, but the sound remained off.

"Marlin is all we're fishing for in the tournament," J.P. said. "But we may get a big wahoo. I heard a good report from the *Lady A* that they had some wahoo action last week at a weed line offshore Baker. Who knows out here? But wahoo or mahi is likely. Plus, you should see the water. The visibility today is probably sixty feet. We hardly ever have that. I'm glad we came out here early."

"We gonna fish all day?"

"That okay with you?"

"Oh, yeah. I'm here for the party. I was just wondering what the plan was."

"I figured we fish easy today; look for bait or rips with a big temperature change and mark them. We motor in to Port O'Connor tomorrow morning or afternoon, depending on how we do–long as we're signed in by five. We have a rest day Thursday so we'll be spry for the tournament."

"I like that plan." Wayne watched Jerry bring a red crescent wrench down on Tom's animated toe. Tom straightened out stiff and board-straight at every leg as his assaulted cat toe grew big and red and throbbed comically.

"I wonder how Stokes's eye looks."

"Like he has a slab of beef melt stuck to the side of his face." J.P. stood and headed outside.

Wayne flinched at the thought, then looked at his cell phone on the surfboard table. No bars. No service. He decided to follow J.P.

"You were right J.P., the water's beautiful. I can't believe we're in the Gulf. You'd never know from the brown water at the beach that it could look like this ninety miles out."

"We're ninety nautical," J.P. said. "That's one hundred and four statutory miles. But I agree, you'd never know it looked like this unless you fish or work on one of these rigs. Fishermen have the better deal."

Within an hour, everyone appeared on deck, enjoying the rarely seen beauty of a Tuesday morning in July, far off the coast of south Texas. The wind had picked up out of the southeast, but remained less than five knots. A slight chop covered the water's surface. J.P. wanted to head out to deeper waters. His plan was to troll lures and cover as much territory as possible in hopes they could find some marlin.

Marlin are long, fast, pelagic fish that spend their entire lives in the open ocean. There was only one way to win the Poco Bueno tournament: blue marlin–a big blue marlin.

"Why not use bait fish instead of lures?" Jordan asked J.P. while they stood in the cockpit.

"I don't want to drag bait today. If we were to troll ballyhoo, we'd pull them around three knots. But we need to do some scouting."

Wayne, Blaine and Jordan were helping J.P. move the big outriggers from their traveling position, pointing up and behind the boat, to their fishing position, which was hanging off both sides at forty-five degree angles. These outriggers held the line from some of the rods that would be trolling lures behind the boat.

"There just aren't that many blues in these waters and there are even fewer in shallow water. When we get deeper I think we may raise a marlin. The big ones are usually solo swimmers. There are six hundred thousand square miles of water in the Gulf, but," J.P. held up his index finger, "we can check out a bunch of ocean while we look.

"Stokesie," J.P. hollered. "When we get these lines set I want you to push us up to nine knots."

"Ten-four."

"How fast is nine knots?" Blaine asked.

He and Wayne both looked at J.P.

"Around ten miles an hour. Ten-three or close to it."

"And we're going to catch a fish going that fast?" Wayne asked.

"That or a little slower, maybe around seven and a half." J.P. saw the perplexed expression on their faces. "Knots," he added. "Everything is in knots."

"I don't remember ever trolling that fast before," Blaine said.

"We rarely do. But, again, I want to cover some ground. And we're going to try something new. Notice anything about these?" J.P. held up a mono leader with a blue and white skirted plastic lure at the end.

Jordan held the lure in his hand. "Where's the hook?"

"We want to find them today, not catch 'em. Maybe we can tease them to the surface and locate our fish for the tournament," J.P. said. "We're only going to use a hook in our farthest lure. I figured we could try it."

"So why use just one hook? Why not no hooks at all?" Wayne said.

"Honestly, it's because I can't stand the thought of knowing I'm not fishing *at all*. This way, at least we have a chance of getting bit."

"Okay J.P., you're the captain."

"You never know," J.P. said. "With this clear water and fast-moving, flashy lures, we're liable to stir up anything. A marlin sees this from under the surface and it's like us seeing a beautiful woman, it gets stupid fast and it wants a closer look. A fish has only gotta do two things: eat and reproduce. That's all its brain is wired for–puttin' things in its mouth and chasin' tail. We don't want to scare 'em off for later if they try a nibble."

All three men chuckled. Stokes listened to this exchange from the helm and thought of Suzanna explaining how to get, and hold, a man's attention. He decided both J.P. and Suzanna were right: there was little difference between men and marlin. If you want to catch one, first you tease 'em up, then let 'em take the bait, and–when you're absolutely sure they have it–you set the hook.

"Plus," J.P. said, "I'm anxious to see if these props will raise fish on this hull. I have my own log of the last four Poco tournaments with my notes on the other boats and their totals. We can fish the rigs, or the

Hilltop, maybe around Hoover Diana. Odds are the rigs are where the most marlin will be raised, or maybe at a floater. But we might also find a good rip. There are ninety boats in this tournament. We can go farther than any of them and faster than most. I'm going to head toward Alaminos Canyon, or maybe even out to Keathley, and look for a rip."

"You're telling me a prop change can bring fish to the surface?" Wayne asked.

"I don't know. Some boats are known for being fish raisers, just from the way their engines resonate or the way their hull cuts the water. This baby . . .," J.P. patted the side of the salon, "is one of those boats." He ran up the stairs to the flybridge and shouted, "Call me superstitious or crazy, but I believe the tune of our old props was wrong. Even so, we raised a bunch of marlin the last two years with the new engines." He turned and continued shouting as he locked the starboard rigger: "John tells me he raised them easy when he fished her with the old engines. Now that our new props are tuned up right, I think we're going to raise even more."

Wayne, Blaine and Jordan stood by in the cockpit while J.P. let the port outrigger lay into position.

"Okay, Stokes," J.P. said, heading back down the stairs. "Let's start throwing a wake and see what happens."

Stokes slipped the twin throttles forward and lightly pushed them with the palms of his hands. The twin diesel engines' staccato exhausts went from a "*blump, blump, blump,*" to a more blended noise as the new blades stirred the saltwater and lifted a swirl of foam to the surface.

The big boat moved forward and Stokes adjusted the weight on his feet, looking back over his right shoulder at the big outriggers. They were fifty-two feet long, cold-drawn aluminum poles whose main function was to help separate the lines they would drag behind the boat. Each shaft was so long it had to be stabilized. Starting at about thirteen feet up and then about every nine feet, criss-crossed aluminum spars, or "spreaders," stuck out at right angles from the main shaft. These looked like gold stars along the silver main. A wire ran from the end of each spar to the outrigger's shaft. Stokes had always liked the looks of their outriggers. There was something exotic about all the criss-crossing wire and metal on their quad-spreaders. And, for some reason, he liked the fact that it took a hell of a lot of engineering just to make a line troll wide and high outside the wake.

J.P. drew three arm-lengths of line from a massive, two-speed Penn International reel. He laid the line over the transom and raised the rod until the lure began to skip on the water. Then he pulled more line and watched the green and blue and gold-flecked plastic, hula-skirted squid, which concealed the lone hook of their entire spread, dance across the surface of the water. He put a thumb on the spool of the reel and let the line feed out at a controlled pace.

"Don't bird nest it," Stokes yelled.

"Fuck you," J.P. responded without taking his eye off the reel. If J.P. were to move his thumb off the cylinder of monofilament line, the spool would spin at a rate much faster than the line leaving the spool. Depending on the velocity of the spin, the size of the line, and the remaining space between the spool and the rest of the reel, the resulting 'bird's nest' could be so tangled that J.P. would have to cut the line and start over. J.P. and Stokes both occasionally got in a hurry and put a nice big nest in a reel.

When the lure had fed out where he wanted it, J.P. took the reel out of free-spool, grabbed the line and yanked hard. The drag made a rapid clicking sound when he pulled. Despite having already burned the line and marked the drag-points on the reel with a piece of tape, J.P. checked the drag lever again, pulled and seemed satisfied. He then set the rod in a holder.

While J.P. set more lines, Stokes turned his attention to the displays in front of him. One had a full-screen view of a chart that he could adjust or zoom. A second was set with a full-screen radar showing surface obstruction or clouds. The third screen showed their speed, as well as their heading and bearing. J.P. had connected this last screen to the computer and GPS. There were endless varieties of data sets that could be pulled off their computer system, their GPS and their components but, when Stokes drove, he wanted to see these screens and their sounder–which showed water temperature, depth and a graph of the Gulf's floor. Anything else he could call up by pressing a few buttons or asking J.P. to press a few.

Above Stokes's head, mounted slightly forward of where he was standing, two identical VHF radios were recessed into a box in the ceiling. The right radio monitored channel sixteen, the left monitored sixty-eight. Stokes had the volume down and the squelch up. The squelch knob basically controlled the static or background noise. With this present setting, Stokes could hear a clear signal at a low volume but little else. They had expected to see other boats but had not yet spotted any. Since no one was on the radio out here, there was no noise. Had they been closer to shore, they would have listened to a relatively constant chatter of boat to boat traffic and an occasional transmission from the Coast Guard. Even with the best antennas, these radios only ranged about twenty or twenty-five miles on a sportfisher.

J.P. spent the next five minutes, with Blaine, Wayne and Jordan's help, setting each of the trailing lures at different locations. A pair of flat lines skipped in their wake at seventy-five feet. Stokes watched while J.P. pulled the lanyard from the port rigger, which worked like a line on a flagpole. He snapped the clip from the rigger onto the monofilament line from the big rod he had just set down. He then quickly hoisted the lanyard up the port rigger with a hand-over-hand motion.

It always amazed Stokes how quickly and methodically a seasoned fisherman could perform this feat. A novice, watching on deck, would not understand the mechanics of what had just occurred. However, the same novice would immediately understand *why* it had all happened when he saw the lure dancing forty-five feet farther outside the boat's wake than it had been moments before.

When J.P. finished, the short outrigger lures bounced over the surface of the water; one at thirty feet, another at forty. A daisy chain of bowling pin-shaped teasers trailed from a clip on the starboard corner of the transom. This staggered set allowed them to turn the boat without tangling their lines. Another rig, the first they put out, was the farthest back–about a hundred and fifty feet–and held by a center rigger similar to the outrigger. J.P. had this center line, or 'shotgun,' as far back as possible, but close enough so they could see a swirl if a fish rushed the lure.

CHAPTER TWENTY-NINE

After the lines were set, Stokes looked at his phone. No signal. He asked Wayne to take the wheel, then went below and into his cabin, crowded with clothes and bags and towels. He thought of Suzanna and wished she were here, not for her cleaning ability, but for her company. She would enjoy being out on the Gulf on such a spectacular day and seeing the unusually clear water. Putting his hand to his sore eye, Stokes reconsidered. *Perhaps it's better she's not here.* He pulled the chair out from under his desk, visualizing Suzanna at the Safari Club dinner: *striking, confident . . . .* He sat down and moved the mouse for the computer, then clicked on the Verizon icon. When a box came up on his screen, he clicked 'connect.' No service. *Oh. Same as the phone.*

Stokes reluctantly reached below his desk and picked up a black nylon case about a foot square and four inches deep. He opened it and withdrew a black metal box. When he pulled out the satellite phone, its hand-held receiver fell from the bag and dangled from its cord. He dreaded trying to use this thing. It was ancient and cumbersome, a relic from John's time on the boat that J.P. had preserved, and it rarely worked. Stokes rummaged through one of the desk drawers until he found the laminated card that contained the instructions for using the phone, read them through, then plugged the phone's co-ax cable into the wall jack next to his desk. Ten minutes and five slow readings of the instructions later, a ring tone signaled through the speaker of the hand set. Stokes sighed with relief. Melinda Witt answered and Stokes said, "Hello."

"Mr. Summers. I'd planned to call you this morning."

"Call me Stokes."

"Call me Melinda."

"Okay, Melinda. I talked to John last night. I know you've talked with Vincent & Gump."

"Oh, yes. I've done more than talk. Yesterday, Monday, I filed everything I could file with the court and I had a private process server serve the papers before noon. They're quick. I've never seen anyone react so fast. They filed their answer yesterday. They've asked for a temporary restraining order and the judge just set their hearing for Thursday at 10 a.m. I'm negotiating now--"

"Wait, wait, please," Stokes said. "This Thursday?"

"Yes."

"I can't do anything this Thursday. I'm on vacation, out of town."

"We can move it. But the hearing has to happen within fourteen days."

"Okay. Move it. But what papers did you file?"

"Everything I could. The divorce petition, interrogatories, requests for production, requests for admissions, subpoenas—"

"Subpoenas?" Stokes said. "Subpoenas for what?"

"Tax returns, bank records, minutes of meetings, inventories--"

"Whoa, whoa, whoa. Melinda, what's going on? I wanted to play nice. Why did you file all this now?"

"Stokes," she said calmly, "you've never been through a divorce and you've never handled a divorce. You asked me if I could do this in seventy days, right?"

"Correct."

"And you promised me a bonus and triple my hourly rate if I did, and I told you that was next to impossible but I would try."

"Yes, I clearly recall our conversation Melinda."

"And this is a very high stakes divorce for you."

"Correct."

"Well, it's very high stakes for me too. It's high-profile and I want to break into the clique of the top-rung divorce lawyers. No one up there knows me. Being sweet is not really an option. I couldn't just walk into Vincent & Gump, hat in hand, meekly asking them to take little ol' me seriously and wonder if we could get this done in sixty-one days."

"Agreed."

"So I dropped a bomb on them to get their attention," she said.

"Well, I think you got their attention."

"Oh, I did that all right. In fact, we just had a hearing with the judge."

"When? Now? Today?"

"Yes. I was in Judge Clark's court this morning for a couple of other hearings, and a whole team from Vincent & Gump was there as well."

"And . . .?"

"And, the judge wanted to talk to us all about this case. The V & G lawyers were trying to get me to agree to hear their motion sooner. They'd asked for a hearing Friday, but the judge is out. He set it for Thursday and told them all to calm down. They had a whole passel of motions they wanted to argue this morning but he said he'll hear their arguments at the temporary hearing."

"So what are they so excited about?"

"Mainly I think they're excited to be billing hourly for six lawyers on one divorce. But the O'Donnell family is evidently quite excited and a little upset about the possibility of having to disclose their financial information in a court proceeding."

"I could've told you that in advance," Stokes said. "Do we really have to disclose everything?"

"We could agree not to, but we don't want to agree just yet. Your goal is to keep the boat, your salary and interest in your wells, which I don't think will be too hard to do. The real issue is doing this quickly. I haven't conceded or told them anything. They seem very nervous."

"They are that. Right after you served them yesterday there was a big meeting with John at his office. Mimi and Lovey were there. I met with John last night in Corpus. The last thing they want is a public disclosure of their finances, and honestly Melinda, I don't want to make any more waves than I have to in order to get this divorce settled and finalized. But you hit a nerve."

"Sounds like it. Are you upset?" asked Melinda. "You sound a little better now."

Stokes heard someone in the master bathroom. The sound distracted him momentarily, then he answered: "I am. I'm better. I got a call from my secretary. She said Mimi was crying yesterday morning, but John was cool last night. I just want to know what I'm dealing with. What makes you think you can move the hearing?"

"I clerked for Judge Clark for a year after law school. I teach his kids at Sunday school and we live around the corner from each other. After the hearing, he called me into his office to show me pictures of all the speckled trout he caught this weekend. He said this hearing Thursday is going to screw up a good fishing trip if it goes too long. Don't worry Stokes. I can handle this."

"Touché. I had a good feeling about you Melinda. Call if you need me."

"Do the same and keep your nose clean. If you get any more information about what's happening with the O'Donnells, call me."

"I will."

Stokes put the handset down as Wayne opened the bathroom door to the suite.

"Everything okay in here?" he asked.

Stokes looked up from his desk through his unswollen eye. "You know what's better than knowing the law?"

"What?"

"Knowing the judge."

Wayne nodded. "Yeah, I agree with that. I'm going back outside. Come join us," he said, then closed the door.

One more phone call on this modern antique. Stokes looked at the laminated card and recommended pushing numbers on the box-top keypad, hoping he could remember what he had done to make the damned sat phone work. With the receiver to his ear, he dialed the numbers and codes umpteen times. Nothing worked. He thought about asking J.P. for help, but couldn't bring himself to do it. J.P. would tease him about not being able to work the phone, that was a given. Stokes could handle that. But he would also tease him about calling Mimi–and that might piss him off. He did not want to talk about Mimi with J.P. right now.

Beep, beep, beep, beep . . . It did it again.

"This son of a bitch!"

Stokes slammed the plastic receiver down onto its cradle. It hit the box like a champagne flute striking an anvil; pieces flew everywhere. He stared at the broken receiver in his hand. A cone-shaped speaker, liberated from years of confinement inside the molded plastic, spun on the desk like a tiny figure skater. Its rotation slowed, then it rocked, wobbled, and finally broke from its spin and rolled forward toward him in an arc. He watched it stop, balanced precariously over the front edge of the desk.

"Mother fucker."

He hurriedly stashed the evidence in the black nylon case.

* * * * *

After fishing for two hours, J.P. pulled up all the lines and ran hard forty nautical miles to the southeast to scout another location. They deployed another lure spread, and initiated another long troll.

"Any action?" Blaine asked, exiting the salon around two in the afternoon. Wayne sat next to J.P. on the mezzanine bench, watching their wake.

"Nada," Wayne said.

"Some days the man conjure the fish, most days the fish conjure the man," J.P. said with a wink. He scanned the wake.

"So, what's that mean?" Blaine said.

"It means we usually don't catch anything," J.P. replied. "I actually think the water is too clear–if that's possible. We've had some whites and sails come up and take a look, but nothing of any size. I think we need to catch some big blue runners or skipjacks and live-rig for the tournament. And, we need to find out where the big fish are and stay with them this weekend."

"Who's driving?" Blaine asked.

"Captain Elsa," J.P. said.

"What if we hook a fish?"

"We're only pulling one lure with a hook. The rest are teasers. Plus, it'll take me about ten seconds to scale the stairs."

"Good. I'm going to go upstairs to stare and dream."

"Do more than dream. I think she likes you."

Blaine smiled. "That's convenient. I think I like her too."

Other than a budding unilateral romance, nothing came to the surface for the better part of the afternoon. They covered another fifteen nautical, traveling east-southeast.

CHAPTER THIRTY

Two hours later, Stokes had taken over driving from Elsa. He continued to worry about how to get in touch with Mimi. He had promised John he would call and he knew if he had time to explain things, he could defuse the volatile situation; but his cell phone was inoperable, and he had destroyed the satellite phone. As a last resort he could use the VHF radio to get a roughneck on a rig to patch him through to a telephone, but he didn't want to have such a personal phone call that way. Nor did he want to tell J.P. they needed to go in just so he could make a phone call.

Taking the boat in was almost out of the question. It was a rule between them that once they were out, they never went back in until they had planned to. If everyone became seasick, they stayed out. If someone cut off the tip of a finger, they stayed out. Anything short of a serious risk of death was not reason enough to go back in. Every guest was informed of the rule before they left the dock. And the rule had never been broken, even though there was usually at least one occasion on every trip when someone really wanted to go in. But Stokes had worried about Mimi all day and now *he* really wanted to go in. Nothing was biting, despite the seemingly optimum conditions. He decided to talk to J.P. about getting to port.

A metallic scream erupted from the back of the boat, so shrill it made Stokes jump to his feet.

"Marlin! Marlin!" J.P. shrieked at the top of his lungs.

Wayne banged on the glass wall of the salon with three sharp pumps of his fist as he rose from his seat on the outside mezzanine bench. Stokes hit the throttles to set the hook, then pulled back thinking it was unnecessary at this speed.

"Let's get these lines in," J.P. yelled.

Stokes turned to see Wayne run across the cockpit, grab a slack rod and start reeling.

"No, this one's yours Wayne," J.P. said. "Get that center rod. This is a very big boy. Get that latch on. Hurry."

J.P. reeled furiously on a loose line. Bodies poured out of the salon and into the cockpit while J.P. screamed orders. Mishka teetered out with a large camera on his shoulder. His cousin followed with the audio recorder.

Elsa had been stretched out on the couch to the left of Stokes in the shade of the flybridge. She had intended to keep him company but had fallen asleep an hour ago. Now she observed the action below with a sleepy expression.

"I guess I'll go down and take some pictures," she said.

She came around the driving console, sat on the bench, then reached into her purse which rested on the floor. She withdrew a small digital camera and a bikini top, placing them on the dash in front of her. With her back to Stokes, she grabbed the bottom of her tight tee-shirt and raised her arms, pulling it over her head.

Stokes forgot what was happening below. He tuned out J.P.'s screams. It was as if someone hit a mute button. He looked down Elsa's back. A red spandex bikini bottom covered her derriere. Sitting on the

white vinyl bench, her pretty rear formed the base of a long, provoca-
tive hourglass figure: hips curved in toward a slim waist, her backbone
a thin valley between two long, firm muscles flowing up to her arched
neck. Her shoulders formed a vee from her waist; light blond hair was
piled on her head with a clip. When she leaned forward toward the
dash to grab her bikini top, Stokes saw the top and side of her right
breast. The cream-colored skin, the pale pink of her upturned nipple.

What is it with these girls? They strip without hesitation. Stokes
felt his dick pressing against his shorts. He sat down on the bench
next to Elsa.

Keeping her back to Stokes, Elsa slipped her arms into her top like
a detective slipping on a gun holster: first one arm through a set of red
straps, then the other. Stokes saw first the left side of her left breast and
then the right side of her right breast. Now strapped in spandex, she
casually pulled down on the material to expose the top of her tits. She
cupped them both and lifted, then checked her cleavage with one last
look and tuck. Stokes held the stainless wheel with his right hand and
adjusted his package with his left. Elsa turned toward him. He was sure
she saw him realigning his shorts.

"Sorry if I flashed you Stokesie," she said with her deep, accented
voice.

She stood up, smelling of coconut oil and holding her little camera
by its cord, and stepped behind the driving bench, leaving her purse on
the floor. She slipped past him, grabbing his shoulders to steady herself. He felt her boobs brush across the back of his head and thought
he could even feel hard nipples.

"I've never seen this," she said.

"Left!" Stokes heard J.P. screaming. "Left. Motherfucker. Left!"

Stokes pulled the wheel left and spun his head to the right, planting his left eye firmly in Elsa's left tit, which was settled under her red
stretched top. The soft collision pushed his sunglasses up off his eyes.

Elsa shuffled to the side. Stokes only had time to grab his glasses off his head before he saw the slack belly in the line and realized he had turned with the wheel. He grabbed the throttles to straighten up, then turned to look forward.

J.P. screamed: "Fuck!"

"What. The. Fuck. Are you doing?" J.P.'s voice cracked he yelled so hard. "Stokes. Are you fucking watching? That was a horse; a fucking horse. You gotta watch the line dude. Jesus. Fucking. Christ."

Wayne protested from the fighting chair: "I didn't do anything."

Stokes put his right hand to his forehead, pressed his thumb to his temple, closed his eye and shook his head. Then he turned to look over his left shoulder. J.P. stood on the port side of the cockpit, his feet firmly planted on the deck and his hands resting on his hips, looking up at Stokes.

"Stokes, what the fuck man?" J.P. said in a quieter voice.

"Sorry dude . . . Sorry."

J.P. dropped his head, then looked back at the wake.

Stokes looked at the wheel and considered how badly he just screwed up. *A fish is never fought with the wheel. Only the throttles. That's automatic–reflexive. You've never done that. And that's the least of it . . . you have to pay attention.* He turned to look at Elsa. *Not to her!*

Wayne reeled in the line that had held the fish and lifted the last portion of the twenty-foot double line and the sixteen-foot leader over the transom. Blaine picked up the skirted lure; the steel hook was bent open. These were twelve-aught Mustad J's. One hook completely filled the palm of Stokes's hand. They all knew it took a heavy fish to bend that hook. Any man would need a vise and a sledge hammer to straighten and open it up like this monster had just done. Stokes decided this was a bad time to tell J.P. they needed to drive over one hundred and fifty nautical miles to Port O'Connor, on an ideal day, the Tuesday before Poco Bueno, so he could call Princess.

"Let's get these lines out," J.P. said. "We've had some lookers. We could find a bunch of fish before dark. But no more hooks, just teasers. If we want to catch some dinner, we'll wait till we have a trailer and pitch to it."

Elsa stepped back behind Stokes, grabbed his shoulders firmly and began to massage his neck with strong hands. "Sorry pooh-kee. I modeled in Milan, Hamburg and Paris since I was fifteen. I got used to sitting in front of all sorts of clothed artists while I was nude. I didn't mean to distract you." She stopped rubbing his shoulders and bent down to kiss his bruised left eye. "I hope I didn't make your eye worse."

"It was the other eye," Stokes said, obviously lying.

Elsa adjusted her position slowly, rubbing against him. Her breasts pushed into his neck and shoulders. "Sorry pooh-kee." She brushed her left cheek against his right temple and held there. He felt her breath. He heard the wet parting of her lips as she kissed him again, taking her time. "Please forgive me," she whispered.

"It can be our little secret." Stokes turned away to assess the situation with the lines being deployed. He tried to get his mind off Elsa's naked back; that and the fact he had a huge woody.

CHAPTER THIRTY-ONE

Stokes sat alone on the flybridge, driving.

"Heytu, load new canister," Mishka yelled from the cockpit.

J.P. laughed and yelled back from inside the salon, "Heytu? His name is Heytu? I thought his name was Cousin."

All three sliding salon doors were locked open, making the entire salon and cockpit a large, unobstructed area. Mishka, Heytu, Jordan, J.P., Wayne, Blaine and Sophia had been moving in and out of the cabin, trying to get where they each wanted to go without tripping over each other. It was a familiar dance. They often had six to ten people aboard while fishing, but today the deck was even more congested because Mishka and Heytu were filming. J.P. was excited to have the cameras, but it had become obvious after they hooked the big fish that these guys would be in the way without a better scheme. J.P., Mishka and Heytu were discussing their options when the blender turned on and then cut off.

"Shit!" Dr. S yelled.

The boat blender was a valued piece of hardware: a Waring commercial bar model. It had a five amp motor which, J.P. had proudly explained, was the strongest motor of any of the blenders he could find. Stokes had burned up a blender motor about every two months making margaritas until J.P. bought this beast. It was never worth having an old blender repaired, so Stokes had to keep buying new ones. Yet he hung on to the old glass canisters because he hated to throw them out. He now had a whole collection.

From his seat at the helm, Stokes surmised that Dr. S had tried to use the blender without putting the top on its steel canister. This always resulted in the same series of events that took place in less than three seconds:

1) Switch on

2) Tequila, triple sec, ice and frozen limeade meet the fury of spinning steel blades

3) Ice cubes turn to slush

4) The green mixture forms a ninety-proof whirlpool and the blender blades suck a hole down into the middle of the liquid, forming an air pocket in the bottom, and then . . .

5) A huge gob of frozen, sticky, partially-blended margarita flies out clockwise from the back of the canister, banks off the right hand side, then plasters itself into the eye sockets of the person holding the switch.

It does that every time.

Each blender disaster left the unfortunate operator with sticky syrup in the hair, tequila and lime juice stinging the eyes, and a cold, sticky mess on the boat's gorgeous cherry floor. Fortunately, Stokes had installed bronze pool drains along the perimeter of the salon and galley floors—spills were an expected part of the routine.

The thought of all this made Stokes thirsty. His water bottle in the dash holder was empty.

"Stokesie, salt or no salt?"

"Salt. Mucho salt."

"Right flat. Big boy in the wake," J.P. screamed. "Tease him up Blaine."

"What?" Blaine asked.

"Reel up. Quick. Yank it. Tease him. See if he'll hit it."

"Where is he?"

"You see that?" J.P. pointed to a long, dark shadow coursing through the boat's wake, just behind the flat-line off their port. The slicing edge of a dorsal fin trailed behind the shadow.

"No . . . oh wow. Wow. Look at the size of that fish!"

"Jig it!" J.P. yelled. "Reel up."

"Holy shit, it's a locomotive," Wayne said. "Sophia, get out here."

Blaine slipped into the fighting chair. He reeled an International and yanked on a heavy custom stick with a bent butt that allowed the rod to sit at an angle in its holder.

"Is he still there?" Blaine asked.

"He's under there somewhere," Stokes yelled from the flybridge. "Hey J.P."

"Yo!"

"That was a damn big marlin."

"I know. Did you mark it?"

"Yep, but you better double check me."

"Hold on. Let's see if he comes back," J.P. said.

Unfortunately, he never did.

Ten minutes later, J.P. surveyed the rods, scanned their wake, then ascended the steps to the flybridge with four bounding leaps. Stokes watched their lines while J.P. pushed buttons on the chart screen. Two fish icons appeared.

"I'll date these later. You did good Stokesie. Keep marking. I hope we found our fish."

They did; find the fish that is. They found a weed line marking a rip–an upwelling current in the middle of the Gulf.

Deep in the southern Gulf of Mexico, large vortices of water are spawned off the northwest end of Cuba. These clockwise-flowing gyres are the progeny of the Yucatan Current, a massive underwater flow which rushes past the Yucatan Peninsula at speeds up to two knots. The Current flows north, famously sweeping a few divers off the reefs of Cozumel every year, then continues into the Gulf between Mexico and Cuba. In order to exit the Gulf, it curls toward the Florida Strait. Much like a mountain brook twisting around a large boulder, eddies form as this sub-sea torrent makes its turn. Periodically, huge gyres are pinched off and sent spinning across the Gulf basin in a northwestern direction. When they hit the undersea canyon walls off south Texas, these deep ocean rivers of cold water swirl to the surface, teeming with nutrients and zooplankton. The bait fish feed on the plankton and the bigger fish feed on them. This upwelling current, or rip in fishing parlance, was the holy grail of what they were searching for today, two full days before the fishing began in the Poco Bueno tournament.

Over the next five hours, the *Break Wind* raised three more blues, two of which stayed in their lure set for several minutes. One of these slashed at a teaser, then shot across the spread, knocked another hookless lure out of the water and disappeared. They also spotted a marlin sunning itself; the fish swirled and sounded as they approached. Assuming they were right and the first fish was a marlin (they had lost some of their shared confidence on the identification of the first fish), that made six marlin for the day. They did not try to hook another because anything caught now would take time away from scouting and would not count in the tournament. They did, however, have six icons on their chart in a fifteen mile area along a curved line that ran southwest from where they had marked the first fish, and *that* was what they had come for.

Just before dark, they snared three blackfin tuna. The blackfin were thick in spots and they watched the tuna chase the closer baits and the bowling-pin teaser set trolling off their transom cleat. J.P. decided to catch one for dinner but their crew had so much fun catching the first one they hooked two more. Each tuna weighed about twenty-five pounds. The second made a startling run, spooled out over half the line on a TLD thirty, then broke off. They also landed a small wahoo. All four battles were captured on film.

Sophia became the hero of the day after Blaine made her take the rod on the third, and last, blackfin; a fish shaped like a big football and built for speed. Even a twenty-five pounder can put up the sort of fight that makes for months of bragging. Sophia reeled with her arms, pushed with her legs and quickly established a routine: pull up on the rod, reel down, hold, brace, pull up again, reel.

Despite the burning pain in her arms, she fought the fish for nearly fifteen minutes. Sophia and the tuna were equally exhausted when she brought it to the boat. J.P. grabbed the line with a gloved hand to release it, as he had done with the wahoo. He pulled his dive knife out of its sheath and brandished the blade in the fading sunlight.

"Don't you dare," Sophia screamed. "You're not releasing *my* fish."

J.P. sheathed the knife and gaffed the healthy blackfin. It was rather upset. It beat the outside of the boat furiously, flinging dark blood as J.P. raised it over the side. He dropped the flapping fish onto the deck and held the razor-sharp gaff out of the way while the tuna danced on its side across the pleated white deck, leaving a crimson trail of splattering blood. The tuna worked itself into the back port corner and then stopped fighting. In the ten seconds it took to hit the deck and flip itself into the corner, its brilliant blue-green skin faded to a dull gray. The fish gulped at the air as it lay in its own shallow, burnt-red pool. Sophia looked pensively at her catch. The tuna's eye sat fixed in its bullet head: a large black orb, devoid of any emotion. The body made one last reflexive shudder.

"It's sad to see their color fade," J.P. said.

Sophia kept staring at the fish. It did not twitch.

"He'll make a great dinner," J.P. said, trying to lighten the mood. He hesitated. "Nothing beats a fresh-grilled tuna steak."

Wayne, Blaine, Jordan and Elsa observed Sophia's response to the tuna's demise. Stokes looked down from the flybridge. With a master's touch, Mishka silently zoomed his camera for a close-up, hoping for tears of remorse and a tender cinematic moment. Heytu held his position and slowly zoomed his camera back from a tight shot on the black eye of the fish to a broader view that included Sophia in the fighting chair. He pulled focus off the fish and onto the innocence of Sophia's youthful face, trying to capture her reaction.

"You okay?" J.P. asked.

J.P. thought Sophia was about to cry. She turned her head to look directly at him, giving Heytu's camera a three-quarter frontal.

"Let's catch something else!" she said.

CHAPTER THIRTY-TWO

Dr. S made another round of Ritas–this time with the top of the canister firmly sealed. He flipped the toggle switch and white frost bloomed on the metal side of the blender's pitcher. The tuna steaks had been buttery and delicious, and there was nothing left of Sophia's fish. A large, half-eaten bowl of salad sat in the middle of the table. Bread crumbs covered two cast metal trays the length of a loaf of French bread.

Stokes rotated a white foam cup between his thumb and forefinger while licking the small amount of remaining salt from its rim. On the cup, "SPIDER ARMS" was printed inside a graphic of eight thin intersecting lines depicting both the stylized crosshairs of a rifle scope and the legs of an arachnid. The margarita inside had long since ceased being frozen. He polished it off.

"Fellas; ladies; I'm exhausted and I'm going to bed. Enjoy yourselves but I can't handle any more."

They were no longer in the deep ocean they had cruised earlier. At Stokes's insistence, they made a long run back into shallower water and were now anchored inshore of the East Breaks in two hundred feet of water. Their anchor line measured over five hundred feet–four hundred was chain–and J.P. had let it all out. They rode at what Stokes thought should be a good anchorage. J.P. knew better. He had never owned up to Stokes that five-to-one was the required scope, and anchoring in two hundred feet of water required a thousand feet of line. J.P. always used their same five hundred feet no matter their depth, and assured Stokes they were fine. The truth was their present line length gave them only about ten percent of the holding power the correct ratio would have given them.

"J.P., will you–"

"Set the anchor alarm. Yes, mom, I already did."

Stokes worried about the anchor coming loose every time they set it. He believed a shifting wind or current could pull the anchor in the middle of the night and allow the boat to drift into an offshore pipe or oil rig; or worse, a moving ship. J.P. was unconcerned. If it were up to him, they would have stayed offshore, drifted all night and kept watch, but Stokes had other ideas. The anchor alarm was a neat deal which J.P. had rigged specifically for Stokes; if the bearing of the boat varied more than ninety degrees, or if the coordinates on the GPS changed by more than a quarter mile, an alarm went off.

"Night, night."

"Good night Stokes," Sophia said. A half-dozen voices echoed her.

Around two in the morning, Stokes woke to a series of loud pops. From the guest room window, he saw green sparks falling slowly in the sky. *Fireworks.* Easing over the stainless steel bar that formed the edge of the fabric bunk, he planted a foot between two Chechens sleeping on the queen-sized berth below. They stirred when he stepped on the wooden frame, but neither woke.

Stokes made his way to the salon. The blinds were down. Wayne sawed logs on the couch. His snores were so blatant Stokes wondered how he failed to hear him earlier. Stokes opened the salon door and froze. Immediately in front of him stood an unwelcome sight: the naked backside of J.P., bent over in front of the open transom door. J.P. straightened up and turned around, dripping wet, his package hung out for all to see.

"Stokesie, you gotta get in."

Stokes stepped outside. The underwater lights illuminated the boat from below. The water appeared as transparent now as it had been that morning. He walked out onto the mezzanine deck and cleared the porch. Something stirred above and he looked up.

"Waa–hoo!" Sophia's nude figure fell from above, arms cart-wheeling in the air. She hit the water with a sharp "whoosh" immediately to Stoke's left. Elsa's inverted figure followed on the opposite side of the boat in a practiced dive. Her long, sleek body, and a Brazilian strip, cut the surface with barely a splash. As Sophia emerged, Blaine yelled "Geronimo!" from above.

Stokes looked up again to see Blaine's heavy frame in mid-air, descending feet first from the tuna tower, with his arms outspread and his pecker happily flying along for the ride. He landed twenty feet from Sophia with an exploding splash and all the grace of a safe hitting concrete.

Stokes stepped onto the lower cockpit deck toward the starboard side of the boat where Sophia was swimming and Blaine had just disappeared. With her hair wet, and her eyeliner and mascara washed away, Sophia's fresh face bore the charm of a spirited teen. But that face inescapably presided over a luscious, well-developed form. He was spying on the naked body of this water nymph treading sensually through the lights and shadows when her radiant eyes suddenly flickered up at him. Blaine emerged out of the clear, light green water in a flurry of silver bubbles and Sophia turned as he surfaced with a gasp.

"Dude, you gotta get in! But cover your balls when you land 'cause I just got racked." He winced.

Stokes watched J.P. lean over to pull Sophia out of the water. Her skin glistened: full breasts, narrow waist, firm legs; all completely bare and unashamed.

This is becoming commonplace.

Once J.P. helped Sophia into the boat, he turned to assist Elsa, who emerged from the water like a gazelle.

Same thing, different wrapper. What is it that makes her so distinctive? The high forehead? The impossibly well-defined cheekbones? The long legs? The bearing of a princess? The steady stare of a lioness? Stokes was getting hard again.

"Get in," Elsa said to Stokes in her sultry voice.

It's the voice.

She sauntered past him, so at ease that her nude figure seemed to float across the deck like smoke swirling in still air. She grabbed a couple of towels from a stack on the cushioned mezzanine bench behind the salon's glass wall, but rather than covering up, she walked back down to the cockpit and handed one to Sophia, one to J.P., and then held the last towel to her chest. She made no attempt to cover her backside as she stood near the transom door. Blaine climbed out of the water and Elsa handed the last towel to him. Stokes stared at the back of her long legs and studied the vertical lines that defined the muscles of her thighs. She had the legs of an athlete, or perhaps a race horse, which met to form a butt that Stokes decided should never be covered; cloaking it surely violated some principal of aesthetic law.

Art. Pure fucking art.

Elsa turned and strolled back across the deck, wearing only a few remaining drops of seawater. She climbed the two stairs to the mezzanine and picked up another towel off the bench. The others were already heading back upstairs. Elsa shook out the towel and wrapped it around herself, holding it open in a sheath, her arms outstretched.

The plush terry made a hallway which ended in her nude torso. She held it there and took several slow, swayed steps toward Stokes.

"You really should get in."

Stokes realized it was an obvious entendre' meant only for him because the others were gone. While the towel was open, he enjoyed an unobstructed view of Elsa's nude, sun-browned front. She was justifiably proud of her assets. He glanced at the manicured strip of light brown hair thinly covering her crotch, then looked up quickly and met her eyes. She smiled, slowly closing the towel and tucking its thick, white cloth deep into her cleavage. The bottom edge *only just* concealed the union of her long legs.

"I'm going back to bed."

"Suit yourself pooh-kee . . . but this is fun."

"It looks like fun," Stokes said, holding her gaze. "But I can't. Not tonight."

Elsa shrugged and proceeded up the stairs. Stokes watched. The higher she climbed, the more exposed she became. When she knew her bottom was clearly visible beneath her towel, she turned on her toes and looked over her shoulder at her prey.

A bottle-rocket shot off the flybridge, fizzing into the sky and then exploding. The intense noise brought Stokes back to earth and he jerked his gaze higher. Elsa smiled wickedly and blew him a kiss. He turned toward the door, hoping the shadows and his quick movement would hide his flushed cheeks.

J.P. has the rocket launcher out, Stokes thought, forcing carnal thoughts from his mind.

He tried to visualize the rocket launcher: its long handle of stainless tubing with the rod holder mounted at a ninety-degree angle on the far end. One person lit the bottle rocket and dropped it into the rod holder while another held the handle end. Once lit, the handler swung the rocket out away from the boat.

No use. The only image he could see was that of Elsa's long, smooth, wet legs on the stairs.

Stokes closed the glass door and reached down for the second time today to move his hard cock around in his pants. Then he noticed Mishka sitting at the bar in front of him, wearing a root-suit and placing a thirty-five millimeter still camera into a water-tight plastic case.

"Boat will look good from water at night. I take good shots for you," Mishka said.

"Try and keep them P.G.," Stokes said, heading for the steps. *Mishka must have seen all of that.*

CHAPTER THIRTY-THREE

The horn was blasting: short jarring blasts, each followed by a pause and then another set of blasts. The horn did not usually sound like that. But, it was definitely the horn.

Whann . . . whann . . . whann.

Someone was screwing with the horn trying to wake everyone. Stokes turned over and rearranged his pillow, refusing to get up. He looked out the port window next to his bunk. Black. Stars. No more fireworks. It kept blasting. *J.P.*, thought Stokes. He was pushing the horn button in an awful, steady sequence–almost a mechanized sequence.

Shit! The horn is blasting!

Stokes rolled off the fabric bunk, stepped on the leg of Mishka or Heytu, he couldn't see which, fell into the cabin door as he opened it, and finished falling into the dark hallway.

Whann . . . whann . . . whann.

"What the hell's going on?" a man's voice bellowed.

Stokes felt his way up the stairs. All the lights were off but he could make out a silhouette standing in the middle of the salon. It was Blaine.

Whann . . . whann . . . whann.

The noise was disorienting. Stokes fumbled along the wall, searching for the light switch.

Whann . . . whann . . . whann.

With the light on, he stepped up to the navigation station. He grabbed his hair and scoured the controls for the source of the alarm.

Whann . . . whann . . . whann.

He couldn't think. *Where is J.P.?* He pushed the horn button a couple of times, but it did nothing but make the real horn honk. *Which horn is blasting?* He looked at the "Blue Sea" panels. All the power on the boat went through these panels and all the breaker switches were labeled. Stokes scanned the AC and the DC panels. *Where is the goddamned switch?*

Whann . . . whann . . . whann.

"Turn it off please!" Elsa screamed over the noise. She stood in the galley, wearing only a long, white tee-shirt. The Chechens appeared on the hallway steps, followed by Dr. S and Sophia. Wayne rose from the couch.

Whann . . .whann . . . whann.

Footfalls thumped down the stairs from above, followed by a loud bang just outside. J.P. opened the salon door.

"The GPS," he yelled. "It's on the GPS."

Stokes fought hard to concentrate on the panel and saw the GPS switch was lit up. So why could he not see the GPS screen? He turned to the screen and pushed the power button.

The dark screen illuminated as J.P. came up beside Stokes.

Whann . . . whann . . . whann.

J.P. toggled the cursor to the word "Menu," then to "Anchor Alarm," then hit "enter." He then toggled the cursor again and hit "disarm."

Silence.

"Thank God," Blaine said.

Everyone started talking at once. Stokes turned to J.P.

"The screen was off."

Jordan walked over to them.

"I turned it off," he said over the clamor of several conversations. "I couldn't sleep with all the light."

"Are we moving?" Stokes asked.

"No," J.P. said. "I don't think so."

J.P. turned guardedly and walked outside, with Stokes in his path. Dew coated the exposed cockpit deck. Stokes flipped on a dome light on the roof of the mezzanine porch. The light reflected off a slick area at the base of the stairs where the dew had been wiped away. J.P. cautiously crossed the slick spot and the rest of the deck, then stood at the end of his tracks near the transom. Stokes followed his wake out. They stared at the ripples breaking around both corners of the stern and trailing off behind the boat. The anchor was set.

Stokes put his hands on the covering board, leaned over the transom and gazed at the rippling starlight reflecting off the water's surface three feet below.

"Healthy current."

"I'll reset the alarm," J.P. said. He limped back inside, favoring his right hip. Jordan and Blaine settled into sleeping bags on pads in the salon. Wayne stretched out on the couch. Everyone else disappeared. J.P. looked at his dive watch: 4:15. He went to the kitchen sink, picked up a white towel with writing all over one side, and stepped over to the GPS monitor. After resetting the alarm, he draped the small towel over the screen.

"We have to leave it on to be able to control the alarm Jordan."

"Sorry about that."

"No harm done. I can't stand to have any lights on when I sleep either but we'll leave the rag over it for now."

"Ten-four," Jordan said.

A rolled up sleeping bag sat next to an empty pad on the floor. J.P. switched off the lights and lay down on the pad, emitting a series of low grunts, never even attempting to unroll the bag. Unable to lie on his right side, he settled on his left and quickly fell asleep.

Stokes turned off the outside mezzanine light and flicked on the stair lights. He carefully grabbed the handrail as he went up to the flybridge, then crossed to the helm and turned on the indirect lights that served the seating area. The flybridge was covered, which kept the thick dew off the vinyl furniture. Wet towels sat in soggy lumps on the floor. Coronita bottles were everywhere. A collection of dark brown strings hung on one of the stainless steel handrails mounted on the ceiling. It looked like hemp rope.

Who would leave a wad of rope up here?

Stokes pulled the rope off the railing and studied it. It was a bikini; top and bottom. He arranged both pieces in his left palm and squeezed, closing his fist around the entire suit.

Now that's a new record for itty bitty.

He opened the door under the front of the steering console, pulled out the white plastic trash can and began picking up bottles. It did not take long to straighten up.

While he worked, Stokes noted the arrangement of several opened, dry towels on the u-shaped couch and realized J.P. had been sleeping here. There were no bugs out tonight. There rarely were any this far offshore. He decided this would be more comfortable than the fabric pull-out bunk, so he turned off the lights and lay down. Waves slapped the boat's bow rhythmically. He saw the North Star off the port stern and, for the first time since they left Corpus, noticed he could see out of both eyes again.

Wind changed. That pulled the anchor.

He drew his eyes closed to make all the starlight blur together, then opened and refocused. Seeing stars far out in the Gulf was much different than seeing them in Houston. Out here, with no light pollution and the reflective water, the stars filled every inch of the sky. The Milky Way actually *looked* milky. Falling stars were common. *This is the sky that made poets write and scholars think when Greece and Egypt were in their prime and ruled their seas. And today, hardly anyone ever sees it.*

Stokes did not sleep long. He stirred while the glow from the still-hidden sun intensified and the sky around him grew lighter. The constellations had faded; there were still visible stars, but he had to hold a steady gaze to see them. He shut his eyes and tried to sleep more, but it was hopeless. He felt restless and ready to do something. Fish, drink, swim . . . *I'm on the boat on the eve of Poco Bueno for God's sake; I should be doing something.*

He looked up again, past the roof of the flybridge into the sky, and found himself thinking about his conversation with Jean Paul–the one about mystic bullshit. He watched aimlessly for a while, then had a thought: I'm going to just lie here and stare. *I'm not going to do anything. I'm going to concentrate only on a spot in the sky and nothing else.* He zeroed in on a cluster of faint starlight and committed himself to not move until sunrise.

His mind tried to wander. Fear was trying to creep in.

No, I've already addressed that. Stokes held his focus on the stars. *There's nothing I can do until we get back. I'm going to think about only this . . . I'm not going to move. I'm going to keep my eyes glued to this piece of sky till the sun comes up. I am going to do this.*

A full thirty minutes after he began his vigil, Stokes lay on his back, the surrounding sky a deep bruise of purplish-blue. It seemed as though it took hours, but in his peripheral vision, the eastern horizon slowly transformed, ripening into a whiter, lighter blue set against the dark. He had fallen into a trance, concentrating his gaze on one narrow speck of the universe high above. When the sun finally crested the smooth horizon–an orange ball at the lower left edge of his field of view, not yet sending its rays across his part of the ocean–he allowed himself a satisfied smile and closed his eyes, nodding off while the boat rocked slowly. Minutes later, he woke to the sun's warming rays on his face. Groggy, he rose from the vinyl couch.

He was stiff and his shoulder was sore where he had slept on it. He put his fingers to his left eye. It was no longer puffed up. The plastic trash can filled with Corona bottles reminded him what he had done last night. He pulled down the damp beach towels he had hung on the ceiling hand rails and briefly imagined himself as a migrant worker picking fruit. With an armload of towels and a trash can full of bottles, he turned to leave. Just before descending the stairs he saw the hemp-rope wad of bikini he had contemplated the night before. He stuffed it in the thigh pocket of his board shorts.

Stokes left the trash can on the mezzanine and stepped inside. He came into the galley and set the stack of towels on the black granite bar. J.P. and Jordan were stretched out on mats on the floor. J.P.'s right thigh was black and blue. Stokes balanced one hand on the bar and raised his bare foot above J.P.'s hip. He curled his foot and poked J.P. on his new purple tattoo with a stout punch from his big toe. J.P.'s right hand swung quickly to swat at the offending foot. Stokes raised his leg away and J.P. fanned back, reaching higher. He momentarily grasped Stokes's heel, but Stokes hopped into the galley between the bar and the back of the navigation station, freeing himself.

"Fuckhead," J.P. said.

"Me? At least I waited a few hours to tease you. You made fun of my eye the minute it happened."

J.P. attempted to stand and nearly collapsed when he put weight on his right leg. He checked himself with two straight arms on the floor.

"Crap! This really hurts."

"It looks like it hurts."

J.P. stood up, nodded in Stokes's direction. "You're one to talk. You look like a fucking raccoon."

Stokes turned, took two steps behind the bar, then ducked down to look in the mirror. It was located behind the bottles of booze, in a wooden bar box, above and behind the stove. The light was dim, so he flipped the illuminated switch for the under-cabinet spots and bent down to look again.

"Damn," he said, leaning in to get a closer look.

The glass above the squatty Crown Royal bottle was the largest opening in the mirror. Stokes studied his face, noted the green hues around his black eye, and listened to a *tap, tap, tap* noise. Somewhere in a cluttered rod-closet of his mind he recognized that sound: it was the sound the stove made when one of the knobs was pushed and the piezo switch engaged. He felt a hot sensation in his stomach and turned his head more to the right, examining the purple and black and red and pink colors where they mixed together with the dominant sick green around his eye. *I wonder if that ox fucker broke a bone.*

A fresh stab of pain arose in his stomach and he smelled burning fabric.

"Stokes!" J.P. shouted just as Stokes realized he was on fire.

Stokes snapped his head up, slamming it into the sharp lower edge of the hardwood cabinet. He felt his legs buckle, then watched a fishing-lure handle on a high cabinet door spin and grow smaller in a kaleidoscopic haze of purple, silver and blue. His limp body fell to the floor, coming to rest flat on his back.

Everything was utterly still. It was black, all black. Nothing happened.

Time passed. A second? A minute? Still nothing, just black.

All was quiet.

A thick weight hit him in the chest, a second after he had fallen. J.P. was pulling him up off the floor. Stokes's blurry vision came to focus on his torso while he was lifted, and he watched the pile of damp towels falling off his stomach. A black, circular burn marred his favorite blue polo shirt. A fleck of charred cotton fell away with the pile of towels to the floor.

"Dude," J.P. said, "you trying to kill yourself?"

Stokes raised a hand and felt a bump growing on the back of his head near the top. It already felt like a golf ball.

"I blacked out."

"You fucking scared the shit out of me man."

CHAPTER THIRTY-FOUR

After breakfast, J.P. pointed their bow southeast into the waves and headed for deeper water. They wanted to scout till noon, then haul ass to Port O'Connor to check in and get ready for the Captain's Dinner and auction, where the guys hoped Houston's finest would be on display. Participants always invited the best-looking women they could find to accompany them to the Wednesday dinner. The promoters of Poco Bueno also made sure the liquor flowed freely. The alcohol, and the need to show off, fueled their auction. Each owner's entry fee purchased one-half of his boat for the Calcutta; the other half was sold. Buying half a boat was betting it would win, and most owners bought the outstanding half of their boat, thereby showing confidence in themself and their crew. But there were plenty of bidders for the outstanding halves of the better boats.

Tomorrow, they could all rest up for the tournament's midnight start.

Being out of contact with the rest of the world today was a bad situation, but Stokes knew he could not change things. He needed to take his mind off Mimi and his crumbling financial existence for another eight hours. *I want to win this. But, I also want to pay my bills and be able to eat.*

Stop it!

Stokes spread his arms wide and gripped the front corners of his writing desk. *Do something. Take control.*

The solution hit him squarely, like a dope-slap to the head. He pulled out the scripts he had outlined, intent on mixing filming with scouting. Mishka had shot plenty of film and video on his own in the last thirty-six hours, but Stokes needed to put a show together. His plan was to obtain enough footage for six, twenty-two minute programs. That would leave time for eight minutes of commercials in every thirty minute broadcast. He figured filming while the boat trolled through the Gulf would make a realistic setting.

Mishka wanted to use video so they could begin shooting immediately, but Stokes insisted he use the film camera and the audio recorder. The wind made the microphone whine. After an hour of set up, including repeated efforts to keep wind noise off their microphones, J.P. and Stokes shot a tightly-scripted four minute segment explaining how to turn a spool of monofilament and a spool of dacron into different types of leaders. They shot the scene twice with an Aeroflex camera. The script of each take was identical, but they both improved their delivery on their second go-round. Stokes had planned to stop filming after this one segment but decided to do a second to avoid setting up again later.

Stokes and J.P. improvised a piece on boat screws. Sophia listened as J.P. and Stokes discussed how to film it and rehearsed some lines. She rolled her sparkling, Italian eyes and said, "You both just lost any chance of me watching."

While they filmed, she helped hold and position the lights Mishka used to avoid shadows.

"Brass . . ., steel . . ., phillips-head . . ., slotted . . .". J.P. removed a screw from a rib below the deck to explain a point.

When they finished, Stokes was encouraged by Sophia taking back her previous comment. "That was actually kinda interesting," she said. "That" had been J.P. explaining the literal nuts and bolts of a saltwater boat.

J.P. then shot a third segment describing different metals found on a sportfishing boat, their properties, and the primary considerations when choosing metals for certain applications.

Elsa had taken Sophia's place helping with the equipment. She blessed J.P.'s four minute lecture on metals as "not in-tahh-lerable."

J.P. and Stokes figured that was a win. Still, they decided to film it again; this time with Elsa asking questions of J.P.

Why would anyone care about which metal was which?; Why use 316 stainless, why not splurge and buy 317?; Why would it matter if the parts touched?

The second take was better, but with a few modifications, Stokes and J.P. teased some slightly humorous lines out of the dialogue by prompting Elsa to ask the more mundane questions in a stilted tone.

They filmed it a third time. J.P. loved the camera, as did Stokes. They also loved Elsa's thick accent. Mishka's only concern was ordering more film stock since they were quickly burning through his supply. For a while, they forgot about pre-fishing the tournament, and Stokes forgot his troubles.

Around 10:30 a.m., they turned their attention to fishing. They were still a long boat ride from where they had marked marlin the day before. The plan was to hit several new locations but, unfortunately, the water had changed. A strong, new southeast wind was raising the seas to between two and three feet. The clarity of the water was half, or less, what it had been, and with the waves breaking, the visibility was poor. While Mishka filmed and Heytu positioned the audio recorder, Stokes took the wheel, explaining to the camera what they were doing. J.P. then put out lines with the help of the rest of the crew.

They trolled again with a five-teaser spread, but today, there were other boats. At eleven-thirty, Stokes saw another sportfisher and decided to avoid her. He made a turn and the vessel hailed them over the radio. It was the *Commodore* out of Lafayette. Stokes identified himself as the *Break Wind*, but made no reference to the name *Princess*. He knew the *Commodore* and Jeff Regan, who owned her, but he did not want to share any information or give any advantage. A half-hour later they lost sight of her.

A number of captains were talking to each other on the radio. Stokes and J.P. remained silent. In truth, they were nearly too tired to talk. Neither had slept much in the last twenty-four hours and Stokes hadn't slept more than a few hours at a stretch since they left Houston. They were also beat up. With the seas growing noticeably rougher, they conceded they'd found what they were looking for the day before. Mishka needed more equipment: jibs, arms, more stock. He had not believed Stokes was willing to pay for film and he had anticipated shooting more video. They needed to get to shore so Mishka could try and order it all out of Houston. The earlier they could get in and get settled in Port O'Connor, the better.

Turning toward shore just before one, Stokes felt relief. He knew that once he was within twenty miles of land, he could get a signal on his phone. J.P. set their helm for Port O'Connor and throttled up in a following sea. For the hundredth time in twenty-four hours, Stokes was glad he owned a seventy-foot boat. The trip to shore was smooth, even in building four-footers.

CHAPTER THIRTY-FIVE

Around 3:30 p.m., Stokes was on the flybridge when he received the phone signal he had been waiting for. He tried to be nonchalant. First, he went down the stairs to find a place to make the call. Then he went to his cabin, but the signal was too weak to register. He wandered the boat, finding his way back outside, then back to the helm where the phone reacquired the signal. J.P. was driving. Sophia, Jordan, Dr. S, Wayne and Blaine were there, observing their approach to land. Stokes considered what to do. He went to the cockpit and, fortunately, the phone maintained the single bar it had shown at the helm. He dialed Mimi's cell. She answered.

"Mimi?"

Silence.

Stokes looked at his phone. The call had ended according to his screen.

Stokes hit the "send" button again and heard two ring tones. He thought she answered.

"Mimi?"

Silence again.

He wondered if he was just having trouble hearing over the wind noise and the engines.

"Mimi," he repeated.

Silence.

Frustrated, Stokes looked at his phone again.

He hit "send" once more. The call went directly to voicemail.

"Mimi. Call me. I tried to call you just now but something's wrong with the phone. Please call me."

He hung up, wondering what to do next. He sat in the fighting chair and studied the batik print on the board shorts he had been wearing since Corpus. Salt particles had formed on the dry cloth. He thought of Hawaii, or more specifically, the harbor in Maui where he bought these shorts with Mimi. He looked at the phone's screen. Two bars now. He pushed "send" twice. Again, the call went straight to Mimi's voicemail. He ended the call, then punched Big John's cell number into his phone. Again, voicemail. John never checked voicemail. Stokes hung up. He punched in another number, the "bat phone" behind John's desk, and put the phone to his ear. He heard a ring tone then, "Yeah." That was how John always answered his private phone.

"John, I'm glad I caught you."

"Don't fucking talk to me. If you can't follow a simple request, you're on your own with this."

John hung up.

Stokes was stung. *John was upset.* Rightly so, Stokes decided. *I should have called Mimi before we went offshore.*

He thought about calling Melinda. *Screw that. Who? I have to do something. Pat? No. I can't keep involving Pat. Should I call Melinda? No. I need to talk to Mimi.*

His phone rang. He pushed the "send" button, hoping it was Mimi.

"Hello."

"Stokes," a female voice said. "Where have you been?"

"Fishing." *Is this Mimi?* He could not recognize the voice over the background noise. He walked up to the mezzanine.

"We're leaving Corpus. What highway do we take to Port O'Connor?"

Corpus?

"Oh shit," he said, realizing this was Suzanna. He started up the stairs. "Sorry Suzanna. I don't know what highway. Hold on. I'll get J.P."

"Stokes?"

"Yeah."

"We're heading up highway 77 and plan to exit south at the Port O'Connor signs, but I thought maybe there's a better way."

Stokes rose to the top of the stairs with a bounce in his step. "I doubt it, but J.P. is right here. Ask him. I can't wait to see you," Stokes said as he rocked up and down on the balls of his feet and handed the phone to J.P. That garnered a look from everyone on the flybridge.

"What?" Stokes asked the crowd. "This is gonna be a great weekend."

Just as J.P. took the phone and began to speak with Suzanna, a clear signal came over the VHF radio. "Princess, Princess, is that you? Over."

Stokes felt a sudden pang of worry. His feet settled flat on the deck and he looked at the radio.

"Princess, come in Princess. This is Bounty. Do you copy?"

Dave DeMarcay owned the *Bounty.* He was a regular at sportfishing tournaments all along the Gulf, and was also a great fan of gossip. Stokes grabbed the microphone. The rest of the group watched with growing interest.

"Hello Bounty. This is Break Wind, formerly Princess."

"Whose idea was Break Wind?"

"That would be me, her proud owner."

Wayne smiled at Stokes and carefully mouthed the words, "I love our new name."

Stokes nodded and pointed a finger at his chest while holding the microphone, responding: "Me too," without a sound.

"What's this I read about your donnybrook in Corpus, Stokesie?"

Wayne looked at Stokes as J.P. ended the call with Suzanna.

"The fight," Wayne said.

"Oh, that was nothing," Stokes said into the mike.

"The paper made it sound like a riot," Dave said.

"What paper?"

The crew on the flybridge was suddenly more attentive.

"Tell me you haven't seen the paper?" a second voice said. "You're a fucking hero for popping Shelby Worth."

"Who is Shelby Worth?" *That name's familiar.*

"The cardiologist," the new voice said.

"Never heard of him," Dave said.

"He's a dick," the second voice said.

"Who's this I'm talking to?" Stokes asked.

"This is Serenity."

Serenity was Abe's boat. Abe was from Corpus.

"This Abe?"

"Yep."

Stokes keyed the mike. "I've heard of Shelby Worth, but I'm not placing the guy." *How do I know that name?*

"That's nice. Now, so has half of Texas," Dave said.

Elsa came up the stairs and sat next to Sophia, who leaned her head on Elsa's shoulder.

"Texas?" Abe said. "Hell, that was an AP story Dave."

"What the fuck man? Ask him what he's talking about," J.P. said.

"What do you mean?" Stokes asked.

Dave came back on the radio. "Oh Stokesie, you really haven't seen a newspaper?"

"No. Tell me what you're talking about."

"Let me read the caption to you," Dave said. "'Chicken King in Scuffle.' That's the headline.

"'Witnesses say Texas billionaire O.L. Kaplan, seventy-four-year-old C.E.O. of The Gulf Company and its most well-known subsidiary, Chicken King Restaurants, Inc., intervened in a fist fight between Shelby Worth, a Corpus Christi cardiologist, and Stokes Summers, of Houston. Kaplan was visibly shaken but appeared unhurt after the fight. Kaplan was a guest of honor at a fundraiser in Corpus Christi and was accompanied by a large group from O'Donnell Oil in Houston, including its C.E.O., John O'Donnell, and Mr. Summers, its Vice-President of Operations. Sources were unclear on who started the fight. No arrests were made but the Corpus Christi police department is still investigating.'

"And the picture is a beaut. It shows Kaplan's old butt pulling Worth up by the collar like he is about to whip the guy's ass! But what we all want to know is: Who is the brown-haired girl on the floor next to you with the come-hither cleavage? And who is the Norse goddess leaning into the camera to help cleavage girl get up?"

Stokes stood with his feet shoulder length apart and laid his head back as far as he could, staring up at the ceiling of the flybridge.

"Fuck!" he yelled. "Fuck, fuck, fuck!"

He wrenched his head forward, making himself dizzy. The bump on the back of his head throbbed and he felt blood rushing into the sore spot around his eye.

"Where did this run?" Stokes asked.

"Everywhere. Like Abe said, the AP put it out on its wire. You're a star Stokes."

Stokes keyed the mike again. "Perfect."

He turned and spoke to J.P. "I'm fucked."

Elsa glanced at Sophia's chest. "Come-hither cleavage, huh? That's a nice compliment for the Italia twins."

"Norse goddess," Sophia answered, crossing her legs and leaning in toward Elsa. "I can't wait to see the picture. I wonder if Suzanna knows about this."

"Who is Shelby Worth?" Stokes asked Dr. S. *I swear I know that name.*

"Never heard of him."

"I gotta go downstairs," Stokes announced to the group. He descended the stairs and ducked into the salon, then into the hallway. The Chechens milled about the guest cabin, both talking on their phones. Stokes found refuge in the master bath. He closed the door and locked it, then set his phone down, turned on the water in the sink and looked at the picture his mom had given him.

Seeing the picture suddenly aggravated him, so he picked up the pewter frame and tossed it, glass down, onto the stack of towels. He took a step toward the toilet. He turned, took two paces back toward the door, put his hand to the back of his neck and turned around again. Two more paces, turn. The water ran.

Focus. What am I going to do?

A knock on the bathroom door broke his thoughts.

"What?" he said.

"Need talk."

Mishka. Stokes took a deep breath and exhaled forcefully. *It's not his fault. Be cool.*

Stokes turned off the water and tried to open the door. It would not open. He yanked the doorknob hard, then harder again.

"Lock," Mishka yelled from the hall.

Stokes pounded the door with one hand and yanked with the other.

"Lock," Mishka screamed.

Stokes decided to just pull the son of a bitch off the frame. Then he looked at the door's chrome handle, saw the latch above it, realized what Mishka was yelling, and flicked the latch sideways. When he touched the handle, the door swung open and he faced Mishka.

"Yeah."

"Need address of tournament."

"What?"

"Address. Address of tournament."

"Port O'Connor, Texas. It's not a big place. The marina, or Alligator Head or dock. I don't know what it is Mishka. Ask J.P."

Mishka turned with his phone next to his ear.

"Will ask," he said, heading down the short hall.

Stokes closed the door again, then turned and looked around, feeling trapped. As nice as it was, this was a small bathroom. The lane between the sink and the steam-shower door measured twenty-two inches wide and six feet long. Although Stokes did not remember the dimensions, he still felt trapped – *very fucking trapped* – mentally and physically.

With his right hand he picked up his phone off the counter, then opened the door to his suite with his left. He stepped inside and hurled the phone at the headboard. When it hit, the battery broke loose from the shell and flew sideways, landing on the floor next to a discarded bra. The plastic battery cover bounced back toward Stokes and landed at his feet. The rest of the phone fell on a white down pillow at the head of the bed.

"Fuck."

The boat bucked. They were hitting choppy water. The movement would be more pronounced in here at the front of the boat, less so at the rear. The floor bucked again under Stokes's feet. He felt slightly nauseated and decided he had to leave.

Wayne and Blaine were in the galley, lighting cigars. Stokes swung out a bar seat and sat down. Blaine slid a crystal high-ball glass full of ice and a golden liquid in front of him.

"Single malt," Blaine said, squeezing a lemon half into the mix. "Good for what ails ya."

Stokes looked at the diamond cuts in the crystal and smiled warmly.

"Thanks."

He took a sip. The scotch burned his mouth. He swallowed and it burned his stomach, inciting another light wave of nausea.

"When I was in high school, I used to keep a bottle of Cutty in my car," Stokes said. "I drank it hot, right out of the bottle, so I could learn how to drink scotch."

"Not a good idea," Blaine said, lighting a long, thick Churchill. "You need to drink it with lots of ice and one of these."

He handed Stokes a cigar identical to the one he just lit: a bright red paper ring girded its distinctive square shape.

"Where'd you get the CAO's?"

"Wayne brought 'em. Join us."

Stokes took the cigar and the torch lighter Blaine handed him. He pushed the igniter button firmly and it made an audible click, sparking the flame. The sound triggered a memory—Stokes felt the back of his head throb while the bright blue flame jetted out, making a nefarious hiss.

"Careful," Blaine said. "That thing's just a few degrees shy of plasma."

Stokes held the lighter and puffed the cigar as he lit it. The smoke tasted good. He exhaled and then breathed in. A small amount of smoke went into his lungs with a soothing effect. He took another sip of the scotch. It was cooler now, as was the crystal.

"Thanks."

He looked out the back glass wall of the salon. The sea behind the boat roiled with whitecaps. In the distance, another sportfisher followed in their wake. The *Break Wind* pounded the water hard and the entire salon moved; glass clinked glass in the cabinets and the bottles in the bar box above the stove rattled against the mirror.

J.P.'s voice came over the intercom: "Hold on down there. We're in the chop of the jetties and we have traffic."

Stokes saw movement to his right and then saw the stern of the *Serenity* heading out. They had hit her wake and they were awfully close–too close to be in the open water. *We must be in the Port O'Connor channel.* Then he realized J.P. had just said as much over the intercom. The salon door opened and Dr. S, Sophia and Elsa tumbled over each other, teasing and giggling as the three of them came inside.

"Let's break out that fuckin' blender," Dr. S said. "We're about to be in Port O."

CHAPTER THIRTY-SIX

Port O'Connor is situated on the north shore of the Intracoastal Waterway. The Port O' Gulf jetties are five miles from town by channel, less if you cut across the shallow sand flats of Matagorda Bay. Another pair of smaller, rock jetties lines the ICW where it meets the bay, and then the town begins. Restaurants, houses, marinas and stores border the waterway on the north side and their docks line the channel for a mile or more. To the south, a couple of football fields across the channel, there are only marsh flats. Arriving from the Gulf, the *Break Wind* headed west into town on the Intracoastal.

J.P. idled the last eighth of a mile to their pier. He passed their slip, shifted to neutral, then reversed at a speed just above a slow drift. He loved speed, but he loved the *Break Wind's* paint job even more, and he swore half the damage done to a boat occurred from the elements, the other half was from docks. Unlike many of the hot-dog captains here, J.P. liked to go slow when docking. The tide was slack and the wind blew them straight back into their berth. With ten people on board, they had plenty of hands, but there was no shortage of volunteers on the dock either. Amazingly, guys stopped working on all sorts of important projects and left their boats just to lend a hand to secure Elsa and Sophia's boat. J.P. laughed at their hospitality.

Stokes, having donned sunglasses and a wide-brimmed planter's hat, threw a rope to a familiar face on the dock. Sophia tossed a second rope to another volunteer on the opposite side of the boat.

J.P. popped the shifters to forward in order to stop the boat's momentum, then tapped the thruster twice to the left.

"Pull us in there, will ya?" J.P. shouted to the man holding the rope Stokes had thrown.

"J.P. Gilpin," the man on the dock said. "I thought you and Stokes were fishing together still."

"We are Greg. Who do you think just threw you that line?"

Greg worked as a mate on charter boats out of Kemah and Galveston and had fished with J.P. A Guatemalan, Greg had a bowl-cut hairdo, dark, chocolate-colored arms, and a golden-brown face. He looked like someone had taken a buffer to his skin, polished it until it glowed gold, then oiled it. His natural, permanent smile and distinctive appearance made him easy to pick out of a crowd.

"Stokes," Greg said, effecting his best south L.A. Latino gang accent, "you holding out on me dude. When did you change the handle of your ride? *Break Wind* is a bitchin' name man."

"Yeah, thanks Greg."

"What's wrong my friend? Why you hidin' under there?"

Stokes had planned to wear the hat and glasses to cover his black eye. He felt silly doing so now and quickly gave up the disguise. He stooped as he peeled the glasses off his face and looked at Greg.

"Dude, put 'em back on!" Greg laughed while he looped a line under both horns of a thick, shiny, galvanized dock cleat, then wrapped a figure-eight. "What the fuck happened?"

Another man took a rope from Stokes and lashed it to a new cleat forward of the cockpit.

"Stokes was in a big fight in Corpus. His name is in the paper and everything," the second helper said.

"It wasn't a big fight." Stokes gave a half shrug. "I got sucker punched, that's all."

"Yeah." Greg safety wrapped the bitter end around the base of his cleat. "I guess I should wait to see the other guy."

"No, the other guy is fine. I never even got to swing at him."

"Bummer."

Stokes kicked a loose rope under the transom wall, then stepped over the gunnel and onto the dock. Wayne, Blaine and the rest of the crew, excepting J.P., piled off the boat as well.

"J.P., I'm going to show everyone to the condo," Stokes said.

The "condo" wasn't a condo at all–it was a five-bedroom house– and like most buildings in Port O'Connor, it stood on piers. It sat next to a canal off the ICW, a couple blocks outside the fenced-in horseshoe of houses known as "The Alligator Head," but Stokes liked that because it afforded them some privacy. They had rented this place for the last three years. It was close to the weigh-in dock. It was inexpensive. It had awesome air-conditioning.

Their crew headed up the dock. Every time Stokes saw someone he knew, they made a similar comment: "Stokes, how was the fight?" "Stokes, aren't you a little old to be mixing it up like that?" It went on up the dock and down Maple Street, and commenced again when Stokes returned.

CHAPTER THIRTY-SEVEN

In Stokes's mind there is a picture–a picture of the "T-head" dock at Poco Bueno. It is dusk on Wednesday night, the night of the Calcutta. He stands at the base of the T, looking down six wooden steps to the pier below. Planks form the deck that stretches out one hundred thirty feet from the bank into the Intracoastal. On each side of the main pier are the finger piers that form the boat stalls. Of all the prime dock space at Poco Bueno–this is the primest.

Sportfishing yachts are backed into every stall. Four boats sit on each side of the dock; four more are at the top of the T. Their sterns range from sixteen to twenty feet in width. Most have hulls painted white, though one is dark blue and another is a light baby-blue. Some are trimmed in teak; two have teak and holly soles. Most of the decks are white fiberglass.

On every boat the lights are aglow, shining into the rigging and onto the decks, reflecting off the stainless steel and anodized aluminum surfaces. Captains, mates and crews are getting ready for the tournament dinner. Stout rods sit in holders, their reels glistening with bright new colored lines. The boats are polished and shined and prepped and readied in accord with the decades-old tournament recipe which calls for equal parts of carnauba wax, diesel fuel, and testosterone. Ladders rise from every boat, slanting away from the pier toward the tuna towers high above, forming an outside row of uniform, shimmering, metal columns horizontally striped with steps. White outriggers sprout from white boats like the antennas of albino lobsters. Every boat has a fighting chair prominently displayed in the center of its cockpit.

Above this maze of metal, fiberglass and lights, small American and Texas flags flap and pop in the stiff breeze. Fittings on taut lines beat a percussive symphony while the wind whips through the rigging. The outriggers point skyward, alongside the antennas and rods, collectively slanting toward the pier. Like rapier swords, they reach into the night sky, their tips forming a white archway above the long, wooden aisle: a fiberglass and metal rendition of an outdoor cathedral–without any deities, excepting the fish. And tonight, these battle wagons have raised their long swords so Stokes can walk down the aisle to his coronation.

At the end of the pier, four more boats are backed into their stalls. Each is broad and sleek with sweeping sheerlines. The sleekest is twenty feet wide and seventy feet long, with a new name on her stern. She waits for Stokes alongside the others in a stable of racing machines, the modern day equivalent of Victorian thoroughbreds. In the distance, water blends to air on the gray horizon.

Small bands of people stroll the pier and crowd the boats. Large, white ice chests with white vinyl cushion lids sit askew on the pier and finger piers. The walkways are littered with white, five-gallon plastic buckets plastered with colorful tackle stickers. On one boat, seven or eight people are talking and sitting and milling about in the cockpit; on another, two mates work on reels. Underwater lights cast a bright, green-white glow between two of the boats. A swarm of shadows darts across the illuminated water. Mullet.

Music floats from the boats; various songs and beats mix together.

The metallic ping, ping, ping of nearby rigging registers in his ears. An engine roars to life then abruptly dies.

Then Stokes can hear people: chatter, laughter, shouts ride the air. After a day of changing out lines, loading boxes, stocking pantries, filling igloos, clearing rod closets, fueling up, washing decks, and waxing everything in sight, the crews have cleaned themselves up. They rest on their boats wearing light-colored caps and visors with boat names on them. Earlier today, their tasks were done in sweaty tee-shirts and old, favorite visors with frayed bills and oil stains. Now, the old visors–the ones that were new just a few weeks ago–have been replaced. Every member of every crew wears a new lid.

Boat owners and their guests are also here, of course. Blue and white and crawfish colored fishing shirts have their tails tucked into pressed, white shorts. Only the "sports" wear the white shorts; the crews prefer khaki, or better yet, board shorts. You can feel it in the air–Poco Bueno is about to begin.

Although he had watched similar scenes at a host of fishing tournaments, to Stokes, this picture in his head portrayed Poco Bueno and no other. He looks down the T-head, taking it all in again while the picture materializes in front of him. The sky is not as dark as the picture in his mind; it is early evening, overcast with purple, ominous clouds, and lights are on. The wind is whipping his shirt and hair, blowing at a constant twenty knots, quartering him left to right. He had been daydreaming. This is not a picture in his head–this is reality.

"Wake the fuck up," Stokes said quietly to himself.

J.P. came up beside him and put a hand on his shoulder.

Stokes turned. "God help me J.P.," he said, thinking of a line his uncle Matt still used, "but I do love this cruel world."

"Amen to that. Is everyone settled in?"

"Yep. And every swinging dick in this town knows about that damn fight."

"Tell me about it. I just now chased the last visitor off the boat. You're a celebrity, but everyone assumes you got your ass kicked because of your sorry looking eye."

Stokes narrowed the insulted eye at J.P.

"Well, I really don't care about that. And I guess I did get whipped, considering he landed the only punch thrown."

"Correction Kemo Sabe. You said he probably broke his hand on the bathroom wall."

"True, but it doesn't matter. My eye will tell the only story that's going to be of any interest at the tournament."

"Don't worry Stokes. I defended your honor. I told everyone who came by that the guy broke his hand. I told 'em you have an iron jaw and used to box Golden Gloves in Louisiana."

"I was ten."

"I told 'em the dude's hand was mangled and bleeding after he sucker-punched you."

"Thanks. I appreciate you lying for me."

"No sweat. That's what friends are for. Plus, I don't want to be known for running with a pussy."

"Again, thanks. What would I do without you?"

They walked down the short flight of wooden stairs to the dock. The *Break Wind* lay moored between the finger piers and the creosoted pilings of the last berth at the end of the T.

Looking away from their boat and stopping at a new custom, Stokes said, "Now that is a gorgeous yacht."

"Bobby just picked it up in Fort Lauderdale," said a young, barefooted mate who stepped down into the boat beside Stokes.

In front of them sat a creation from Paul Mann: a plank-on-frame masterpiece that cost as much as a small island. Momentarily infatuated, Stokes studied the woodwork as the mate's bare feet crossed the sole of the cockpit. The deck was dark teak, with a darker trim between each plank. *Every piece of wood looks like it was hand-picked to fit with the board next to it. It looks brand new.*

"Every piece of wood was hand-picked to match the grain of the board next to it. She's brand new," the mate said before disappearing into the salon.

Stokes stared after him, his face screwed sideways. He felt a hand on his shoulder.

"What do you think, Stokes?" J.P. asked. "Would you trade her for the *Break Wind*?"

"No, but I sure do like the looks of her."

While they walked the dock, this routine repeated itself a few times. Like Mimi and Lovey in the shoe department at Neimans, Stokes and J.P. could not walk a dock at a tournament without stopping, over and over, to gawk and talk about the boats. Most of them they had seen before, but it was always a treat to see the newest models and admire the craftsmanship.

When they reached the *Break Wind*, J.P. approached the refrigerator.

"You want a beer?"

"No, I started on scotch earlier. I think I'll stick with it."

Stokes poured two shots of Cutty into an empty foam Spider Arms cup that had lipstick smudges on its rim. He sipped from it.

"Careful, you drink that neat and it'll sneak up on you like tequila."

Stokes opened the ice maker, scooped up a small mountain of ice and filled his cup until it overflowed.

"It's better that way," J.P. said.

"Amen."

They held the cup and the Corona bottle together.

"Poco Bueno," they said in harmony.

CHAPTER THIRTY-EIGHT

Stokes's cell phone was badly damaged and he had tried to duct tape it back together. He confessed his sins toward the satellite phone to J.P., who made him feel better by declaring, "It was a piece of junk anyway." The whole group planned to attend the Captain's Dinner tonight, but Stokes could barely keep his eyes open. He peered at the ice inside the foam cup on his desk, heard thunder outside, and thought he better have some more whiskey.

In the salon, J.P.'s cell phone rang. Angie and Suzanna had made it to Port O'Connor and J.P. directed them to the condo by phone. As J.P. finished talking to Angie, another call came in. J.P. found Stokes in his room, looking at text on the computer screen.

"Stokesie, Molly wants to talk to you."

"How'd she get your number?" Stokes asked when he took J.P.'s phone and held it to his ear.

"I looked at one of your old phone bills and guessed the most frequently dialed number was J.P.'s," Molly said.

Stokes was impressed: impressed she heard him and impressed she thought of that.

"Good thinking."

"Did you see the papers?" Molly asked.

Thunder rolled outside and the ceiling shuddered.

"I'm looking at the story on-line now."

"I was out yesterday and today, but I planned on going in tomorrow to get caught up and open the mail. I left you a message both days. I didn't want to go in unless you were okay with it."

"No problem."

Thunder rumbled again in the distance. Mishka clunked down the hall and spoke to his cousin in the guest cabin. The door shut, muting their conversation.

Stokes had no idea what would happen if Molly went into the office with all the turmoil underway. "I think you might get ushered out, but give it a try."

Then Stokes remembered John's words to Molly.

"On second thought Molly, don't. If you go in, you might get hit with a subpoena, or they might make you go through my files with them. Stay out tomorrow. If anything changes, I'll call you. But if I don't call, don't go in."

"Okay."

Stokes hung up and sat at the desk, thinking. He knew he should call Melinda Witt. He had known it all day, yet he decided to put it off. He left his duct-taped phone on the desk as he stood, holding his cup and J.P.'s cell phone. *First call, when I get my phone fixed, will be to Melinda Witt,* Stokes thought while he walked up the stairs. *Right after I try Mimi, I will call Melinda.* He continued toward the couch where J.P. lay stretched out, then amended his plan in the process of handing the phone to J.P.

Shit. I better call.

He pulled the phone back from J.P.'s grasping hand and moved toward the bar, ignoring J.P., who looked after him and dropped an extended arm to the floor. Stokes swung out a bar stool and leaned against the seat.

"I need to make one more call," he said, removing Melinda Witt's card from his wallet.

"Hey Melinda."

"Stokes, I've been trying to reach you. I couldn't get the hearing canceled. We might have a problem."

"Why? What's the hearing about?" Stokes glanced outside at the dark skies.

"It's their T.R.O. hearing. The same thing we talked about yesterday."

"I thought you said moving it wouldn't be a problem."

"Well, usually it's not, but those creeps at Vincent & Gump like to play chicken-shit games."

"That's not exactly a secret," Stokes said, inching back on the bar stool. "What happened since we talked last?"

"I called the lead lawyer handling the divorce, a woman by the name of Marguerite Ficher."

"Oh no." Stokes moved back up to the edge of his seat. "Marguerite is handling this?"

"Yes. Do you know her?"

"Only by reputation and the pink leather on the Queen Anne chairs in her office. Pat says she kicks puppies, bleeds ice water and hates to hear the word 'no.'"

J.P. snickered and sipped his beer.

"That sums up the woman I'm dealing with," Melinda said. "Tuesday afternoon I told her you were on vacation and couldn't make the hearing Thursday. I asked if she would agree to move her hearing and she said, 'Send over something in writing,' which I did. Tuesday evening, she hadn't sent back the agreement and she wouldn't take my calls. I sent it over again this morning. Then after lunch, her secretary claimed they didn't receive my fax. I talked to Marguerite around two and she said: 'I'm sure my clients will agree to move the hearing,' and she again acted like she hadn't received my letter. So I e-mailed it and faxed it a third time. Then from three to four she ducked my calls again. So I had to file a written motion to continue the hearing. I sent a copy of my motion to her and instead of an agreement to move it, I get a response back in forty-five minutes. They prepared and filed this thing in forty-five minutes, arguing they have to have a temporary restraining order tomorrow because you're a spendthrift, you're going to waste community assets at a fishing tournament, you'll spend tens of thousands of dollars betting on boats, and they insist the court enjoin you from spending any money or incurring debt, or even using the boat."

"Jesus Christ on a stick!" Stokes said, jumping up from the stool. "Can they do that?"

A lightning bolt split the sky several miles to the south and a thunderclap shook the boat.

J.P. laughed. "You're going to hell for that."

Stokes waved his hand in the air to quiet J.P. so he could hear Melinda.

"Technically, yes; practically, no. I don't think any judge would grant what they're asking unless he was in their pocket. And Judge Clark is in no one's pocket. When he finds out how deceptive Marguerite was with me over a simple continuance, he won't be happy. Of course, I *did* file every document possible when I filed the original petition, and we *are* pushing to go fast, and you *are* at a big fishing tournament, and I *did* agree to this hearing in chambers on Monday. That's unusual, so she'll argue this is an extraordinary divorce involving extraordinary sums of money. Even so, Judge Clark probably won't sign their T.R.O., even if he hears their motion tomorrow. He's agreed to hear our motion for continuance before the hearing on their motion. He faxed a letter to both our offices around five-thirty saying as much."

"So, what do you think will happen?"

"I think the judge will be aggravated at Marguerite but he'll hear her out unless she pulls something else. I think he'll grant the continuance, since any money you spend this weekend that could be considered community property can be immediately replenished from your separate assets, given your means. And, I think the hearing will last less than ten minutes because Judge Clark wants to be out of town by noon so he can go catch trout. But, there's some risk that he will grant their T.R.O."

Stokes leaned against the seat. "And if he does, what happens?"

"If he does, you're technically enjoined from spending any community assets or incurring any debt and a myriad of other standard things which I'll explain to you . . . that is, *if* he grants it. Even then, if you violate the order, you're not held in contempt of court; they just get to claim you violated the order and they'll require you to pay back the community share of what you spent in the final decree."

"So what's the point of the hearing?"

"I get the feeling the point is that Mimi and Marguerite are going to fight us every step of the way and this is going to be a *very* nasty fight. They're going to try and money-whip us to death. I've never heard of anyone filing an answer on the day they were served–that's sending a message. The hearing is at ten tomorrow. If there is any way you can make it, that would help."

"Wonderful," Stokes said. "I'll be there. But don't bank on the judge being in any hurry to leave to go fishing."

"Why's that?"

"The weather. It looks like it's about to rain again here and the wind is howling. I wouldn't want to be fishing in East Bay in weather like this."

"I'll try not to mention that. I'll see you at ten at the courthouse."

"Adios."

Stokes fell back into the lap of the bar stool, popped J.P.'s phone closed and set it on the bar. "I need to be in Houston by ten tomorrow. It's two and a half . . . three to be safe . . .". He spun the phone with his fingers. "I have to get up at six J.P. But let's make a deal. Let's not mention this again for the rest of the night."

"Deal. Maybe you should get ready so we can get the hell up there."

"Ten-four."

Stokes tilted his cup to look inside; half the ice was still there. Rain pounded on the roof.

"I better have some more whiskey to get ready," he said.

"Hurry the fuck up," J.P. replied.

CHAPTER THIRTY-NINE

The water was warm, really warm. It pelted Stokes in the face. A few streams hit his teeth and ran down inside his lower lip, then ran down his chin. He turned around, keeping his eyes closed, and let the water spray onto his neck while he took in a long, deep breath through his nose and focused on only one thing–he could breathe clearly. He had zero sinus pressure. Then he fully considered this physical novelty: In just the last two days, he had smoked two or three big Churchill cigars. He also had several glasses of pinot, a pitcher's worth of margaritas, and a couple tall scotch and sodas.

Maybe this sinus problem isn't all physical. Maybe it's not the smoking and the drinking. Maybe there's a mental aspect to those fucking headaches.

A hallway door closed. He opened his eyes, looked forward into the blue glass tile, then closed his eyes again, tilting his head back into the stream of hot water blasting from the shower head.

John is mad, but will he fire me? Think about something besides money. Focus.

The water pounded his neck. *J.P. put some serious pressure on this system.* In fact, the pressure was only fifty pounds, the same as a house; but the orifices of the shower head were smaller than normal. J.P. had researched shower heads extensively. Besides plumbing fixture designers, only a handful of people have ever read the specs of a shower head. J.P. was one of those people. Stokes considered these facts while he scrubbed the shampoo from his hair and the shower blasted his head, neck and shoulders for another half-minute. He also thought about how, before he had helped J.P. redo this entire boat, he would never have known how much water was on board or even considered how it came out of this shower head at a pleasingly high pressure. He let the water blast into his mouth for a second and then turned around again, rinsed and spit.

Stokes dried himself with a thick, blue towel embroidered with the initials "S.O.S." The towels were a gift from his mom. He told everyone she was a great joker and the towels were for the boat. *What else?*

The towel was warm from the warming rack on the starboard wall, above the head. The shower's hot water heated the rack by flowing through this array of stainless tubing. Stokes's idea: he drew it up, the marine architects tweaked it, and J.P. made it happen. He was proud of it, but it wasn't the best design. Granted, if you remembered to put your towel on the rails, you had a hot towel after your shower. But, if you forgot and grabbed the bars, you could burn your hand.

Stokes held the big, warm, terrycloth towel to his face, raised his eyebrows and thought, *Why the fuck am I thinking about this?*

Oh yeah. Because I'm trying not to think about Lovey, Mimi and an army of the smartest, most expensive, ruthless lawyers in the free world destroying my fucking life.

J.P. banged on the door of Stokes's suite and then opened it.

"Let's eat!"

CHAPTER FORTY

Stokes, trailed by a hobbling J.P. and the Chechen duo, exited the boat. Suzanna sailed comfortably along the dock toward them. She made no effort to hide the fact she was happy to be there. Her alluring smile said it all.

She gave Stokes a long hug, then put her hand to his eye.

"You poor baby. Does it hurt?"

"No, not a bit. Not anymore. The swelling has gone down. How was Phoenix?"

"Wonderful. Dry, no humidity. It was one hundred four degrees both days but it felt better than Houston at ninety."

Stokes had been outside all of thirty seconds and had begun to perspire. He pinched the fabric on the front of his shirt, pulled it away from his body and let it fall back, circulating some air; some stifling, sticky, marsh air.

They approached the big, white central tent of the Poco Bueno tournament under dark, threatening skies. The dining area covered several concrete tennis courts, and tables spilled out from two sides. There were a hundred round tables, each with ten chairs, and the space was full of people. The Captain's Dinner had been held under a tent at this location every year for over thirty years.

Lightning flashed periodically to the south, and thunder constantly rolled in the distance. Gusts of wind blew at their hair as they filed into the line to get inside. When they stepped up to the gate of the cyclone fence that ringed the perimeter, the majority of the men present turned to check out Suzanna. Stokes hesitated a moment to let J.P. catch up. He nodded toward Suzanna. "Get this."

While Suzanna continued toward the back of the tent and the serving area beyond, a lane opened up in the crowd and men stopped talking spontaneously.

J.P. finished scanning the scene and his gaze rested pleasantly on Suzanna's sashaying backside. "I've stretched biminis that weren't that tight."

Just then, a feminine drawl hailed "Hey Stokes" from a nearby table.

Nell Stevens leaned back in her seat and grabbed his hand. J.P. sped up to catch Suzanna and avoid being part of the conversation. Heytu noticed J.P.'s new haste, matched it, and bumped into Stokes as Nell spoke, prompting a few choice Chechen insults from Mishka and a deep "My opologee" from Heytu. Stokes told them to go on and he would catch up.

Next to Nell sat four Houston women Stokes vaguely recognized.

"That's a mean looking eye," Nell said. She was a Houston socialite and an acquaintance of both Mimi and Lovey. She was also staring after Suzanna.

"War wound. You look great Nell. Is Mike fishing?"

"Always the charmer. And of course Mike's fishing. This is bigger than Christmas to him. The girls," she nodded to the other women at her table, "and I are here for the weekend at the condo with the kids. The older ones want to watch the weigh-in. We have a sitter tonight, but tomorrow it's going to be the beach and sun all day."

Thunder rumbled.

"Or, so we hope," she said.

Hearing the emcee testing the microphone, Stokes said, "I need to get a plate."

"Have fun," Nell scoffed, still staring at Suzanna's wake.

Stokes smiled broadly. "Thanks. You too."

The cats at Nell's table stiffened: they narrowed their sharp eyes and breathed in to puff their chests, tilting their smirking faces up ever so slightly. Stokes took ten steps then looked back. Every one of their heads leaned inward at their table and all their mouths moved at once. Purses were opening and cell phones were being drawn. He turned and walked toward the close-clipped grass where steaks were being served off large grills mounted on trailers.

Stokes joined the line beside J.P., who turned to him with a huge grin.

"Dude, that will get back to Houston within the hour."

"If it hasn't already."

Just then Angie came running across the lawn and impulsively hopped onto J.P.'s back. She put her hands over his eyes and teased, "Guess who?"

"Mighty Mouse." J.P. laughed and stumbled sideways, but maintained his footing as Angie hopped down beside him. She saw his black and blue thigh.

"Oh baby. What did you do?"

"Something stupid."

"Are you okay?" she asked, leaning down and lightly touching the bruise with her fingertips.

"I'm fine." J.P. raised a flattened hand, then violently slapped his injured leg. The sharp sound made Angie jump back.

J.P. swaggered, smiled triumphantly at her reaction, and said: "If you're gonna be dumb, you gotta be tough."

$\smile$

He playfully winked at Angie.

She hugged him again, kissed his cheek, then turned to Stokes.

"Hi, Stokesie. I like a man with a sexy black eye! You got these girls some good publicity."

"So ya'll aren't mad about the story in the paper?"

"No, I thought the girls looked cute," Suzanna said. "Plus, being associated with O.L. Kaplan helps."

"I never heard of him till now," Angie said. "Did he really tell the president of Mexico to kiss his ass, face-to-face, on national television?"

"He did," Stokes said. "I actually saw it live. He wanted to feed greasy fried chicken to the masses, but President Gortari wouldn't let him operate there."

"Pretty nervy dude," Angie said, wrinkling her nose and pushing her glasses farther up on her face.

"Yeah." Stokes smiled. "Pretty nervy dude."

He thought of telling some O.L. Kaplan stories, he knew a hundred of them, but decided another time would be better.

"Can I have your attention please," the Master of Ceremonies addressed the crowd.

Fishermen fell silent. This was serious.

Fish talk.

J.P. and Stokes loaded up their plates.

CHAPTER FORTY-ONE

The Calcutta. That was Stokes's favorite part of the Poco Bueno tournament. It grew old fast, it went on for hours, and most people left long before it ended; but that is what everyone talked about; that is what everyone remembered. The Calcutta.

The *Break Wind* came up for bid early. The name elicited laughs from the fishermen and eye rolls from the female sector. The bids opened at three, and she almost went for four. Then, the emcee pointed out she was Stokes's boat – the former *Princess* – John O'Donnell's fish raiser that he never used. Stokes and J.P. were learning fast, the emcee told the crowd. They were not pros, but they caught fish and they'd been improving every year. They obviously were doing something right.

Rain fell from the sky in wavy sheets, forcing the crowd to pack together under the tent. The auctioneer said "going twice" and raised his gavel. Stokes was about to own her for five thousand–then the price shot up. In the back of the tent a pair of bidders whom Stokes could not see were competing to buy his boat out from under him. The price blew past sixteen. Then eighteen. In what later seemed like only an instant, she sold for twenty-two thousand dollars. William Tyler Busch V placed a bet that the *Break Wind* would beat the other ninety boats in the tournament and catch the biggest marlin in the gale now blowing outside.

Rain pelted the big tent in blasts that went on for five or ten minutes, then subsided before roaring to life again. With every blast, the wind howled and the vinyl roof shook. People screamed to be heard above the din. A few unlucky men on the outer perimeter were soaking wet. Inside, clusters of people huddled between the tables.

Stokes seethed. He had wanted to buy his own boat; it was good form. More importantly, *he knew* they were going to win this, but he had panicked. At twenty thousand he had second thoughts and, in a moment of weakness, he let it go. A week earlier he would not have flinched at twenty grand. He clenched his fist without realizing it. *Thank God, Busch bought it.* Winning a few hundred large would surely endear Busch to their cause.

"Have we ever gone that high?" Wayne asked J.P.

"Nope. Last year we went for sixteen. Twelve the year before. We've never hit twenty. You told him didn't you?"

"No. Scout's honor. I haven't breathed a word to anyone," Wayne said.

"Well, he's throwing a bunch of money at a game he knows nothing about."

"Maybe," Wayne said. "But maybe he likes you guys and believes in you already. Look at it as a vote of confidence."

J.P. shrugged. "Nice vote, considering he has yet to meet us. You swear you didn't tell him?"

"Again, I swear."

"Stokes is a good gambler. He must be more twisted up about this divorce than he's letting on because he just forfeited half his bet on a sure thing."

Wayne thought about J.P.'s comment for a moment then asked, "So, you're that confident you're going to beat out every other boat here?"

"I have never, *ever*, been more confident," J.P. whispered in a conspiratorial tone. "We raised more big marlin yesterday than I've ever seen off the coast of Texas in one day, and no one else was around. In fact, I've never marked that many marlin in half a day *anywhere*. Yeah, I'm confident."

"Well, Busch seems awful interested in all this. He said he's bringing his boat up from New Orleans, and he made that bet the minute he walked in. Maybe we have a sponsor."

J.P. and Wayne were deep in a conversation when Angie approached.

"What are you boys plotting?" Angie curled into J.P.'s arms, squeezing between J.P. and Wayne. She giggled and her blue eyes darted up behind her thick, dark frames. "This is truly insane J.P."

"What is?"

The rain had stopped. Wayne looked at Angie but did not speak. J.P. had spoken for him.

"This," Angie said, laughing and shaking her damp blond hair. "All this."

"What's insane about it?" J.P. demanded indignantly.

Angie uncurled herself from J.P.'s arms and pulled him toward a corner of the concrete deck, still inside the eaves and the drip-line of the tent. She waved at Wayne and Elsa to follow. Suzanna scooted over, sensing gossip. The five of them stood in a close circle. Angie leaned in.

"This is insane J.P.," she repeated. "This town. This tournament. Have all you guys lost your minds?"

"What's so insane about it Angie?" Wayne asked. "These guys bet on every tournament."

"It's not the money. Well . . .". She blew a stray strand of her bangs off the black frame of her glasses. "That's insane too, in its own right."

"It's this place," Suzanna said. "It's . . . it's . . ."

$\mathcal{CJ}$

"A dump!" Elsa said.

"Thank you," Angie and Suzanna said in concert.

"A dump?" J.P. felt totally offended. "What's wrong with Port O'Connor?"

"For God's sake," Angie said. "It's a cow pasture bordered by water. It's a good place for a mosquito, but there's nothing here. When we were talking to you on the cell coming into town, we were in the middle of a field dotted with mesquite trees and skinny, starving cows. There's nothing on the highway for thirty miles. Then there are ten blocks of low buildings and the road ends at the corner of a brown beach and St. Joseph's Catholic Church. It looks like it's the nicest building in town, and by nicest, I mean it looks like a cinder-block church you would find in central Mexico. What do you guys see in this place?"

"What about these houses?" Wayne motioned to the horseshoe of houses around them that formed the Alligator Head compound.

"Okay, we'll give you that–ten houses in a dump," Angie yelled. People turned to look at them.

"This is Poco Bueno," J.P. said. "The best tournament of the year."

"Exactly," Suzanna said. "'Poco Bueno' the fabled fishing tournament. You and Stokes and the rest of these guys," she paused and looked around at the crowd huddled under the tent, "dream about and talk about this all year. You actually worry whether you'll get an invitation to this. Most of these big Texas tycoons have the money to do anything they want, anytime they want. Why in the world do you guys choose to come to this berg--"

"This dump," Angie said.

"--in the middle of a pasture, to play?"

"Why not hold it in Rockport?" Elsa said. "The marina at Key Allegro was bue-tah-ful. Not Cannes, but bue-tah-ful."

"Plus there are some restaurants and stores and . . . civilization in Rockport," Suzanna said.

"It wouldn't be Poco Bueno," J.P. said.

Rain suddenly drummed the top of the tent. They all moved further inside.

"May I have your attention," the emcee called. "It's already ten and we need to speed things up here, but we have the tally for the first third of our boats gentlemen. Ninety paid entries. With the first third auctioned, *including* all entry fees, we are at four hundred forty thousand dollars. If we keep up this pace on the auction, this year's total purse will be . . . Are you ready?"

Hoarse yells broke out all around. "Tell us!" came a voice from the front. This was repeated throughout the crowd. The rain battered the tent more intensely than before.

"The total," the emcee shouted over the deep, prolonged rage of the rain, "will be over nine hundred and fifty thousand dollars!"

"Waaa-hoo," Angie screamed.

The rest of the revelers went ballistic: Applause broke out among a wild frenzy of whoops and hollers which rose from the crowd; men beat their chests with their fists; open hands slapped together above the sea of visors and heads.

Over the noise of the crowd and the rain on the vinyl above them and the rain falling into the puddles, Angie shrieked into J.P.'s ear: "This is a very nice dump!"

* * * * *

Two hours later, the crowd had thinned and the rain had stopped. Their group, which now included Bill Busch, had taken over a table. It turned out Busch thought he was doing Stokes a great favor by bidding up the *Break Wind*. When he arrived, twenty boats had sold, with the best bringing between fifteen and thirty thousand. Busch was worried when he saw Stokes's boat was about to sell for less. It was an understandable mistake, but the game was to get everyone else's boat to go for a high price and to buy your own as cheap as possible. That way, the pot grew large while your own bet was small. It made for a funny and embarrassing story at Busch's expense, but he was a good sport, predicting the story would get funnier with time.

A voice said, "Good night ladies."

Stokes turned around. A good-looking guy about his age walked toward him wearing a green ESPN sports coat.

Suzanna and Stokes stood up. "Jack, this is Stokes. Stokes, Angie and I met Jack earlier, he's covering the tournament this weekend."

"Stokes Summers," Stokes said, extending a hand.

"You fishing?"

"I am. And filming." Stokes nodded across the table where Mishka and Heytu were sitting. "We heard your crew was going to be here. Let us know if you're light on any equipment. We have a store."

"Are you filming or shooting video?"

Stokes began to explain and Morgan wanted to talk more. J.P. joined in, as did Suzanna and Morgan's cameraman. Before long, they commandeered a second table and were joined by Mishka. The auction concluded shortly after one. Stokes was intoxicated and kept waiting for a chance to exit so he could get some sleep. Finally, he decided that despite the importance of this meeting, tomorrow's court hearing was the more critical. It was time to go. He stood up.

"It's late," he said, looking at the cup of beer he'd been nursing for twenty minutes. "In fact, it's beer-thirty already." He lifted the cup and downed it in one shot.

"What did you just say?" Bill Busch asked.

Stokes belched softly.

"Stokes!" Angie hit him lightly on the shoulder with a tiny, balled-up fist.

"Scuse me. Beer-thirty Bill. Damn that was good."

The die-hards who had stayed for the entire auction were filtering out of the tent. Stokes's crew rose to leave. Abe Scarborough and several others walked out with them. Stokes had not had the chance to talk to him all night. Abe approached just as Suzanna gave Stokes the key to her rental car.

"Abe man. I want you to meet Suzanna Stacey, a friend of mine and a new business associate. Suzanna, this is Abe Scarborough. He's the guy we talked to on the radio coming in."

"I wasn't there honey. But hello Abe. It's very nice to meet you."

"Charmed," Abe said.

Sophia came up beside Suzanna and they began to talk. "Excuse me," Suzanna said to Abe as she fell back to speak to Sophia. Wayne took her place in the group and they continued toward the exit.

"My God Stokes, she's something else," said Abe. "You move fast."

"She's a friend."

"I'm sure that's what all married guys say about women they date."

"Ha, ha."

The crowd leaving the tent compacted to pass through the narrow gate, where hired patrols made everyone throw their drinks in the trash.

"So Stokes," Abe said, "what do you know about Shelby Worth? That eye looks good by the way."

"Only that he's Mimi's cardiologist. She sees him about every three months. Swears he's some great wonder-doctor," Stokes said as he stepped through the gate ten feet behind J.P.

Abe, J.P., Dr. S and Wayne stared at him. No one had any idea who Shelby Worth was until this very second. Now they all knew–all except Stokes. Stokes took three steps, absently contemplating the disbursing crowd. Then he seemed to remember something, broke stride, and turned to the men. All four stood aghast and watched him pull up short.

"Dude," J.P. said. He paused, carefully considering whether to continue. "Shelby Worth's the guy who slugged you in Corpus."

Dumbfounded, Stokes stood before his friends: mute, assaulted, and confused. All he could do was blink.

* * * * *

Stokes decided against sleeping in the condo for a variety of reasons. He was disoriented, but not because of the alcohol: his thoughts swirled while he tried, once again, to make sense of "the fight." When he went inside his room, he pulled his binder out of his desk. Then he sat down and looked at his financial notes. Nothing had changed. He was just torturing himself—regretting his decisions—but this time, he faced the truth by putting it into words: "I put everything I made into this boat. I'm a fucking idiot."

He turned in his desk chair and looked at his cabin. *But, I can't fish a tournament without a boat. And I didn't come here to watch.*

So why did I come here? To escape? To win?

He looked back at his notes. *And why did I put every dollar I could earn or borrow in this boat?*

He put his shaking hand to his neck and felt how warm it was. When he was tired, really tired, he became feverish and jittery—and worried. But tournaments did that. Before every tournament he rushed around for weeks: buying, fixing, planning. And before the first bell of every contest, he was already beat. This one was no different. Then he'd dreamed up the notion that the show could save his ass and stayed up most of Sunday night writing. He shook his head. *So why do I do it?*

He moved to the bed and rested against the headboard. A phrase came to him: *Never expected to win. Just wanted to box.* The waves from the Intracoastal Canal made a constant muffled slap outside his suite. The noise deadened all other sounds.

Then that fucking blind-sided punch, that fucking ox guy, Worth . . . . He thought about Mimi and his crumbling future as he touched his left eye socket. *But John won't fire me.* He pushed back into the mountainous pile of down pillows.

* * * * *

"Stokes! Hey Stokes!"

Stokes yanked himself sideways and opened his eyes. He was lying on the bed, in his clothes and in his room, drool stained his pillow. J.P. stood above him.

"It's six-fifteen."

"I set my clock for six-thirty," Stokes said, turning off the alarm. He opened the drawer of the side table and removed his tie, then dutifully showered, dressed and walked into the salon.

J.P. was just coming back on board. The fabric blinds across the stern wall of the salon were up. Two kids were on the dock, and it was still dark and overcast outside. J.P. opened the sliding door, but did not come in.

"Just checking to be sure you didn't hit the sack again. It's almost seven dude. You need to get going."

"Thanks. I'm leaving. I've got to fix my phone in Houston." Stokes held up his duct-taped phone and smiled. "This shit's not going to cut it."

"Okay," J.P. said. "I have some helpers. I'm gonna wash and wax the boat."

CHAPTER FORTY-TWO

Stokes emptied the last drops from the plastic water bottle, then tossed it on the passenger floor with the others. The cool front, the rare north wind in July, was gone. Last night's storms off the Gulf had saturated the farmlands and the sun now steamed the air. The speedometer read eighty. The driver's window was down and the air-conditioner blew nearly as hard as the wind coming in the window — only much cooler. An hour out of Port O'Connor, about to merge onto 59, Stokes figured he would be in Houston in another hour and a half. Sweat poured off his forehead and the back of his shirt stuck tight to the vinyl seat. He had purchased three bottles of water and a bottle of Advil in Port O'Connor. Minutes before his visit to the Kwik-Stop, he vomited most of what he drank last night. The open window served as a precaution, but the waves of nausea seemed to have stopped. He was starting to feel normal, except for his headache, which he fully expected. He raised the window when he entered the highway. Without the additional noise, he enjoyed the cold air and considered the dash clock, hoping he could make it downtown with time to spare.

* * * * *

After he parked, Stokes walked across the street to the courthouse and finished cinching his tie to his neck. *She was fucking around on me and I didn't even know it.*

The puzzle pieces had slowly been coming together since last night, and despite his best efforts, he couldn't help thinking about them. He had arrived early and decided to wait in the empty courtroom, correctly assuming this hearing would not take place in chambers. Two lawyers filtered in while he sat alone on the back bench. Then Melinda came in and asked him to step down the hall. *I had no idea.* They talked for ten minutes and returned to the courtroom. Mimi, Lovey and Marguerite were inside. *I know she was.* Stokes told Melinda he would be in the restroom and excused himself as Marguerite rose to meet Melinda and hand her a new pleading. *And she has the nerve to fight me over the boat.*

When Stokes returned, the bailiff entered the courtroom through a door beside the bench. He announced Judge Clark's entrance. Lawyers and litigants stood for the judge and then they all sat at once. When the proceedings started, Stokes looked down at his chest and stared at the interlocking stirrup design on his tie. Then it hit him: the last piece. That was what he couldn't figure out. *That's what's been bugging me since Corpus. His fucking tie!*

Four years ago Mimi announced she'd been diagnosed with some sort of heart problem . . . *she doesn't have any more fucking heart problems than I do* . . . that needed monitoring and she'd been referred to a specialist in Corpus. *Which I bought.* Of course, she had some explanation, and she said it was minor, and she didn't want to talk about it. But Houston is the biggest medical center in the south. *I believed a Houston doctor would refer my trust-fund bride to a heart specialist in Corpus? We're the home of DeBakey and Cooley.* Every three months for a couple years Mimi went down there. *She stayed at the Hyatt every time she went.* Then she stopped for a while. Last winter she started up again, *right after she and Lovey came back from Paris with those fucking ties.*

His hand clasped at his throat.

She bought me Hermes ties. That's what heart-boy was wearing the other night. Guess where he got his tie?

His hand gripped the knot in a tight fist.

A surgeon wouldn't break his hand over a group crashing his party. No fuckin' way. That asshole was jacked at me for upsetting Mimi, or screwing up his deal, or whatever. Fucking Aggie.

Tighter.

I know what I saw. I know what my marriage has been like for the last few years. I'm going to trust myself on this one. Cardio-dick and Mimi have been rendezvousing at the city called 'Body of Christ' for years. I'm a sap. I'm a fucking idiot.

He laughed quietly. His right hand now hovered in the air. Slight tremor.

He was sweating as he sat alone at their counsel table in the cool, air-conditioned courtroom. He began removing his tie. While he did so, he thought about playing football at Jesuit. Every senior on the team gathered together, no coaches, and agreed not to drink until the end of the football season. He went to ten parties that season and didn't touch a drop of alcohol. *Not one fucking beer.* His buddy Roger did the same thing. Then a week before their last game, all the seniors were together and he proposed they lift the pledge off the entire team so they could drink that weekend at a field party. Brook Camden and Sam Ayoub looked at him like he was crazy. Sam said: "Hell Summers, we've been drinking all season and so have all the juniors. Get your head out of your ass." *That's what Sam told me. Get your head out of your ass. I have never once cheated on Mimi and she has been fucking this big faggot in Corpus for years.*

The silk slipped silently from his neck. He fingered the mother of pearl button that bound the starched collar to his perspiring throat. Then he stopped. Instead of unbuttoning his collar, he put the four fingers of his right hand into his tailored choker and pulled. Once the cloth was drum tight, he arched back with his neck. The cloth ripped; the button popped into his palm. He placed it on the desk before him, enjoying the fresh air on his throat.

He listened to the lawyers' voices rising near the bench. *Melinda was quiet.* Good sign.

She was ahead, so she shut up. *Good lawyer.*

The Bubba Gump crew whined on. Then, Judge Clark banged his gavel and Stokes watched him stand up in his black robe. He liked the feel of his open collar.

Stokes stood, Melinda motioned him outside and they stepped into the hallway. Melinda pulled him by the arm, but he ignored her grasp and turned to face Mimi directly when she stepped from the courtroom. Before Lovey, or Marguerite, or the rest of Mimi's team reached her side, Stokes silently placed the silk tie with the interlocking stirrup pattern in her hand. Mimi's attention fixed on the fabric, then her head jerked up.

In the beat of a heart, in the time it took for Mimi to meet his spent eyes, Stokes knew the truth.

Bitch.

Without a word to anyone, he turned and exited the courthouse; leaving Mimi, and the lawyers, and six years of his life, there in the hallway.

CHAPTER FORTY-THREE

Stokes crossed the street from the Harris County courthouse anncx to the lot where he had parked. He scrutinized the space for a Suburban, then remembered the sedan baking in the July heat two aisles away was his. He approached the car and thumbed the Hertz key chain; the locks opened.

"Stokes."

He turned and saw Melinda hustling toward him carrying her briefcase.

"Stokes, would you like to talk about this? Maybe get something to eat?"

"There's not much to talk about." Stokes paused, then added, "Thank you Melinda. Seriously. Thanks for how you handled things in there; and for the offer. But I really don't want to go to lunch right now. I have some errands."

"Stokes." Melinda put her hand on his arm and then released it. "Are you okay?"

Stokes felt his blackened eye and his sore cheek twitch reflexively; he glanced down and then back at Melinda.

"Come on Stokes. How're you doing in there?"

"How am I doing?"

Stokes searched the sweltering asphalt lot and saw no one. He took three steps between his car and another, then turned to look at Melinda while she walked with him. His eye twitched again.

"I've been asking myself that for a week now. This morning, I was driving in and I asked myself that exact question. To be honest, I don't *know* how I'm doing. I'm happy, I'm sad, I'm angry . . . I feel like a fuc . . . like a failure. I got here and I was fine. Then we go into the courtroom and I have to listen to that bitch Marguerite lying about the boat being a wedding present--"

"She was doing her job Stokes. Her clients are lying."

"She only has one client! I don't care if Lovey is calling the shots. Marguerite was lying."

He stopped and glanced at the ground. A few seconds ticked by.

"So yeah," Stokes said. "I'm not sure how I'm doing. I'm annoyed at being in this courtroom, I'm embarrassed, and at the same time, I wanted this but . . . I'm . . . fucking pissed off! Sorry." Stokes stared at the ground again, then back at Melinda. "I feel like hitting something or throwing something right now. I've been drinking in the sun for four days, I'm worn out."

And I feel like I'm fucking losing it.

Stokes's brow had broken out in a sweat and his starched, white oxford stuck to his back. Melinda put her hand on his forearm again and held it there.

"I have a number for a counselor I want you to call. Will you do that?"

"I have some buds I can talk to Melinda. I think I'll try that first, okay?" He blinked his tired, red eyes and set his jaw.

Melinda saw the resolve on his face.

"Okay, but you have my number. If you want to talk, call me. I'll give you that counselor's number too. Talking to him won't hurt any-thing."

"Thanks. We'll rain check on lunch."

"Deal. Take care of yourself."

* * * * *

For lunch Stokes did something he hadn't done since law school. He ordered a Quarter Pounder with fries, sat in the restaurant and ate it–alone. He looked out under the yellow arch in the window while his mind wandered. *My whole life is collapsing around me, so why is it all I really want to do right now is go fishing?*

After lunch, the sales manager of the phone store on Kirby, near his house, activated and programmed yet another new phone for him. They were getting to be good friends. She gave him the latest model, which looked like a pack of gum it was so small and narrow. Stokes protested. He wanted simple and liked the forty-nine dollar job in the display. But the manager said he needed a nice phone. She didn't want him walking around with a piece of junk. He was a good customer and she told him he was getting "a huge discount." She was cute. Stokes always liked dealing with her. She was decisive and took care of business quickly. All Stokes had to do was sign and leave. *And, she has nice tits . . . I am a fucking dog.*

Stokes left the store and slipped the phone in his pocket, noting how small and light it was. It rang. He held it up, studied its keypad and felt relieved to see that, like the last four or five phones he'd owned this year, it had one green button labeled "send" and one red button labeled "end." He felt like a technical genius and, despite this morning's calamity, he grinned like a wino who had just found a twenty on the sidewalk. He pushed the green button and confidently held the phone to his ear.

"Hello."

"Mr. Summers, will you hold for Mr. O'Donnell please?" Linda said.

"Sure."

The phone went silent for a moment. Stokes held it away from his head and looked at it. When he brought it back to his ear, John was yelling, "Can you hear me?"

"Yes, John, I hear you." There was background noise. It sounded like John was on a speaker.

"You're fired Stokes. I want you to clear out your stuff and get out of the office."

Stokes was quiet.

"We clear on that?" John barked.

"Yeah John, we're clear."

The line went dead and Stokes closed his miniature phone. He quietly climbed into the low sedan, started the engine, heard a familiar country tune and angrily spun up the volume knob. As he left the parking lot, the phone rang again, barely audible over the music. He pushed the tiny green button and held the phone up to his ear with two fingers and a thumb.

"How did it go?" J.P. asked.

A horn honked, then another; tires squealed and skidded, but George Strait soothingly sang on. Stokes stomped the brake and looked to his left. A pickup careened past the hood of the sedan, its driver angrily gesturing.

"I'll call you back J.P." Stokes flipped the little phone closed.

A foot. He watched the truck speed away. *Maybe less. That would have crushed me. I almost fucking killed myself. If he hadn't slammed on the brakes, I would have killed myself.*

Fuck! Focus, dumb shit. Focus. Either get your head out of your ass or die, Stokes thought, entering the traffic.

You're fired Stokes. We clear on that?

Numb. That was how he felt. Numb.

We clear on that?

He drove, turned, accelerated, braked, watched, accelerated, rubbed his temples, tried to keep his eyes open, and drove.

You're fired Stokes.

South of the loop, he pulled off the highway, into the parking lot of an abandoned patio furniture store, and shifted into park.

Clear on that?

He turned the key. The air stopped, the engine stopped, the radio continued.

You're fired.

He punched the volume knob, which fortunately doubled as the radio's power switch. In the now quiet car, in the empty parking lot, while the unconditioned air began to heat, Stokes's eyes filled with fluid, and when they could hold no more, the tears fell. He put both hands to his head, palms to his temples, fingers splayed through his hair, and cried.

"What the fuck do I do now?" he asked through the salty streams falling from his nose. "What . . . the fuck . . . do I do . . . now?"

He was asking someone else–someone who he didn't believe could hear.

He couldn't admit, even to himself, who that someone was. It would make him cry harder if he ever did.

Stokes had always asked *him* his questions. Even when Stokes had known the answers, he still asked. Lately, they were just rhetorical questions; Stokes knew there would be no answer.

Since he was a kid, he always asked *him* everything. *He knew.* Not once in nine years had Stokes acknowledged to himself *who* he was asking questions to, when he asked them alone, like this . . . but once again *he* was asking *him*, and *he* wasn't there to answer. *He* was no longer a phone call away. Stokes couldn't just drive up and see *him*. *He* couldn't have a scotch with *his* youngest son anymore. *He* was dead. *Stokes* was the lead elephant now.

Dad was gone. And now, so was John.

The car was a furnace when Stokes finally got hold of himself. So much so that opening the door helped. The sticky, ninety-five degree air outside was an improvement. He walked around the lot thinking of John's tone, of Mimi's betrayal, of his own impossible debt, of the *total fucking meltdown* of his life. He was alone, he said to himself, and there was no possible way out of this.

Back in the car. *Think of something else. What was I thinking before? What . . . he looked at the phone . . . oh yeah . . . .. These phones are really simple now. Breathe. And kind of cute. Breathe. But, should a phone be cute? Breathe. Stay on track.* He started the car, cranked the air and pulled onto the service road.

"If you work hard and stay focused, you can achieve anything."

He said that to me all the time.

His hand shook like he had a palsy. He pressed the side of his hand against the top of the wheel to stop it, then looked at the phone and closed his palm around it. Passing cars now, doing eighty. *Time to get back to the boat.* He looked up at the road, then down at his fist again, trying not to grip too hard. *Get it together.* His hand shook, he couldn't stop it. He watched the road, holding his gaze on the lines.

"I trust your judgment."

You said that all the time. What you think of my judgment now?

"You'll make the right decisions, you always have."

You said that too, a lot. But this time I obviously haven't made the right decision, have I?

"I'm proud of you."

Stokes burst into tears again. Uncontrollable. *That was the last thing you ever said to me.* He let himself cry. He glanced back at his clenched fist through brimming wet eyes. *I'm going to keep trying. I promise you. I'm going to focus. I'm going to work my way out of this . . .*

His right fist clenched the phone tighter.

Crack.

The noise confused him. For an eighth of a mile he puzzled over the origin of the sound as he glanced at his white knuckles. Then he warily opened his hand, not really believing what he saw. He had just broken the shell of his brand-new phone.

While he exited the highway, Stokes called J.P. back with his tiny–cracked–phone and listened to the voice mail greeting. He left the message he would be back at the boat around eight. He drove aimlessly through neighborhoods just past the second Rosenberg exit, found a small park, pulled in next to two empty tennis courts, and sat under a tree. For over an hour, he petted and conversed with an overly friendly basset hound-mix that was in desperate need of a bath; then, having fully collected himself, he drove off, in search of some iced tea and a place to wash his hands.

By the time he returned to the highway, he was in another storm; but this one was easily solved with the wipers.

CHAPTER FORTY-FOUR

Stokes parked the rental car in front of the condo, but rather than going inside, he walked to the boat. Preoccupied by dire worries of debt, failure and ruin, he did not observe the big blue van, emblazoned with the yellow words, "PHOTO SUPPLY," parked sideways at the base of the T-head. As he passed beside the van, a massive, lumpy polyester butt protruded from the side door, shifting back and forth and bulging like the sides of an over-inflated tire; even this escaped his notice. Finally, a long, labored gasp–not unlike the sound of air being sucked from the regulator of a scuba tank–caught his attention. The occupant of the lumpy pants wheezed as he removed a bundle of three-inch poles. Stokes studied the van's contents, then his brain engaged and the words plastered on the side of the door suddenly registered in his mind. *More supplies, more gear . . . more money.*

Mishka and Heytu stepped from behind the opened back doors of the vehicle, each holding a box.

"What's this?" Stokes gestured toward the butt that was reentering the van.

"Equipment, film, supplies," Mishka said.

"For what?" Stokes snapped.

"The Technical Sportsman," Mishka said, smiling. "This where they film it, right?"

"Right," Stokes said, encouraged.

Lumpy waddled back out of the van, vacuuming air left and right and dragging a large box toward the door. Stokes grabbed one end and pulled. When it slid out, the weight sunk him to his knees and the box thudded to the ground.

"What's in here?" Stokes said.

"Counterweights . . .". Lumpy stopped and wheezed desperately. "For the boom."

Stokes dragged the box over the wet pavement, away from the door. He had told Mishka to get all the necessary gear, at any cost, as soon as possible, but he now seriously regretted those words. He had not expected Mishka to find and deliver it all to the boat in twenty-four hours.

They brought the equipment into the salon, out of the humidity, and set it on the floor. Lumpy lit a cigarette. The whole open salon looked like a network storeroom. Stokes grabbed his checkbook, and he and J.P. followed Lumpy's ballooning back pockets, his smoke trail and convulsing lungs up to his van to retrieve the last load and pay the invoice. When they returned to the *Break Wind*, a small crowd had gathered around her. Three guys were making no attempt to act like they were looking at the boat. They stood apart and across the pier, gawking at Suzanna's backside and whispering to each other.

"Suzanna is right, J.P. Men are dogs."

"What are you talking about, dude?"

"Nothing."

When they neared the *Break Wind*, there was a commotion. The three guys who had been ogling Suzanna now walked up the pier toward the parking lot. Stokes hesitated, a little longer than he normally would have, before he stepped to the side to let them pass. Suzanna and another small group of men were on the dock watching Mishka in the cockpit. Mishka yelled in his native tongue. Half the men looked toward Mishka, the other half had their bodies facing the boat but kept turning their heads and leaning back to sneak peeks at Suzanna. Walking closer, Stokes realized it was not just Mishka in the boat. Mishka and Heytu were yelling at each other–again. Large, black cases lay open on the mezzanine deck and Mishka held what looked like part of a large camera. Heytu held another piece, and something big and metallic rested on the fighting deck.

"This doesn't look good," Stokes said as he came up next to Suzanna.

"Oh I don't think it's a problem. They've been yelling at each other for several minutes now, but it looks as though they're about done."

Stokes kicked off his flip-flops and jumped down into the cockpit.

"How are we doing Mishka?"

"Fine, fine," Mishka said, then he hurled a string of foreign expletives at his cousin. "This his first time to assemble cranes and Steadicam mount. Not understand instruction written English. My cousin is strong and carries, but no use on put together."

Mishka snatched a part of the Steadicam from his cousin. "We fine, fine. No problem," he said, turning back to his machinery.

Stokes went inside, followed by J.P. and Suzanna, leaving the Chechens and the crowd on the dock. The rest of the crew was at the condo.

"What's the plan?" Suzanna asked.

"We're set to go," Stokes said. "Tonight's dinner already started up at the tent. But, it will be much more laid-back than last night. Everyone slept off their hangovers and then spent the day getting ready. They'll have another captain's meeting; I'm sure they'll discuss the weather. Let me hurry Mishka and his cousin along."

"Tell you what," Suzanna said. "I'm going to go on up with the others. Do you mind?"

"Course not. We'll be up as soon as we can get there."

Stokes went to his cabin. When he returned five minutes later, the salon was quiet. J.P. sat on the L-shaped couch, feet on the surfboard table, eyes closed.

"You ready Stokesie?"

"Yep." Stokes looked outside and saw the Chechens had left the back deck. "Where are the terrorists?"

"They went on ahead; they were both hungry and horny–they wanted to check out the talent."

"There was plenty of it last night; shame everyone was packed together too tight to see it."

"We all managed."

When Stokes and J.P. walked into the big tent, the first thing they saw at a nearby table were four charming faces and two ugly ones. Suzanna, Angie, Sophia and Elsa all sat together, along with the Chechens, laughing, talking and having a good time. The tent was clearing out. Most of the crews had eaten and returned to their boats.

CHAPTER FORTY-FIVE

Precisely twenty-one hours after the Calcutta auction concluded, the rain was coming sideways.

All ninety boats in the tournament were occupied: ghostly figures in yellow slicker suits moved about their decks and surrounding docks, keeping their backs to the wind. They looked like monks in their bulbous yellow hoods. Occasionally someone turned into the wind and a hood flew backwards, eyes squeezed tight, an exposed head was rinsed, and the victim pulled his hood back over his head and held it with one raised hand. Inevitably, the water drained out of the righted hood and ran down the back of the newly baptized boater.

Precisely twenty-one hours and thirteen minutes after the auction, the rain quit.

But the wind continued to gust.

Stokes's little phone rang as he sat at the helm. The driving wind had numbed his senses, but the ringing inside his thick, yellow slicker woke him from his stupor. He considered letting it ring, fearing he would get wet unzipping. *My back is soaked anyway.* Another ring provoked him to unzip and pull the Velcro tab from his dry, front shirt pocket. He felt the split in the plastic shell embedded deep in his pocket and then squeezed the phone between his extended fingers. When he withdrew it, it slipped from his grasp, bounced off the steering console and slid across the wet fiberglass deck toward the stairway. He fell to his knees and thrust two heavily mantled yellow arms toward the phone. It teetered over the edge of the stairwell before he grabbed it, stabbed at the green button and held it to his ear.

"Hello!" he yelled over the howling wind.

"Stokes?"

He barely heard his name. "Hold on," Stokes shouted. He looked around for a place to get out of the squall, then crawled to the space between the driver's bench and the console. He opened the door under the steering wheel, removed the empty trash can and stuck his head in the cramped cabinet.

"Hello. Who's this?"

"Never mind," the voice said. "Can you hear me?"

"Yeah."

"Then don't say who this is."

"Pat?"

"You follow directions so well."

"What?" Stokes yelled. The phone's tiny speaker made Pat's voice nearly impossible to hear. Stokes pushed inside the cabinet as far as he could, contorting his body into a fetal position.

"Can you hear me?"

"Yes." Stokes twisted, spastically jerking inward until he bumped the top of his sore skull on the front interior wall of the cabinet.

"Then listen close," Pat said. "Get the fuck out of the marina as soon as you can."

Stokes finally could hear clearly, deep inside his cabinet turned cave.

"Why? What the fuck are you talking about?" He rolled onto his back, feeling dizzy. His head throbbed. His shoulders were wedged tight and he could not move his arms.

"Listen, I could be thrown out of my own law firm and I could probably lose my law license for calling you and telling you this. Where are you? Are you alone?"

Stokes's eyes rolled, searching the dark cabinet. "Yeah. No one's in here with me. What's the big fucking secret?"

"Your boat is about to be seized by–"

Stokes heard "seized" clearly but lost the rest in the roar of a fresh onslaught. Rain bombarded the front of the cabinet, just a quarter-inch of fiberglass away from the top of his head.

"Did you say seized?"

"Yes. Mimi and Lovey pulled an end run around your judge," Pat yelled. "After he refused their motions this morning, they went to federal court in Galveston and convinced the judge there to sign a writ. Danny swore out an affidavit stating you owe forty grand in fuel charges and the judge agreed to seize your boat for the charges."

"That's ridiculous," Stokes yelled. "I don't owe that."

He paused. Rain beat on the cabinet wall–like it wanted in.

"Well, maybe I do . . . but this is bullshit Pat!"

"Calm down. This isn't about money. This is about fucking with you for embarrassing Mimi. They're trying to ruin your weekend. This is Marguerite's way of showing Mimi and Lovey she has balls."

"Fuck her! The shotgun start's at midnight."

"I know that. But Marguerite doesn't know that."

"What time is it?" Stokes asked.

"Ten-fifteen. If they're not there yet, they may not be able to find you. I just learned about this myself."

"Thanks for the heads-up Pat."

"Stokes?"

"Yeah."

"Please Stokes, don't tell anyone."

"Ten-four."

Pat's phone clicked off. The rain that had been pelting the cabinet's outer side suddenly stopped.

Stokes considered his position for a moment.

While talking to Pat, thousands of raindrops had clung to the top of the waxed dash above, forming a uniform sheet of cold liquid. Inside the dry, dark chamber, Stokes looked at the illuminated keypad of his cracked phone, which he held between his face and the low ceiling–a space of about five inches. With his elbows tight to his side, he lowered the phone and clutched it to his dry chest. Outside, thick drops fell steadily from the mouth of the cave and onto his waist.

He considered his position again. How could he get out of this?

The best way was to stay on his back, put his calves on top of the bench seat, and slip his torso out of the cabinet with a twist. It was a tight spot; it would take the moves of a gymnast. *And, I am up for the challenge.*

He raised his calves onto the seat outside.

The water puddle marshaled for its assault.

Stokes left his phone on his chest, slipped his hands up behind his head, and shoved. His execution was flawless. In one fluid motion, he removed himself from the cabinet, twisted his body, and lay liberated on the floor between the seat and the console. It had taken only a second. Only a drop had dampened the crisp, dry cotton on his chest. Free from his confinement, he beamed a broad, Cheshire cat-grin toward the radio boxes recessed in the ceiling, satisfied with the clever gymnastics of his maneuver.

The water sheet, with characteristics strikingly similar to those of his wife and mother-in-law, finished its own clever maneuver. It had shaken with Stokes's effort, swayed forward when his hands pushed against the front of the cabinet and then, as Stokes's weight shifted to the back of the console, the aft edge of the sheet had broken the invisible dam holding the water on the top of the dash. In one fluid motion, the entire contents of the puddle rushed down the angled backside of the dash, past the thoughtfully laid out screens and dials and instruments and shifters and throttles. Just as the smirk sprawled over Stokes's face in celebration of his emancipation, the puddle–trillions of molecules strong, but only about a cup and half in volume–fell through the air in a wavy, broken sheet and landed deliberately; first on Stokes's new phone and then, immediately afterward, on the still dry front of his fishing shirt. The rain began again and flew sideways in the wind.

At the same moment the water dam broke, J.P. opened the sliding glass door of the salon. He stood inside the *Break Wind*, listening, just as the furious sound of blowing rain began anew. Despite the deafening noise, he heard his buddy Stokes yell two separate and distinct words at the top of his lungs: *"Mother! Fucker!"*

Stokes crashed down the stairs, past J.P., and into the salon. Neither spoke. J.P. closed the door. The air-conditioner kicked off and the whir of air being forced through the metal vents ceased. There was a low hum and a tick as a disc changed inside the stereo cabinet. Stokes stood on the stairs, just inside the doorway, and put his wet phone on the bar. Water trickled onto the floor at his feet. A stream formed and dribbled into a bronze drain. The phone commenced vibrating and tried to ring. It had never vibrated, not in the whole eight hours Stokes had owned it. It made a curious sound, then shook again.

"It's dying," Stokes said.

He flicked one end of it. It spun and rocked while it twirled, like a dead June bug on its curved back. No more vibration. No sound.

"It's dead," J.P. said.

"That was a pretty good phone."

"Pity. We all gotta go sometime."

"Speaking of going, we need to get the fuck out of here," Stokes said.

"Why?"

"Trust me on this, you don't want to know."

"Well, trust me on this," J.P. said. "You don't want to go."

They turned together and stared out the wall of heavy glass doors spanning the breadth of the salon's stern. Each of the four panes was neatly held by its polished stainless frame. They had argued about installing these doors for months while rebuilding the boat, until J.P. found a pressure-lock, and a redundant sensor, to hold the doors open. J.P. knew Stokes–the designer–was admiring the view.

"There's not another sportfisher in the world with a sliding glass wall at the stern of its salon," J.P. said.

"Too bad for them, 'cause that looks pretty damn cool," Stokes said.

Outside, their fishing lights cast a brilliant halo over the cockpit. A fisherman could re-spool a reel under those lights and never want for daylight. Beyond the lights' realm, the world appeared black. The wind whipped the rain in every direction. Spray swirled around the salon like it was blasting from unmanned water hoses, slashing back and forth behind the aquarium-like wall of glass.

Stokes peeled off his slicker top, revealing a yellow fishing shirt soaked to the skin, front and back. Water dripped from the rolled up, button-tabbed bulk of his sleeves and he felt something in the thigh pocket of his board shorts. He ripped open the Velcro flap, then reached inside and removed a hard knot of brown strings.

"Dude," J.P. glanced at Stokes, "you're supposed to zip that top. When I wear one, the water stays on the outside."

Stokes held the cord up between them and shook it. When Elsa's crochet bikini top fell open in his hand, both he and J.P. unconsciously sighed in unison.

"God, she has a great rack," J.P. said.

Stokes tossed the bikini on top of the deceased phone and stared at the rain flying away from the salon windows. "Mimi has federal mar-shals on the way to seize the boat as we speak."

The wind turned a passel of drops to the right and they darted away like translucent minnows in an aquarium. Another group fol-lowed them, then the wind blew the rain straight away again.

"Leave the radio off," J.P. said. "Not even the Coast Guard can make us talk to them if we never hear 'em. The girls are all staying here. Their choice. Blaine feels like he should stay with Busch since he invited him, but he'll go if we need him."

"That makes you, me, Jordan and Wayne," Stokes said.

"And the Chechens," J.P. said. "How long before the marshals arrive?"

"No idea. I'm surprised they're not here already. Listen, I really need to talk to you." Stokes put a hand on the back of a bar stool. "I made some decisions today . . . I need to tell you what I decided."

"I guess you decided to go with the white curtains instead of the dark blue, huh?"

"No. Here's the deal: Like I sort of told you earlier, there's a chance, a good chance, really, that I've fucked up. I trusted Mimi. I thought this divorce would be easy, but it's anything but. I also assumed I owned the boat free and clear. It looks like I was wrong on that too. We sent the paperwork in to transfer the boat a few months after I agreed to buy it, but the title didn't change until months after the wedding. The O'Donnells don't know that yet, but once they do, I have a big problem. If I lose the argument on the boat, I still own half of her but I can't af-ford to buy Mimi out so I'll have to sell. I can buy another boat with the money. Not like this, but another one. There's nothing I can do about all that now. The facts are going to be argued and the O'Donnells will stick together. I'm *persona non grata.*

"So . . . here's where you come in. I've decided what I'm going to do but I don't expect you to feel any loyalty to the cause. You need to do what's best for you."

 ↺

J.P. yawned.

"Here's my plan: Mishka and I talked yesterday about finishing the pilots. Anyway . . .," Stokes stalled, thinking again about John's call.

"I started this project and I intend to finish, even if that's all I finish. Yesterday I hired Mishka and Heytu for another two months. We're going to work 24-7 and crank out a couple of good shows, hopefully on this boat. I also want to hire Suzanna and all three of the girls for any open time they have between now and the end of the month. When I hired this lawyer for my divorce, I told her to move as fast as possible."

J.P. shifted beside him, looking at his watch.

"The judge announced today, at our *ex parte* request, that we'll finish all discovery in this case in thirty days. Now that he's said it, we're in no position to say we want to delay. And, to be honest, if I'm going to lose six or seven years of my life and most of my money and be driven into bankruptcy, I'd just as soon do it quick and start over. If I lose the boat, actually I'm thinking it's *when* I lose the boat, and it could be any minute now," he laughed nervously, "we won't be able to film on it anymore. Even if this works, it'll take a while to package and sell the show. If not, hell, I tried."

Stokes adjusted his feet and stuck his hands in his pockets.

"Oh, yeah, there's another thing . . .".

Stokes jingled the coins in his pocket, thinking once again about John's blunt call today.

"I . . . uh, there is . . .".

He gritted his teeth, the jingling ceased, and he stood there for a full ten seconds.

The silence caused J.P. to turn and look at him.

Tell him straight up. No bullshit. "And John fired me today J.P. I'm no longer employed by O'Donnell Oil."

"So what?"

"So, I'm about to be broke. Mishka and Heytu and all the equip-

ment, hiring Suzanna's firm, purchasing studio time. Other than the
Colorado royalties, which are shrinking fast, I have no source of income if I'm not drawing O'Donnell Oil checks. I've got nothing left to
sell but the boat. I owe a *shit load*. At this rate, I'm burning thirty K a
week. I'll be tapped out in two or three months. And then the bank is
gonna seize the boat if Mimi hasn't already."

They stared at each other for a moment.

"And?" J.P. asked.

"And, what dude? Did you hear me? Tapped out! As in down to
fucking zero."

"And what's the fucking question?" J.P. yelled.

"Are you in?" Stokes yelled back, matching J.P.'s volume and con-
tinuing at the same level. "There might not be an up-side or a future
here J.P. If I fuck this up, I'm toast. I can't pay you a salary when the
money's gone. I won't have any money to live on myself. And I won't be
able to play big boy games anymore."

J.P. shook his head.

"Dude, you seriously think I care?" he asked in a calmer voice.
"We've had more fun together in the last few years than I've ever had in
my life. You're like a fucking brother to me Stokes. A rich brother." J.P.
laughed. "I'm not going to miss out on being a part of this show. We'll
make a hit out of this, we'll get rich, and we'll do it while we fish and
party our asses off. I have no doubt whatsoever that you can pull this
off. I never have. And if we fuck up, who cares? We're right back where
I started. I'll teach you how to get a real job. We can work together in
a shipyard."

They both laughed.

"At least we went for it. After all, we're just a couple of dirt bags.
Adolescent dirt bags."

"We are not."

"Stokes . . . come on. We spent twenty thousand dollars on underwater lights that we only use because they look cool. We spend all our time at fishing tournaments because we like boats. We gamble. We drink. We don't take care of ourselves. Our bodies are being abused 24-7. Angie says we're both so fascinated with tits we remind her of a pair of twelve-year-old boys. And, our great plan is to get rich producing a TV show for other adolescent dirt bags."

"Angie said that? Twelve-year-old boys don't think . . . well, I guess they do."

The stereo played softly over the speakers and the air-conditioner now droned, but J.P. did not respond.

"Okay. You're right. Angie's right. But you know what? Fuck maturity. I like tits. Hell, I like adolescence. I like *all* this shit J.P. I'm sick of living the way other people want me to live. This . . . *this*," he put both his hands to his chest, "This is what *I* want to be when I grow up." He paused, then added, "It'll be a good show."

"Yeah, you picked a good fight."

"What?"

"I didn't see it at first, but this show's a good idea. It's a good place to focus your efforts." J.P. stared at the floor. "The good thing about fishing is you're just fishing. You're not thinking about the past or the future. You're in the moment."

"Seriously," Stokes said. "I'm not trying to be rude, but sometimes the shit you say--"

"By *thinking* I mean *worrying*." J.P. looked up at Stokes's reflection in the glass. "When you're out there, you're not *worried* about your future. You're not *regretting* your past. It's all about the present. The rod, the reel, your buds, the fish—you're just fishing, you're not worrying."

"Okay, I follow you."

"People might forget their worries for a while when they watch your show."

Stokes looked away from the glass and stared at his feet.

"You'll look back on this and realize it was the best part," J.P. said. "It'll be a good show if you throw yourself into it. And you will; you'll mean it."

"We'll mean it."

"Yeah."

J.P. looked Stokes up and down.

"You're already wet. Run and get the guys. I'll undo the electrical and warm the engines. Tell 'em not to bring anything but what they're wearing. We're gonna hit those fish hard, catch 'em, get back here and weigh in. If this shit keeps up, we'll come back tomorrow evening with the winning marlin and take the Friday bonus as well."

Stokes yanked the slicker over his wet shirt and then immediately arched his back as if he'd been shocked. The moist cloth had cooled, and chill bumps erupted on the skin of his arms. He felt his hair stand on end.

"You'll get just as wet the minute we leave," Stokes said.

"I know, but right now I'm dry," J.P. said.

Stokes cracked open the back door. Before he stepped out, he turned to talk to J.P, who had just pulled a beer out of the refrigerator.

"This is my first one of the night," J.P. said defensively.

The wind howled outside and a whistling sound came from the doorway.

"Do you really want to go?" Stokes said.

J.P. handed Stokes the beer he had just opened. Stokes took a swig. J.P. went back to the refrigerator, removed another beer and opened it. He pulled out a bowl filled with dried slices of lime, walked back to Stokes and placed the bowl on the bar. Stokes squeezed a slice into his Coronita bottle. J.P. did the same, then pulled two plastic-tipped cigars out of a red and white paper box in his chest pocket and handed one to Stokes. He peeled off the clear wrapper, as did Stokes. J.P. pulled a yellow plastic lighter out of his pocket, cupped his hands and lit his cigar. He then held the lighter toward Stokes.

They stood there, smoking and watching the rain. Neither said a word. The wind gusted harder now and made its weird whistle at the door. J.P. blew a cloud of smoke towards the opening and the pressure sucked the smoke cloud outside. Raindrops raced in the wind.

"Nobody else knows about that rip," J.P. said. "Nobody else knows about those fish. And nobody else is going to win this tournament. We ain't gonna let some fucking federal marshals stop us without a fight."

Stokes puffed hard on his cigar, clutched his beer and stepped outside. When he cleared the mezzanine's porch, he clenched the white plastic tip in his teeth and drew hard again, knowing the cigar would go out. Rain assaulted him. The cigar got doused. The paper cover went from its normal light brown to a dark, syrupy black, the burning tip from red to ashen.

Stokes hopped over the gunnel and onto the finger pier, put his left hand to the top of his hood and hustled down the dock, holding the last few ounces of beer in the bottle in his right hand, his shoulders up against the rain. The cigar swelled heavy with the water it absorbed. He winced and shivered as a stream of water snaked down his left forearm, passed his elbow, and chilled his armpit. He squeezed his upper arm close to his chest, cocked his head to his left shoulder and ran on, keeping his hand on the brim of his hood. When he reached land, he straightened his head, released his grip and relaxed his left arm. The jostling movement of his feet hitting the asphalt parking lot broke the wet cigar where it joined the white plastic tip. The hood flew backwards. The waterlogged cigar fell away, tapping lightly on the chest of his yellow slicker before plopping into a puddle on the ground. He ran toward the condo, shoulders down, head exposed, smiling like a goon in the driving rain.

CHAPTER FORTY-SIX

The rain quit. Heat lightning pulsed in the east every ten or twelve seconds. All but one was aboard and ready to head out.

"We good?" Stokes asked, rubbing his hair with an S.O.S. towel and stepping up to the nav station to sit next to J.P. on the ottoman.

"Muy bueno," J.P. said. "Where's Jordan?"

"He'll be here. You still want to leave now?"

"Yes." J.P. punched in numbers on a calculator then made notes on a pad. "We'll wait in the ditch. We have a well-marked route going out. This weather's going to slow us down at first, but I'm thinking they won't cancel the tournament. These squalls are just training in lines. They're violent little fuckers, but they ain't gonna cancel. With this wind, we'll cut across and then cut back here." J.P. pointed at the screen. "So we'll get out past the rigs in the middle of the night."

"Feels weird, doesn't it?" Stokes asked as they both stood up.

"What's that Stokesie?"

"I just came back from Houston and I haven't even been to my house . . . or my office . . . hell, I no longer *have* an office, and soon I won't have--"

Jordan met them at the door, stepped between them, simultaneously patted them both on the shoulder, then continued inside.

Stokes's hands balled up into tight fists. J.P. decided to change the subject.

"Let's cast off," he said, heading up the stairs.

Rain fell in big, sloppy drops. For several seconds, Stokes watched them plunk into the water. The regret of losing his house, and the life he had led for years, had distracted him once more. He struggled to get back on track. Then he stuck his head into the salon. Jordan leaned over the sink in the galley. Neither Wayne nor the Chechens were in sight.

"We're leaving Jordan. You sure you have everything?"

"I'm loaded. Let me finish cleaning this pot and I'll give you a hand."

"No. Keep cleaning. I can get the lines."

Mishka looked up from the front stairway. "Need us?"

"No," Stokes said. "Just wanted to be sure you boys are on board."

"We storing stuff. Will be out."

Stokes closed the salon door and stepped off the boat while the intensity of the rain increased and the raindrops fell at a slant, re-soaking his newly dried hair. He untied ropes from the foredeck, then walked around the finger piers through the bright cockpit lights to untie the other side, thinking again about his job, his house, his life, his . . . about Mimi. He stopped, stood still for a moment, tried to let his eyes adjust to the brighter light, then uncleated the port stern line and spring line. He climbed back into the cockpit just as the salon door opened.

Mishka came out, holding an encased camera on his shoulder. Jordan stood at the counter drying a bowl with a white *Princess* bar rag that had writing all over one side. Through the open door Jordan yelled to Stokes the single word: "bueno."

He meant it as a question: "Bueno?" as in "Are you good out there?"

Stokes heard it, despite the increased noise from the rain hitting the water, and yelled back, "Bueno!"

J.P. shifted into gear and eased forward on the throttle. The boat pulled ahead and sideways, and Mishka lost his balance. They were barely moving, but all seventy feet of her lurched and then banged hard against the finger pier on their starboard side. Stokes turned, looked at the starboard stern line tied fast to a shiny, galvanized cleat, and felt like an idiot.

"Fuck," J.P. yelled from the flybridge.

"Sorry dude," Stokes said, jumping off the boat.

J.P. turned and revved the throttles to stop the stern from slamming back into the dock from the recoil of the line. He strained on his toes to look over the edge of the boat at Stokes.

"How bad?"

Stokes jogged forward along their starboard side to assess the damage. He squatted down and pulled the tight, front spring line out of the way. Several deep scratches crossed the freeboard paint and a few wood splinters floated in the water, but otherwise, all was well.

"We're okay J.P."

"Hop in. And can everyone hear me?" J.P. screamed.

Five voices screamed back "yes" through the noise of the rain and engines.

"No one say 'bueno' again!"

Stokes's remorseful expression burst into a shit-eating grin as J.P. continued.

"I don't want to hear the mother fucking word 'bueno' unless it's from a mother fucking Mexican in mother fucking Mexico . . . deal?"

"Si, si," Stokes yelled, and the rest of the crew yelled "deal."

The boat had floated back into the middle of the slip and they were well-centered for their exit. J.P. shifted to forward, accelerating slightly faster than normal because of the current and wind. He looked over his left shoulder and watched the gap widen between the transom of their big boat and the wooden dock. When he turned to look ahead, they were clearing their berth and he gave it more throttle. High above, the rain clouds broke up, and the sky opened overhead. A loud crack rang out. Another crack followed, then a splintering sound and a sharp ping. The boat lurched right again while J.P. reflexively throttled and swiveled his head. He heard a whizzing sound, like a bullet or a whip, then ducked as something flew past and crashed into the water in front of him.

"What the fuck was that?" he yelled, shifting into neutral.

Stokes came out of his crouch at the top of the stairs and looked back sheepishly. One of the front timbers of the finger pier was now missing a new cleat. Below that timber, wood splinters, brand-new ones, floated on the water at the front corner of their stall. The boat's blue spring line hung from a stainless cleat on their side, near the starboard back of the salon. A strong outgoing tide slowly pivoted the boat, bow left, stern right. J.P. throttled to gain control. Stokes could see nothing in the dark water ahead.

"What the fuck? I thought you had all the lines Stokes." The situation was so absurd J.P. laughed.

They motored slowly down the Intracoastal in a heavy shower. Stokes leaned off the flybridge and looked back to inspect the timber with the fresh scar.

"That was the fucking spring line off the front," he said. "It shot that thing a long way. That cleat could have killed me."

"Us," J.P. said, still laughing.

CHAPTER FORTY-SEVEN

For the next hour, J.P. shifted in and out of gear while the boat drifted in the Intracoastal Waterway a mile from the T-head and only a half-mile from the Coast Guard station. Rain pelted the water, thunder rumbled and shook the air, lightning crackled, and wind whipped the vessel from side to side. As far as they could tell, no federal marshals had shown up at the dock. They kept all the cell phones and the VHF radio turned off for good measure. If someone wanted to talk to them, they would have to find them with a boat first. In this storm, there were not many boats running around, but there would be soon.

The shotgun start at midnight signaled the beginning of the tournament. No one actually fired a shotgun; the tournament officials simply announced over the radio that the boats could leave. The *Break Wind* joined an armada of million-dollar-plus fishing boats motoring out of Port O'Connor in the ICW. The boats raced across a portion of Matagorda Bay, in a five-mile-long line of lights, then into the channel toward the end of the ocean jetties. Horns honked from the vessels and from the shore, crowds screamed, someone even managed to light a few bottle rockets, but the usual midnight celebration was subdued by the rain which fell again in sheets and waves.

There was no light in the sky. When they reached the channel inside the Gulf jetties, the water was as rough as J.P. had ever seen it. The jetties of Port O'Connor, like the jetties of nearly every navigable entrance to the Gulf of Mexico along the Texas coast, are piles of granite rock and concrete which line the channel, jutting out into the sea. In Port O'Connor, these lines of piled stone cut through a barrier island and serve to stop the channel from silting back in on itself, as well as to break the waves of the ocean, allowing the vessels inside the protective walls a smoother passage into deeper water. Unlike every other jetty in Texas, the rocks at Port O'Connor are not parallel. Instead, they neck down, forming a channel that has the shape of a whiskey bottle whose top is pointed toward shore. The long jetty also has no safety cut, a place halfway down the rocks where a small boat can exit. The end of the jetties is the only outlet. When the tide is running hard and pulling water out of the channel, and the wind is blowing into the accelerated outgoing water, it can stir up an awful stew. Tonight, the water inside the jetties looked like the open ocean itself.

A quarter-mile after they passed the narrow inshore entrance of the jetty channel, at the spot where the neck of the bottle meets the body, the depth gauges on the flybridge dash dropped from forty feet to ninety-six feet. Nobody was watching, but the ninety-six-foot depth reading was no mistake. Scour holes have formed inside this choked section of the jetties by past seas just like this, and the sonars were finding them just as the waves were lifting their boat.

A mile and a half from where they begin, the jetties stop; and in another couple of minutes, their vessel would bear down on the end of the rocks. This was often the roughest part of a voyage. The ocean was rocking. Stokes guessed they were in solid ten-foot seas. J.P. knew they were nines. The wind howled demonically out of the southwest. They needed to head southeast. Traveling at night with the wind and waves breaking against their starboard side for well over one hundred and fifty miles would be miserable, and in seas like this, maybe impossible. J.P. knew the waves beyond this point would be smaller. He also knew where he wanted to end up; his waypoints were charted on the GPS display in front of him. But he amended his plan.

J.P. turned and screamed at Stokes, "We're gonna follow the pack out for twenty miles, then head east another forty, then we'll turn into the wind and take the waves on directly."

They nervously scanned the riot of black waves surrounding them. J.P. also kept glancing at the radar screen, which clearly showed the jetties and the other boats. Small mountains of water formed where the jetties stopped. The tide was strong and outgoing, the wind stronger and incoming.

Their vessel headed out to sea with all her curtains closed. On a convertible sportfisher, the flybridge can either be exposed or enclosed. When Hatteras built her, *Princess's* flybridge was enclosed by glass windshields. Stokes decided to make the flybridge open when they refurbished her. He explained to the designers and architects at Sparkman & Stephens that they could close their clear plastic curtains if needed. After all, how often would they be driving her in torrential rain? Stokes thought about that now. An additional thought came to mind: *Dumb shit.*

While they rode the flybridge through the gale, J.P. stood behind the wheel. Stokes stood by his side and held onto a stainless handrail on the ceiling. Mishka held a ceiling handrail on the opposite side of J.P. and tried to hold the camera steady on his right shoulder. The base of the boat now moved with the unusual seas and the flybridge acted like a lever at a ninety-degree angle–seventeen feet above the water line–swaying and rocking and pitching in random, thirty-degree arcs. With their equilibriums gone, stomachs lifted and fell, feet constantly shifted, and knees bent to cushion the blows; and every time their bodies adjusted, the momentum of the flying bridge stopped, reversed, and accelerated in a new direction; and then, as soon as it started that way, it abruptly shifted again.

"Now this," J.P. screamed over the wind's noise, and the rain beating every surface of the boat, and the salt spray blowing back off the bow, and the roar of the big waves, and the engines' whine, and the generators' drone, and the rolling thunder, "this is fucking scary."

"Amen!" Stokes yelled. He glanced at J.P., looked behind, and then looked ahead. They were following a thirty-eight-foot sportfisher. Less than one hundred yards separated their bow from the stern of the smaller boat. The waves looked like dark houses moving before them. At the crest of each blue-black house, the water broke, making a long cap of scattered white spray. Above the hurricane-like roar, they could hear the high-pitched sizzle of the spray on the waves around them. The waves grew and, as they left the jetties, the boat tilted violently forward on the back side of a swell the size of a two-story house, their speed increased, and spray whistled off the top of the wave behind them. Stokes fell forward two steps and then, at the top of his lungs, he yelled, "Where's that boat?"

J.P.'s eyes opened wider into the spray, his mouth said the words "Oh shit," but no noise was audible. A violent kick from a wave moved them left twenty degrees. At the same time, the most important screen in front of J.P., the radar, went black. He made a snap decision to keep this fact to himself.

Mishka kept the camera on J.P. while filming, but looked forward. He saw nothing. Just a blue-black wall of water. No horizon. No boats. No lights. He spun the camera forward and composed himself, thinking there was nothing he could do but document the event. He held the camera at the bow, recording, then panned back to J.P. and Stokes.

J.P. pulled back on the throttle. All seventy feet of the boat slid down into a trough: a black hole of water. He spun around to look at the transom, then forward to the bow, and saw only a black, shiny re-flection. He yelled at Stokes, "Unzip those fucking curtains!"

J.P. looked at the transom again. A wave was coming. He looked in front of him. The bow of the boat pointed down into the water, black on black. No depth perception. He was blind forward. He had no choice but to throttle ahead. They gained speed.

Stokes fell forward and yanked a zipper from top to bottom. Half of a clear plastic curtain beat at him like a manic flag. He yanked the next zipper and the curtain released and flew into his body. He gripped it with his left arm and tried to hold it while he looked ahead. Their bow torpedoed into the base of a mountain of dark blue water. Stokes fell into the opening created by the missing curtain, then managed to pull himself backward. Their yacht rose, water falling off her foredeck in massive slices while she ascended the wall of ocean. J.P. turned right, correcting to his previous path. For a moment, they were level.

Stokes looked forward. The thirty-eight-foot sportfisher they had been following had disappeared. An ocean-going yacht, with ladders and a tuna tower and radars rising over forty feet off the water's surface, had disappeared in front of them. A football field had separated the two yachts. Now she came into full view as their own vessel dropped into a trough. Huge drums were lashed in her cockpit. It looked like they were about to ram into her transom.

J.P. pressed the throttles to turn starboard, heading into the on-coming waves. "Watch them!" he yelled to Stokes while he throttled up on the front side of a monstrous haystack. They seemed to be barely moving. More throttle. The other boat appeared to be slipping back-ward toward them. At the very moment Stokes believed there would be a collision, their swell began rising and the other boat's swell fell. As their vessel crested its swell, they accelerated away from the other boat.

"We're clear," Stokes yelled.

The other boat seemed to have stopped, suspended atop the crest of a massive wave while the sea around her raged; then her bow dipped, her stern rose and her props sprayed water out from under her while she slid into another trough.

J.P. pressed the port throttle forward and pulled back on the starboard and they banked off a wave. They were about to cut back behind the boat they had been following.

"What're you going to do?" Stokes yelled.

"Head east," J.P. yelled. "We can angle off now. Fuck our waypoints."

"What if we hit someone? We're too fucking close to shore. Keep this course," Stokes yelled.

Stokes disagreed with J.P.'s plan but either way, on this heading or another, this was insanely dangerous; especially right now. They could plow into another boat head-on. This very second they were surfing across the path they had just taken. They made it, and crossed their previous course. No boats. Stokes worried about rigs and pipes. There were not many unmarked pipes, but one was all it would take. But J.P. was driving, and driving in this storm was incredibly difficult. They had their radar. Stokes would let J.P. decide the path.

Stokes focused on that decision for a moment and put everything else out of his mind: the monstrous waves, the fierce wind, the punishing spray of the saltwater, the needle-like sting of the rain. The unworldly noise. The absolute roar. Was this the right decision? Should he take the wheel? No. J.P. was just as good a driver as he was. J.P.'s night vision was no different and he had just navigated those gigantic rollers without hitting the boat in front of them which, evidently was having some kind of problem powering up the big wave. No, this was the right move.

If we sink, it will not be J.P.'s fault. We have a bunch of boats out here in the worst possible conditions. We don't want to kill a crew by running over them. We have life jackets.

They were riding down a wave again. A seventy-foot yacht—surfing.

They porpoised and rose and leveled, and accelerated and surfed again.

This is crazy. They should have called off the tournament.

Porpoise. Level.

But we know where the fish are. Were.

Throttle. Spray. Surf. Stinging rain. An eerie seethe–like a thousand angry snakes–followed them.

Stokes turned. The white cap of the wave they now rode broke behind them, projecting a shrill strain. The crest followed at their eye level and only thirty feet behind the flybridge. They were truly surfing.

Stokes stepped back beside J.P. and saw one of the screens was off.

Jordan pulled his way up the stairs. He held out dive masks. J.P. stared at them. Jordan grasped the wheel. J.P. fell back on the driving bench, slipped on a mask and then retook the wheel.

"Awesome!" J.P. yelled when water spangled his mask. "What'd you do? I can see. The water is beading off!"

"Rain-X," Jordan yelled.

"You're a fucking genius!"

Stokes skeptically took a mask from Jordan and pulled it on. He could see. He struggled forward, half-hanging onto the stainless bar above him. Jordan took the plastic curtain from Stokes. Stokes took another step forward and slashed down on a second zipper. Again, the freed curtain beat into him. He slashed again. Now they could really see.

Jordan, J.P., Stokes and Mishka looked at each other with their masks on. J.P. cracked up laughing.

"We look like the four biggest dorks in the world," he yelled.

"Why did you cut the radar off?" Stokes yelled.

"I didn't," J.P. yelled. "It quit."

Stokes stared out of his mask, wide-eyed and silent. The four of them rode the flybridge for another hour.

The rain stopped and started. When it was bad, they used the masks. They made fifteen miles on the chart. The seas were calmer. They were out of the horrendous chop caused by the outgoing tide, the incoming wind, and the brutal currents off the end of the jetties. The wind eased, shifting more south. Perhaps the worst of the storm was over. *Perhaps.*

They planned to start fishing at dawn, along the northernmost boundary of the curve that marked the weed line the marlin were prowling. The turbulent ocean would put them many hours behind schedule. It would be impossible to run straight or fast in these seas. The fish had been here two days ago but, more importantly, the rip line–the line between the cold, upwelling current and the warmer sur-face water–had been here. Throwing a line out in the middle of the Gulf and hoping for a bite may have won a big tournament–once. It had never won the Poco Bueno.

What often won in the past was live-baiting around the big oil rigs. The best known, a rig called "Tequila," is seventy-five nautical miles off Port O'Connor. Not far from Tequila are two other popular rigs called "The Cervezas." In this weather, with little chance of visually locating bait or fish, many of the boats in the tournament would choose to fish these rigs. Several other fixed rigs and semi-submersibles would also see their share of boats, as would the big rock structures ten to fifteen miles south of Tequila called "The Hilltops," and another rig about one hundred forty miles off the Port O'Connor jetties called the "Hoover Diana." Each structure provided cover for bait fish which attracted the bigger pelagic species.

By first light, boats would be lined up, waiting their turn to circle a rig, hoping to draw a big marlin up to their lines. To a land-locked lake fisherman, it may sound like a boring way to fish for the undis-puted kings of the ocean, but it was effective and it was an adrenaline rush. The industrial rigs, the intrusion of man-made structures in the unspoiled wild of the open sea, were quickly forgotten when a five-hundred-pound marlin appeared in the wake, charged, and then viciously crashed a bait. These fish, predators and hunters in every sense, are the blue-water equivalent of a lion on the plains; sighting, scenting, stalking, and running down their prey in a brutal and merciless display of what they do every day for their own survival–eat. Watching this spectacle, even once, was the fisherman's equivalent of smoking crack: one time and you were addicted. It did not matter if a couple of oil rigs or thirty production platforms spoiled the view. More often than not, the Poco Bueno was won by a boat circling a rig. Today, however, J.P. and Stokes hoped to beat the odds.

They had plotted their strategy for two days. The general current of the rip was subject to move. With this weather, they assumed the rip would either break up or move northeast. If it had held together, they hoped to intersect it and follow its edge, the point where the colder water met the warm, where the weeds accumulated in an arcing line, where the marlin hunted and where they would hunt for their marlin.

CHAPTER FORTY-EIGHT

Just before dawn Stokes was driving with Jordan beside him on the flybridge. The Gulf had calmed significantly from the fury of the previous night. Large waves–with white spray covering every crest–blanketed the surface of even larger swells in the open water. Their bow rode upward at a slight angle on the sharper swells, then tipped forward again and leveled off while the bulk of the hull cut a deep groove into the water. A smaller boat, a lighter boat, would have ridden the larger waves and swells to their crests, then dropped into the next trough, jarring the boat and its occupants. Stokes knew that was exactly what was happening on the other boats in the tournament right now. In the shorter boats, the crews would be standing in order to cushion their bodies from the intense pounding of their banging hulls. Stokes pictured John among a circle of attentive admirers at a cocktail-party, saying, "Fishing in a boat under fifty feet is just a very expensive form of torture." That line was always followed by the heavy roll of John's laugh and an appreciative peal from the gallery.

Stokes refocused and thought of his current competition. At seventy feet, the *Break Wind* was bigger than all but one entry in this year's contest. There were several other boats at sixty-three feet, one at sixty-eight and another at seventy-two. Stokes felt pity for those poor souls in boats under fifty—pity for their lack of comfort, but not for the fact he was about to beat their best efforts, take their money and win the tournament. They would be fishing in an hour and a half, it was five-thirty. Stokes increased their speed with the growing light, intent on reaching the spot where they had marked their fish.

Another twenty-five minutes passed.

Jordan stirred.

"You tired?" he asked.

"Yes and no," Stokes said. "Yeah, my eyelids are warm. I have a fever from lack of sleep. I'd kill for a hot shower and a still, dry bed. But, no, I don't want to sleep. We're getting close. We're about ten nautical from the arc of the rip. I'm mad at these fish. We're about to win Poco Bueno for the first time. How do you feel?"

"Like shit, thank you."

They rode another minute. Up, up, up more, then down. The throaty, wet exhaust changed pitch each time they angled down.

"That was insane last night," Jordan said.

"Agreed," Stokes said. "That shit around the jetties was insane. And, I don't know what was wrong with that boat in front of us."

"Spending the last six hours trying to concentrate to avoid hitting anything was no picnic either." Jordan stopped short. "Did you hear that?"

They listened.

Zee. Zee.

The sound came from behind them. Jordan turned, listening.

Zee.

"Oh cool. Look at this."

He motioned to the dark, upper corner of the flybridge. In each corner of the ceiling, mounted to the ladder that went to the tuna tower, was a small, black camera.

"Mishka must be operating them remotely."

Jordan stood, grasped a ceiling handrail with one hand, then plucked the microphone from its clip with the other. He released the microphone and let it hang, tethered to the ceiling by its pigtail cord, while he adjusted a setting on the radio to intercom. Then he sat back down and grabbed the dangling mike.

"That you down there Mishka?"

"Yes," came a deep, thick, gravelly voice over the speaker.

"Nice try J.P.," Jordan said.

"I can see you guys," J.P. said, " and hear you on the headphones. This is some cool ca-ca."

"How do we look?"

"Like hammered shit. I have coffee; you guys want Baileys?"

Stokes looked at Jordan. "Yes, lots. And doctor it up some more," Stokes said.

Jordan keyed the mike. "Ten-four. Baileys and booze of your choice in one. Baileys and no booze in the other."

"Ten-four, but I heard him the first time."

Zee.

"Cut that shit out," Jordan said into the microphone.

"Must get shot," J.P. said, again in his best thick Chechen accent.

"Can't you get a remote mike?" Jordan asked Stokes.

"Yeah, but we just bought these twin radios. It's a waste of money. I told J.P. the remote mike was back-ordered."

"Don't worry," J.P. said over the intercom. "I called Jimmy right after you told me that Stokesie. We should have the remote next week, and if not, at least before the Legends tournament."

"This is bullshit J.P.," Stokes said. "We're not keeping these spy cameras up here."

"Relax," J.P. said in a silky, late-night D.J. voice. "We'll take the cameras out of your bedroom and the heads and the flybridge after the tournament."

"Ha ha."

They rode another few minutes in silence. The salon door opened and closed and J.P. came up the stairs with three mugs. "Breakfast is here boys."

"You're feeling chipper," Stokes said, taking a mug.

"Other one," J.P. said.

Stokes handed the mug he held to Jordan, then took a sip of his. He coughed immediately. It tasted like hot cough syrup with a mint flavor. He drank a long draw. When he swallowed, his throat burned and he coughed again, getting liquid in his windpipe. That made him cough harder, repeatedly. The last cough hurt.

"That's good booze," he said hoarsely.

"Thanks," J.P. said. "Schnapps, shine and Community with chicory. The shine gives it that gasoline touch."

"Yeah, I noticed that," Stokes rasped. Then, recovering his voice, he added, "Very mellow."

"Speaking of that," Jordan said, "how are we on fuel?"

"Bueno," J.P. said.

Stokes rolled his eyes. "Don't forget our new deal."

J.P. nodded in agreement.

"How much do you guys carry?" Jordan asked.

"We can hold three thousand two hundred and fifty gallons," J.P. said.

"Jesus. We could go to Mexico on that."

"That's the idea. And we can go a lot farther than Mexico."

Zee. The camera panned from Jordan and Stokes at the wheel to J.P. in the front of the helm on the u-shaped couch.

"Mishka's got the con," J.P. said. The lens extended toward him. "Do you ever take a rest?" he asked the camera.

"Behave," Stokes said. "This is our new career. We're gonna make you a star."

"Three thousand two hundred and fifty gallons of diesel. We rarely load more than two thousand gallons but we have bladders in the spine of the hull for about twelve hundred and fifty more," J.P. said, warming to his topic. "We burn eighty-five gallons an hour at twenty-four knots, fully loaded. Our range is ninety percent of three thousand two hundred fifty gallons. So we can range twenty-eight hundred. That gets us to Mexico and Cuba and into the Caribbean."

"That's a take," Jordan said. "Why so much fuel?"

"We designed her to travel anywhere on her own bottom. We didn't want to pay to ship her across an ocean on a transport. If we fish Cairns or Africa, it will be a blast just making the passage."

The salon doors opened and closed and Mishka came up the stairs with a camera running as J.P. finished talking.

"We can fish farther out and different water than most. With this much fuel we can go anywhere."

"What about weight?" Jordan asked. "How can you possibly move with thirty-two hundred gallons on board?"

J.P. smiled at the camera. "Well, for one, we usually run with two thousand gallons or less; and two, we laid our reserve tanks forward in fixed ribs in the bow. That balances the load and we just transfer to the main tank from there."

The camera lens retracted and moved back to Stokes. The remote port camera turned toward the bow and re-focused for the horizon.

"This is fucking weird," Stokes said. "I need to piss."

He stood up and stepped to his left while Jordan slipped into the seat behind the wheel. Stokes walked around the front of the steering console and J.P. knocked back his drink. Stokes stepped by J.P. and grabbed his mug. "Otro?"

"Sí."

Five minutes later Stokes returned to the flybridge and handed J.P. a fresh, fully-loaded drink, then took Jordan's old seat.

"You know even though your back was to the lens, it looked like you were playing with it," said J.P.

"I know you didn't put a camera in the head J.P."

"Okay. Think what you want. But you're gonna be embarrassed when your taking a piss makes the edits."

"Did you see the drums on the back of that boat we were following last night?" Stokes asked the group, changing the subject.

"See 'em?" Jordan said. "I was staring at them. If those things would have busted loose they would have torn the side off that boat."

"Precisely the reason we have so much capacity," J.P. said. "Half the boats in this tournament used to fill their cockpits with fuel drums. If anyone went down last night, I'll bet they had drums strapped like that. That's about the stupidest thing you can do in my book."

"Why?" Mishka asked, his shoulder cam at the ready.

"It's just like Jordan said." J.P. paused and shot an annoyed look at the camera, but his rigid expression diffused and he continued in a pleasant tone, "You lash a fifty-five gallon drum standing upright on the deck of a boat and you have around three hundred ninety pounds of liquid in a can. That can is usually held to either a ladder or a handrail with a rope or strap. If the fuel sloshes and the can moves six inches quickly, it gains enough inertia to snap a two thousand pound test strap. Once it's loose, the inertia builds. You slide it across twelve feet of wet deck to the other side and something's going to give. You strap five drums on your deck, like those idiots had last night; put yourself in rough seas, like all of us idiots were in last night; and start to lose power with all the extra weight in your cockpit, like our friends; and if you go down, you are one lucky mother fucker if you survive."

The red light went off. Mishka leaned away from his viewfinder.

"You want shoot last part again and leave out mother fucker?"

J.P. raised his mug to the camera. He took a long swig, then tilted his head toward the ceiling and gargled the words: "mother fucker, mother fucker, mother fucker," as a high-octane coffee cocktail spilled from his mouth, down the sides of his cheeks, and ran down his neck. He held his lighter to his lips, spewing brown liquid, and sparked the flint. A blue flame flared for an instant.

"Very nice." Mishka stopped filming and put his camera in his lap.

Ten minutes later, the dark wall of clouds broke in front of them, and sunlight shopped between distant columns of rain. The seas were still confused, but the wind had abated and changed to a more typical south-easterly direction. The sky brightened. Stokes watched bait fish, flying fish, and occasionally small pods of dolphin, riding the pressure wave off their bow. The water was much clearer than he had expected after last night's seas. J.P. had rods rigged and set in holders in the cockpit. Stokes finished a potato and egg burrito at the flybridge when J.P. came up the stairs.

"Anything?" J.P. asked.

Stokes had not been paying much attention. With a mouth full of food, he raised his head and pointed forward, intending to tell J.P. he hadn't seen anything.

He and J.P. spotted the weed line at the same instant.

"Holy shit," J.P. said.

Stokes yanked back on the throttle. The boat's rate of motion dropped so quickly it sent J.P. falling forward. He grabbed the top of the dash and caught himself.

They slowed to an idle and Stokes turned down sea while they surveyed the tightly-packed weed line. Clumps of reddish-brown sargassum and trash stretched in front of them. They would have intersected it at a ninety-degree angle if they had kept motoring.

J.P. did not take his gaze off the horizon. The boat rolled with the still sizeable waves.

The wave height diminished over the last two hours, Stokes thought.

"I think we found our rip," J.P. said.

"It's closer to where it was than I would have guessed."

Stokes pushed the chart menu and hit the range button. He punched the range key to ten miles and exited. Their boat's position was at the center of the screen. The icon for one of the fish they had marked was between them and the edge of the screen.

"We're less than two miles north of one of the fish we marked."

J.P. looked behind the boat, slowly scanning the horizon around them. "I don't see anyone else."

"Yet," Stokes said.

The salon door opened. Mishka and Heytu came up the steps, followed shortly thereafter by Jordan and Wayne. J.P. looked at them all, one at a time. No one spoke. The others were looking at the sea. J.P.'s inspection prompted Stokes to examine their crew: faces sagged from alcohol and exhaustion; wet hair, slick from the salt spray, stuck close to heads; their eyes all bore the same whipped expression. But the night was over and the first day of their tournament was about to begin.

CHAPTER FORTY-NINE

They moved just above idle. The ship's faithful had congregated around J.P. on the flybridge and every one of them held onto something. J.P. prepared to address the men; Stokes steeled himself to keep his mouth shut and not interrupt.

"Gentlemen," J.P. said.

Stokes coughed a sliver of flour tortilla in J.P.'s direction. He looked up at J.P. from his seat at the helm.

"Sorry," he said.

J.P. studied him, wondering if Stokes was about to heckle his speech.

Here it comes, Stokes thought. *He'll open with "old enough to gaff a fish," then he'll leave out twenty years of his life.*

J.P. had worked on a charter boat one summer between sixth and seventh grades, but afterward, his primary contact with fishing boats was in shipyards, where he slaved from the age of fifteen until he met Stokes. Granted, he loved to fish, he'd been around boats his entire life, and he'd crewed for numerous trips and a few big tournaments, but neither he, nor Stokes, had fished seriously or professionally until they'd finished *Princess* three and a half years ago.

Still, we've learned a lot in three years, and what these guys don't know won't hurt them. Plus, lying is an important part of fishing.

"Gentlemen," J.P. repeated. "As soon as I was big enough to gaff a fish, I took a job as a deckhand on an offshore boat. You boys just rode through some of the roughest seas I've ever been in. But now, you're gonna get your reward. See that weed line? That's what we came for."

He gestured forward, past their long white foredeck and into the seas. The boat pitched along with the swells, and the sun peered over a blue and black bank, illuminating a long bed of weeds sprawling in front of them. Behind that spot of light, other clouds moved slowly in the sky, casting massive shadows that slid over the water. The floating sargassum looked like a long peninsula on the surface of the rollers.

"Do you need some help rigging up?" Jordan asked.

"All done," J.P. said. "But today we're pulling meat, not lures."

"Meat?" Mishka asked. "What meat?"

"Meat as in trolling 'hoo." J.P. looked past the camera lens at Mishka's empty expression and added, "Ballyhoo." Same expression.

"Halfbeaks," J.P. continued. Then he smiled. "Just messing with you comrade. Bait."

J.P. looked into the lens of the camera Mishka held on his shoulder and said, "We've got a few more minutes. Come with me."

He turned and headed down to the mezzanine. There, he opened one of the new ice chests to reveal layers of foot-long silver fish on trays of aluminum foil. A small coil of monofilament line was attached to the head of each fish.

"This is a horse ballyhoo," he said in a strong, solid voice.

He knelt and picked up one of the rigged fish. Brine fell away from the cold carcass. Then he stood and turned toward the camera.

"We order them frozen out of Florida. They're from a family of fish called halfbeaks because they have a long lower bill and a much shorter upper bill, see." He spread the beak of the little fish. "We break the bill after we rig 'em but you get the idea. A marlin is just the opposite; they have a long upper bill and a short lower. Anyway, these little fellas are a great bait. They can be trolled for hours without washing out. All the big pelagic fish love 'em and they can be rigged different ways, depending on conditions and what you're gunning for."

Stokes yelled from the flybridge, "It's six-fifty."

A wave slapped harshly at the boat and J.P. spoke even louder: "They're a close cousin to the flying fish and they're found all over the world . . . in tropical waters anyway. I'll teach you how we rig 'em later."

He set the bait back into the chest, closed the lid and stood again, reverting to his normal speaking voice.

"It will be the same as the other day when we were scouting, only our goal today is to catch a marlin, not just find a marlin. When we were dragging teasers and lures, we ran between eight and ten knots. Today we'll move around three or four knots when we pull these."

J.P. stared at the camera on Mishka's shoulder.

"We good?"

Mishka filmed another few seconds while one hand tightly gripped the back of the fighting chair, then he lowered the camera to his hip and said, "Sí."

A wave slapped the transom. J.P. looked around while Mishka raised the camera again and backed up. J.P. contemplated the Gulf. The waves had calmed from last night but it was still rough. He calculated the height between the crests and troughs of water before him. "Four feet," he said absently, "maybe three and a half at eight seconds."

He considered turning on the weather radio to check the forecast, but quickly put the thought out of his mind. Whatever the weather, he was going to fish. Plus, leaving the radios off was a nice touch. Having never left them off before, he had enjoyed the silence.

"I don't care if we get ten-footers at six seconds," J.P. said, "we're either going to sink the boat or win the tournament. To hell with the conditions."

He studied the rods around him with a determined expression. Mishka captured it on film.

Again, J.P. spoke to no one in particular: "This crew's not ready for live baiting . . .. Novice crew be damned. There are marlin here. We have to at least try live bait."

"We need some mahi or blue runners," he said, picking up a small, spinning rig. "Stokesie!"

Stokes leaned back from the cushioned vinyl driver's bench on the flybridge. "Whatie?"

"Ándele."

"Sí, sí boss."

Stokes eased the throttles forward, barely tapping them. The boat seemed not to move at first, but he let the props work until the forward motion was noticeable and the boat had reached its full momentum, moving slowly through the water toward the line of dark brown and crimson floating in front of them.

"Six fifty-five," Stokes yelled.

"I need my crew," J.P. yelled.

"Yeah boss," Jordan said. "We're coming."

Jordan and Wayne went down the stairs to the cockpit. J.P. handed each a spinning rod.

"We need to make bait. As we pull along the weed line, troll short and watch. If you see any activity, cast those fairy wands to it."

Wayne studied the rod and reel in his hand, then looked at the thick, stout offshore rigs sitting in their holders around the cockpit. "Oh," he said, looking back at the thin, whippy rod in his hand. In any other setting, this was considered a substantial spinning outfit.

"Where's Heytu?" J.P. asked.

"Operating remote cameras," Mishka said.

"Get him out here. This won't be much to watch. But if we get into some good bait fish, we need to work fast. I want as many rods working as possible."

Mishka stopped recording and went inside. A few moments later, he and Heytu returned to the cockpit. J.P. looked at Mishka and then at the camera. Mishka raised his camera and pushed 'record.'

"All right boys," J.P. said. "Let me clarify what we're doing. The prize money is nine hundred forty thousand dollars. Out of the ninety boats registered for offshore, sixty or sixty-five left at midnight last night, and half of those probably turned back. But they'll all be out this morning. Seven boats can make the board at the tournament, but only the top six are paid and sometimes there are only one or two marlin caught."

A large set of waves jostled the boat just as J.P. completed his sentence.

Stokes sat at the flybridge helm, smiling. He thought J.P.'s speeches were a waste of time, they could start fishing in two minutes, but J.P. always gave a similar sermon to their tournament crews. It had been three and a half years since they christened the new *Princess*, and J.P. had refined his speech at each tournament. This was the third time Stokes had heard it during Poco Bueno.

J.P. always warmed up the same way and was about to make his big point: Do you boys want to settle for third or fourth place or do you want to win big? Stokes wanted to screw with him now, but decided against it. This was the first time J.P. had made this speech on camera. Stokes would let him have the stage to himself. He checked their heading again then turned his head to watch J.P. in the cockpit below.

"Out of the top six, first place gets sixty percent. That's five hundred sixty-four thousand dollars to the winners, in case you guys are slow to cipher. The other five places split up the rest. A tuna, wahoo or mahi will get you a rod and reel. Only a marlin will get you money.

We were two miles from this spot the other day when we proceeded to pull up more marlin than I have ever seen in the Gulf in one day. I've been on boats that placed in this tournament and that was cool, but I've waited my whole fucking life to win this tournament."

Mishka waved his free hand to attract J.P.'s attention.

"Fuck it Mishka."

Mishka turned his palm up, lifted his hand higher, then dropped it to his side.

"We didn't come one hundred sixty miles in blown out seas, at night, to sightsee. We're going to win this son of a bitch! Does everyone agree?"

"Hell yes!" Jordan yelled.

"Yeah," Wayne hollered.

"You tell 'em J.P.," Stokes yelled from the helm. "But it's seven o'clock."

Heytu waited for the yelling to stop and then asked plaintively, "Does crew get any money?"

J.P. looked sternly at Heytu. Mishka zoomed the camera in. The boat rocked through the waves for several moments while a broad, toothy grin grew on J.P.'s face.

"Fuckin' A brother. The boat buyer at the Calcutta gets half, the boat owner gets the other half. The tournament rules say the crew shares ten percent of the winnings, but you boys are on the boat of the world's most generous owner. Our tradition is we split the boat's portion, half to the owner and half to the fishermen. Even though our boat was auctioned, that is still one hundred forty-one thousand. We have three fishermen, so that is forty-seven thousand apiece."

Heytu's jaw dropped, his eyes clouded, and the tip of his tongue lolled on his lower lip.

J.P. laughed. "Just kidding Cousin. We'll *all* split the crew's half. Even our censor behind you gets a share."

Heytu turned toward Mishka and the camera captured a big ivory smile under his mop of curly black locks.

"One forty-one divided by five is twenty-eight grand apiece," J.P. said. "But we don't get shit if we don't catch a winning marlin."

"What if we catch two big ones?" Heytu asked.

"I like your attitude, but I don't think that's ever happened. You can weigh in more than one fish but you would have to–"

Jordan's reel began screaming and then stopped.

J.P. turned, watching Jordan and the line, studying how the fish fought. The little, open-face, spinning reel screamed again. Mishka zoomed in tight. The line flattened out in front of Jordan. The fish was running to the surface.

"What is it?" Stokes yelled from the helm.

"Not very heavy, less than two pounds," J.P. said. "Get those other lines out there."

Wayne drew his rod back and heaved his lure into the crosswind. His three-quarter ounce spoon landed one hundred twenty feet behind the boat and ten feet behind where Jordan's fish was about to surface.

"Nice," J.P. said.

Wayne began his retrieve while Heytu tried to lift the bail of the spinning rod he held. His silver spoon fell to the deck.

"Wayne," Stokes yelled.

Wayne looked up at Stokes, stopped reeling, then held up his hand. He handed his rod to Heytu.

"Take this one. These reels are tricky unless you've used them before."

Heytu pulled his reel away from Wayne. "Have to help fish."

Jordan's fish breached the surface and made a low, arching jump.

"Bingo," J.P. said. "We got chickens."

Wayne lowered his voice and spoke to Heytu: "Cousin, you have nothing to worry about. J.P. just made a deal and neither he nor Stokes will break it. You just do what you can. If J.P. says fish, fish. If he says camera, film. Bottom line: you do all you can and we all win."

Heytu smiled and accepted Wayne's rod while handing Wayne his. Just as Heytu took Wayne's rod, he felt a yank. Heytu's eyes bulged. Another yank. He took a step towards the transom.

Jordan had the first small dorado, or chicken dolphin as J.P. called them, on his line twenty feet behind the boat.

"Leave him out there," J.P. said. "Crank up the drag on that reel. The others will follow him. They're school fish."

J.P. looked at Heytu's rod tip and it yanked down again.

"Use the rod more," J.P. said.

Heytu looked at him, perplexed.

"Raise the tip."

Heytu did so and his reel clicked twice.

"Keep it there."

Another click. Then another.

"That isn't a blue runner; maybe a dorado," J.P. said.

Click. Click.

"Pull up a bit."

Heytu raised the rod, feeling a solid response as his line tightened. The reel began to sing.

"Hold on," J.P. said.

The reel sang its metallic song.

"Don't touch the line or the reel. Just let him run."

"What do you have?" Stokes yelled.

"Shark," J.P. said.

Heytu watched the reel as the line angled deeper and the fish below swam sideways.

"Or maybe a big dorado," J.P. yelled to Stokes.

"Maybe wins tournament," Heytu said.

"Maybe not," J.P. said.

"Keep going," J.P. said to Stokes. "Get him up so we can make sure, but it's probably a small shark."

"How can tell?" Heytu asked.

Mishka panned the camera to J.P.

"Sharks hit fast and then run hard when they feel the hook. This one ran a solid six seconds. Probably a five-foot sand shark or a silky. Once they finish their first hard run, they wear out. They run out of oxygen, and their muscles fill with lactic acid. This guy will give you a couple more big tugs on the way up, try to head for the bottom and then come in. When he sees the boat he might get religion again and run, but we'll cut him loose if he's a shark."

"Why?" asked Heytu, a tinge of panic in his voice.

"We have to work on marlin or bait for marlin. Trust me."

Stokes listened to this exchange from the helm and smiled. He knew J.P. did not feel like babysitting another newbie, but he could see Heytu was depressed by the news.

"Sharks are worth zero dollars. You still want him?" J.P. said.

Heytu's expression changed. "Nyet." After a moment, he added, "Trash fish."

He must have been listening close, thought Stokes.

Wayne's reel made a short shriek. His line came to the surface twenty yards from the boat. Heytu was reeling and raising his rod tip repeatedly.

"Keep it up," J.P. coached.

Heytu turned to him to speak and the fish on his line made another run.

"Heavy trash," Heytu said.

"He saw the boat," J.P. said. "Keep reeling."

Wayne had the second small dolphin to the boat.

"They're called chicken dolphin because they're small and plentiful, and they have a firm, white meat," J.P. said to the camera.

"Lift him in," Jordan said.

Wayne lifted his rod tip and five feet of line which held a wiggling, brilliant green and yellow dorado. When the fish came over the side, Jordan held a wet towel intending to grab it, but the small dolphin flipped violently on the end of the short mono leader, freeing itself from the hook and falling to the deck.

J.P. raised the lid of the live well and tapped their agitated prisoner into the bubbling seawater. He then looked behind the boat at the dorado still hooked on Jordan's line.

"Toss it right behind him," he said to Wayne. "There are seven or eight on his tail."

Wayne turned to do as he was told. He made a light cast, concentrating on the water behind Jordan's fish. He could not see any other fish, but as soon as the spoon hit the water, something took it and ran.

"Put that rod in the back holder and get another line out," J.P. said to Jordan.

J.P. looked back to Heytu's line and a long, gray shape broke the surface. It was a five-foot silky. J.P. drew his knife, cut the monofilament line above the leader, and re-sheathed the knife while the shark turned and disappeared.

"Give me the line," he said to Heytu.

Heytu brought up the rod tip and the line flew loosely in the strong wind. J.P. grabbed the line out of the air. Several pre-made leaders hung on a loop of line below the gunnel. J.P. selected an eight-inch, thirty pound mono leader and held a gold spoon in his right hand. With a series of fast wraps, he attached the monofilament line to the barrel swivel, then attached the leader to the spoon.

While he held the rod and reel in front of him, J.P. turned to Heytu. "Watch."

Mishka zoomed in.

"Put your finger on the line like this. That stops it from moving and keeps the line still. Pull the bail away from you like this. That allows the line to flow off the spool when you release your finger. Bring it back over your shoulder like this and look at your target. Then flip it forward and, as you do, let go with your finger and point toward the target."

The spoon rocketed through the air, hit the top of a three-foot wave, skipped, and disappeared behind the crest. J.P. handed the rod to Heytu just as the tip was jerked down and the reel started to sing again. J.P. feigned indifference.

"Don't catch another fucking shark."

Heytu grinned. He was now part of the crew.

CHAPTER FIFTY

By 7:15, they had boxed six live dorado. J.P. announced that was enough.

Stokes objected. "Let's catch all we can."

"We need to get these in the water," J.P. said. "They won't last long in the live well and we can catch more later. Hopefully we'll find some blackfin or skipjack."

Stokes gave in to J.P.

J.P. quickly bridled a dorado with dacron. When he placed the live bait fish in the gentle wake off their stern, it swam awkwardly. He pulled it out, made a fast adjustment to the bridle and set it back. Satisfied, he handed the rod to Jordan and went to work on a second bait.

The blue marlin they were after might be hungry and aggressive, but then again, they might not. If they were picky today, that slight adjustment in the bridle would make the mahi present itself more naturally and might just pay off.

Stokes brought the boat alongside a particularly dense section of the weed line and a field of small fish percolated from the choppy surface. They bump-trolled along the weed line for fifteen minutes while these tiny fish jumped in groups of hundreds in every direction.

Grinning broadly, Stokes turned to watch Jordan, who was trolling a fresh mahi. He saw J.P. grinning back up at him.

"We're gonna win this fucker," J.P. said, his voice barely audible above the noise of the engines, exhaust and waves.

"Ten-four brother," Stokes said.

They trolled.

Nothing happened.

They kept trolling, very slowly, settling into a pattern. Every twenty seconds or so Stokes popped a shifter or a throttle to hold their position, and he constantly turned to watch Jordan and J.P., who stood at the stern holding their rods. The big boat rode the waves. Her crew was comfortable, and confident. But still nothing happened.

An hour passed. Rain fell in sheets for twenty minutes, then quit. They repeatedly cleared weeds off their lines and changed out baits. More time, more bait. Two of their original baits died in the live well and Wayne caught a few more small dolphin. The bait fish were everywhere; but where were the big fish?

After another hour of constant attention to their two live bait rods, J.P. decided they needed to change. The waves had calmed a bit. As much as he wanted to fish live, the reality was that only he and Jordan had the experience to do so. J.P. stood at the stern, reeled in his line, then turned to Mishka.

"Time for ballyhoo," he said to the camera.

In ten more minutes, J.P. and company had deployed the riggers and were pulling their "big fish spread" along the weed line.

After a third and fourth hour of fishing, J.P. paced the cockpit. He went up to the flybridge to check the readings of all the screens and gauges. He fiddled with the broken radar. During hour five, he went below to check the engines and generators.

Mishka shadowed J.P. the whole time, filming.

Watching J.P. made Jordan nervous. After another two and a half hours, Jordan mixed a Bloody Mary and brought it to J.P. on the outside couch.

"No thanks," J.P. said when Jordan handed him the drink.

"Just take it."

J.P. did so and drank a sip. "Good," he said.

Jordan then took another Bloody Mary to Stokes on the flybridge. The sun hid from view, obscured by an overcast sky.

"At least we're not getting baked today," Jordan said to Stokes.

"Roger that." Stokes turned his head for the four hundredth time in three hours and looked behind. "But I thought we would've hooked up, or at least brought something up to the surface, by now."

The boat was cutting a parallel path of the arc they had charted a few days before when they marked the fish. Jordan studied the GPS screen and then the sea around them. They were running along a rip line of clear, dark blue water contrasted by a line of murkier blue water. Dark crimson-brown weeds of sargassum floated in the clearer water. Bait fish occasionally broke the surface. Stokes scanned the waves ahead.

"Maybe we'll get some action at the four o'clock bite," he said, sipping his drink.

Jordan went below. He found J.P. still sitting on the mezzanine couch with the bottom of his foam cup tilted up to the sky. Jordan walked over, held out his hand, and J.P. handed him the cup. Five minutes later, Jordan emerged from the salon with a fresh drink. J.P. had not moved. Jordan saw J.P.'s eyes were closed. Thinking J.P. was asleep, Jordan set the cup in a drink holder.

"Thanks." J.P. put his hand to the cup, raised it to his mouth, took a drink, then put the cup back in the holder without opening his eyes.

Jordan stared at their wake.

"Do we need to change baits again?"

J.P. checked his dive watch: 3:30.

"We haven't seen so much as a swirl all day. Let's give these some more time."

Tick, tick, tick.

Jordan looked excitedly at the center rod whose reel had just ticked. He shot a nervous look at J.P., whose eyes were closed again.

"I just lightened the drag on that one," J.P. said. "Exciting, huh?"

Jordan turned to go upstairs to check on Stokes. He looked at the sky. "Dark sky at three-thirty. Not good," he said, reaching the top of the stairs.

"Can you relieve me a minute?" Stokes said.

"Sure."

Stokes rose, stretched, and went downstairs as rain fell lightly.

Jordan held the stainless wheel tenderly with his right hand; then he looked forward, past the couch and the open flybridge, and out to the dark horizon. Despite the occasional shower, all the curtains were rolled up and the bridge exposed. He brought his gaze back to the flybridge and studied the horseshoe-shaped couch. The white vinyl was new. J.P. said Stokes had just replaced it because the first upholstery job was done poorly. He considered the seams. This job was flawless. The fiberglass deck and ceiling were meticulously kept; salty from a long run and dirty from foot traffic, but nothing a water hose wouldn't cure. He looked at the dash. Three screens sat side by side. The layout was intuitive: the whole dash comfortable to the eye, every dial easy to read and understand, and everything well-kept. Jordan noticed the whole front dashboard opened on a piano hinge. If a gauge or wire or screen needed to be replaced, the dash could be lifted to access the back of the dashboard. He turned to look back over the cockpit, then shifted his gripped hand over the stainless wheel again.

"You look pretty happy up there," Stokes said over the intercom.

Jordan was startled. A camera motor whizzed over his left shoulder. He turned to look at it and the camera zoomed.

"That you Stokes?"

"Ten-four."

"I fuckin' love your boat."

"I'm glad. I just wish we could love her with a big marlin aboard right now."

J.P. walked up to the salon nav station.

"Where are we on our arc of fish markings?" he asked.

Stokes looked at the GPS screen and pushed some buttons. J.P. sat on the ottoman next to him. Wayne leaned on the bar, nursing a beer.

"Wayne," J.P. said. "You mind babysitting the rods a minute?"

"No problem."

Heytu rose from the couch. "I watch rods with you," he said to Wayne as they headed outside.

Stokes had the chart up on the screen. He changed the distance settings and Jordan's voice came over the intercom.

"Tell me you guys are messing with this screen up here."

"Ten-four," J.P. said into the mike. "Give us a minute and we'll put you back to where you were. Meanwhile, keep tracking the weed line."

"Ten-four. I have a visual and we are tracking," Jordan said, imitating an air traffic controller.

The range on the screen hit twenty-five miles. J.P. and Stokes could see their location and the icons where they had marked the fish.

"We're too far south," J.P. said.

"Agree. Let's turn around."

"Good idea. Soon as I take a leak."

J.P. went to the head; Stokes made a fresh drink.

In another minute, Mishka came up the stairs holding another camera.

Then Jordan screamed over the radio, "Marlin, marlin, marlin!"

Mishka rushed outside. Stokes ran around the bar, followed by J.P.

When they exited the salon, Heytu was in the fighting chair with the live rod in the gimbal. J.P. spoke loudly to him over the din of the reel giving line to a racing marlin.

Stokes ran upstairs to take the helm from Jordan.

"He was in the spread for a few seconds," Jordan said when Stokes reached the helm. "He just took it."

"Okay. Easy there Cousin," J.P. said. "I hope he's hooked good. On three, I want you to push this thing right here forward and then pull back hard on the stick, okay?"

Heytu nodded. Mishka repeated the instructions in Russian.

J.P. counted: "One, two, three."

Heytu pushed the lever and tried to pull back, but the rod would not budge. The fish ran harder.

"That's it. Now let him run. Don't touch that line."

The reel screamed non-stop.

"Something's after the port teaser," Jordan shouted from the fly-bridge.

"Get it in fast Wayne," J.P. yelled. "Cousin, keep your left arm right where it is. Wayne, reel 'em all in quick, this could be a money fish."

Heytu's eyes widened for the second time today. Mishka caught it on his camera.

"Stokesie, take the wheel," J.P. yelled. Stokes was already there.

"Jordan, carry your ass down here and reel in . . . . " J.P. stopped yelling when Jordan ran by him, grabbed a rod and began reeling.

"Money fish. You take rod," Heytu said to J.P.

"No, no, Cousin. You started him, you have to land him."

The reel fell silent. The line slowly headed toward their boat. Stokes hit the throttles, the reel ticked. It ticked again. The line arched to their port side. Stokes eased back on the throttle and the reel screamed again. Wayne reeled in his second line. The fish had hit the shotgun rod. Jordan had one line in.

The reel stopped screaming. One line remained in the water on the port side. Mishka zoomed in on Jordan, who ran to the rod, lifted it from its holder, ducked it under the working line that held the fish, and reeled furiously.

"Good job guys," J.P. said. He turned to Stokes at the helm and said loudly, "Keep doing what you're doing."

"I just come outside," Heytu said excitedly. The smile never left his face.

"Beginner's luck," Jordan said. "We should have put you out here nine hours ago."

"Cousin, I guess I forgot to give you a lesson but you are now on point," J.P. said. "You do what I say, when I say it. Capiche?"

"What capiche?" Heytu asked.

"You understand?"

"Yes, understand all but capiche."

The reel screamed again.

"Capiche means, do you understand?" J.P. said over the sound of the reel. Mishka yelled out something in Chechen.

"Yes, understand," Heytu said.

The reel stopped screaming. It ticked. Ticked again. Then stopped.

"Okay Cousin, raise up in a strong, steady motion and then reel down."

Heytu did it.

"Again."

This time Heytu jerked the rod at the bottom of the stroke, putting a slight bow of slack in the line.

"No, no, no!" J.P. yelled. Then he lowered his voice, "Steady, no slack in that line. Mishka, translate quick."

Mishka rattled off a few phrases. Heytu nodded. The reel screamed and stopped.

"Again," J.P. said.

Heytu raised the rod, reeled down, and then lifted up again in a smooth, uniform series of movements. He watched the line intently, making sure it stayed tight.

"Nice," J.P. said.

Heytu grinned.

"What did you tell him?" J.P. asked Mishka.

Heytu answered: "Make believe line is trip wire and keep tight. Any slack and we all die."

J.P. raised his eyebrows. "Never heard that particular advice but I'll try to remember it for my next student. You're doing good Heytu."

Heytu's grin swelled, then a bead of sweat trickled down his brow. He grimaced when the salty drop stung his eye. Jordan grabbed a towel and mopped his forehead. Confused by the attention, Heytu reacted by pulling his head away, like a spooked horse trapped in his stall during a vet's visit. But, as Jordan drew back the towel, Heytu was smiling underneath it; and again, Mishka caught it all on film.

"Look at the reel," J.P. said. "You're watching the line and that's good, but watch it *at* the reel. Now Cousin, move this lever back. That's the clicker. We want that off now."

"He's coming up," Stokes yelled.

The line cut away from them and the angle of the monofilament in the water flattened. A big blue marlin swam out of the water in a leap.

And just like that, they knew they had won the tournament.

"Big money," Heytu yelled.

Or, maybe not.

"Fuck," Stokes yelled.

"Fuck; why fuck?" Heytu asked.

J.P. and Stokes exchanged looks, then J.P. glanced at his watch. The fish headed starboard. The reel no longer screamed but line peeled off.

"What's he doing?" Stokes yelled.

"Taking line," J.P. yelled back. He turned to Jordan and lowered his voice: "Get Heytu a bottle of water."

Jordan ran inside.

"Why he say fuck?" Heytu asked again.

"This fish is two-twenty, maybe two-fifty. He thinks we need a bigger fish to win."

"We can catch two!" Heytu said.

The fish quit running. With his gaze fixed on the reel, Heytu raised the rod, reeled down, then raised the rod again.

"Keep it up," J.P. said. "He may be bigger. Let's get him in and look."

Heytu reeled again as Jordan exited the salon.

"Any fish we catch today we have to take to the dock and weigh in today," J.P. said. "It's five o'clock. We have to stop fishing at seven–that's the rule."

Heytu strained to lift the rod. J.P. continued talking.

"It will take us a half-hour to land this guy."

Wayne and Jordan stood by, listening.

"So he may be all we get. If we go in now, we have to make the same run back out tonight. But, we most likely have a reception party waiting at the dock who won't let us go out again. The only way this fish is going to win the tournament is if no one else has a marlin."

"That ever happened?" Wayne asked.

"Yep. Several times. And with the seas like this and the weather, this could be the only marlin caught. Plus the Friday bonus is thirty grand. We might win that."

"So what do we do?" Jordan asked.

"I say we keep the son of a bitch, but it's Stokes's decision."

The reel jerked and gave line again. J.P. cut a glance at Stokes above, then looked back at Heytu.

"Don't yank that rod."

J.P. opened the water bottle and fed it to Heytu, who downed it quickly. Jordan mopped Heytu's sweating brow again.

Heytu shook his arm to the side. The reel stopped. The line went slack.

J.P. and Stokes both panicked. Stokes hit the throttle and J.P. screamed, "Reel!"

Heytu began grinding the reel. The line came freely, then it stiffened as quick as it had slackened.

"Great. Fucking. Job," J.P. said. "I mean it dude. That was a fucking perfect recovery. You're a natural."

Heytu was huffing. "Tank you."

"But that was also a stupid mistake," he scolded. "Don't take your hand off that reel again."

Heytu was sweating profusely. His black, curly hair was greasy and sweat beaded around his hair line. His blue tee-shirt was soaked tight to his solid chest. His forearms were bulging.

"How're you doing?" Jordan asked.

"Good. Arm burn, but I good." Heytu pumped the rod and reeled.

"Again," J.P. said. "Fight back some line. We don't want him to run again like that."

Heytu raised the rod, reeled, raised again, reeled, raised again.

"My Got. My body hurts."

"Take a breath," J.P. said, looking at his watch.

Jordan gave him more water from the bottle.

"You've been at it for twenty minutes," said J.P. "Don't rush it now but I want you to reel and keep the pressure on him. You're wearing this guy down. He's close. Let's bring him up."

The line slackened momentarily, then tightened. Suddenly, the dark blue fish broke the water's surface eighty feet from the boat. It came out of the waves, tail-walked sideways for twenty feet, then slammed down on its side. As soon as it hit the water, it headed sideways. Line smoked off the reel, popping and snapping from the grooves on the spool. The fish kept running and running, the line on the reel kept playing out. When it finally stopped, Heytu stared at the reel.

He had spent twenty brutal minutes reeling this fish in, and in less than one minute, the fish took out all the line he had reeled in and much more. J.P. had said he was wearing this fish down.

"Oh Got," he said again, still looking at the reel.

"Pump," J.P. said. "Pump and reel. Don't be a pussy."

Heytu furrowed his brow at J.P. and lifted up on the rod. He reeled down. His arms burned. He raised the rod. His back hurt. He reeled down. His legs were tense and twitching. He pulled up and reeled down.

"That's it Cousin. Reel him in."

It took forty-five minutes from the time they hooked the fish until the time he came alongside the boat. He still had energy, despite a long fight in eighty-eight degree water, but J.P. grabbed the leader and then the bill. As soon as J.P. had his hands on the bill, the fish whipped his head and his tail side to side, throwing water in every direction. J.P. kept his grip on the long sword while the fish strained and flailed, beating the side of the boat.

Jordan jockeyed for a good position beside J.P., then grabbed the leader.

"He's over the length limit but not by much," J.P. yelled. The fish convulsed and writhed as J.P. held fast. "But he's a fat little hoss."

Stokes studied the fish from the helm. *He's shorter than that. If he is legal, he's barely legal.*

The fish thrashed again. *If he shrinks on the way in, which he will– they all do, he might not pass the length limit even if he meets it now.*

"How long is he," Stokes yelled.

"One-o-two, maybe one-o-five. But probably legal and plenty fat!"

They had to decide. The word 'plenty' was a direct reference from J.P. as to his opinion on what they should do, but ultimately, it was Stokes's call. Despite J.P.'s pep talk, any legal marlin was a big deal. The prize money mattered. Stokes thought about how badly he needed his cut; *but that's only if we win.* Just hanging a marlin at the dock was prestigious for any of the fishermen in this tournament. And this one was fat according to J.P.

Stokes thought he was neither legal nor fat. He was just a marlin of slightly above-average proportions. Even if J.P. was right and the fish *was* heavy, could he be heavy enough to win? *No.* Not unless no other fish were weighed. Or only a few other fish. If this fish was legal, he was probably worth tens of thousands of dollars. Maybe even a tournament winner, so maybe hundreds of thousands. But pulling him in just to measure him might kill him.

Stokes did not want to hurt the fish and then determine he was undersized and had to be let go. In a big tournament like this, most captains would pull the fish in and measure. It was against the rules, and no one would admit to it, but it was a fact. Pulling this one in would traumatize him no doubt, and if he thrashed inside the boat, he could strip the protective slime off his sides, increasing the risk of infection or disease and amplifying the drag on his body if they turned him loose. Not to mention a fish this big could injure his skeleton or organs once his weight was no longer carried by water.

"You want to ground check him?" J.P. yelled.

He was screwing with Stokes. He already knew the answer.

"No! Can you measure him J.P.?"

"Jordan, grab that tagger," J.P. said.

The fish swam calmly for a moment. J.P. leaned over the side, resting his own torso on the gunnel. Jordan held the tag stick toward the fish's bill. Trailing behind the stick was a piece of dacron line with two knots in it, one hundred one inches apart. At J.P.'s instruction, Jordan tried to let the first knot ride even with the tip of the marlin's lower jaw. The second knot at the end of the line looked to be even with, or just past, the keel scute of the tail.

The fish jerked violently while J.P. held his bill firmly with both hands. The head of the fish collided with the brand-new tag stick, which flew out of Jordan's hand, landed in the water twelve feet away, and immediately sank. They did not have another. J.P. held the blue by his rough bill. Jordan put his right hand on the point of the marlin's dorsal fin in front of the small sail, trying to be of some help. The fish surged against J.P. and threw saltwater.

"Stokesie, I can't tell from the tag line if he's legal, but I really don't think he's short. What's it gonna be?"

Stokes was ready with a reply. He had considered the weather, the seas, their distance from Port O'Connor. Any fish they caught today had to be weighed in tonight–the tournament rules were strict on this point.

They had missed the federal marshals yesterday, but they would be there today. Lovey would make sure of that. The Coast Guard was probably looking for them right now; helping the marshals. This fish could be worth nine hundred forty thousand, or maybe it would not place at all. He had considered all of it since they first saw him jump. Now he had seen the measuring rope. It looked legal to him.

The fish gasped at the air and began to thrash again.

"Let that son of a bitch go. Let's catch a bigger one!"

Wayne turned to plead with Stokes. This was money in the bank; why gamble?

When Wayne turned, J.P. quickly moved one hand in a looping motion and then raised both hands out of the water. With a swirl, the fish plunged out of sight.

Silence.

Heytu sat spread-eagle in the fighting chair.

Jordan and J.P. stared at the water.

J.P. had never seen, nor heard of, anyone releasing a legal marlin in the Poco Bueno tournament. Had he made the decision, they would have kept the fish and gone in to weigh it. He would have at least pulled him into the cockpit to measure him.

Stokes sat alone at the helm.

"Stokes," J.P. yelled, still looking at the water where the fish had just been, "you have very big cojones."

* * * * *

Rain began to fall. Hard.

CHAPTER FIFTY-ONE

"Let's move Stokes," J.P. said, peeling off his gloves. With the synchronizer disabled, Stokes pushed the throttles forward concurrently with the palms of both hands, keeping his fingers extended. He concentrated on his left hand and muttered, "Focus. This could be the last trip on this boat. Twenty years from now I want to know I went for it. Win this fucking tournament."

"We have an hour," J.P. yelled to Stokes. "Bring her up to three knots. Jordan, hand me that rod. Let's get these lines out."

Stokes pushed the throttles away from him as a burst of wind blew rain into the helm from the left. The screen went from two, to three, then four knots. Then five. He eased back. Rain spat at him again from the front left corner of the flybridge.

The sky darkened; the sun slipped behind foreboding clouds. A curtain of rain engulfed the boat. Stokes watched the seas ahead. Thick, troubled drops were falling on every inch of the surface, but the waves were smaller now.

A chill went up Stokes's spine. He turned and looked at the cockpit again while they pulled along the weed line. He heard a voice in his head say, "Enjoy the struggle, the best part is before you know the out-come." He sniffed and answered silently: *Bullshit. The guy who came up with that didn't owe a million six.*

Ten minutes later, with lines baited and their spread re-deployed, Stokes heard the remote camera whine and turned to it.

"Hey guys," Stokes said. "It's after six o'clock. We're less than an hour from the end of the first day of the Poco Bueno tournament. We just caught and released a small marlin. We're going to try and hook a bigger one to win this tournament. We're one hundred sixty nautical miles from Port O'Connor. Unless we hook up in the next hour, we're going to stay the night out here. Tomorrow we'll catch a winner." He smiled insincerely–and he thought, convincingly–toward the camera, but as he turned away the video captured his expression gravitating to a frown.

Rain pelted him again from the side. He looked down at his lap, felt his injured eye twitch and throb, and observed that he was wet everywhere, which triggered another worry–about being chased–that caused him to shiver. He blamed the tremor on being wet. The sargas-sum weeds were still visible. The water rode flatter where the weeds floated. Their dark brown stems sat on, and just under, the surface. He turned to look in their wake and refocus. Five lines were out.

Three, five and seven. That's what J.P. calls this set-up.

When the boat passed through the water, it separated the sea be-neath their bow. Seventy feet later and six feet below their stern, the hull and props and rudders cut through the very same water, throw-ing a pair of trailing waves in parallel lines behind her; their wake. Swirls of disturbed water from their props, and small waves made by the pressure of their lower hull, broke the wake in pieces. They referred to each of these small pressure waves by their position. The third wave was about thirty-five feet behind the boat. J.P. had set two of their baits here. The fifth wave, at seventy feet, hosted another pair of baits. The final bait trailed dead center at one-twenty. At the center bait there was a swirl, then the rubber band broke out of the rigger with a sharp *snap!*

"Center rod," Stokes yelled.

J.P. was already at the rod.

Stokes watched the bait while it dragged behind the boat. Nothing had taken it.

"Come on. Please," Stokes said.

He dropped back on the throttles as J.P. let line leave the reel. Jordan and Heytu came running out of the salon. Both wore yellow slickers. Heytu hoisted a camera to his shoulder.

Zee.

Stokes ignored the remote camera and looked to the far bait. Nothing.

Wayne came out to the cockpit.

J.P. lifted the rod. Its line usually went up to the center rigger and then back; now it was straight back. This fish had hit hard enough to pull the line from its pin, but they weren't bit yet.

J.P. pointed the tip of the rod toward the stern and yanked, pulling the bait out of the water. A dark shape rocketed out of the deep, crashing the bait. Stokes felt his body lift involuntarily with the excitement of the top-water assault.

A violent strike. A wolf-like, saber-toothed maw snapped around the bait in mid-air, then hit the water in a dive.

J.P. turned toward Stokes on the flybridge above him.

"We got a donkey wahoo," he yelled. "And I'm going to nail him!"

J.P. pushed the drag lever forward and raked back on the rod in a sideways motion. Pain shot through his injured leg, causing him to lose his balance on the wet deck. He fell, with the reel sandwiched between his already bruised hip and the transom. Fire ripped through his thigh. The fish ran sideways, turned and charged the boat.

J.P. twisted–half landing, half rolling–on top of the back gunnel, while he reeled furiously.

Jordan and Wayne lurched toward J.P.

Stokes saw J.P. sliding off the back of the boat. He throttled down abruptly, trying to throw J.P. into the cockpit.

Jordan and Wayne, although swayed by the drop in speed, each managed to grab a leg as J.P. rocked over the transom and passed the rod and reel to Jordan. Wayne reached out and seized J.P.'s arm. Jordan backed up toward the fighting chair, holding the rod and reel, while J.P. and Wayne came tumbling onto the deck in a heap. They both crawled quickly to port, behind the chair, and sat on the deck. The line had gone slack; now it flew off the reel for another second.

Just as Jordan sat in the chair, a loud ping rang out. He watched their wake and the last wisp of a spot in the air right behind him where the line had just disappeared.

"What happened?" Stokes yelled.

Rain beat the deck. Everyone stared expectantly at Jordan. J.P. and Wayne were still on the sole beside the fighting chair. Jordan looked over his right shoulder, first at the two of them on the floor and then up at Stokes, pointing to the reel.

"He smoked it. The line broke. Look."

Jordan wiped raindrops off his face with his forearm and then held up the rod. A single piece of monofilament trailed off the reel.

Stokes had never seen a larger wahoo. It was well over one hundred pounds. *Probably a state record.*

Everyone was quiet again. J.P. was down, sitting on the deck for a reason: he could not stand on his own.

Stokes needed to take over J.P.'s duty as the fishing director in the cockpit, but it was late, everyone was dead tired, and the rain was falling in buckets. He pulled back on the throttles.

"What's the time J.P.?"

"Six-fifty."

"Okay guys," Stokes yelled, "let's call it a day. Jordan, can you carry our fallen captain inside and fix him a stiff drink? The rest of you guys can start reeling in lines."

Stokes throttled back, turned on the autopilot and went down to help. While they slowly motored in the waves, reeling in their lines and taking baits off hooks, Stokes leaned over the transom and rinsed his hands in saltwater. A breaking wave covered him to his elbows. The water was warmer than the rain, and it felt good.

They ate soup and sandwiches and turned in early. The night was spent dragging a big sea parachute and they took turns standing watch. Stokes did not say a word about drifting all night.

CHAPTER FIFTY-TWO

Stokes woke at dawn on the salon couch. They were not moving. It took him a minute to figure out why that was significant. All night the huge boat had gently rocked. He had woken up repeatedly, before and after his watch, worried they might hit something, even though they were miles from any structure. Thankfully, the rain quit at midnight. Now it was still. He panicked and stood up. The windows were glazed with condensation and he wiped his hand across the glass, smiling as his mood changed.

"All right."

They had a calm sea.

Stokes exited the dry, sixty-eight degree cabin and felt his feet tingle in the warmer, humid air outside. J.P. sat in the fighting chair, working on a reel.

"We need to get moving," J.P. said.

"How's your hip?" Stokes stared out at the ball of orange which had just come up on the eastern horizon. For the moment, he could look right at it.

"Nothing a couple of drinks won't cure." J.P. eased forward on the chair. His thigh showed black and purple from the cuff of his shorts to the knee.

"I thought you were going in yesterday holding that rod."

"I thought so too. I was off balance, or at least that's my excuse for not paying attention. Would have made a hell of a story if I landed him." J.P. shook his head. "I hated handing it off with a trophy wahoo on the line."

"It's going to make a hell of a show. That was the biggest wahoo we ever hooked."

"Sí, muy biggo. But something fucked up this reel in the process, or maybe it was already fucked. Who knows? It'll have to be rebuilt, the drag is shot." J.P. stood, slowly putting his weight on his legs.

Stokes grabbed the rod and reel. "I'll put it in the storeroom."

"Mark it somehow," J.P. said. "We don't want anyone to bring it out by accident." He let go of the fighting chair and limped toward the salon door, unable to straighten his injured leg and throwing it ahead like a two-by-four upon which his hip pivoted.

"You're driving today. You'll be worthless down here."

"Not worthless, but I'll be happy to drive."

Stokes stored the reel. J.P. shuffled through the boat, banging on doors and waking their crew.

"Wake up fuckheads!" he repeated as he hobbled lamely from the salon to the master suite. "We're late! It's 6:48."

By the time Stokes returned from the storage room, everyone was standing in the salon. J.P. cranked the main engines from the nav station. The generator had been running all night to power the air conditioners.

"Wayne, Heytu, you guys go up front and pull in our sea parachute, then bag it and stow it in the locker," J.P. said. "Stokesie, you help Jordan bait up."

He turned to Mishka.

"Try and find us something to munch on for breakfast. As soon as the sea-anchor is in, we start fishing. The action was hot last night before we quit. I'm worried it might be slow around noon today like yesterday, but let's see if we can catch two marlin this morning."

Heytu smiled at that and walked out the back door. Stokes put a hand on Jordan's wrist, twisted it slightly and looked at the time on his watch: 6:55.

Hell, we are late. But the water is calm. Low swells. Slight chop. Awesome conditions.

J.P., Stokes and Jordan exited the salon behind Mishka.

"Look at that," J.P. said, pointing south. Tuna were up on the surface a hundred yards from the boat.

They quickly adopted a new game plan.

Ten minutes later, they'd boated four skipjacks. The first line was rigged and out. Two tuna were in the tubes for later. J.P. stood at the helm on the flybridge, motoring along the weed line.

"Let's get that other bait out," he yelled.

"We're on it," Stokes said.

J.P. turned the boat to parallel the rip while Jordan finished threading a dacron bridle through the front of the eye sockets of a wiggling, fifteen-pound skipjack, held fast between his legs with a wet towel. He finished bridling and draped the tuna over their transom, laying it in their wake and scrutinizing it closely. The tuna swam naturally, without listing.

"Damn Jordan, that's about as good a job of bridling as I've ever seen," Stokes said.

"Danke. Big bait. Big fish," Jordan said, playing out line.

"Let's put . . .".

Jordan's bait disappeared underwater. He put his thumb above the reel, careful not to touch it, while its spool spun slowly.

"Did you see that?" J.P. yelled.

J.P. had seen a shadow and a small swirl, then the skipjack vanished.

Jordan kept his head down, watching the reel. His right thumb was now ready to press ever so lightly on the spinning spool of monofilament, if needed. J.P. considered tapping the left throttle to straighten out the boat, but held off. Stokes studied the line leaving the reel. The spool was pulling out faster now.

"Give it time," J.P. said.

The salon door opened. Mishka walked out with a camera by his side.

"You better turn that on quick," said Stokes in a low, urgent tone.

Jordan held the thick rod with his left hand on the foregrip above the reel; the short, bent butt of the rod rested on his left thigh. J.P. desperately wanted to tell Jordan to set the hook, but he waited, letting Jordan be the judge. Stokes was thinking the same thing, but decided it was too important. Line peeled away. Just when he was about to tell Jordan to set it, Jordan took in a deep breath through his nose and lowered the tip of the rod.

"Get ready," Stokes said.

Jordan pushed the drag lever forward with his right hand, then took hold of the rod with both hands and pulled upward. The rod flew up six inches and then bent. The fish on the other end responded with a yank. Jordan weighed two hundred and twenty-five pounds. One hundred nineteen feet of line and leader now connected him to something even larger: something that was in its own element, something that was hungry, and something that had a freshly-sharpened twelve-aught hook deeply embedded in the firmest part of its upper palate. That something was thirty feet under water when Jordan pulled up. Monofilament line, even one hundred-pound test like the line on this rod, will stretch and give some over a distance. But at one hundred nineteen feet, twenty feet of which is doubled mono and another sixteen feet of four hundred-pound leader, there is little stretch. The fish on Jordan's line instinctively bent his body, slashing sideways, jerking his head away from the boat.

Despite his best efforts to brace himself, Jordan was unprepared for the fish's reaction. He stepped forward, placing all his weight on his right foot. Unfortunately, his leather deck shoe came to rest in a pile of tuna slime. For the second time in two hook-ups, a fisherman flew into the transom of the *Break Wind*. Jordan crashed into the low wall. His left hand gripped the rod while colliding with the bridge of his nose. The reel hit him in the chest, but his legs and hips took the force of the blow, flat against the back of the boat. The collision was spontaneous and violent, but Jordan was unfazed. Line peeled off the reel with a wild, piercing screech.

"Get your ass in that chair!" J.P. yelled.

Stokes tried to support Jordan, holding his shoulders. Mishka kept filming.

The salon door opened and Heytu ran out with a bottle of water and rushed to Jordan's side.

Jordan's reel lost line with blinding speed and at a high pitch that sounded like a kite string cutting the air as it followed the running fish.

"If we can survive this first big run, we might have a chance," Stokes said to Jordan.

Jordan glanced nervously at Stokes, then back at the unwinding reel. J.P. shifted into neutral, then threw the shifters into reverse. The line stopped. Jordan reeled. J.P. pulled up on the throttles and threw the gears into neutral. Jordan backed up to the point just in front of the fighting chair. J.P. shifted into the forward gears as the line angled toward them, then he accelerated to keep ahead of the fish.

"What is it?" Jordan yelled to J.P.

J.P. was mum, but Stokes answered: "Something really, really big."

"Marlin?" Jordan asked.

"I don't know. If it is, we just . . . I don't want to jinx this. Let's just see."

"The chair," J.P. yelled.

"Let's just see," Stokes repeated.

Jordan worked himself into the fighting chair with Stokes's help. He kicked off his wet leather shoes, set his bare feet firmly on the footrest, then pressed back, trying to lift the rod. He pulled harder and harder on the rod, until the reel gave line. It felt like he was hung on something. He lowered the tip, reeling all the while, then tried to raise the rod again. Once again he strained, pulling upward on the shaft. The reel gave out another inch of line. It seemed as if the fish on the other end was anchored in place.

Stokes pulled on Jordan's hip and Jordan looked down to see Stokes fastening the fishing harness. He quickly redirected his focus to the rod and reel in his hands. The line was as tight as a banjo string and emitted a low hum. Then the big fish turned and swam at will. All the reel could do was spin in protest. Line was peeling or smoking or dumping off the reel, but it was coming off at a faster pace than any of the reels had peeled or smoked or dumped line in the last couple of days. It stopped. After a few seconds, Jordan pulled up on the rod with all his strength; it felt as if the fish was a stationary object.

"I don't know what this is," Jordan said, "but I've never fought anything this heavy."

The fish ran again, peeling off another fifty feet of line. When it stopped, Jordan tried the reel against it. Its response was to take more line. Stokes felt like this fight had just begun, yet close to a third of the nine hundred fifty yards of monofilament line was gone from the eighty-wide reel. This was a big reel. It had enough line to land almost anything – *almost*. The eighties were the second largest reels on the boat. The one-thirties were the largest, but Stokes disliked using them. He felt they were just too big to handle. Now he wondered if a one-thirty would have helped. J.P. reversed the boat while the fish took line, then stopped, then took line again.

"He's taking line!" Stokes yelled as the fish took more.

J.P. reversed hard. Another fifty yards of line was gone.

"Stokes, this is a big son of a bitch, isn't it?" Jordan said.

"Yep."

Line peeled off the reel again for a short burst.

"You think it's a marlin?" Jordan asked, managing to pull up and reel down, gaining line. He lifted up and reeled again, repeating the process over and over.

"Keep it up," Stokes said. "Take back everything you can Jordan."

The fish ran.

"We're dumping line J.P.," Stokes yelled.

Again, they traveled backward. J.P. pushed the throttles. Water broke over their transom, splashing Mishka's camera.

"Heytu," Mishka yelled. "Camera is wet. Hurry!"

Stokes stared at the reel. *Oh shit. It could spool it.*

Jordan could only watch while line peeled off the reel. For a split-second, he stole a glance at the bottle of water Stokes held in his hand. The sun seared Jordan's burnt face.

"Can you pour some of that on me?" Jordan asked.

Stokes did so, then turned to grab another bottle from the sink. The reel lost line again.

Heytu ran out of the cabin, handed a film camera to Mishka, then took the camera Mishka had been using and wiped it dry.

"Get trash bag," Mishka said.

J.P. continued in reverse. The monofilament snapped and popped again as it ripped from the spool under stress.

The fish stopped running and Jordan lifted the rod, reeled and lift-ed again. Deep beneath the water's surface, the fish turned and swam deliberately toward them. Jordan reeled faster with surprisingly little effort while using his thumb to guide the line on the reel. J.P. shifted into neutral and then forward. He throttled up. Jordan reeled, keeping the line tight. Line built up on the reel. After what seemed like five or more minutes, Stokes noted the line was now well past the mid-point. Then the fish stopped moving. Jordan reeled down and tried to lift the rod, but could not budge the fish. He pulled harder. The grudging reel gave up bits of line, first an inch, then another.

"Jesus Christ," Jordan said, "whatever this is, it doesn't seem very tired."

"What's he doing?" J.P. yelled.

The reel lost line again.

"We're losing line J.P.," Stokes yelled.

J.P. reversed the boat once more. When the fish stopped running, it had peeled off another sixty yards. It ran again.

Heytu returned with a plastic bag, shook it open, then maneuvered it over Mishka's arm and the camera. He stretched the bag tight and poked a hole in the plastic to reveal the lens.

J.P. had not said much. Stokes was tight-lipped too, and he had not answered Jordan's question.

"What's wrong?" Jordan asked Stokes.

"What? What do you mean?"

"I mean . . ."

The line ran off the reel for another three second stretch. Jordan tried, unsuccessfully, to raise the rod.

". . . J.P. hasn't said shit. You're not talking. What's wrong?" Jordan gasped.

"I don't know about J.P., but I'm just praying this is a big fucking blue," Stokes said as he poured water over Jordan's shoulders. "I'm also wishing we could have seen it hit the bait."

The reel lost more line. Jordan could not lift against the fish.

"How long has it been on here?" he asked.

Stokes turned to the flybridge.

"J.P., what's our time."

"Thirty-five minutes."

Stokes was stunned. It seemed like ten, fifteen max.

"If we could get this fish to make the wrong move and come to the top, we could tire it out," Stokes said. "And that's the other odd thing. Big marlin usually jump early. I'm worried this may not be a marlin."

The reel stopped. The fish seemed to be making shorter runs. It was well off to starboard now.

"Should we spin the boat and chase it?" Stokes yelled to J.P. "We could earn some line."

"Nada. We ain't that sophisticated. Let's play it safe. Lift up on it Jordan. See if it's still as stubborn as it was."

Jordan pulled up on the rod. It bowed, yet the tip barely moved.

"It's still on there."

He reeled down and tried to lift again. This time he regained some line. He repeated the maneuver. The line slanted to the side. Jordan reeled one revolution, then another. He reeled faster, raising the rod in sequence. The fish swam sideways rapidly. The reel lost line yet again.

"It might be coming up Jordan. Mishka, it might jump here," Stokes said.

The reel stopped giving line. Jordan reeled. There was a huge belly in the line. The fish had turned. Jordan kept reeling, gaining line quickly. The changing angle of the line in the water showed the fish was swimming toward the surface.

As Jordan continued to reel, the line went slack.

"Oh shit," Jordan said.

Stokes yelled "J.P." as J.P. slammed the throttles forward.

"Keep watching," J.P. screamed, "and keep talking to me."

Jordan watched the reel. J.P. throttled back and the reel suddenly smoked line.

"It's testing the hook," Stokes said. "Don't give it any slack."

"I can't help it if it's bolting toward us."

"I know, I know." Stokes held a bottle of water to Jordan's mouth.

Jordan took a sip, keeping his gaze fixed on the spot where the monofilament left the reel.

"You're doing great. Keep working it," Stokes said.

Jordan reeled down, pulled up on the rod and reeled down again. He kept at it.

"It's moving," Jordan said.

He repeated the 'lift, reel, lift' maneuver several times while the line angled away. Suddenly, the surface of the water in front of them exploded. Two hundred and thirty feet behind the boat, a raging blue marlin missiled out of the water: a dark, sword-like bill followed by a wild eye searching for its tormentor. Above a gaping mouth and a silver-white underbelly, a dark blue stain covered its long bill and swept down its back like a tailored cape; a sharp dorsal fin sat at a right angle against its lateral line, and a black pectoral fin protruded like a wing from its shining side.

The fish rocketed straight up, completely out of the water, angrily waltzing on its sickle tail, trying desperately to shake the hook. At the peak of its jump, the small, lateral ridges at the base of its tail were visible. For a split-second, a brilliant white spray of saltwater framed the spectacular fish against the deep, dark blue of the ocean. Its wet, muscular torso glistened, bathed in sunlight, as it hung in the air. Then it twisted its massive body and fell back toward the surface. In a cascading splash, it landed flat on its right side, skipped from the momentum of its fall, and flailed its thick, mermaid-like tail as if trying to swim in the air. Then, just as quickly and unexpectedly as it had surfaced, the marlin sounded. The reel began to lose line; the fish ran harder, the speed of the exiting line increased.

Stokes screamed: "Back up! Back up!"

J.P. shifted both engines into reverse, shoving on both throttles. Line burned off the reel as Stokes watched in horror, knowing the fish would spool them. After all their effort, when the line reached the end, it would snap like sewing thread.

J.P. increased the throttles. The blunt, square stern of the *Break Wind* plowed into the light Gulf chop, causing the boat to lurch backwards into the crest of each low wave. The digging motion of the stern rocked the boat; each time they dug, the stern rocked in deeper. Water splashed in larger and larger waves, then flooded over the transom and into the cockpit.

Stokes stood on the right of the fighting chair, futilely watching the nine hundred and fifty yard spool become smaller and smaller, getting sprayed by the sheets of water breaking over the transom, and praying the fish did not reach the end of the line. He worried the friction from the dragging line could cause it to break. *That's not possible. This is one hundred pound line.*

The fish kept running.

But that's a seven-hundred-pound blue. Of course it's possible.

Mishka positioned himself on the left side of the chair, filming in the frothing water coming over the back of the boat. Their reverse speed increased. J.P. had no choice but to press the throttles. It was either that or lose the fish. Wayne stood behind the chair, holding on to the backrest, wondering if they might flood the engine room.

Jordan braced himself in the fighting chair, bare feet on the stirrup board, his left hand on the foregrip of the rod, his right hand on the handle of the reel. His lost shoes floated aimlessly around the cockpit. Each time the brine drained down, his shoes settled on a spot, shuffling on their own. Then another flood floated and animated them.

Water breached the stern gunnel again and again. The fish had slowed and the boat was reversing as fast as the fish was swimming. J.P. let off the throttles. The fish stopped. Jordan lifted the rod. The marlin turned hard and, once again, line peeled away.

J.P. increased the right throttle and decreased the left. That sent the starboard prop spinning faster than the port. The boat turned with the racing fish and the bow swung wildly, but still the line raced off the spool. J.P. hit the thruster toggle and neutralized its swing. He kept reversing the boat in pursuit of the fish; his hands flew across the controls, switching from gear shifter to throttle to toggles. Water no longer sheeted over the transom. The big diesel engines growled a low, bubbling rumble–unheard by anyone on board. Instead, each heard only the sound of his own voice and that of the men around him screaming:

"Ahhh, Hooo! Mother! Fucker! Look at that big, beautiful son of a bitch!" Stokes yelled.

"Seven-fifty!" J.P. punched the air. "If she isn't seven-fifty, I'll kiss your ass!"

"She's huge," Wayne yelled.

"Monstrous. Fuckin' monstrous," Jordan yelled.

"Did you see its girth?" J.P. yelled.

Heytu, now on the flybridge filming next to J.P., mumbled, "Oh Got."

"What do you think, Heytu?" J.P. asked. "You like this kind of fishing?"

"Yes. Very much. Yes, I like very much," Heytu said, gazing at the water.

Heytu's voice was reverent–the kind of voice used in church.

"Work her!" J.P. yelled. "She's green as hell Jordan. You've got a lot of work ahead of you dude. Don't give her any quarter. Take some line!"

"How the fuck am I going to take line from a fish pulling the boat?"

"She's not pulling it now. Try it candy-ass."

"Fuck you!"

Jordan reeled down and tried to pull up. Nothing. He could not budge the fish. But the movement aggravated the big marlin. It pulled line again. When it stopped running, Jordan pulled up on the rod, moving the fish a few inches, then reeled down.

"You think she's seven-fifty?" Jordan asked.

Stokes held a water bottle toward Jordan. Jordan leaned his head back while Stokes tipped the bottle up.

"No, but she may break seven," Stokes said. "Good job Jordan. Now let's get to work."

Jordan lifted the rod but the line held firm. It felt as though he was hooked on the bottom, only the bottom lay forty-six hundred feet below. It was probably the fish. As line again raced off the reel, Jordan concluded it was definitely the fish.

Jordan lost himself in his thoughts and the singular task before him. He was burning up, covered in sweat, his muscles ached, and his right thumb was red and swollen and tender from nervously squeezing against the reel's handle for forty-five minutes.

The fish ran. She stopped. Jordan pulled up, pushing with his legs. He reeled down. The fight continued.

J.P. throttled and thrusted, sending the boat forward and backward and sideways, in an attempt to help Jordan make up line—and keep that line tight—while Jordan fought the fish from the chair. J.P. was impressed with Jordan's innate understanding of the fight. It was simple really. As long as slack was kept out of the line and pressure stayed on the hook, the fish would find it difficult, but not impossible, to throw the barb. Keeping the line tense was job one. After that was the fight—getting line back on the spool at every opportunity.

Pulling in the seven-hundred pound fish would require wearing the beast down before it wore Jordan down. Getting the fish to surface was their best weapon. But it was also risky since the fish's best chance of throwing the hook was when it jumped. It would tire quicker jumping. It would lose oxygen. Lactic acid would build in its muscles just as J.P. had explained to Heytu when he fought the shark. Evidently this marlin was unaware of the biological difficulties it faced. It swam hard, like a charging horse. *A fucking Clydesdale,* Stokes thought. Jordan cranked and reeled, gaining back line and keeping pressure on the fish.

Another thirty minutes passed.

Wayne emerged from the cabin with more water.

"Open," he said, lifting the bottle. Jordan leaned his head back and drank while his eyes strained to look down at the reel.

"Oh, that's good," Jordan said.

"Here," Wayne said, holding Jordan's hat in one hand and pouring water over him with the other.

Even as he enjoyed the cold shower, Jordan kept his attention on the rod. The fish gave line easier than before. Jordan reeled down, lifted and reeled. Again. And again. And again. The marlin ran. Another hour passed.

Two hours and fifteen minutes after it was first hooked, the big fish jumped again. This time the reel was full of line and the marlin rose sixty yards off the port side. It shot into the sky as if it had been launched from a sub, then thrashed back into the water, falling tail first. It lunged upward again, the morning sun reflecting off its silver scales as it quivered in flight like an unbalanced arrow. It jumped a third time, and then a fourth. With the first two jumps it appeared indomitable, but after the fourth, it seemed to falter before retreating beneath the waves.

"I'm glad she did that," Stokes yelled to J.P. "She deserves to show off."

"And we have it captured forever, right Mishka?" J.P. yelled.

Mishka gave a thumbs up.

"Yes. Beautiful picture."

Jordan pulled up on the rod and the fish exploded out of the water again. This time it completely cleared the surface, spun on its back, and arched its body. Its heavy, silver belly flashed the sky. As its body fell, the fish threw back its massive head and flipped its fantail sky-ward above the saltwater spray. Then seven hundred pounds of pelagic muscle knifed back into the water, heading straight down. Line raced off the reel in its all too familiar way. Jordan expected it to stop, but the fish kept diving.

"J.P.!" Jordan yelled.

J.P. threw the gears and throttled. The boat spun and backed toward the fish, then slowed as J.P. let off the throttles. The reel was still smoking line, but the fish was diving straight below them. J.P. shifted the gears again and they eased forward. The fish stopped to recharge. A third of the line was gone.

"That's impossible," Jordan said, his body slumping into the chair. "I can't do this man. I'm worn out."

"Just try and catch your breath." Stokes lifted Jordan's brown, floppy hat, poured more water on his balding head, then replaced the hat.

"Okay. I'm ready for another three hours."

Fortunately, it did not take that long. The jumps and the long, extended run that followed were the big marlin's last campaign. An hour later, they pulled the monster blue along their side and opened the fish door. Stokes seized the thick leader with two gloved hands, then gripped the bill while J.P. swung a ten-inch flying gaff down and the fish reacted by shaking violently.

With the flying gaff set firm, J.P. grappled with the line and pulled fast. He staggered momentarily, handed the line to Jordan, then sunk another ten-inch gaff into their catch, discarding the pole as Wayne nervously clutched the second line.

The mass of thrashing marlin yanked all four men toward the transom several times in rapid succession, but Stokes had collared the coarse surface of the big, tapering bill and secured the fish's most lethal weapon while Wayne and Jordan pulled firm on the gaff lines. J.P. finally looped a rope over the tail of this fish that refused to die and it was almost over. Together, they wrenched and wrested the heavy blue out of the water and into the boat. When the tail was finally contained inside the cockpit, the revelry began.

"We're gonna win Poco! Fucking! Bueno!" J.P. yelled.

"Yeah baby," Jordan screamed as he high-fived J.P.

Mishka kept filming, determined to document the moment despite his elation, but Heytu ignored the camera on Mishka's shoulder. He laughed and screamed and grasped and hugged Mishka's neck, then jumped with excitement, his feet bouncing in a semi-circle around Mishka's stationary body.

"We rich cousin! Rich! Rich! You love Texas, yes?"

"I thought you were nuts yesterday Stokesie," Wayne yelled, "but you're a genius now." He laughed and patted Stokes on the back.

When the yelling and the slapping of palms and the laughter died down, J.P. and Stokes climbed the stairs. The huge blue on the floor of the cockpit below was the largest marlin they had ever caught.

"It could easily win this tournament," Stokes said quietly.

The static of the VHF radio sputtered behind him. Without looking at the helm, he knew J.P. had just turned it on and adjusted the squelch and volume to find out if they were in range to hear and transmit to any other boats.

"What's our time captain?" Stokes asked.

"Ten-forty."

J.P. picked up the microphone of their "broken" radio and called a committee boat to tell a tournament official they were having radio problems, but they had just boated a big fish.

CHAPTER FIFTY-THREE

Stokes stood in the cockpit, holding a margarita glass full of scotch and admiring the massive marlin, whose tail girth he had just measured at seventeen and a half inches; 'twenty at the tail' was the shorthand number for a marlin to break a grand. Neither he, nor J.P., had ever been on board a boat that landed a blue or a black that weighed a thousand pounds, but that was the long term plan.

J.P. leaned back from the helm. "Let's ice her best we can. How big?"

"Seven plus." Stokes sipped his drink. "What do you think?"

"I agree. Great proportions. But she's gonna shrink before we get back. With this water, we can haul ass and be at the dock early."

"Not too early. The scales don't open till five."

"Aye-aye. I'm gonna burn off some diesel."

J.P. checked the instruments on the dash, saw they were heading south, and slowly pushed the left throttle forward while holding the right throttle back. The compass card rocked and floated in the clear mineral oil which filled the domed glass of its case. The *Break Wind* spun to a west heading, then northwest. He flicked the synchronizer switch on the dash and eased the throttle forward. Her momentum built steadily, the RPM's increased, the engine noise rose and she laid into the low sea, effortlessly breaking the light chop. At eighteen hundred RPM's, he stopped accelerating and the boat planed. He tapped the right throttle until the RPM's hit twenty-fifty, then settled into his seat for their cruise home.

Stokes drained the remaining half of his drink. From his position near the stern, he felt the vessel lift out of the water along her lateral line when J.P. hit the trim tabs. *The same line on a marlin where it feels the temperature of the water,* Stokes thought. *And the line on my balance sheet where my assets are about to be cut off.*

* * * * *

Once the fish was on ice, the crew's energy hit a lull. Mishka and Heytu arranged cameras and took fresh film out of the refrigerator to warm. Stokes, Jordan and Wayne secured rods and straightened up, putting away baits and lures and hooks. Each had a drink or two in the process and now it felt like a Sunday morning, but their excitement still simmered. They knew it would soon be Saturday night. At Poco. At the winners' table.

Stokes went outside to marvel again at their catch. He placed his drink on the covering board of the transom door and held it there with his left hand. At his feet lay the graying fin of the marlin's tail. Behind their stern, the boat's speeding mass gouged a hole in the Gulf, exposing their outside stern wall down to the trim tabs, but that void sucked shut in a boiling surge at the surface just two feet back, where a thick, white trail of bubbles swirled in the sapphire-blue water, so clean and clear that it made Stokes think of the pure waters of the arctic. He watched their wake recede in the distance and held his glass out toward the turbulent, fading track. Something inside him, faintly responding to the scene, made him think for a moment that the boat was like a person, traveling through the world and making its mark;

yet the evidence disappeared rapidly, leaving things as they had been. The words *"regretting your past,"* interrupted his reverie, but he was tired, and tired of thinking, so he decided to forget the past, and instead, drink, and smoke, and enjoy the ride back on his boat with his buds–perhaps for the last time. He went up top to talk with J.P.

"You know what my favorite part of this whole trip was?" J.P. asked in a serious tone.

Stokes sat on the couch in front of the helm, his feet and arms splayed to both sides, his drink rocking and threatening to spill from the wide-rimmed glass. He almost shouted above the noise of the wind.

"Yep."

J.P. took his focus off the horizon and stared at Stokes. "Okay. What was it smart guy?"

"It damn sure wasn't the ride out."

"Nope," J.P. said.

"It wasn't when we found the rip intact."

"Yeah. You're right. That wasn't it. But that was pretty cool."

"It wasn't when we let the little one go."

"He wasn't that little," J.P. said.

"And it wasn't even at the end there when you gaffed the big girl and took her out of the game, or when we struggled to pull her across the goal line."

A glint of worried curiosity passed through J.P.'s eyes.

"So, what was it? What was my favorite part?"

Stokes stood and leaned in over the helm, holding his beverage off to one side. "When the tension was the highest . . . when the line was tight . . . when our adventure still had some clothes on her, but was showin' lots of cleavage--"

"It's this warm scotch." J.P. snatched the margarita glass from Stokes's hand and emptied the last few drops of McCallum onto the deck. "I told you to be careful with this shit."

The scotch beaded on the white sole, forming a line of jiggling, fluid, butterscotch pearls that blew off the back of the flybridge in a neat row. Stokes continued in a sober tone: "The best part was when we were in the middle of the fight. When we were worn out and worried . . . a long time before we knew what the hell was gonna happen. It was when we had that big fucker on the line . . . before we knew what it was."

A look of pure, unadulterated amazement resided on J.P.'s face. "How'd you know that?" he asked earnestly.

"My best friend . . .". Stokes burped. "Is a wicked-smart, mystic motherfucker. He splained it to me before we ever went on this trip."

CHAPTER FIFTY-FOUR

By the time their antennae were in range of the boats fishing Hoover Diana, the radio was alive with captains comparing notes, bragging, complaining, and razzing each other. Serious fishermen were out here in numbers, vying to win the most prestigious bill-fishing tournament in the Gulf, so there was plenty of gamesmanship going on. And they were all talking about the *Break Wind's* "Big Fish." Inside the salon, everyone listened to the chatter. Alone at the helm, J.P. picked up the mike and remarked over the intercom that every boat they heard had fished inshore from their location.

"After all," he said, "what idiot would come this far out, in the middle of nowhere, to look for marlin?"

The occupants of the salon chuckled at the commentary. J.P. smiled smugly to himself, knowing several other boats had come out this far, or farther, but one–in particular–had found their marlin. Then his mood darkened. He kept the mike at his mouth, but did not depress the key. "This might be the biggest fish we ever catch on this boat," he said to no one.

A labored pant wafted up the stairwell, preceding Wayne, who arrived on the flybridge with a heavy sigh. "I'm getting too old for this shit," he announced before plopping down next to J.P. and removing his hat. "But I'm glad I was here to witness." He wiped his forehead with the crook of his arm, then set the hat on the seat. "That's one enormous fish."

J.P. turned to the cockpit. Their marlin bag–a sheath of white, insulated plastic, open at both ends and sealed with Velcro on the sides–bulged with their fish and all the ice they could stuff into it. Her wide, sickle tail jutted out from one end, blocking the fish door in the transom. She now resembled a massive, whole-fish burrito, with her tortilla-like shroud stretched across the entire length of the cockpit, up the steps, and under the mezzanine's roof, where the bag terminated at her gill plates, leaving her head exposed. Beyond J.P.'s view, the tip of her bill reached toward the salon door. A black, anodized pipe elbow protruded from beneath the roof, but J.P. paid no attention to it.

"She's a beauty," J.P. said.

The two of them stared out at the Gulf while they rode. Wayne seemed preoccupied, pulling at the leather lace of his Topsider for a few minutes, then turning and glancing furtively at the remote cameras, and finally whispering: "You know, our boy's stepped in a world of shit. Reality's gonna set in the minute we hit the dock, assuming the Coast Guard doesn't stop us on the way."

"Yeah. I've been wondering about our plan for fishing the world." J.P. shook his head and removed his sunglasses. "Lovey'd like nothing more than making Stokes suffer. Even if he manages to keep the boat, this is a rich man's sport. Without his job . . . our buddy's about to be a lot poorer."

Wayne bobbed his head, as if considering whether J.P. had made a valid observation, then stopped bobbing and concluded his analysis by saying, "Relax. John won't fire him."

It was J.P.'s turn to glance over his shoulder at the remote cameras and wonder if anyone else was listening.

"John did fire him," he said solemnly, replacing his glasses. "Right before we left."

Wayne chewed at the inside of his cheek.

* * * * *

"Sportfisher . . . of any . . . this . . . cockpit or fighting deck . . . ."

Stokes was talking to someone below. J.P. could not catch all of it, and judging by Wayne's puzzled expression, neither could he. J.P. was about to yell at Stokes when Mishka screamed "again," then a loud crack split the air.

They both recognized the sound of Mishka's clapper, and Wayne smiled approvingly.

"If Stokes doesn't make a marketable show out of this, it won't be for lack of effort," Wayne said. His grin widened as he leaned forward, rubbed his thighs and then patted his knees. "And I'm damn sure willing to bet on him." He put his Stetson back on and stood, peering over the rail to catch a glimpse of what they were filming.

"Amen brother," J.P. said. "Safe bet."

Twenty minutes later, the blender roared.

Stokes danced up the stairs bearing two green margarita glasses, their wide, shallow bowls filled with frozen, light-green slush and rimmed with chunky salt crystals. He had purchased these glasses after much debate, carefully experimenting with half a dozen types–for a month–before settling on these: they fit precisely in the boat's glass rack, felt good in the hand, and their edge held the sea salt well after being smeared with lime.

"Maestro," Stokes said, handing J.P. a glass.

Wayne received a similar offering from Jordan.

As the sun burned at J.P.'s right shoulder, he took a swig. With its tart flavor and generous dose of Patrón, the frozen fluid was the perfect antidote to the Texas heat.

"Un . . . fuckin' . . . be . . . lieve . . . able," J.P. gargled.

Stokes sat next to J.P. on the driving bench and pried up the narrow, brass nail of a cedar box with a filet knife. Inside the small chest, beneath a thin sheet of red wood, six Churchills lined the top in an unbroken row. For a moment, Stokes felt like he was alone in his Mom's kitchen, having just discovered a hidden box of chocolates.

He plucked out a cigar, held it in his fingers like an inflated pencil, and jammed the rounded end into the deep, indented center of his glass for a ten count. He slit the wet tip, handed the cigar to J.P., then took another from the box, repeated the process, and passed it to Jordan. At twenty-five knots the wind made it difficult to light up, but they managed.

Everyone was excited and talkative except Stokes–Stokes was quiet. After a week of frantic running and worrying and drinking and erratic sleep, he was thoroughly exhausted. But he knew he would not sleep for many hours. He drew on a big Cuban, holding in the smoke, relying on it to boost his energy and wake him up. He wondered about John–not John the father-in-law, that John was gone–but John the boss: the guy he used to hunt with, before he ever called him Dad. He opened his mouth and let the wind draw the smoke out over their wake. *Maybe that John is still around.*

He had not been listening for a while when he heard Jordan ask, "So what's that formula for figuring the weight of a marlin?"

Mishka motioned for J.P. to wait. He moved to J.P.'s side, readjusted the film camera on his shoulder, and then the light came on. Heytu held a boom mike near J.P. that looked like a feather duster.

"Most figure the weight of the fish by using length times girth," J.P. said. "Or that's what they call it. The formula is length, times girth squared, divided by eight hundred. You're supposed to measure the girth behind the pectoral fin and the length from the bottom jaw to the fork of the tail. But the formula is wrong. Not all marlin are shaped the same, and a big one, eight or nine hundred pounds, will be off by forty or sixty pounds, usually on the low side. If you put two together, they even *look* different. Some are ugly like Cousin, and others are cute and cuddly like me."

J.P. grinned at the camera. Stokes was amazed. Once he quit bitching, J.P. seemed even more himself when the camera was recording than when he was having a conversation with someone. He was completely at ease.

"You get fat ones and skinny ones, and some are more muscle-bound than others, like our girl down there." J.P. motioned with his thumb to the cockpit below and then continued, "The problem with the math is weight has to do with a cross-section of the torso times the length. The secret formula for marlin, the deal I just mentioned, is using the distance around the fish, the circumference, instead of the cross sectional area. You follow?"

"Not really," Jordan said.

"Put it this way: you could get a better estimate if you measured *through* the fish rather than *around* it."

"Okay. I get that, but why the eight hundred deal?"

"Dividing by eight hundred is a shorthand way to account for how the fish's body is shaped. It doesn't matter how the cult of Pythagoras arrived at that, it's just the best anyone can do to account for the general body proportions of a fish."

"Okay." A look of doubt registered on Jordan's face.

"I'll put it in terms you might better understand. Angie is five foot five and has a twenty-two inch waist. I can hold her whole butt in one of my hands. She probably weighs one hundred five pounds. When I was in eighth grade I was about the same height and same waist, but I weighed one fifty. That's a forty-five percent difference. Change that to a thousand-pound animal and it makes you realize the formula is just a rough estimate. But let's get back to our girl back there in the body bag, the one that's about to make us all a bunch of money. You saw the way she holds her girth through her middle? Her anal girth behind her lower fin wasn't much less than her pectoral girth. That's a stout fish. You add about fifteen percent for a fat fish to the secret formula, then you toss all the numbers out on their ass and use your best judgment. I'm guessing our girl is seven-fifty, but then again, I'm prejudiced."

Drunken laughter filled the flybridge.

"One question," Stokes said, joining in the mirth. "What are the rest of Angie's measurements?"

More laughter. The tinkling of glasses. The rhythm of the water washing the hull. More unseen reflection taking place inside Stoke's head. It was a long ride in.

The waters grew crowded with boats the closer they came to Port O'Connor. Several trailed them, riding their broad wake as they neared the twenty-mile mark in choppy seas.

The radio traffic picked up too. "Stokes . . . *Break Wind . . . Princess,* whatever your name is today; I know that's you in front of me. Are you listening? What did you do man, kill somebody?"

Stokes rose from his seat, reached toward the ceiling and turned the radio off, then he surveyed the bloodshot eyes of his crew.

"Okay lads," he said, removing the blunt butt of his fourth cigar from his mouth. "Like we discussed Thursday night, the radios were broken but we went out anyway. The tournament officials might be a little peeved at us 'cause we managed to call in and tell them we had a big fish, even though somehow we did not have a working radio all weekend."

"Or a radar for that matter." J.P. raised the dash by its hinge and pulled out a small, blue, plastic square. "Turns out we blew a fuse."

"And we didn't find a spare," Stokes said.

J.P. cocked his hand back and flung the little fuse off the side of the boat.

"So you fellas are not an accessory to anything. Must have been shitty wiring," Stokes said.

"Go to hell," J.P. said.

"Be sure and pack anything you'll need for a few days because I suspect the guys who are really going to be annoyed with us are not going to let us back on the boat once we land," Stokes said.

"I'veneverbeenarreshtedbyafederalmarshalbefore," Wayne said, all in one word. "Heck, I'veneverbeenarreshtedatall."

"It should be uneventful," Stokes said. "They don't have any beef with us. They were just ordered to arrest the boat. But remember, don't say anything if you don't have to and if you do, just say we didn't know a thing about this."

"And," J.P. said, "if anyone asks, we left the dock early Thursday night to avoid the crowd. Tell 'em we do it every year."

"Doowe?" Wayne asked.

"No," J.P. said. "But next year remind me Wayne. We've started a new tradition."

"And remember guys, we had our phones off when we left," Stokes said. "So, are we good?"

Everyone raised their glass.

"Bueno," J.P. said, prompting laughter and multiple alcohol-mangled bueno's from the crew.

"No one's going to believe us," J.P. said to Stokes.

"So what? Mimi lied, Lovey lied, Danny lied, they all lied, and their lawyer encouraged it. They did it just to fuck with me in a fishing tournament. Any judge would have their ass for that."

"I'm not talking about judges. I'm talking about tournament officials."

Stokes nodded. "You know more about electronics than ninety-nine percent of the guys here. Forget the fuse story. Just babble statistics and ohms and radio stuff till their eyes get blurry and convince them we had no radio."

J.P. put his hand to the bill of his visor and gave a half-hearted salute. "Okay boss."

Stokes tipped his glass to J.P., downed what remained of his margarita, then went below to call Melinda Witt. The radio question about 'killing someone' confirmed what Pat told Stokes the night they left. He planned to tell Melinda only what she needed to know–so as not to draw her into anything–and to ask her to go to federal court in Galveston first thing Monday to set a hearing and lift the B.S. seizure order. But when he reached her, Melinda said she had been served with a copy of the writ late Friday–twenty-four hours *after* she should have been served and too late to respond.

"I know absolutely nothing about maritime law, but I've been at the law library at South Texas College all day, researching," Melinda said.

Stokes raised an impressed brow. "Bottom-line it for me."

"Okay. It's legal to seize a vessel *in rem* for fuel charges–which they have an order to do. But you've bought your fuel this way for years– which was never mentioned in the petition. And, it looks like Danny fabricated the theft allegations in his affidavit. If so, both judges are going to be pissed. But in the meantime, the marshals are under orders to seize your boat. I'm shocked they haven't already."

"So, what do you suggest?"

"I really don't know *what* we can do. I'll be at the federal courthouse in Galveston when the judge gets there Monday morning. If we get some good evidence to prove Danny was lying, we'll show it to Frost, but otherwise, Marguerite's firm is too close to him to be worried about his reaction."

"Call Molly as a witness if you can schedule a hearing. She knows the accounting better than anyone," Stokes said.

"I've talked to her twice today," Melinda said. "I'll call her if I need her."

They continued to talk for a few minutes, then Stokes went back upstairs. When the boat hit the heavy swells at the end of the jetties, J.P. used his cell phone to call a tournament official to confirm they were coming in with a big fish, and Jordan raised an upright marlin flag, proudly signaling they had a marlin on board.

Stokes's hands shook as he thought about the rest of his conversation with Melinda. On Thursday, he had told her he wanted to discuss a settlement, and he assumed he had the boat to bargain with. But Melinda was now worried Mimi might succeed in claiming that the boat was community property. Stokes purchased it before the marriage–that should make it separate–but in one of their many motions Thursday, Mimi's lawyers had raised the issue. Lovey claimed she and John forgave the note and the boat was a wedding present–making it community. Stokes contended it was an exchange: he was owed a bonus, the boat debt was deducted from the total, and John tore up the note before the marriage–that made it separate. He thought he had written a letter documenting the transaction, but Molly could not find it, nor did she remember ever typing such a letter. That left an argument, but no clear answer. Melinda felt certain they would end up litigating, and the judge was likely to agree to some sort of restrictions on Stokes's use of the *Break Wind*. Things were getting worse, and a nasty divorce meant the chance of John asking Stokes to come back to work was almost zero. The possibility of cashing a winning tournament check was suddenly a very big deal.

CHAPTER FIFTY-FIVE

Stokes piloted the *Break Wind* into the Intracoastal, toward the city dock that held the Poco Bueno scales, weaving through a chaotic flotilla of barges, pushboats, coastal fishing skiffs and larger offshore fishing craft. Water Street, which adjoins the dock, was packed, as usual. The high-stakes tournament and its weigh-in party were prestigious events for this tiny town, and both were promoted heavily by the city throughout the year. The weigh-in was open and accessible to all: no entry fee, no barricades, and no master of ceremonies. Just a great excuse to hold an outdoor party for visitors who would spend money in Port O'Connor. The rest of the tournament, including the highbrowed dinners, the auction, and the after parties, were invitation-only, police patrolled affairs that took place behind the private, chain-link confines of the Alligator Head Club. But the weigh-in was public, seriously public.

A bait n' hook carnival of fishing fanatics, boatniks, bikini stalkers and garden variety beer-guzzling bikers were drinking, dancing, and buying tee-shirts and koozies and corn dogs and pork-on-a-stick at the year's biggest shindig. Mixed in with this raucous crowd were a few hundred dressed-down, big-city types from Corpus and Houston and Austin and Dallas and cities beyond.

ZZ Top blared from speakers mounted on the back of a flatbed semi that would serve as the stage for the award ceremony when the scales closed at eight. Gray puffs of smoke from the Port O'Connor Volunteer Fire Department's hot-link and fajita sale blew across the canal. The smoke stung Stoke's eyes and the smell of barbecued meat made his mouth water. Upon their arrival, a throng of onlookers swarmed the shoreline: word was out the *Break Wind* was coming in with a big marlin.

At the water's edge, two young, federal marshals–pissed off because they'd been ordered to stay here, without a change of uniform, for three days–waited and sweated in the still scorching five o'clock heat; forty-caliber Glocks rested on their hips. Five Coast Guardsmen kept watch nearby.

"Leaving the radios off turned out to be a really good idea," Stokes said to J.P. as he pulled past the scale and shifted to idle while another boat exited.

Stokes maneuvered slowly, backing toward the wharf. He stood, facing the stern and the anxious crowd, working the throttles and shifting gears with his hands behind his back–feeling like he was steering a float through a Mardi Gras parade.

J.P. grinned as he scrutinized the marshals.

"I'll handle this."

"Don't say shit!" Stokes said.

Without explaining, J.P. went below. The mob on the shore crammed shoulder to shoulder, trying to view the bagged marlin. A low tide placed the boat at rest well below the bulkhead, and J.P. threw a stern rope off their starboard side, then limped to port, where the marshals scrambled aboard.

Jordan jumped onto the foredeck and manned their front lines.

Once cleated fast, Stokes killed both engines. For the first time in ten hours, the burbling baritone of the boat's exhaust fell silent, but ZZ continued to rock Water Street.

In the cockpit, J.P. and the marshals were now laughing next to the tail-end of their catch. Stokes wondered what was happening. He scanned the surroundings and noticed a small wave ripple through a group of frat boys clustered near a beer truck. Angie and Suzanna materialized from the scrum of wide-eyed college men.

"Stokesie, get down here," J.P. yelled. "We need to show these guys around."

"Gentlemen," Stokes said, descending the stairs. "What can I do for you?"

"Stokes Owen Summers?" one of the marshals demanded.

"That's me."

"Your name's not Owen," J.P. said.

"Later," Stokes said, shooting J.P. his best shut-the-fuck-up look.

"Mr. Summers, we're here to arrest this vessel." The marshal held out a typed document. "This is a writ of seizure signed by Judge Frost in Galveston, sir."

Stokes pretended to be caught unaware while he slowly read over the writ. He shook his head and looked up at the marshals. "This is stupid."

Behind the marshals, a uniformed set of ten legs caught Stokes's eye and he glanced further up at the faces of the Coast Guard contingent, who were staring back down at him and hovering on the bulkhead like a row of pelicans waiting for a meal.

His voice rose and he addressed them all: "I paid for every gallon of fuel on this boat. I'm telling ya'll, this affidavit is a damned lie."

"You'll have to tell that to the judge sir," the young marshal declared. "We'll need to escort you to secure your vessel. We have dock space here in Port O'Connor at the Coast Guard station and we have authority to allow you to berth your vessel there."

The pelicans nudged each other and nodded approvingly.

"That's mighty civil of you officer; thank you," Stokes said, ignoring the pelicans and trying to think of what to do next.

"We done?" J.P. asked.

The young officer turned to J.P., dropped the stiff inflection for a more down-home tone, and said, "Yeah, J.P., that's it for the official crap."

"Then come on boys, you gotta see this rig."

J.P. ushered the marshals across the cockpit, past the body of the marlin and up the steps. Stokes followed, leaving the now downcast, long-billed guardsmen at the stern among the multitude of onlookers. J.P. slid open the salon door, and when the marshals moved inside, J.P. leaned back, still holding the door's handle.

"Jimmy Ebarb," J.P. nodded toward the salon. "Went to school in Dickinson together. Great guy—give me a minute alone with him . . . . If I need help, I'll wave an S.O.S. towel, *Owen*." J.P. pulled himself toward the door, then swayed back and added, "Partner's name is Barncy something."

"Hey baby."

Angie flew over the side of the boat in a cheerleader vault, planting her feet together on the deck. She landed with a thump, took four bounding steps alongside the white vinyl bag, then leapt onto J.P.

"Oh my gosh, you stink!" she said, crinkling her nose and wriggling away.

Suzanna stepped down precisely onto the deck.

"You know how to make an entrance honey, I'll give you that," Suzanna said, ignoring the monstrous fish. "Did you miss me?" she teased, with a forefinger under Stokes's chin.

"Absolutely."

She smiled and lifted his sunglasses. Stokes drew back, having completely forgotten about his eye.

"It looks much better. But still manly."

Suzanna turned and curiously regarded the imposing head and sword of the otherwise plastic-wrapped trophy, as if deciding whether she liked it there, in the middle of the walkway. Then she looked Stokes up and down.

"ESPN is interviewing another crew down the wharf."

The door slid open and Wayne stepped outside, appearing newly showered.

Suzanna continued: "Jack wants to talk with you guys fresh off the water. Hello Wayne."

Wayne removed his Stetson and teetered forward to peck Suzanna on the cheek.

"Darwin."

Stokes stepped back to make way for Wayne. "That's probably not – ouch!" The sword had poked him in the back and he hopped to the side.

"Okay, TV time," Suzanna said, clapping her hands. "Angie, get J.P. inside quick and make him comb his hair, and pick out a better shirt. No stripes. Stokes, you look like hell. Go wash your face and put on your best shirt. Something white if you have it, white shows your tan. Lose the glasses. Angie help him."

While Suzanna ordered the crew about, Stokes spotted four tournament and city officials huddled near the scales, twitching over the scandal they perceived being caused by the combined presence of the marshals and the small squadron of Coast Guard backup. The officials were conflicted, wanting to entertain the visiting masses with the *Break Wind's* large fish, but also desperate to get the federal police–and the boat they wanted to arrest–away from their respectable street party.

"Suzanna," Stokes said, a little more sharply.

With her head turned away, she held an extended left arm toward Stokes's waist, wiggling her fingers in an invitation for him to grab her hand. That request went unanswered as she moved closer to Wayne, calmly stroked the brim of his cowboy hat with her right hand, and said, "Wayne, will you help me clear absolutely everything off this deck except what must stay out?"

Jimmy Ebarb stepped from the salon and onto the crowded mezzanine behind Wayne. Barney remained in the doorway, tapping a polished combat boot on the frame.

Suzanna addressed them: "Oh boys, don't you love it inside? Come see the flybridge. Stokes, give them the upside tour."

Barney moved forward abruptly, saying "excuse me," and Jordan popped out from behind the sliding door, looking as fresh as Wayne.

"On second thought," Suzanna said, "Jordan, be a dear and show our guests the flybridge. Stokes needs to clean up."

"Can I talk to you for a moment?" Stokes snapped.

He led Suzanna away from the door, down the steps, to the tail of the marlin.

"We need to keep these law men entertained," she whispered. "They'll look good in the background."

Robert Earl Keen blasted from the speakers on the stage.

The weigh-master yelled with fading patience: "Stokes, we need to get moving."

Before Stokes could respond, Suzanna piped up.

"Give us a minute," she shouted.

She turned toward the salon to see if her instructions were being followed, but no one had budged, so she clapped her hands twice.

"Chop, chop!"

The crew scudded off toward their stations.

Exasperated, Stokes waved the writ in the air.

"The marshals are not here to sightsee or model Suzanna. They just gave me this. They're seizing my boat."

"I heard," she said, glancing at the phone in her hand. "But we're about to launch *The Technical Sportsman* with millions in free publicity to a national audience. You take care of the show, I'll handle the boys in blue."

Suzanna smiled and met Stokes's eye. He cocked his head. Recognition morphed into hope, then transformed into full-blown enthusiasm as his booze-addled brain realized she thought they could spin this and pull off an interview *before* the boat was seized.

She climbed off the boat, went to the scales, chatted briefly with the worried officials, then found Elsa and Sophia and returned to the cockpit. The marshals stood beside Jordan at the top of the flybridge stairs, about to descend.

Suzanna turned to Elsa. "You're on sweetie. Time to modify their behavior." She helped Elsa into the boat and they both helped Sophia. Elsa slinked straight up the stairs, purring "Hello pooh-kee" when she reached the bridge.

"Good," Suzanna said to Sophia. "She has them penned in. They don't stand a chance."

Wayne loaded beer bottles and cans in a bag and Suzanna approached.

"Hurry honey, I'm calling the ESPN crew now."

She pushed a button on her phone, crossed the deck and began to talk and laugh. Then she put four manicured fingertips over the speaker of her cell and held it away from her.

"Go tell Stokes and J.P. to get out here *now*. Then call your brother and get him and Bill Busch here quick. The ESPN guys are on the way. We're filming in just a minute. You look great Wayne," she added.

Wayne smiled, but was careful not to speak. He was being flattered and manipulated, and he liked it. He reached into the front pocket of his pressed, white shorts and pulled out his phone.

The *Break Wind* was moored next to the *Wasabi*, whose crew was weighing in game fish, but no marlin. Six more boats now idled in the Intracoastal, waiting to off-load their catch and weigh in. When the

ESPN crew arrived, the *Wasabi* pulled out and *Marduke* took its place. J.P. and Stokes, clad in their best tropical-fishing-dude attire, stood in the cockpit with the weigh-master, Captain Kent, taking a measure of how best to lift the fish out of the boat.

Stokes quit listening to J.P. and Kent, and instead, looked up to the flybridge. Above him, Elsa wore a thin gauze shirt over a bikini top and tight khaki shorts. He thought of her on the stairs, the night of the fireworks, and strained to see her now above his glasses while he directed his head toward J.P. and Captain Kent. He nodded periodically as if participating in their discussion. The movement of his head, the skewed position of his eyes, the heat, and the booze he had consumed, all combined to stretch the already long legs of Elsa's silhouette, making her look like a Barbie doll. Then Temptation Barbie arched her back. Stokes felt something, realized what it was, and fell back to earth. He briefly adjusted the fit of his shorts. *Two plus two is four, four plus four is eight, eight plus eight is sixteen . . . .*

"We gotta move this boat J.P.," Kent pleaded. "We have six more waiting to weigh fish."

"Will that chain reach the boat from here?" Suzanna shouted to Kent from the crowd on the bulkhead.

Kent was a long time member of the club that hosted the tournament. He liked J.P., but he had never met Suzanna and he was both annoyed and amused by her question.

"Yes ma'am," he yelled back. "We can reach her just fine from here, with twenty feet to spare, but as I just said, we need to get a move on."

"Good. Then move the boat out three more feet and tie her down there J.P."

J.P. glared at Suzanna. His shoulders rose, and Stokes—knowing J.P. was about to tell Suzanna exactly where he was going to leave the boat and why—clamped his right hand on J.P.'s left collar bone and squeezed hard. Startled, J.P. dipped, spun and grabbed Stokes's wrist.

"Cut that out dude. She--"

"Stop, stop, stop."

J.P.'s mouth sprang tight; his jaw muscles flexed and a knot of veins rose on his temple and pulsed blue. Stokes put both hands on J.P.'s upper arms and turned him toward Mishka and Suzanna, who were standing next to the scales and deep in conversation, both gesturing at their boat.

"It's for the camera angle J.P. This is theater. She wants the transom and our boat's new name in the shot when we raise the fish. Let the woman do her job. It'll make us look better."

Jimmy Ebarb appeared beside J.P.

"Let's talk," he said.

Stokes and J.P. followed the marshals up onto the bulkhead as Suzanna stepped past and back into the cockpit. Stokes swiveled his head and scanned the crowd, grateful the pelican guards had flown away.

"Gentlemen," Jimmy said, reverting to pompous mode, "this vessel is under seizure by order of--"

"Aw, c'mon Jimmy." J.P. scowled. "You don't want to seize the boat with a dead fish in it."

"Not my problem."

"It will be once it starts to stink and you realize you can't remove it without a hoist," J. P. said. "And all these people might lynch you if you ruin our shot at winning this tournament."

"That's a chance I'll have to take," Jimmy said.

"But you can't take the liability for a five-million-dollar vessel can you? I mean, do you even know how to pilot a boat like this? Because if you wreck it, you have to deal with the pissed off lawyer who owns it. Did I mention Mr. Summers is a lawyer? Plus, you'll have a serious issue with the entire O'Donnell family and their own legal army at Vincent & Gump. That would suck, huh?"

"J.P., you–"

"And half that fish is owned by Bill Busch the fifth, heir to the beer fortune. The winner's cut might be as high as nine hundred and forty thousand dollars, which is some serious beer money. So let's make a deal guys."

While he spoke, J.P. made his way behind the marshals, forcing them to turn and direct their attention to the boat's cockpit below, where the girls were working on makeup. Angie wore a white bikini top, khaki shorts, and her black, rectangular glasses. Sophia caused more of a stir than the bagged marlin. She wore a dark, iridescent-blue bikini that shimmered in the sunlight. It was more conservatively cut than the sets of strings she had been wearing, but she drew every eye on the dock—male and female. Elsa seemed overdressed compared to the rest.

It was now obvious to Stokes that the marshals were men first, law men second. They scarcely considered J.P. as he spoke.

"You give us ten minutes, we'll get this giant guppy out of your way, you get to watch four of the most beautiful women in Texas from right here, and then we'll park the boat for you in your stall. Y'all will have done your job and allowed us to finish ours."

"We simply can't–"

"Please dude. I'm begging you. Ten minutes. This could be a very important ten. My job is on the line here," J.P. said.

Jimmy and Barney exchanged looks.

"You have five minutes J.P. But remember, my ass is on the line here too," Jimmy said, looking around nervously.

Stokes and J.P. returned to the boat, pushing through the crowd that had tripled in size. All were craning their necks, trying to see the women and the marlin.

J.P. stepped back onto the deck, knowing he had saved the day, feeling his liquor, and dreaming of getting his hands on a big check while he wondered what the deal was with all the blue flashing lights ricocheting off the glass of the salon.

Three white Coast Guard pickups now lined Water Street. There were no sirens, but all had light bars on their roofs, sending their strobes across the street and the canal.

The five missing Coast Guardsmen reappeared, led by a new commander holding a bullhorn. They filed onto the boat and began untying lines.

"This vessel is under arrest. You have ninety seconds to vacate," the commander yelled.

He climbed to the flybridge, briefly surveyed the dash and flipped on the blowers, then lifted his bullhorn. "Captain Blake, in sixty seconds you are to arrest anyone on deck."

A clarion blast from the engines and their exhaust startled the crowd, and everyone rushed to exit the boat.

The commander lifted the bullhorn again. "Thirty seconds Captain Blake."

Exactly a half-minute later, the *Break Wind* was released from the dock, occupied only by six members of the United States Coast Guard–and one very large fish.

CHAPTER FIFTY-SIX

S tokes, and the majority of his stunned crew, helplessly watched the *Break Wind* turn into the Intracoastal and disappear behind a tug. On the bulkhead, amongst the disappointed crowd, a teary-eyed Mishka finished folding up a tripod then hugged his cousin.

"What's wrong?" Stokes asked.

"My fortune in cameras is taken. Must start all again."

"Dude . . .," Stokes said. He thought better of that. "Mishka, no one is taking your cameras. It's just the boat."

Mishka sniffed and rubbed his nose.

"Can take anything if you are government. Believe me."

Stokes let it go.

Farther back, near the stage, J.P. argued with the two marshals. As he pleaded, he brandished his arms toward the surrounding crowd, as if he had been appointed their protector; but the marshals were having none of it. When they turned to walk away, J.P. fell into a violent fit, screaming at their backs, kicking a discarded beer can across the asphalt, and then tearing at his hair. He turned and searched for Stokes among the breaking lines of the pedestrian army. When he found him, he shook his head gravely and held up his palms in defeat. They walked toward each other in the dispersing crowd and the rest of their crew met them.

"What now?" Busch asked.

"The marshals say that's it," J.P. said. "Game over. The order says seize the boat and they seized it. There ain't nothin' anybody can do."

"What about the fish?" Busch continued. "We still have two hours. Can we transfer it to another boat?"

"That's a damn good idea," J.P. said.

"Any others?" Blaine asked.

"The tournament officials might argue with us," J.P. said. "You can't give another boat a fish, but this is different. It might work."

Dr. S squeezed in beside Stokes and held a cigar toward him.

"Can we call John?" Blaine asked.

"I've tried," Dr. S said. "Just now. Can't reach him."

"Based on my last conversation with John, I don't think that would accomplish anything anyway," Stokes said, taking the cigar. "J.P., we need you to keep talking to the marshals–try anything, but keep trying. Bill, why don't you and Blaine figure out our best argument and make it to the tournament officials. Get the rule book, call some lawyers if you have to, but try to get them to agree to allow us to transfer the fish and weigh it in." He looked at Wayne.

"I'mgonnastayherewiththegirls," Wayne said.

Bill Busch, Blaine and the four girls turned toward Wayne, wondering what he had just said.

"Good idea," Stokes said. "Suzanna, see if you can keep the ESPN guys around and tell 'em to keep their cameras out and ready. I'm going to the Coast Guard station to try and reason with them."

"How exactly are you going to *reason* with them?" J.P. asked.

"Do you have a better plan?" Stokes asked.

"No," J.P. said. "But don't try to steal the boat. They have guns. They could sink it."

"I'll drive you over," Dr. S said to Stokes.

Stokes followed Dr. S past the flashing lights of the abandoned Guard trucks and down Water Street, until the swarm of sweating Bubbas thinned. A Coast Guard van filled with replacement truck drivers passed them when they reached a side road.

Dr. S clicked his tongue audibly against the roof of his mouth and then spoke: "I did some research on Shelby Worth."

"Forget it," Stokes said, sounding annoyed. "I know all about him and Mimi. What happened with your trip?"

Dr. S wrenched his jaw sideways then nodded, understanding.

"My wife left for Europe without me. She's kinda ticked." Dr. S bit off the end-cap of his cigar, spit it out, then flicked a gold Dunhill lighter as they made their way to his car parked three blocks away.

"When I got home Friday night . . ."

He puffed contentedly, lighting the fifty-four gauge Robusto.

". . . I found a note on the kitchen counter under a Viagra bottle. There's nothing subtle about Lisa's sense of humor. We have sex maybe once every three months. I don't know how she found that bottle, but it was a scrip for ninety pills and three refills, and, the bottle was empty. She left a lovely little missive under it, referring to me in several endearing terms like 'S.O.B.' and 'sorry ass' and . . ." He puffed. "I thought this was particularly well put: 'lecherous, swarthy, prurient, bastard.'"

Dr. S took another long draw on his cigar, exhaled, and spoke while smoke flowed from his lips. "You don't see the word 'prurient' in print much. Pity. It really is an excellent word. Very descriptive. Gets right to the real essence of the subject, doesn't it Stokesie?" He huffed out the last wisp of smoke. "I thought it tied in well with the Viagra bottle. That Lisa . . . I tell you, for all her faults, she has an excellent sense of humor.

"One thing the note did not say was where exactly, in Paris, we were going. She didn't leave me a ticket, or a flight number, or even the name of the hotel."

Dr. S studied at his cigar and spun it between his fingers. A trickle of sweat ran down his neck as they walked. "I'm thinking I may go to Cabo. Or Vancouver. There's this killer hotel in Coal Harbour where I--"

"What are you doing tomorrow?"

"Refilling that prescription, of course."

"No, seriously. Can you do me a big favor?"

"Anything."

"Can you get some money and let me write you a check, but not cash it for a few weeks? I hate to ask Doc, but I'm paranoid Mimi's lawyers might be watching my account. Plus, I'm trying to figure out where my next paycheck will come from."

"Sure Stokesie. I know you're good for it." He puffed again. "And don't worry so much, you'll have plenty after the trial."

"There's not going to be a trial. That was never my intention."

"*She* cheated on *you*."

"Why'd you come with us last Sunday? Why'd you come back?"

Dr. S paused, slowed his pace, and then said innocently, "I wanted to be with my buds."

"Exactly. And how long have you known me?"

Another verbal stall.

"Since your engagement."

"And can you remember when I didn't own the boat or wasn't working on it?"

"No. Em . . . vaguely. Did you own it before you guys were married?"

"Mimi and I loved each other Doc. At least I think we did. That's why we *got* married. But we moved to Houston, I started on the boat and I quit hanging out with her. She tolerated all my friends in law school, but I wouldn't deal with her mother. When your friends won't hang out with you . . . well, you make new friends."

Dr. S walked to the driver's side of his Bentley and unlocked the door with a remote. When they climbed inside, Stokes faced the opposite direction, tears forming in his eyes.

"You okay?" Dr. S asked.

Stokes thought of saying, *Yeah, except for the money. And John, and failure, and Mimi, and bankruptcy, and embarrassment, and bills I can't pay,* but instead, he drug a fist across his eyes and answered, "Peachy."

A bead of sweat released off Dr. S's clavicle and ran down the center of his chest beneath his black silk shirt, catching on the pendant of his gold necklace.

Having regained his composure, Stokes spoke up as the car started: "Compared to some of the old salts in this tournament, we don't know shit about big-game fishing. I don't know why I think we can pull off a TV show on the subject."

"Oh, please. You were good enough to win."

"We were lucky to catch it."

"We both know you can hire all the experts you want for a show. And don't forget pal, we all need some luck now and then."

Dr. S brought the car to a stop behind a boat being towed by a pickup. The long shaft of a mud motor jutted out toward their grille. He drew on his cigar again, watching the truck turn, taking its trailer, boat, motor, and potentially Bentley-grille-piercing-prop along with it.

Stokes squinted at the road ahead and snapped his head back, seeming to wake from a momentary nap as they approached Maple Street.

"Turn here," he said. "Most of this is my fault Doc. I'll let my lawyer maneuver a while longer, but I'm just trying for a fair settlement. This was never about a trial. I'm not going to punish Mimi."

"You're wrong of course. It's not your fault." Dr. S twisted his cigar over the burl-faced tray and tapped off a virgin rind of ash. "I'll give you fault: At my wedding, I distinctly remember standing in the nave of that gorgeous Orthodox church in Prague and watching Lisa come down the aisle, one dainty foot in front of the other. The whole time I was thinking how much I'd like to get in the maid of honor's pants. Lisa knows I've never been faithful, but I'm sure it was my lack of effort to be discreet lately that led to her early departure for Europe. But you told me just the other day how you never cheated on Mimi. That's amazing. Especially considering your running buddies. Hell, just between hanging with me and Big John, I don't know how you did it."

Stokes was not sure what to say.

The Coast Guard station was just ahead on their left. Dr. S pulled over.

"You think John would let me come back to work later?" Stokes asked. "I mean, if we can settle the divorce and all and keep it civil from here forward?"

Dr. S shifted to park, then glanced at the dark, undulating fronds on top of several palm trees that were hiding the *Break Wind's* tuna tower. He watched them sway back and forth and back again, until Stokes thought he was trying to count them.

"Johnny will let you do anything you want. You just need to figure out what that is."

Dr. S met Stokes's eyes.

"Don't sell yourself short buddy. You're a safe bet. Everyone you know has figured that out, especially the O'Donnells." The clock on the dash ticked; smoke slowly curled away from Dr. S's cigar. "What we're all wondering is: Why is it taking *you* so long?"

Stokes pursed his lips together and nodded. "Thanks Doc."

CHAPTER FIFTY-SEVEN

Stokes explained to the ensign on duty at the Coast Guard station that he was, essentially, homeless, and he needed to get some personal effects out of the *Break Wind*. That gained him entrance to see the commander, who was in his office. He appeared to be satiated after having asserted his authority in front of such a large crowd, so Stokes proposed the notion of allowing them to remove the fish from the boat. The commander exploded with expletives and ended by saying, "Nothing is coming off that boat."

Stokes reverted to what he had told the ensign, meekly pleading to get some clothes out of his room. The commander agreed, and even added, facetiously, "Take your time."

* * * * *

Stokes stood beside his boat, lamenting the terrible waste of the bagged marlin lying in the cockpit. He stepped on board, walked up the stairs and gave her snout a regretful pat. Once inside, he loaded his gym bag and grabbed the pewter frame out of the bathroom. Then he thought about how unreasonable the commander had been and decided he would, indeed, "take his time."

When he reached the top of the hall stairs he was sweating and breathless in the warming salon, so he decided to make a gin and tonic. *Maybe that's my problem,* he thought as he poured a measure of Boodles into one of the margarita glasses. *I'm off my tonic.*

He puffed on the Cuban and looked in the fridge for the bowl of week-old limes, then squeezed two dried-out slices over his drink, drew again on the cigar and stirred the ice in his glass as it tinkled softly. Alone in the galley, he realized what he had told the ensign was true–without the boat, he was homeless. He decided to survey his domain one last time. *After all, that's what I'm fighting for.* He turned and looked over his shoulder. *What's left of myself.* He stood there, drink in one hand, cigar in the other, struggling to grasp a thought which had just come to him, one that had been dancing just past the edge of his consciousness since before the tournament began.

"Damn it."

His voice reverberated across the cherry floor, over the granite bar, off the glass walls, and echoed in his head.

The battle's not out there, it's in here.

It's not the tournament. Not the divorce. It's me.

That's the fucking fight.

He snatched the pewter frame up off the counter; two intense, determined eyes stared out at him.

I traded my ambitions for a comfy life and I lied to myself about doing it.

I'm depending on the O'Donnells.

I was worried about John firing me because I was too scared to quit. Now I'm hoping he'll hire me back because I'm too scared to go out on my own. Doc is right. I need to take control. I've got to stick to my plan and believe in myself.

With a stiff drink and a fresh resolve, he headed outside. He ignored the great fish and forgot about the military men in the building next to him. Instead, he climbed up the stairs to complete his self-analysis. When he reached the flybridge, he decided to capitalize on his newfound courage by climbing into the tuna tower, thinking he had not been up there lately.

The only way to the tower was to climb one of the ladders which functioned as supports for the roof of the flybridge. As Stokes began climbing, his legs wobbled from the day's alchohol and nicotine, and he remembered why he hadn't been up there lately. *This is fucking dangerous.* He cleared the remote camera and the roof, and gazed at the long, white, rotating radar antenna, the satellite dome, and the four VHF radio antennae which were mounted there. The radar had a gash in its fiberglass housing. He set his drink on the roof, gripped the cigar in his teeth and reached out, breaking a shattered piece of fiberglass away from the housing and studying it. Flakes of silver zinc–the remnants of something–were embedded in the fiber. Then he remembered the airborne projectile that whipped past their heads as they left the T-head, and he tossed the glass chip overboard, wondering if he should tell J.P. how the radar broke.

He slid his glass onto the center of the tuna tower's floor, then ducked and pulled himself up under the rail. From the sloped fiberglass deck, he looked down at the plastic-wrapped fish lying twenty-six feet below on the cockpit's sole. *Jesus*, he thought, contemplating a fall, *that would hurt.*

He wondered why he risked his neck and came up here: *Oh yeah. My domain. All seventy by twenty feet of it.* He blew a puff of smoke, which immediately dissipated in the stiff breeze.

Standing in the control center of the tower, holding onto the guardrail that surrounded the six-foot-wide pulpit and listening to the music of the weigh-in party breaking up on the wind in the distance, he leaned down and picked up his drink off the floor. The gin smelled like juniper, like cedar trees in the Texas Hill Country. Across the street from the station, scrub cedars covered an empty lot. In the distance, the beach houses of Port O'Connor perched on tall piers, standing mute sentinel over the surrounding marsh flats. He glanced southeast, toward Pass Cavallo, and thought, *I could travel to Mexico, the Caribbean and the world from this spot.* Then he looked back at the station and frowned. *I should have been so lucky.*

He pulled on the guardrail. *Solid.*

The contrast and the irony were obvious to him: his boat–which he was losing–was solid; but his life–which he was stuck with–had completely unraveled in little more than a week.

Focus. No way this is the best part, but I made a promise. I'm going to keep trying.

A diesel Mercedes clattered up to the side of the Coast Guard station, sounding like an industrial sewing machine. The black sedan pulled off the oozing asphalt and into a shell lot, sending a puff of white dust leeward. As the dust cleared, Dennis stepped out of the driver's seat and closed his door with a thump. Then John exited the passenger side, followed by Pat from the back seat. After a short interval, Stokes yelled.

"Hey guys."

The three men scanned the area.

"Stokes?" John said.

"In the tower."

The men looked higher, hands above their eyes, searching above the roof of the Coast Guard station, through the swaying palms, until they saw him.

"I'll come down."

When Stokes reached the lower deck, John came around the corner of the building with Dennis, but Pat did not appear.

"Why haven't you answered your phone?" John asked.

"It's broken," Stokes answered. "Dr. S tried to call you. He couldn't get through."

"Hmmph!" John snorted. "Mind if we come on board?"

Stokes waited, ready to help John maneuver his big frame into the boat. When John and Dennis reached the side, they both halted and stared down at the fish in the cockpit.

John swallowed, hard. "God damn."

"I know," Stokes said dismissively.

John set one leg astride the gunnel, sighed, and spun with a groan, dropping his bulk to the boat's floor. He ushered Stokes along the side of the marlin and toward the upper mezzanine deck, leaving Dennis behind to ogle the broad sweep of the tail.

"When I came back this morning and got an update from the lawyers, they told me about the seizure. Pat's been trying to track down the judge for the last two hours, but he's having trouble now. The cell service is for shit down here."

John forced a scant laugh, then his expression grew somber and he put his big hands on Stokes's shoulders, holding him out at arm's length and gripping him tight.

"Lovey was on my ass to fire you all week. She had me on my last nerve when I . . . . God-damn-it son," he shook Stokes solidly, "I'm sorry I made that call." John gulped, stared at Stokes, then lowered two penitent eyes. "Please forgive me."

"There was never any question she would have my ass," Stokes said, chuckling lightly. "But thanks for comin' down here to say that in person. That means a lot to me."

John motioned for Dennis to join them. Stokes held the sliding door open, considering whether to throw out his cigar. In the last six years he would have done so automatically. John eyed the burning stogie. Stokes placed the Cuban in his mouth and slid the door closed.

In the galley, Stokes poured two Cokes. John quaffed his greedily, then struggled to shed his sport coat. Stokes attempted to help, but succeeded only in aggravating John.

"I'm not a fucking cripple," he barked, yanking his arm away.

"Okay, okay," Stokes said, hands raised in surrender.

"Why don't we go upstairs and talk," John said.

"You head on up and I'll catch you in a second."

Stokes pulled a nearly empty box of Churchills from the humidor cabinet. He removed two cigars and set the box on the bar next to the picture frame, which Dennis picked up and examined.

"You were a stick," Dennis said.

Stokes ducked his head—hiding a scowl for the briefest instant—while he pulled on a pink Mirror-lure handle. He reached inside the top drawer and removed a box of matches. Beside him, Dennis looked over and thought perhaps he recognized the pink Mirror-lure.

Stokes sensed, rather than saw, what Dennis was looking at.

"Have a cigar Dennis," he said, pocketing one in his shirt and heading for the door with a malicious grin. "There are more lighters in the top drawer."

Dennis squinted at the photograph through the base of his thick tri-focal lenses. He saw the kid in the picture casting a fly line and recalled the last time he was on this boat. Then he had an epiphany, remembering Stokes's back-cast and the force that had ripped his ear open. He spun his head and his eyes riveted on the pink Mirror-lure door handle. His right hand flew to his scarred ear. He gaped at the lure and involuntarily began to shake his head–like a hooked trout.

* * * * *

John was still working his way up the stairs and Stokes followed him to the top, where John plopped onto the flybridge couch.

Stokes set the extra cigar on the vinyl cushion and motioned toward it with his hand. "You want one?"

"You know I hate those things."

Stokes blew a piece of tobacco off his lip and said, a bit more arrogantly than he intended, "Thought you might have changed your mind."

"No," John said. "And I assume you haven't changed yours."

Stokes considered that. *He's talking about the divorce of course. Nothing about my job. Yes, he's talking about the divorce. Mimi would not have fessed up about her lover. There's no reason, except revenge, to tell him now.*

Stokes did not want revenge.

"No John, I haven't."

He struck a Ritz match, shielded it tight in his hands, and let the harsh flame resurrect his dead cigar.

"After you appeared in public again with that woman, Mimi and Lovey resolved they were going to beat you one way or the other," John said.

That meant the Captain's Dinner.

"But this will all pass son. I want you back at the office, if not in the family. We can work this out." John paused and drained his glass. "The lawyers tell me they made a mistake."

Stokes thought he was talking about the seizure. "Really?"

"Really," John said. "Seems if you don't fully list all your assets in a pre-nuptial agreement, it's null and void."

Stokes was shocked, but held a poker face while he drew slowly on his cigar. *This is news.*

"The fucking nimwhit who drafted the pre-nup only listed three trusts for Mimi. He left out four others, including a particularly large one left by my daddy. As you know, Dutch loved his grandbabies."

Ice cubes clinked in John's glass.

"You mind?"

Stokes took his glass. *What's he telling me? That I can go after the family's assets? That I can have all the money I want, but he wants me back in the office?*

When he returned from the galley, John was looking south across the Intracoastal at the pass and the barrier islands. Stokes handed him a fresh drink.

"So, like I was saying, Dutch left my little girl and my bouncing baby boy some trusts with lots of zeroes in them. Your mother-in-law didn't think they needed to be listed in the pre-nup. Now the lawyers tell me we're exposed for millions. The pin-stripes at Bubba Gump think, that I think, it's their fault; but I guarantee you, Lovey had a hand in all of it. I swear, I didn't find out about any of this, or the boat, till this morning. If I had known it Thursday . . . I never should have let Lovey convince me to make that call. I'm truly sorry son."

Condensation dripped down the deeply cut crystal of John's glass. Stokes watched a drop fall through the air and splatter on the white-checkered fiberglass deck.

"That shark you found is pretty damned good," John said. "And she's about to learn just how good she is. When she gets the information about the trusts, she'll smell blood."

John took a sip, keeping his gaze on Stokes.

"What do you want son?"

Stokes looked up from the deck with a start.

"Just what we agreed to before the wedding. I told Mimi that already. I want the boat because it's *mine*. I purchased it with the royalties I earned. She can have the house and everything else: the cars, the art, the furniture. I sold all my interest in the wells except for the Colorado play and the Emmit deal. I think I own those. Other than that . . . we're square."

"What about the money?"

"It's Mimi's money."

"Lovey tells me you're in debt up to your ass son."

Stokes shrugged. "That doesn't change our deal."

"Maybe you didn't hear me. The Bubba Gump group says--"

"I heard you. Failure to disclose all the material assets voids the pre-nup, and you're wide open on this. But ten more zeroes on Mimi's balance sheet wouldn't have changed anything when I married her, and it doesn't now. I signed that contract." Stokes took a long, satisfied pull on his cigar and exhaled confidently as he spoke. "I don't want a dime of Mimi's money . . . but I want every fucking penny of mine."

* * * * *

John had sized Stokes up as they talked, at first thinking he was still dealing with his top earner, the prize bull he had long hoped would add a new bloodline to his family; his ambitious, restless, impulsive son-in-law, whom he believed he had to control and tamp down, lest he try and wrest the reins John intended to hold for many years. But as Stokes had talked about what he wanted, John's expression changed. He was no longer speaking with the prickly V.P. of operations who had sulked around the office for the last few months.

"You want to chat with your lawyer?" John asked.

"Nope."

"Do we need to have the deposition and produce all the papers?"

"Nope. Not if we have a deal."

John held out his hand.

Something in the way Stokes held himself as they shook made John recall his first sight of Stokes at his front door, seven years earlier, in his cut-off jersey, thirsty, sweating–and smiling.

John lowered his gaze, knowing the answer to his inquiry before the words left his mouth.

"So, you won't come back to the office?" John looked at Stokes.

Stokes looked him straight in the eye. "No . . . . You and I are cool. We can work things out between us. But I'm not coming back John . . . not to the office . . . and not to the family."

Then John did something completely out of character, something Stokes knew he would remember for the rest of his life: John returned Stokes's stare and, in a steady, clear voice, said, "Son, I envy you."

CHAPTER FIFTY-EIGHT

Pat opened the back door of the Coast Guard station and dashed out, waving his hands madly above his head like he was being pursued by a hive of bees.

"The order is lifted," he yelled, running towards the boat. "The arrest is off the yacht!"

He stopped at the gunnel, his arms frozen like branches. He looked down into the cockpit, then his eyes tracked up into the mezzanine.

"God damn."

Pat looked up at Stokes on the flybridge and their eyes met.

"I know," Stokes said.

Pat looked at his watch. "You've got forty-five minutes before the scales close."

* * * * *

Pat called J.P. with the news while Stokes cranked the engines and went below to start the generators. They were preparing to leave when J.P. called back to report the crowd was buzzing, the ESPN cameras were in place, the lights were on, ready to record the boat's arrival, and Suzanna had the girls ready to play their parts. Only one other marlin had been brought in, it weighed less than five hundred pounds, and all other boats were accounted for. If Stokes could get to the scales in the next fifteen minutes, they were the winners of Poco Bueno.

Stokes wanted the three men to ride with him to the scales, but Pat suggested they drive over in their car and leave Stokes to arrive alone–like a champion at a major, holding a three-stroke lead as he walks up the fairway toward the eighteenth green. Stokes laughed at the suggestion, but John took it seriously; in fact, he insisted.

* * * * *

Stokes stood alone at the helm; the canal ahead was clear of traffic. Despite having less than a mile to travel, and ample time to weigh in the fish that lay behind him, he nailed the throttle. He removed his sunglasses, set them on the dash and clutched the pewter frame with his left hand. Beneath the shade of the flybridge roof–with a wide grin on his face and wind sweeping at his hair–he held up the frame to look again at the picture. Instead, he saw a clear reflection of himself in the frame's glass.

Something was different.

He was looking at a set of unfamiliar, yet intimate, eyes.

He considered the paradox.

How could his own eyes, in his own reflection, be strange to him?

He slowed the boat and turned in toward the city dock, oblivious to the cameras and the cheering crowd waiting on the shore.

Then it hit him.

He recognized the eyes.

These were the same eager, determined eyes that belonged to the kid in the picture. He tilted the frame to remove the reflection and smiled affectionately at the ambitious boy staring out at him.

Glad you're back.

ACKNOWLEDGMENTS

My most sincere appreciation goes to my assistant of many years, Gina Youngblood, for her unwavering dedication to this project, and to my extraordinary publisher Joseph Daniel - and the team at Story Arts Media - for shepherding this work into print.

A special thanks to my editor, Wes Smith, for his help in cultivating the story from the clutter. Thanks also to Barry Brooner, Tim Parks, Chuck Grehn and Murray Stacy, for their expertise in the oil business; Art Fahrenholz, for his knowledge of boat construction; and Mark Bunting and Micheal Parks, for their contributions regarding photography, television and film production. I am particularly grateful for the vast store of nautical knowledge derived from Captains Scott McCune and Larry Kent; and mariners Mike Cooper, Richard Davis, Dr. Tom Sanders, Dr. Michael McCann, and David Dies. I would also like to thank the many who read drafts with fresh eyes and open minds, including Mark Robbins, Barbara Fahrenholz, Ted Moor, Jack Wiener, Jeff Baker, Doris Sanders, Andy Henschel, Dr. Ken Barton, and fellow authors Bruce McCandless, David McGee, Kevin Kelly, Denise Huddle, and Brent Carter.

Above all, I owe a special debt of gratitude to my best friend and most trusted advisor, my wife Melissa. For twenty-six years she has encouraged me to write, knowing, more than anyone, what it means to me. When I began *Poco Bueno*, she put up with me reading to her, day after day. As my harshest and most valued critic, she read and edited dozens of early drafts, and when the manuscript lay finished, she read it cover to cover and proclaimed, "You've done it. You've got a book; it will be here forever."

Chris Parks, 18 December, 2012
Boulder, Colorado and Port Arthur, Texas

IF YOU LIKED POCO BUENO

T hen you probably know a guy who would like to receive it as a gift! Poco Bueno is perfect for Father's Day, graduations, birthdays and birth-of-a-child days, weddings and bachelor parties, the day a pre-nup is torn up or a divorce decree is signed, Christmas, New Years, the first day of fishing season, Duck-Eve, that long plane flight, just about any holiday, or for any of those moments in life when someone you know could use a healthy dose of adventure and inspiration. Please visit www.pocobuenobook.com to discover all the ways you can share this marvelous tales.

Author Chris Parks is enthusiastically available for interviews, speaking engagements, book signing events, club meetings, etc. Please visit www.storyartsmedia.com for further information, and to learn more about our other fine books.